Favorite Daughters

LAUREL OSTERKAMP

Black Rose Writing | Texas

First printing

ISBN: 978-1-68513-016-9
PUBLISHED BY BLACK ROSE WRITING
www.blackrosewriting.com

Printed in the United States of America
Suggested Retail Price (SRP) $21.95

Favorite Daughters is printed in Baskerville

*As a planet-friendly publisher, Black Rose Writing does its best to eliminate unnecessary waste to reduce paper usage and energy costs, while never compromising the reading experience. As a result, the final word count vs. page count may not meet common expectations.

Author's Note

I began writing *Favorite Daughters* in 2015, at a time when no one could have guessed how much the political landscape in the U.S. was destined to change. Through the years, I rewrote and revised multiple times, always to reflect our ever-changing reality. All I can say is, my final version of *Favorite Daughters* is vastly different from the original. That said, it is a work of fiction. I am an English teacher from Minneapolis; I love following politics, but I have no firsthand information. While the characters and situations in my novel might reflect real people and events from our recent history, I drew upon my imagination (and a bit of internet research) while writing it.

And, while several characters may be inspired by people from the political world, they were also inspired by the women who have impacted my life, including my mother, my aunts, my teachers, my co-workers, and my best girlfriends. This novel is for them, but it's especially for my daughter, Pauline.

Pauline, I love you so much. I want to give you everything. I can't, but I *can* give you this:

"Never grow a wishbone, daughter,
where your backbone ought to be."
–Clementine Paddleford

Favorite Daughters

Chapter 1
Columbia University

It's quiet up in the stacks and the light is dim. I squint through my smudged glasses and read all about nineteenth century gender politics. Sometimes my Feminist Research Methodology class seems pointless, especially when I become aware of how little things have changed in the last hundred years. Not to dismiss the sacrifice and toil from trailblazers like Susan B Anthony and Elizabeth Cady Stanton, but let's be honest; politics is still a boy's club. This unoriginal realization leaves a sour taste in my mouth as I sit cross-legged on the floor, flipping through the book's yellowing pages that smell like a thrift store suitcase. The words blur in front of my eyes. *Numerous nineteenth-century feminists protested the underlying rules and repercussions of our social welfare system and policies…*

Heavy footsteps interrupt my lack of focus. Suddenly a pair of thick, black leather shoes are in my line of vision, and somehow, I know without knowing: those shoes belong to a Secret Service agent. More importantly, they belong to Aubrey Adam-Drake's Secret Service agent.

I'm shocked, not at my potential celebrity sighting, but that a Secret Service agent would wear such shoes. I mean, they don't look very conducive for running. Don't Secret Service agents occasionally need to chase after bad guys? Sneakers would for sure be more practical, but maybe a pair of Nikes wouldn't give off the air of gravitas most agents seem to have. (I've only ever seen these agents on TV or in movies, but still…) I'm so consumed with pondering this question that my stomach doesn't flip, and I hardly even register that the only girl who has the distinction of belonging to two royal families must be nearby. Her fame comes not just from her father, Anton Adam, Liechtenstein's younger-sibling prince who will never inherit the crown, but from her grandfather, Howard Drake, the 42nd president of the United States and patriarch of the Drake political dynasty. The Drakes are the closest thing America has to royalty. Aubrey's mother, Eleanor Adam-Drake, is currently running for the New York Senate, and people say that in a few years she'll run for president and will most definitely win. After that, her younger brother, who's also a politician, will probably take office, and speculation has already begun that Aubrey will follow in her family's footsteps.

Wow. Aubrey Adam-Drake. This is the beginning of my junior year at Columbia and I've yet to lay eyes on her, but I guess that's about to change.

"Student ID?" The Secret Service agent demands. I reach into my backpack, fish out my ID, and hand it to him. He checks the ID, looks at my face to make sure the image matches, and gives it back. "Why are you up here?"

I cock my head. "Umm, to study?" I use just a touch of sarcasm, but he doesn't respond. Instead, he turns toward the female voices that are fast approaching. Then it hits me, this moment is a two for one. Just past the Secret Service agent, with Aubrey Adam-Drake, is Marina Hunt. She had her own reality show in the late 90s, where cameras followed her as she balanced her studies at an elite private high school, went on countless modeling gigs, and had love affairs with the hottest celebrities at the hottest parties. It was like a real-life version of *Gossip Girl,* except nobody ever actually thought Marina's existence was real-life. She first rose to fame because her dad, Oliver Hunt, worked as a lawyer for the country's most notorious mob bosses, and then he went on to become mayor of Atlantic City, where he owned several properties and soon expanded his luxury hotel chain nationwide. Now he's everywhere, always spouting his outrageous opinions on some political commentary show and thus making himself a household name. And while Marina and Aubrey's backgrounds are certainly different, their fame has made them allies. Everybody on campus knows they're best friends.

I tell myself not to look up from my reading, not to gawk, and definitely not to rubberneck.

"You are so wrong!" Marina says with a laugh.

"No, I'm not. He said 8:30. I promise." Aubrey's answer comes out breathy yet strong, exactly like how she always sounds whenever she's answering a reporter's question about either side of her family. It's funny that she's so familiar, when her parents tried hard to protect her from the limelight. She was only six when Howard Drake was elected, and the press were warned to tread lightly with the combo first-granddaughter/princess. The warnings mostly worked, but every now and then some mean-spirited commentary would pop up, criticizing Aubrey for her gawkiness. Because of how smooth and sophisticated both the Drakes and the Adams all are, she's been called an ugly duckling more than once.

"I don't care," Marina replies. "You're the one dead set on meeting him."

"Right." Aubrey sounds exasperated. "Because one of us needs to take this seriously."

I look up. I can't help it. Aubrey is leaning against a shelf, her back to me, her waves of brown hair cascading down her back. She is by no means short, even when slouching in her flats, but nonetheless, it's clear that Marina is still several inches taller. Marina faces Aubrey, and her auburn hair is slicked back into a flawless bun. Her makeup is also impeccable; her plum-shaded lips part and her perfectly arched eyebrows rise at Aubrey's tone.

Neither of them notices me, as I'm crouched back and sitting in the shadows.

"I don't see why we need his help," Marina says. "We can handle this on our own."

"He's the student body president! If you want to start a revolution, you begin at the top."

Marina rolls her eyes. "We *are* at the top."

"I don't want to use our families' influence for this, Marina. It's not right."

"So, we're going to a student government geek instead? That's just as twisted."

The Secret Service agent gestures toward me and mumbles something that sounds like, "Ma'am, you have company." Aubrey shifts, making her face visible, and her wide mouth sets into a concerned frown. "I'm so sorry," she says to me. "We thought it would be empty up here, and yet we totally intruded." She shakes her head and speaks to Marina. "See, this is what I meant before. We'll live up to our entitled reputation if we go around demanding that people bow down and leave every time we show up."

Marina shrugs. "Who's demanding anything?"

"We came up here to speak in private," says Aubrey. "Maybe we could go up a floor?"

"But you said we'd meet him on this floor." Marina sighs.

I clear my throat. "Hey, no worries. You can have your private conversation, and I won't listen. I have way too much studying to do, anyway."

Marina narrows her eyes. "What's your name?"

"Elyse Gibbons," I reply.

"Do we have class together?"

"Um, no," I say to Marina. I look to Aubrey. "This is actually the first time I've ever seen either of you—in person, that is." I cough. "You know what I mean."

"You look familiar," says Marina.

"Can't think why," I respond, but that's not entirely true. There are lots of girls on campus who look like me: average height, athletic build, long brown hair. I suppose my most distinguishing feature is a set of rather large hazel eyes. Chances are Marina doesn't recognize me, she recognizes my type. You know, the type who tries to look smart but comes off as appropriately pretty in a non-threatening sort of way. On campus, girls like me are a dime a dozen.

We hear someone new approach. Aubrey's Secret Service agent moves toward the entrance, obviously prepared to protect if necessary.

"See," Aubrey says to Marina. "That's him. I got the time and place right. But we should go somewhere else, so ..." she turns to me. "What's your name again?"

"Elyse." I answer.

Aubrey talks to Marina. "We should go somewhere else, so Elyse can return to studying."

"Hello ladies." The guy who greets them is almost as famous around Columbia as Aubrey and Marina. Finneas Beck, student body president, is handsome in the way that young actors who star in movies about guys at New England boarding schools are handsome. His nose is charmingly crooked, and his light brown hair is longish in the front yet short in the back, but most of all, he has that air of wealth and privilege that only comes from birthright.

"Hi, Finn," says Aubrey.

"We have to move our party somewhere else," Marina says. "Our new friend Elyse is using the space to study."

I try to think of something that won't give away how desperately I want them to stay in my vicinity and blurt out, "Don't mind me, I'm pondering Schrodinger's cat." Gosh, where did that come from?

Finn looks at me amused. "You know that's a hypothetical situation. The whole point is the cat can't be both simultaneously alive and dead."

"Yeah, but hypothetically, what did he have against cats?"

Aubrey bursts out laughing, Marina looks annoyed, and Finn chuckles appreciatively as he glances down to the book I'm actually reading. "*Revolutionary Women and Gender Politics*? Are you taking Dr. Kent's course?"

"Yeah. How'd you know?"

"I took it last spring."

Aubrey laughs some more. "Seriously, Finn? You took a women's studies course?"

He shrugs. "Sure. I could check off a box for my poli-sci minor, so why not?"

"This is all really fascinating, but I have to be somewhere in an hour." Marina sounds borderline pissed, but the pinch in her voice is tempered by a silky lilt to her words. "Can we get down to business?" She stares at me pointedly.

I remain still, but I blink a couple times. "The thing is, all the books I need are here." I make a sweeping gesture to the library shelves and to the piles of books in front of me. "I've got a lot of reading to do, but it won't bother me if you stay."

"Are you sure?" Aubrey asks.

"It's totally fine," I respond, the calmness in my voice belying my rapidly beating heart.

They exchange looks. Aubrey points to a spot a few feet away, and they move out of my line of vision, closer to the entrance, which is still guarded by the Secret Service agent. I continue reading, but of course I can't help but overhear their conversation.

"Do you know if there's been anyone else?" I hear Finn ask.

"I've heard rumors," Marina says.

Finn speaks again. "Nothing confirmed?"

"We can get proof," Aubrey says. "But even if it's only Marina, that should be enough."

"Yeah, we're talking a major sex scandal here," says Finn. "We can't just throw around allegations unless they can be backed up."

"Fine," Marina retorts. "I'll give you all the details to back the allegations up." Then she talks ...and talks and talks.

I take furtive notes, which is basic instinct for me as I'm a reporter for *The Spec*—short for *The Spectator* —Columbia University's student paper. Its reputation is the reason I'm here instead of at West Chester University where my mother teaches, and where I could have attended for almost nothing. But I'd insisted on Ivy League, with a chance to work for and with the best and the brightest —people like Aubrey Anton-Drake, Marina Hunt, and Finneas Beck. How else will I ever become one of the best and brightest myself?

If the three of them had asked me if I was reporter, I would have instantly said *yes* but they didn't ask, so here we are. Tomorrow I'll get to *The Spec's* office right when it opens. I've been a junior staff member for a while, but so far, the biggest story I've covered was about Parents' Weekend.

Nice to meet you, Big Break. My name is Elyse Gibbons.

Chapter 2

I don't get the headline I was hoping for because my editor doesn't think it's a viable story. "Not all parties have been interviewed. No one has spoken on the record. Right now, this is all just conjecture."

She says this after she reads my write-up: "Ethics Professor Implicated in Sex for Grades Scandal."

"Interview your sources," she tells me. "Give Professor Martin a chance to comment. See if you can find other students who will back up Marina's story. Then maybe we'll run it."

"How am I supposed to do all that?" I ask.

She arches her eyebrows and somehow that simple action shames me. "Do you want me to assign this to someone else?"

"Of course not. It's my story."

"No. Just because you happened to be in the right place at the right time doesn't make it 'your story.' You earn that by doing the leg work. So, figure it out and get it done, or I will assign a new reporter. Hell, maybe I'll take the story myself."

Chastened, I exit *The Spec's* office and go out into the gusty morning. Today I have three classes with exams coming up. Blowing off my studies is ill-advised for sure. But I sense a time limit in that "figure it out" ultimatum. I don't want to look back one day and wonder "what if *I'd* been the one to break the biggest story on Columbia's campus in over a decade?" I mean, this could become national news. The implications are huge.

I pause for a moment, buttoning up my heavy gray cardigan which has become my autumn jacket (another ill-advised move, since I hate the smell of wet wool). Where am I even going?

I let my eyes pass over The Alma Mater statue that sits at the entrance to Columbia's library. Two months into my junior year, I still feel reverence every time I see Athena sitting with her big book and an owl hidden in her robes. Right now, all the people who walk by her seem to have a definitive destination, with their backpacks slung over their shoulders and sleeved cardboard coffee cups in their hands. Meanwhile, I stand still while my mind races. If I go to Professor Martin before I talk to Marina and other possible witnesses or victims, that could kill the story. So, I should try to interview Marina first. But how? Even if I could track her down, I doubt she'd tell me anything that I didn't record the night before.

Then I remember Aubrey telling Finn, "We can get you proof." I should talk to Aubrey right away; she was the one intent on 'starting a revolution." But it's not like I can just look Aubrey up in the student directory, find out her schedule, sail past her Secret Service agent, and convince her to speak on the record.

No, my best option is to head toward Lerner Hall which houses the student government. I know from covering the minutes of student council meetings that members of the executive board keep office hours. Maybe I can find Finn, and maybe he can get me in contact with Aubrey.

I walk to Lerner Hall and exit from the rain into the high ceilinged, steel and glass constructed building. It reminds me of a modern art museum, with its strategic lighting and shiny floors, like it could be the setting for a futuristic film where everyone must travel through warehouse-like tunnels because we can no longer safely breathe outside. I look at a building directory posted on an exposed brick wall and find the location of the student government offices and travel down the hallway as if I belong here.

When I arrive outside the door with "Finneas Beck" posted on the nameplate, I find it ajar. What luck; he's here and he's alone.

I knock lightly, and he turns around.

At first his face is open, like he's a store clerk happy to help me find the right sized jeans. Then recognition skips across his features, and his mouth twists into a semi-frown. "It's you," he says. "I had a feeling you'd show up."

I lean against the door frame and smile, acting more confident than I feel, aware that he hasn't invited me to come in and sit down. "Maybe I'm reading it wrong, but you don't seem happy to see me."

"No, no…" He shakes his head. "It's not personal. But last night I remembered that I've seen you around before." Finn leans back in his office chair and peers at me with eyes that match the navy-blue Henley he wears. "Because of your hair," he states simply. "Do you always wear it in a knot on the top of your head?"

Involuntarily, my hand drifts to that soft spot at the top of my neck, where wisps of escaped hair linger, having released themselves from my bun. "I suppose," I answer, feeling self-conscious. My long, dark hair is a source of pride; I love how thick and shiny it is. Doing my one hundred brush strokes every evening has become part of my daily relaxation ritual. So even though it's difficult to manage, I don't have the heart to cut my hair short. Instead, I always wear it in a bun at the top of my head, because if something is working for you, why change? "What's wrong with my hair?"

Finn's mouth drops open just a little and his cheeks pinken slightly before he forms his response. "N-nothing," he softly stammers. I would say he embarrasses far too easily except that in the next moment he projects confidence by letting his gaze capture me in a stronghold. His eyes lock on me for a moment too long, and a pull of attraction takes me by surprise. "You have pretty hair," he states. "But it made me remember you." He taps his finger against his lower lip, and then – dammit – I'm thinking about how kissable his mouth his. "You cover student government meetings for *The Spec*. You're a reporter."

I step inside his office as if accepting a challenge. "The way you say I'm a 'reporter' makes it sound like I'm a criminal."

He laughs, one charming dimple appears on his left cheek, and suddenly he's not so intimidating. "Sorry. I didn't mean it like that, but if you're planning to expose either Aubrey or Marina, then we have a problem."

Well, he's got the nice-guy schtick down: complimenting me, acting self-deprecating, and then saying something confrontational in this charming, non-threatening sort of way. I tilt up my chin and harden my voice just a little. "It's not my intention to expose either of them, but I believe there's a story here that needs telling."

He raises one eyebrow and crosses his arms over his chest (which I can't help but notice is nice and broad.) "It's not up to you whether or not the story should be told. That decision belongs to Aubrey and Marina."

I sit on the chair opposite his desk, unzip my backpack, take out a notebook and poise my pen, ready to quote him for the record. "Oh, come on, we know it's more complicated than that. Look, why don't you tell me what happened with Marina Hunt and Professor Martin? That way we can hold him accountable."

Now Finn's laugh is dry and slightly cynical. "I'm not telling you anything. I promised Aubrey and Marina I'd be discreet."

I let out a huff and allow my spine to slacken just a little. "Then can you at least tell me how to find Aubrey? I'd like to interview her."

"I'm sorry, but I can't."

A voice comes from behind me. "No worries, because here I am."

I turn and do a doubletake, sure that I'm dreaming. Maybe it's a life-sized projection, a pixelized version of her. But no. For the second time in twelve hours, Aubrey Adam-Drake stands before me.

She steps into the office and Finn's mouth goes slack. "Aubrey. I didn't know you'd be stopping by."

"I wanted to follow up after last night's conversation."

He nods frenetically, which causes his bangs to flop into his eyes. "Sure." He gestures toward the chair I'm sitting in and then turns his head, meeting my eyes while blinking. "I think you should go."

"No," Aubrey states flatly. "Elyse, I want you to stay."

"She's a reporter, Aubrey." Finn's voice is tight, almost like he's scared.

"Good." Aubrey sits in the only other chair in the room, a folding metal one that was probably pulled in at some point as an afterthought. "That saves me the time of having to go to the media myself." She flips her long braid off her shoulder and uses her hand to smooth the damp frizz that grows atop her head. Then she speaks over her shoulder to her Secret Service agent, who stands out in the hall. "Do you mind, Jerry?"

He gives an almost imperceptible nod and closes the door so he's on the other side, watching and vigilant, while Finn, Aubrey and I sit together in the tight space. She sighs like she's just taken off a pair of uncomfortable shoes. "Okay, let's talk. We have work to do."

"Are you sure about this, Aubrey?" Finn taps his fingers against his lip again. "I mean, if you're going to talk to the press, shouldn't Marina be here too?"

Aubrey's eyes meet mine, as if it was me, not Finn, who just posed that question. "You understand why we need to talk about this without Marina here?" she says. "And you won't screw us over?"

I nod. "Yes," I struggle to say. "I mean, yes, I understand. And I absolutely will not screw you over."

"Good," she replies. "Because for some reason, I want to trust you."

Suddenly, the window shakes from a gust of October wind and rain pellets against the glass. Outside, it's like the world might end. But inside, this might be the moment when my world finally begins.

Chapter 3

Aubrey gets me everything I need. She convinces Marina to go on record about Professor Martin, and then, magically, she convinces some other girls who were harassed by him to go on record too. Finn makes "Professorial Power Abuse" an agenda item at this week's student government meeting, and he personally invites Professor Martin to attend. Aubrey, Marina, and several of Professor Martin's other conquests are there. I'm there too, covering the whole thing for *The Spec*. The evening seems endless as I sit through discussions about parking regulations and rooftop garden permits, my chest tightening as I wait for the fireworks to go off.

My palms are damp, and it feels like there's something stuck in my throat, like maybe burrs or a scouring pad. Am I having an anxiety attack? That would be ridiculous. If anything, I should be happy that before the meeting began, Aubrey found me sitting in the front row, my little tape-recorder ready and my heart beating at twice its normal rate. "Is the article ready to go?" She'd asked.

"Yes," I'd replied. "Now all I need to do is add an account of this evening's meeting. I'll stay up all night writing and submit it tomorrow morning."

She'd nodded vigorously and squeezed my arm. "I owe you one, Elyse."

"Don't be silly. I owe you, for giving me such a huge story."

"No." She'd stepped in closer, taking on a conspiratorial tone. "I can't believe how good our instincts were, trusting you." A soft laugh punctuated her words. "You know it wasn't an accident, right? Marina and I chose you."

"Huh?"

"We knew you'd be in the stacks that night," she'd said, her smile taking up her entire face. "Tomorrow evening, after the article is published, we'll go out for drinks and I'll explain. For now, just enjoy the most explosive student council meeting in Columbia's history."

Enjoy the meeting? Her words have the opposite effect. At the moment, I'm fighting the compulsion to puke while staying glued to my seat, and doubts and confusion are roiling through my mind, so *enjoyment* is not going to happen. Seconds tick by like they're dying a slow death, but eventually, all the meeting agenda items except the last have been covered.

Finn sits at the table in the front of the room, and he sighs before speaking. "Lastly, 'Professorial Abuse of Power' is a specific concern." He pauses and directs his words to Professor Jake Martin, who sits in the third row. I've never taken one of his classes, but I've heard that on the first day of his most popular course, *Persuasion and Propaganda,* he tells his students to call him "J.M.". I've also heard that he always makes the top five on "the hot list" for Columbia's professors. I've seen J.M. around campus; he's usually wearing jeans and a corduroy shirt, as if he's going for the lumberjack look with his longish hair and two-day beard growth. And I guess he lives upstate and commutes from his self-sustaining farm, where he churns his own butter and chops a lot of firewood.

Tonight, his hair is combed, and he's freshly shaved, but he looks pale, like he's constipated or in pain.

"Professor Martin," Finn continues, "I urged you to attend this evening's meeting so as not to deny you the chance to speak and defend yourself, and Sir, you will be given the opportunity to do just that. But first…" He looks to Marina, "I believe our guest, Ms. Marina Hunt, has something to say."

Marina stands and walks to the podium. She may as well be a model traveling the runway; her fashionably clad, long-limbed body, her smooth auburn tresses, and her politician-serious-smile all amount to the sort of composure I know I'll never have. I wonder, should she thank nature or nurture for this flawless self-possession?

"Good evening," she says, her face the exact right distance from the microphone, and in her black tailored jacket and cream silk t-shirt, she projects the perfect amount of dignity. "I am here tonight, speaking not just for myself, but on behalf of other female students who trusted the wrong man. I thought I'd be safe, visiting Professor Martin during his office hours. He claims to prioritize our well-being, but he used his power position to violate me and several others. Professor Martin, otherwise known as J.M., is guilty of chronic sexual harassment."

She pauses, takes a steadying breath, and I wonder if she's nervous or if her vulnerability is for effect. "A couple of weeks ago, I had questions about my term paper. I stopped by during J.M.'s office hours. He invited me in, closed his office door, and listened intently while I described analyzing the ramifications of yellow journalism during the Spanish American War. Then J.M. said he was hungry, and we should get something to eat. We went out for a burger and a beer, and we stopped talking about William Randolph Hearst and discussed our personal lives instead. Then he walked me home and said goodnight and that was it. I felt flattered by his attention.

"The next time I saw him was in class and he asked me to stay after. He said, 'let's walk back to my office,' and I agreed. But once we got there, everything went wrong. His hands were all over me. He grabbed me and shoved his tongue down my throat. I pushed him away, saying no, and he laughed and told me not to be shy, that if I wanted an 'A' there was an easy, enjoyable way to get it. I yelled at him to stop, and he said I'd regret it once grades came out.

"I ran from his office, and afterwards, my best friend, Aubrey Adam-Drake, consoled and calmed me down. But then she and I set to work. We believed that I couldn't be the only student who J.M. had ever pressured for sex. We asked around and discovered that several others have similar stories of mistreatment, but all have been too intimidated or ashamed to speak up."

Marina's voice sounds choked, and she sniffs back tears, which I assume are real. "J.M. abused his power, and when I gave him the chance to apologize, he blamed me for his inappropriate actions. He told me that I'd been the one to come on to him. But I'm the one who's been violated! Nobody should be treated like that. That's why I believe that Professor Martin should be fired."

"You realize, Ms. Hunt, that student government officials have no power over the hiring or firing of professors," Finn says, almost apologetically. He has this look, misty eyes combined with a determinedly set jaw, and I wonder if he wants to fix all the world's problems just for her. For a moment I find myself wishing Finn would look at me like that too. Then I shake it off. After all, I'm a feminist, and wishing for a man to "take care of me" is like embracing the notion that men are, in some way, superior to women, and I refuse to do that.

"I understand," Marina answers. "My purpose tonight was to make my story public. I want his pattern of abuse to stop. I am prepared to go through the proper channels and file a formal complaint tomorrow." She ends her little speech with a firm nod of her quivering chin, and then she gets up and glides back to her seat.

The room is silent.

I wait for J.M. to say something, to yell in anger, to bluster his way through this awful, awkward moment. But he just sits, staring at the floor, looking like he might vomit. Then another young woman stands by her chair and speaks. "He did the same thing to me."

She launches into her story and people start talking over each other, and it's chaos until Professor Martin jumps up and nearly runs from the room. After that, any hope of regaining order is lost. I rush off as well, and go back to my dorm, where I keep my promise and spend all night finishing my expose'.

It's published the very next day, and then students stage protests outside J.M.'s lecture hall. My story is picked up by the wire services, making national headlines, and news outlets like CNN and *The New York Times* send their own reporters to Columbia. Marina's father, Oliver Hunt, is quoted: "An older man should never use his power to prey on a young girl. It doesn't matter who he is; it doesn't matter who she is. Any guy who'd do that is scum, end of story."

Professor Martin is put on unpaid leave while the university conducts a formal investigation of misconduct. Everyone thinks that J.M. won't be back. They're not wrong, but they also don't understand the full story. Once J.M. was up against the awesome power of Aubrey Adam-Drake and Marina Hunt, he never stood a chance.

Chapter 4

"To our success!" Aubrey raises her Mai Tai, Marina raises her Manhattan, and I raise my diet coke, which I had to order since it's a few more months until I turn 21. (When we sat down, they told me that Aubrey's birthday was in September, and that Marina never gets carded. Of course she doesn't. She's Marina Hunt.) We're at a bar near campus, Tiki Tessa's, and our glasses meet and clink together, hovering over the middle of the table.

"To our success!" the three of us gleefully repeat.

After we each take a drink, I dare to ask, "So, what did you mean that you and Marina 'chose' me?"

Marina raises her perfectly arched eyebrows. "You told her?"

"Sure." Aubrey shrugs. "Elyse would never tell on us. She's too excited about breaking the story." Aubrey turns to me, putting both her palms flat against the table, like she's confessing or explaining something complicated. Maybe both. "Okay, so Marina and I came to Columbia wanting to make a difference, but given our notoriety, we had to be careful. Then we heard about what a perv J.M. is. The rumors were awful, but nothing ever really caught up with him. And everyone knows that men get away with sexually exploiting women *all the time* while the victims get questioned and harassed."

"But we knew that nobody would question or harass either of us," Marina adds. "It's a perk of fame and power. So, I signed up for J.M's course and led him on a little, you know? Sure enough, he came on to me." She tilts her chin. "I had to do it that way. We weren't going to get him fired until we had proof."

"But isn't that entrapment?" I ask.

"Who cares?" Marina flips her hair off her shoulder as she speaks. "He's still guilty. He harassed so many girls, but nobody would listen to them. Go ahead and question our methods. I'll never regret giving these girls a voice."

Heat rushes to my face. "I—I wasn't suggesting you should have regrets," I stammer. "I'm just surprised you'd take such a huge risk. What if you got exposed in all this?"

"Is that your plan?" Marina demands. "To expose Aubrey and me?"

"Elyse wouldn't do that," Aubrey insists. Her trust in me is flattering, unless she thinks I'm too docile, too simple, to do such a thing.

But I go with it. "No, of course I wouldn't." I speak directly to Marina. "But what if word gets out through some other source? Aren't you worried about your reputation?"

Marina's shoulders sag and for a split second I wonder if she's going to cry. "I figure, what the hell?" She straightens herself in her chair and squares her shoulders. "I'm no stranger to bad publicity. When my parents got divorced my mom wanted to send me off to a Swiss boarding school because every day, *The National Enquirer* had some new, salacious story about one or both of my parents, and I got teased constantly. But I told her no. I was only twelve at the time, yet I knew this would be an issue my entire life. I had to develop a thick skin and not care what people say."

Aubrey reaches across the table to squeeze Marina's hand while speaking to me. "We had to be selective about how we got the story out and not just use our families' influence, you know? So, we researched all the reporters on *The Spec*, found you — I *love* that you're taking so many women's studies courses and how you're a volunteer at that refugee's shelter close to campus, and you did that internship last summer with the U.N., — anyway, we set things up so you'd be the one to break the story."

I take a gulp of my diet coke, wishing it was more than zero proof. I could use a little liquid fortification right about now. "You should have told me."

"We did," says Aubrey, still smiling.

"No, you should have told me from the beginning."

"You're upset," says Aubrey, twirling the tiny pink umbrella that came in her drink between her fingers. "Gosh, that's too bad. I was hoping you'd be cool with it."

"Well, you can't say anything," says Marina. "We'd deny the story, you'd have no proof, and you'd only hurt yourself. And certainly, don't talk about it with Finn."

I grip my diet coke glass, which is slick with condensation. "Why would I say anything to Finn? Unless I'm covering a student government meeting, I'll never even see him again."

"No, actually, you're about to see him right now," says Aubrey. She points to a cluster of fake palm trees near the entrance of the bar. Finn stands next to them, scanning the bamboo-filled room, clearly looking for us. Aubrey waves and he waves back. "He's coming this way."

My heart does a loop-de-loop as he navigates toward our table, past electric tiki torches and underneath paper lanterns that hang from the ceiling. I see he's wearing another Henley like the one he wore in his office last week; this time the sleeves are pushed up, revealing a pair of strangely attractive sharp elbows. "Hello, ladies," he says, as good-natured as if we're all good friends. "Mind if I join in the celebration?"

"Pull up a chair," Aubrey says. "We're so glad you could make it."

Finn sits. He offers Marina a dazzling smile and gives me a quick lopsided grin, which I return. I can't help it; I want Finn to like me. But I barely register on his radar as he immediately turns to

Aubrey. "I saw the interview with your dad in *The Atlantic.* Sounds like his charitable foundation is going well."

Aubrey's large eyes grow wider. "Yeah, I hope so. He's really worried about his image after… well, you know." She doesn't have to complete her thought; we all know exactly what she means. A year ago, Prince Adam authored a book called *The Myth of Prince Charming*, where he gave his advice on making modern marriage work. He wrote, "The alpha male is an outdated notion. A true prince will respect his wife's power and ambition and find her more desirable for it." He did the talk show circuit, espoused his relationship philosophies, and swore up and down that he doesn't regret leaving Liechtenstein or marrying into the Drake family. He insisted that he loves how driven his wife is and that he hopes to one day be "First Gentleman." Three months later, he was caught having an affair with a New York socialite half his age.

"That's why I'm done with living in the public sphere," says Marina. "There's so much pressure to be perfect. Nobody talks about all the philanthropic things Prince Adam has done, only where he put his penis."

Aubrey cringes. "Marina, please. That's my dad you're talking about."

"Exactly." Marina taps her French manicured index finger against the rim of her cocktail glass. "The press and the public act like they're entitled to all his secrets, like they know him. It's so wrong."

"I agree," says Finn. He looks directly at me, arching an eyebrow and smirking, causing that one dimple of his to appear. "Reporters need to be reigned in."

I swallow roughly. Are his challenges a perverse form of flirting? Surely not. "But…," my voice comes out weak and soft, so I clear my throat, determined to sound strong. "Journalism safeguards democracy. I bet the student body would be super interested to hear their president's opinion regarding the first amendment. I'm going to assume you were being flippant, but if not, well, then we have a problem." Ha! Two can play that game.

Finn, Marina, and Aubrey all turn towards me, clearly shocked that I'd say something a tad bit subversive. At least, I think that's why they're all staring at me with knitted eyebrows and slightly parted lips. But come on, if journalists are "reigned in" to protect the elite, we're heading down a slippery slope towards tyranny.

Marina and Finn both stay a little bit pinched up until Aubrey laughs and playfully punches me in the shoulder. "I like you, Elyse. You speak the truth."

I let Aubrey's giddiness infect me and I join her, laughing. Briefly, I forget that Marina and Finn sit at our table, and for a moment, the room is only large enough for me and my new friend, Aubrey Adam-Drake.

Chapter 5

A day later, Aubrey calls. "I realize you've done Marina and me a favor," she says, with barely any preamble. "There's nothing to stop you from publishing your side of the story, including our confession that we pretty much entrapped J.M."

"True...," I say, not adding that I'd gone so far as to write something up, in the same way one might compose an emotional, I-need-to-get-some-stuff-off-my-chest-letter to an ex, the type of letter you know you're never going to send.

"So," Aubrey continues, "since you've given up one story, I thought I'd make things right by throwing a different story your way. What are your plans for tomorrow afternoon?"

"I'm pretty open," I respond. "Why?"

Aubrey tells me that she's gotten me an interview with her mom, Eleanor Adam-Drake, and, if sheer nerves can cause cardiac arrest, consider me gone. Eleanor is more than a politician, she's an icon, and with all the television and print interviews she's done over the course of her career, I'll for sure be the most inexperienced journalist she'll have ever encountered. I just hope I don't make a fool of myself.

***

"Mom, this is my good friend, Elyse Gibbons," Aubrey says the next day the moment we walk into Eleanor's office at the back of her campaign headquarters in Queens. "Elyse, this is my mom, Eleanor."

Eleanor Adam-Drake must have one of the most recognizable faces in the entire world, but I grin at the introduction like she's surprised me somehow, and meanwhile, resist pinching myself. This is actually happening. If I could choose one woman I'd like to become, it's Eleanor-Adam Drake.

She stands and steps from behind her desk, giving me full view of her tweed slacks paired with a black cashmere sweater. Eleanor always dresses like she's about to go horseback riding, and her bushy brown hair (which she passed down to Aubrey) usually looks windblown. "It's so nice to meet you, Elyse. Thanks for coming all the way to Queens to do the interview."

We discuss education reform, universal healthcare, and national security in a post-9/11 world. I try to ask tough questions, but as promised, I stay away from anything that's connected with her marriage to Prince Adam. After twenty minutes, Eleanor looks at her watch, looks at Aubrey and then back at me, and says, "Well, I hope I was able to answer all your questions. But I'm afraid we need to wrap this up."

She stands, Aubrey and I stand, and the awkward goodbye dance begins. I thank Eleanor profusely, she acts like it was no big deal, and she and Aubrey hug, making plans for dinner later that week.

Afterwards, Aubrey and I walk to a bakery rumored to have the best cupcakes in New York. I offer to pay, but she dismisses me with a wave. "My favorite is red velvet," she says, "but if you like chocolate, you've got to try the fudge buttercream." She orders before I can tell her that I love chocolate. I guess her Secret Service agent doesn't, however, because for him she orders a vanilla with pink frosting. We walk in Cunningham Park as we eat.

"What was it like growing up, having Eleanor for a mom, and being a part of the Drake dynasty?"

Aubrey licks a dab of cream cheese frosting off her thumb. "Is this part two of your interview?"

I laugh even though I'm unsure if her question is a joke. "No, just genuine curiosity. I won't publish this conversation."

"My mom is my hero." Aubrey punts at a mini pile of dried leaves on the walking path, and they scatter and separate like her unruly hair in the autumn breeze. "She's a great mom. She was always there for me and nobody believes it, but she always put me first, above whatever she was working on. The hard part was all the other stuff – you know, the expectation that everyone in the Drake family will one day hold elected office, coupled with all the criticism my grandpa gets and how we have no privacy. It's why I still need Secret Service detail. Normally grandkids of past presidents wouldn't have it, but I'm a Drake, and that means there will always be threats against my family and me."

"Yeah, I can imagine that would be rough."

"No, you can't imagine it. You have no idea."

The weight to her voice, the firm set of her mouth, and her unblinking eyes momentarily paralyzes my insides. "Sorry," I say. "I didn't mean to overstep."

"You don't need to apologize, Elyse. I'm the one who should apologize for snapping at you." She sighs, puts the last of her cupcake into her mouth, chews and swallows it down. "God, that's good. They really might be the best cupcakes in New York." She turns toward her Secret Service agent. "How was the pink frosting, Jerry?"

He gives a brief nod, and Aubrey turns back around.

The clouds hang low over our heads. They have gone from pale ashen to a deep charcoal in the minutes we've been talking. The wind picks up and I long to be in my dorm room, wrapped in my blankets and basking in the bright warmth of my reading lamp. "We should head back," I say.

Aubrey nods and we turn around. As we walk toward the car, she's quiet, resisting all my attempts to engage her in conversation.

Finally, I say, "I feel bad that I got us talking about something that upsets you. I totally put you in a bad mood, didn't I?"

"It's not your fault." She tucks a frizzy curl behind her ear and lifts her chin. "But maybe now you understand why Marina and I are friends." Half of her mouth twists into a smile. "I know we seem like opposites; she's been on the cover of *Seventeen* while every photo of me might as well be published in the Us Weekly 'Don't' section. I'm always captured in a yawn or on my latest bad hair day."

"That's not true. Don't be so hard on yourself."

"It's okay, really." She makes this laughing-sighing sound. "I know how the world sees me. But Marina is gorgeous. In her entire life, I don't think she's ever had an awkward moment. Yet she and I both understand what it's like to live in the public eye, to have everyone believe they know you, and judge you and your family all the time."

I think about my own family. I never met my dad. He lives somewhere in Ecuador, and my mom didn't get a chance to tell him about me because by the time she knew she was pregnant, she'd come home from traveling and teaching English overseas. I guess my dad was the type of one-night stand where phone numbers aren't exchanged. It was just her and me for many years, living in our townhome in West Chester, a mile away from the campus where she's a professor in the ESL department. Then mom fell in love with her yoga instructor, and he convinced her that marriage is a worthwhile institution. Now they have twin boys. I try not to resent her new family, and we both work on keeping our mother/daughter bond strong.

I guess every family has their own, unique brand of drama, but mine is generic and low-key compared to what Marina and Aubrey have gone through. "I get that I'll never understand you the way Marina does," I tell Aubrey. "but I'd really like to be friends, and I hate that I made you feel bad. Is there anything I can do to make things better?"

She turns to me with a sudden intensity. "Just be honest with me, Elyse. I have dozens of people who say whatever they think I want to hear. But I want the truth. Promise to always tell me the truth."

"Of course, Aubrey. I promise."

She smiles, we link arms, and continue our walk while pressing our sides into each other. I'm so pleased by this new bond, that it barely occurs to me how difficult it might be, keeping the promise I just made.

Chapter 6

The year I turned twelve, I got a subscription to *Popular Science* for my birthday. Every month, I read each issue from cover to cover, and among other things, learned about the migration patterns of bees and the far-reaching power of the internet. But there was one article that changed my young life. It was a time-lapse photo essay that showed the quick disappearance of the glaciers and explained how ice is its own ecosystem.

You see, with the glacier's deterioration, we lose more than clean drinking water. I mean, sure, rising sea-levels are dangerous, but that's not the point. With every drop of ice that melts, we surrender a vital part of our world. I was twelve, reading how this was happening right before our eyes, and nobody cared enough to do anything.

I panicked.

I'd have this recurring dream where I'd be standing on a glacier that would turn to slush beneath my feet. I could feel the cold and damp, and right before I'd wake, I'd try to scream. But as it always is in dreams, no sound came out. Instead, the Arctic Ocean would fill my lungs as I sank into the watery depths of our failing planet.

My mom was worried about this preoccupation of mine, about the dark circles under my eyes and how I'd stopped talking about normal things, like volleyball practice or auditions for the school musical. She wanted me to be well adjusted and not a weirdo who spent all her free-time researching global warming. But none of Mom's attempts to distract me worked, so she took me to a therapist, a new-age guy named Phil who burned incense and had me sit in a bean bag chair during our "chat" sessions. Surprisingly, Phil was helpful. He listened to me explain the importance of ice, how we can't let it melt even though we *are* letting it melt, and he asked me, "So, you feel powerless?"

"Yes, of course," I replied.

"Then you need to find your power. What can you do, that will make a difference?"

We talked and together, came up with a two-part plan. Part-one entailed activism: I would write my congressmen and send letters to the editor of the local paper. I would find a teacher to help me start an after-school program that did fundraisers for Sierra Club, and we'd set up more efficient recycling efforts.

Part-two of the plan entailed my preoccupation—okay, my fear—of ice. Because despite my crusade, my glacial nightmares continued. "You need to take control," Phil had told me. "How do you think you can do that?"

I'd shift on his beanbag chair, take in a whiff of the sandalwood incense he'd burn, and close my eyes. Behind my lids I'd see ice, slick and shiny, and I'd feel overwhelmed by its majesty. I'd realize that I had to harness that frozen power, and the only way to do so was to conquer it. I envisioned myself gliding across it. "I need to start figure skating," I told him.

I gave my poor mom no peace until she found a rink at the West Chester community center where I could take lessons and eventually join a league. Most girls started younger than me, like at six or seven, but there I was, a twelve-year-old learning her double toe loops at a painfully slow pace. But the sound my blades made when they carved into the ice, the indoor rink that was always freezing no matter how unnaturally warm it was outside, and the power of my limbs as they glided over the hard surface: it was the remedy I needed.

My nightmares stopped, and a new obsession began. And I don't use the word "obsession" lightly. Once I begin something, I never, ever quit. It's a quality that's admirable in theory but not so attractive in real life, yet my obsessiveness got me into an Ivy League school on a partial scholarship, and maybe one day it will propel me to even greater heights, like into a position where I can truly effect change. But for now, Aubrey is thrilled that I've volunteered for her mom's campaign. Not everyone feels the same way, however.

"But don't you need to study?" my roommate Sandra asks me. We're in our tiny dorm room and I'm talking to her reflection as I put in my contacts. Then I fix my long brown hair into a high bun atop my head. Sandra stands behind me, disapproving of the fact that I'm getting ready to go work the phone banks for Eleanor's senatorial campaign for the third time this week, and it's only Wednesday.

"I'll study later," I reply, taking a hairpin and wedging it into place so my bun doesn't fall apart the minute I step out into the breezy autumn night.

"Whatever." Sandra turns away, plops down on her bed, and takes out a psychology textbook. She pages through it ruefully, clicking her tongue in this chastising way. "I just don't see how you're going to keep up with all your classwork, what with your newspaper job and now all this campaign stuff. Something's gotta give. Are you going to quit skating?"

"I can't. I'd lose my scholarship." I silently count to ten to refrain from telling Sandra to chill, that she's not my mother and I can take care of myself. But I also want to come home tonight, fall into bed and get a good night's sleep so I can wake up for a 6:00 AM practice. And if Sandra is mad, she's likely to make that impossible. We'll most likely need to have a "heart to heart" until the wee hours of the night as she tearfully releases all her angst over our struggling friendship. I know this because this happened once before, and I've since managed to internalize any and all caustic remarks to prevent it from ever happening again. "I'm taking a break from volunteering at the refugee center," I say, "at least until the campaign is over. So, it's not so hard, making time for everything."

"I get it," Sandra says. "Mingling with the powerful and elite is a lot more fun and glamorous than helping all those needy immigrants."

I bite my lower lip, fighting the urge to take the bait. It's not easy, but luckily, I'm saved by a knock on our door. "Who's that?" Sandra asks.

"No idea." I assume it's for me because people don't often stop by to talk to Sandra, and when I open the door, I find Marina standing on the other side, perfectly clad in a fuzzy, pale pink sweater. Her distressed blue jeans have tiny rips in the knees that probably doubled the cost. "Oh," I say, stunned. "Hi, Marina."

As soon as Sandra hears me say Marina's name, she jumps from her bed, making her psychology textbook fall to the floor with a thud. Then she stands behind me, gawking without apology. I'm instantly mortified.

Marina, however, seems unfazed. "Aubrey said you were working the phones tonight and asked me to pick you up, so you wouldn't have to take a train."

"Wow, that's so nice of you. Let me just grab my stuff." I awkwardly step past Sandra. I feel bad about not introducing her, but if I give Sandra an opportunity to start talking, we'll never get out of here.

I grab my wool cardigan and the oversized canvas messenger bag that contains pretty much all the contents of my life. I say, "Bye Sandra, good luck studying," and step out into the hallway, joining Marina and shutting the door to my dorm room.

"That's your roommate?" Marina asks.

If there's attitude or judgement behind the question, I can't detect it. I resist saying, "Yeah, we were assigned to each other," and say instead, "Yeah. She's not perfect, but she's a good person."

"Hmm." Marina smiles slightly. "Aubrey has said the same thing about you."

***

The drive to Queens is long. There's a lot of traffic and extended, wide spaces in our conversation. "I didn't know you were volunteering for Eleanor's campaign," I say, an attempt to fill the silence.

We sit in the back seat of Marina's limo. She has a compact out and I'm awed by how she's mastered the art of applying lipstick in a moving vehicle. "I guess you could call it volunteering," she says, smacking her lips together. She snaps the compact shut, closes the lipstick, and drops them both into her Louboutin purse. "I'm organizing a celebrity fundraiser," she says. "My dad is going to be involved."

"That's cool. I didn't know your dad's a Democrat."

She shrugs. "He doesn't really have a party affiliation, just loyalty to certain candidates. But I believe in Eleanor, so I convinced him to help out." Marina smiles as she flutters her long dancer-like fingers. "We're going to do a skit where my dad teachers Eleanor how to be 'street smart' enough to represent New York."

Oliver Hunt began his career by representing mobsters in court and getting notorious criminals off on technicalities. Now there's speculation that his mafia connections got him elected as mayor of Atlantic City and that his hotels enjoy funding from illegal sources. So, there's no doubt that Oliver Hunt is street smart, but is that really the sort of endorsement Eleanor Adam-Drake needs?

I sit and contemplate, rubbing a loose piece of yarn from my sweater between my fingers. "I don't get it," I say, after a moment that was probably around thirty seconds too long.

Marina tilts her head in confusion, as if my ignorance is charming. "What don't you get?"

"Well, Eleanor has tons of knowledge and experience. And isn't going through some staged scenario to win your dad's approval sort of demeaning?"

"It's supposed to be funny," Marina answers, her voice sticky. "People like candidates who'll laugh at themselves. Eleanor usually comes off as too serious, strident even."

"Yeah," I say, not to agree, but to acknowledge that I heard her. "I hate that word, 'strident.' Men don't get called strident, and a guy with her resume would never be accused of inexperience."

Marina raises her eyebrows, and her mouth coils into an annoyed little circle. "But Eleanor isn't a guy. She's the former first-daughter, and she has an image problem. People say she's too ambitious, so we need to soften her, make her more likable."

"By staging some farce where your dad teaches her to be corrupt?"

"Wow. You really don't hold back, do you Elyse?" I neither confirm nor deny her statement because she starts laughing, as if to dismiss my bluntness as a personality quirk. She shifts in her seat, crossing her legs and looking slightly guarded. "People like my dad *because* of his flaws, not despite them. Meanwhile, Eleanor comes off as too pristine. This will make her authentic."

I smile. "Isn't *making* somebody authentic a paradox?" She doesn't smile back but I do get an eye roll out of her. "How will you frame the skit? Will it be like, 'is Eleanor New York enough to be our Senator? Does she know how to eat a big slice of pizza, and can she figure out how to buy a subway token?'"

Marina adjusts herself again, shrugging slightly. "Maybe."

I figure I've probably talked way too much and have possibly offended her, so I don't say anything else for the rest of the car ride. Thankfully, we arrive after a couple of minutes and I get out swiftly, saying over my shoulder, "Thanks for the ride, Marina." I go into the now familiar campaign office and find my spot at a table with a phone.

I like calling people, even the surly ones, so I can remind them to vote. We're not supposed to argue with anyone, and I don't, but if they give me some attitude I'm not above giving some attitude back. I figure it's my job to convince the doubters that it's in their best interest to get off the couch and vote Drake.

I'm in the middle of a conversation with a retired postal worker who isn't sure she can trust Eleanor, when Marina steps into my line of vision. "Come with me," she says, pointing to the room in the back that is Eleanor's office.

"Hold on a second," I say into the phone, and then I hold the receiver away from my mouth. "Why? I've almost got this lady convinced."

"You're needed in the back, to work on the fundraiser." Marina leans in, nearly whispering. "I told them about your idea, and they want you back there. This is a step forward, Elyse. Don't blow it."

"Hello!" The retired postal worker's Brooklyn accent blares through the receiver. "What's the idea? A telemarketer putting me on hold?!"

"Hey," I answer. "I'm not a telemarketer, and you weren't put on hold." Marina crosses her arms over her chest, tapping her foot with rapid impatience. *Wrap it up,* she tells me with her eyes. I sigh. "Vote for Eleanor," I say into the phone. "If you don't trust her then you're buying into all the right-wing talking points. Don't let them trick you. Now... good night."

I hang up and stand at my desk. "Okay, I'm ready."

Marina shakes her head. It looks like the corners of her mouth are trying to relax into laughter, but she won't let that happen. "Yeah. Getting you off the phones is a good idea. Come on, let's go."

She leads me back to Eleanor's office, to where I'd interviewed Eleanor not so long ago, but now several people are here, and I don't recognize any of them. I see neither Aubrey nor Eleanor, so I ask where they are. "Some campaign event in Harlem," Marina tells me.

"What about your dad?" I ask. "Is he on his way?"

She laughs. "No. Of course not."

"Then how is he going to know what to do for the fundraiser?"

"We'll fill him in," a woman who must be on Hunt's staff tells me. Or maybe she's an Adam-Drake campaign worker, but either way, I've never seen her around before. She has a Princess Leia hairdo with a bun on either side of her head, crooked teeth, and the air of self-satisfaction. "That's how this campaign stuff works. We, the underlings, plan, but the stars don't get bothered with the details."

I resist smirking. I mean, she can't be more than thirty, so how experienced could she be at this "campaign stuff"?

I hazard a glance at Marina, who looks annoyed at being labeled an underling. I bet she could rip Princess Leia a new one. But Marina just says "Right," because as usual, she's composed and restrained.

I mean, I could I learn a thing or two from her.

"Elyse," Marina continues, "tell them what you said to me about the fundraiser. I think you have some interesting ideas."

I lay out my ideas about Eleanor eating pizza and riding the subway and of course they're "tweaked" but people do listen to what I have to say. I realize that Marina's right; stepping into the back room *is* a big step forward. I might still be an underling, but for now, I'm also part of the inner-circle. At one point, Marina and I meet eyes, and the smile she offers me is genuinely warm and welcoming. I attempt to offer her an equally effusive smile back, but she looks away. I'll have to find a way to say "thank you" later and to recognize she's the one who got me back here. I suppose I should also recognize, if only to myself, that what Sandra said is true. Even though I've been working harder than I ever thought possible, at the same time, mingling with the powerful and elite is fun.

Chapter 7

I'm invited to attend the fundraiser, and it's probably the biggest thing that has ever happened to me. A-list celebrities will be there, including Oliver Hunt, Anton Adam, and possibly, the former president, Howard Drake. Marina loans me one of her dresses, I guess to prevent me from wearing something embarrassing. I arrive at the banquet room of Hunt Tower in a little black dress by Michael Kors, and if I do say so myself, I look good. Except, my wool sweater has left a bit of lint on the dark velvet. When Marina sees me, her nostrils flare. She's obviously piqued that I didn't achieve her brand of perfection.

"Seriously, Elyse." She uses her hand to brush and pick the fuzz from my dress. "Sometimes I think you've been living under a rock your entire life. How did you make it so far in figure skating like this?"

I don't ask how she knows about my skating career, and instead say, "What do you mean? Like what?"

"Like you're so oblivious. I thought figure skaters were supposed to be disciplined and pristine." She finishes removing the lint and straightens my dress strap. "There. Now don't spill anything on yourself. Can you manage that?"

"Yes. Of course," I say, but I do feel like a child in this swanky, low-lit room full of adults talking business while sipping cocktails. It's like visiting a foreign country.

"Good. And remind me later to give you a coat. I have at least three that I don't use anymore. I'm sure one of them would work better than that wet glob of wool you cloak yourself in."

I'm torn between indignance at her condescending tone and curiosity over what sort of coat she might give me. It's probably too late to act proud; I mean, I'm wearing one of her dresses, after all. But I'm not a charity case, and I *am* relatively accomplished as a figure skater. I'll never be Olympics level, but I didn't win the division championship my senior year of high school by being a hot mess. Maybe I'm not pristine, but nobody can fault me on that discipline thing.

I press my lips together to keep from saying anything stupid, and Marina takes my silence as a sign that I'm overwhelmed. "Don't worry," she says, smiling and patting me on the shoulder, "you look great and everybody here is really nice. Get a drink and enjoy yourself. You've earned it." She air-kisses me on the cheek, waves to someone in this crowded room, and walks away.

I shouldn't feel abandoned, but I do.

I head toward the bar, where I order a Bacardi and Coke. "I'll need to see your ID," says the bartender.

"I forgot it at home."

"That's a shame," he says. "So, what can I get you? Shirley Temple? Chocolate Milk?"

"Wow," I reply, stunned at his arrogance. "That was unnecessary."

"No," he says, his voice hard, "it was *so* necessary." He leans towards me, menacingly. "You wanna know what I hate? Over-privileged, underage girls like you, batting their eyelashes and flashing their cleavage to get me to serve them alcohol. I know your type, and I know you'll never follow through. You'll just get my bartending license suspended."

I size him up. He looks like a former high school linebacker disappointed by life: broad, big, and angry. "Okay, obviously I struck a nerve, but what do you mean: I won't follow through?"

"You know *exactly* what I mean. Don't talk down to me." Now he's shoving his face so close to mine that I can smell the alcohol on his breath. I guess he's been sampling the goods.

"Fine. Never mind. Can I please have a soda water with lemon?"

"Aren't we fancy?" He sneers. "You want something that will look like I gave you a real drink, just so you can get me in trouble."

"I think I'll try another bartender. Thanks anyway." I start to leave but he grabs my wrist, which I had stupidly placed on the bar.

His whisper is fierce. "You tell anyone lies about me and you'll regret it, understand?"

"Is there a problem here?"

I turn toward the voice behind me and realize it belongs to Finn. It's sort of dizzying, how good it is to see him. The bartender immediately releases my wrist and stands up straight. "Not at all," he says to Finn. "What can I do for you?"

"You can leave my friend alone," Finn replies, clipping his words in a somewhat threatening tone. But if he's genuinely angry, he drops his ire almost instantly, and says, "and you can get me two G&Ts." He's already holding out his ID. The bartender glances at it and silently prepares the requested drinks.

My urge is to run off, to take a private moment, catch my breath, to shed a tear or two after that strange and scary interaction. But I can't let the bartender see that he's intimidated me, and I'd be mortified to have Finn catch me thinking that he's my hero. So, I hide my shakiness by playing it cool, and I lean against the bar like there's nowhere I'd rather linger. "Hello, Finn," I say. "How are you?"

"I'm good. How are you, Elyse?"

I shrug. "Not sure. I mean, I was excited about tonight, but I'm rethinking that now."

He leans against the bar as well, angling toward me. Finn's wearing a worn white t-shirt with a blue collar and Levi's. But he also has on a gray blazer that I bet is cashmere and cost more than my entire yearly clothing budget. Unlike me, his unkempt look is deliberate, suave even, and the errant lock of hair that hangs down onto his forehead broadcasts an attitude, like he doesn't care or even realize how good looking he is.

"I thought you were amped about the skit. Didn't you help with it?"

"Yeah, and I guess I'm amped. It's just…" Biting my bottom lip, I try to ignore what I know to be true. Tonight, I'm out of my depth. "Never mind," I say. "What brings you here?"

"My dad is a campaign donor," he tells me. "Milton Beck. Haven't you heard of him?" I shake my head and Finn continues. "He's a real estate developer? He founded The Beck Companies."

Finn says this like it should ring a really loud bell in my consciousness. But it doesn't. "Sorry," I say.

Finn turns toward the bar as the bartender places down his drinks. "Thanks, Man," he says, slipping a one-dollar bill into the tip jar. Is that a jab for the bartender's treatment of me? Finn doesn't strike me as a stingy tipper. He takes the drinks, one in each hand, and then he looks at me. "Come on," he says, with a tilt of his head.

Feeling grateful for his help, I follow him. Finn crosses the room until he finds a little table that he can set the drinks on. "Here." He scoots one of the drinks across the table, so it's right in front of me. "Drink up." Then he lifts his drink to his lips and takes a hearty sip.

"I don't get it. Is this for me?" I look around the room, as if to locate Finn's date, someone who is surely highly desirable. Okay, some of the ladies here are stout, middle aged, and matronly in their cocktail dresses. But there are also a lot of young women who look like models taking a break from the runway. Surely one of them is here with Finn.

"You wanted a drink. I got you a drink," he says.

"Thank you," I say, gesturing toward the G&T. "But didn't you come with someone?"

"Just my dad." He does this little sideways shrug, half-smiling at me like I'm cute. "Are you going to drink with me, or not?"

"Okay." I take my first sip of a gin and tonic: not bad, but not something I can guzzle.

"What do you think?"

I swallow down a bit more. "It's good, but I'd have preferred a Bacardi and Coke."

"If I'd ordered that, the bartender would have known it was for you, and he wouldn't have given it to me. Besides, that's a sorority girl drink. You're better than that."

"Really?" I flush a little at the semi-compliment. "How do you know?"

"I'm extremely perceptive." He laughs. "For instance, I'll bet you five dollars I can guess your favorite author."

I scrunch up my face, puzzled. "How would that work? Even if you guess correctly, I could just lie and say it's someone else."

He shakes his head. "Nope. Because I'm ninety-nine percent sure you packed a pen into that teeny little purse you're carrying. Take it out, and write down the author's name on this cocktail napkin."

I laugh because he's right; I did manage to squeeze a pen into my evening bag. I mean, you never know when you'll need to write something down. I take it out and start scrawling on the damp cocktail napkin Finn passes to me. It's difficult, as the napkin tears a little under the pressure of the pen, but I manage to write my favorite author's name legibly, ostensibly keeping it hidden from Finn's view.

"Okay. Who is my favorite author?" I'm torn between hoping he'll guess correctly (which would mean he *gets* me) and hoping he's wrong, so I can tease him about his overconfidence.

"It's so easy," he chuckles. "Margaret Atwood, obviously."

"Why?"

He shrugs. "It's a formula. You're not a lit major and you're clearly a feminist, meaning you'll go for some woman from the 20th century. You're bright and analytical, yet also emotional, so that puts you in one of two camps: Sylvia Plath or Margaret Atwood.

Both authors are a major downer, but Plath is so depressed that she can't get outside her own head. That's not you." He squints his eyes, peering at me gleefully. "Atwood has a sense of humor and underneath all her grim projections, she encourages activism." He smiles and waves his fingers in a jazz-hands sort of way. "Voila! Your favorite author is Margaret Atwood."

"Great explanation," I concede. "But your logic is flawed. Since, as you said, I'm not a lit major, why would you assume I'd prefer a novel to an autobiography? You didn't even consider someone like Emmeline Pankhurst."

"Who?"

I raise my eyebrows in pretend shock. "She was a British suffragette who wrote that putting the vote in women's hands was desperately necessary. And when she advocated for poor, unprotected mothers, her critics labeled her militant." I take a sip of my G&T, letting the ice tinkle as I raise and lower my glass. "Did you not learn about Pankhurst in the same women's studies course where you studied Plath and Atwood?"

"I must have been sick that day." He reaches out, his right index finger briefly gliding over my left hand as it rests against the table. "But admit it, Elyse; I guessed correctly, didn't I?"

Something about Finn's soft, unassuming tone, coupled with that dimple when he smiles and oh yeah, his glittering blue eyes, gets my heart fluttering. Do other people go through this sort of thing?

Be cool, Elyse. I tell myself as I take a breath. "Okay, sure."

Finn reaches across the table and grabs the napkin which, yes, has Margaret Atwood written upon it.

"Hurrah!" He cries. "You owe me five bucks."

"Yes, except you made up your 'formula' as you went along." I smirk. "You watched me write on my napkin and that's how you figured it out."

Finn raises his eyebrows and grins, causing his dimple to reappear. "I admit nothing." He downs the rest of his drink. "Do you want another?"

"Shouldn't I buy, seeing as how I owe you five bucks?"

"Don't worry about it. We'll figure out a payment plan later."

He gets up as if to head back to the bar, but I stop him by saying, "Hey. Who's your favorite author, Finn?" It suddenly feels urgent that I find this out.

He surprises me by walking around the table and standing close to me. "I'd tell you, but then I'd have to kill you." He lightly chuckles at his own silly joke.

"Seriously, though." I peer into his eyes. "Who do you like?"

He leans in, his breath is warm against my cheek, his words softly reaching my ears. "I don't have a favorite author yet. I'm still figuring out what I think and who I like. Except, I know I like you."

Our eyes are locked, and for a moment I almost think he's going to lean down and kiss me in this crowded room. And if he did, I would so totally let him.

"Hey, there you are." Aubrey approaches and gives me a quick embrace. "You look amazing."

"So do you," I say. In the middle of feeling flustered, and half-relieved/half-disappointed that the moment between Finn was broken, I'm wondering if Marina was also Aubrey's stylist for the evening. Her hair is slicked back into a knot at the base of her neck and she's wearing a strapless gown in burgundy velvet. The result is stunning, even if she looks slightly self-conscious at showing so much skin.

"We'll start the skit soon. You should come back now and meet Oliver and say hi to my mom, because afterwards they'll be super busy talking to all the donors."

I take a swig of my G&T and try not to cough any of it back up. "Okay," I rasp. "Let's go."

"I'll come too." Finn states. "I've always wanted to meet Oliver Hunt."

"Great," Aubrey replies. "Follow me."

We let Aubrey lead us into this little area that I guess you could call backstage. I recognize an actress from a TV sitcom, a pitcher from the NY Yankees, and a comedian from one of those shows on Comedy Central. They'll each perform in the skit, but they may as well be the wait staff, because all the oxygen in the room is taken up by Oliver Hunt. Even though he's surrounded by celebrities, he moves and speaks like he's the only one who matters, looking in real life just like he does on TV. He's wearing his trademark suspenders, and his tall, lean body (save a bit of a paunch) moves fluidly. Except for an angry jolt of energy here or there and an energetic jerk of his balding head, he emits an aura of supreme self-satisfaction. And everyone lets him command the space as if it's his God-given right.

"I get it." He speaks to Marina in a gravelly voice and flips through some papers, which I assume is the script. "I make the audience laugh, and at the end I praise Eleanor. But you know I'm gonna add in some of my own lines, right? Otherwise I can't have fun, and believe me, you want me to have fun."

Before I think better of it, I start talking. "Actually, I helped write the skit, and we agonized over every line. You know how this sort of event can go: say one wrong thing and it makes headlines for a week. You should probably stick to the script."

Marina glares at me like I just killed a kitten with my bare hands, but Oliver Hunt seems more confused than angry. "Who the hell are you?"

"This is Elyse Gibbons," says Aubrey, coming between us. "Marina and I are school friends with her, and she's been working on my mom's campaign. She also writes for *The Spec* and was the one who broke the story about—"

Oliver cuts her off. He looks past me at Finn. "You're Milton Beck's boy, aren't you?"

Finn steps forward, his hand outstretched. "Yes. It's an honor to meet you, Sir."

Oliver shakes Finn's hand and gives him a friendly little slap on the back. "Likewise, likewise. And don't worry. The ugly rumors — no, lies—about your dad: nothing will come of them. We'll make sure the people who started it will pay. We'll *make* them pay."

Finn clears his throat, and for a moment I worry he might cry. "Thank you, Sir."

Suddenly there's a flurry of activity as Eleanor enters. "Okay, I'm here. Are we ready?"

If Oliver commands all the oxygen in the room, Eleanor claims every bit of psychic energy. Now that she's arrived, I feel guilty for giving anything but her most pressing issues more than a moment's thought. Her entrance is like a slap in the face, and I'm not sure that's a good thing.

"Hello, Eleanor. Good to see you again." Oliver looks her over, his expression contradicting his words. It's like he's blanching in the presence of a woman who doesn't get her power from youth or beauty.

I mean, she looks fine. She wears gray wool pants, with a cream-colored tunic that has mother-of-pearl buttons. Her hair is set into waves that frame her face, and the injustice of it all hits me. She must have spent far longer than Oliver did on her appearance, but only Eleanor will be critiqued over her looks, over her voice, over everything; that's the danger of being a female politician.

This isn't lost on her, especially not the "politician" thing. She works the room, saying hello to everyone and thanking them for being here. "Elyse!" she says when gets to me, "It's so nice to see you again."

"Thank you," I reply, pleased that she remembers me. "Good luck with the skit tonight. I have a feeling it will go great."

"Thank you. Thank you so much." She smiles that broad smile of hers, and I get the feeling she didn't really hear me or that my words didn't register. I bet she couldn't even say what she's thanking me for.

"Ms. Drake, it's an honor to meet you." Finn extends his hand. "I've worked with Aubrey at Columbia, and nobody on campus has such a great mind and sense of integrity as your daughter."

If Eleanor's eyes were slightly glazed over a moment ago, they sharpen into focus now. It had to be the mention of Aubrey, a surefire way to break through any of Eleanor's trances. She shakes Finn's hand. "Thank you," she says warmly. "And what is your name?"

"Finneas Beck."

Eleanor opens her mouth to respond, but Aubrey breaks into the conversation.

"Mom, come on. It's time." She shepherds Eleanor, Oliver, and the others onto stage, leaving Finn, Marina, and me behind. I hadn't even realized that Marina was still in the room.

"I'm surprised you're not playing stage manager," I say to her now. "Wasn't the sketch your baby?"

Marina shrugs one shoulder and heads for the door. "Whatever," she says lightly. "Aubrey likes to be in charge, and everyone always assumes that between the two of us, she's the smart one."

"And that doesn't bother you?" I ask.

"Nope. If people have low expectations of me, it lets me off the hook. And tonight, it means I can enjoy the party."

But as Finn and I follow her out into the banquet hall where we can watch with the rest of the guests, I wonder what thoughts really brew beneath Marina's head of gorgeous auburn hair. For all her perfection, does Marina harbor insecurities? Is it possible that she's jealous of awkward, ugly-duckling Aubrey?

I don't harp on this for long. The skit is a hit and the evening plays out like a dream. Howard Drake even makes an appearance, and when I get to meet him, I realize everything they say about him is true.

"Elyse, this is my grandad, Howie." We're standing at the build-your-own sushi table when Aubrey introduces us. He turns all his attention on me, and for a moment I believe I've become the center of his universe. "Well, hello Elyse," he says, in his warm, slow drawl. "Thank you for coming out tonight. Aubrey says such wonderful things about you. I just love getting to meet her friends."

"Thank you, Mr. President. I have to say, I'm a big fan."

His rosy cheeks rise as a lopsided grin takes over his face. "Well, thank you," he says, as if I'm the first person to ever pay him such a compliment. "But from what I hear, you'll have your own set of fans one day. Aubrey says you're very bright, very talented. And you're a figure skater? Tell me, are those moves you do as dangerous as they look on the Olympics?"

I fill him in on the risks of triple toe loops, and he listens, riveted, while we compose our spicy tuna rolls. There are so many questions I want to ask him, like *how does one get elected president,* and, *what is it like, having the awesome power and responsibility of leading the free world?* But somebody new grabs his attention away. He apologizes, repeats how happy he was to have met me, and is on his way.

"I saw that you got to meet the great Howie Drake," Finn says to me, about an hour later. I had gone to find a bathroom, and on my trek through the gilt-covered lobby, I encountered Finn, sitting with school-boy good posture in one of those gold upholstered chair/couch things that are everywhere in this hotel. They're pretty, but they don't look super comfortable. I'm afraid if touch one, I'll leave a stain.

"You were watching me?" I ask.

"I was watching Howie Drake," says Finn. "And not out of admiration. I was curious how many women he'd hit on tonight."

I come close, but not too close to Finn and the loveseat that he's perched upon. I don't want it to seem like I'm angling for an invitation to sit next to him. "Howie Drake wasn't hitting on me."

Finn laughs. "Obviously."

"Wait. Why 'obviously?'"

"Because you're a friend of his granddaughter's, she was standing right there, and even he has boundaries. Don't worry, I wasn't commenting on your level of attractiveness."

"I wasn't worried," I respond quickly, realizing I sound defensive or like I'm lying. Suddenly I'm tired. I want to be home, and not home in my dorm room, but home in my childhood bedroom where the most challenging thing I'd do all day is get up early for my rink time, practice my latest routine and hope I don't fall on my ass. "What are you doing out here?" I ask. "Why aren't you in the party?"

"Just waiting while my driver gets the car ready. I'm going back."

"Oh." I look at Finn and really see his heavy eyelids and drooping mouth. He looks as tired as I feel. "Okay, well, have a good night."

"How are you getting back to campus?" His question comes out loud, abrupt, and full of nerves, but that can't be right.

"I was just going to take the train."

"Alone? At this time of night?" He blinks at me a couple of times, and then he stands. With one hand extended, presumably for me to take, he says, "Let me give you a ride."

Then I do something totally crazy. When my hand rises, I let it join with Finn's. We're *holding hands*, which is strangely intimate and wonderful. We make our way to the coat check to get my sweater and bag, and we're still holding hands when an older version of Finn approaches. "You're heading out?" He says to Finn. "Without saying goodnight?"

Instead of releasing my hand, Finn grasps it more tightly. "I'm sorry, Dad. I thought you saw me wave as I left the banquet hall."

Finn's father is tall and broad, with a head of thick white hair that compliments his perfectly tailored evening suit. "I expected more than a wave, Finneas." Somehow, even though his voice is soft, it stings with disapproval. "Come around on Sunday. Your mother wants you to."

"Of course." Finn says this to his father's back, as he's already walking away. Then Finn turns his head toward me. "Sorry I didn't introduce you. It wasn't the right time."

"Don't worry about it."

I let him lead me out front, where his car waits. We climb into the back, with its plush, cushiony seat, low lighting, and soft hum of classical music.

"Did you have a good time tonight?" Finn asks.

"I did," I say. "What about you?"

He nods. "It was cool to meet Oliver Hunt. I've always admired him."

I don't respond because if you can't think of anything nice to say, don't say anything at all. I feel my brain-activity dip, like it was a sharp line, full of angles, but now it's a sloped curve, weighted down by fatigue. "Hey," I murmur, "did you mean what you said earlier?"

"You'll have to be more specific. What did I say?"

I almost answer with: *You said that you know you like me.* But suddenly it feels pathetic to bring that up. So instead I say, "You told the bartender that I'm your friend. Am I?"

He squeezes my hand and turns his head toward mine. "Sure." His voice is warm, his tone yielding. "I mean, I am if you want me to be."

Now my heart must be overcompensating for my brain's malaise. It jumps and bangs against my ribcage in a single, glorious bolt of rebellion.

"Yeah, that sounds good." I smile at Finn and he returns my smile. For a second, I again wonder if Finn is going to tilt his head down and kiss me, and my body goes both warm and cold at the prospect. But the moment passes, nothing happens, and I turn my face away from his. "I'm exhausted," I say.

"Yeah, me too. You can nap if you want."

In the expanse of the backseat, we're sitting way closer than necessary. I let my head drop to his shoulder and close my eyes. He smells like limes and cedar, and the cashmere of his jacket is like a blanket against my cheek. I wouldn't have thought it possible, but sleep comes almost instantly.

Chapter 8

I decide I should cover the second Parents' Weekend of my college career for *The Spec* since I covered the first, and I have it on strict authority that Oliver Hunt will be participating in the campus events. "It should be very newsworthy," I tell my editor, and she agrees without argument that I can be the one assigned to it. I guess my connection to Aubrey and Marina gained me some clout.

Then my mom calls.

"I'll arrive on Friday afternoon," she says, as if we'd already discussed it. "See if you can get me a guest room in your dorm."

I take a breath before answering. "Mom, registration ended a long time ago. It's way too late to get you a room."

"No problem," she says. "I'll just crash on your floor. Baby, it will be fun, like we're having a sleepover."

"Sure," I mutter, gulping down unease. "But I might be really busy this weekend. I have a lot to do for the paper."

"I promise I won't get in your way."

I don't dispute it even though of course she'll get in my way. But it's useless to say so. That would hurt her, and hurting my mom is at the very top of my list of things I hate to do.

On Friday when my mom arrives, we first head to my dorm room. Luckily Sandra is out when we get there. Still, I dread having to introduce my mom to my roommate. I can already hear Sandra's passive-aggressive sighs as she communicates the imposition of my mom sleeping on our floor. Scratch that. I'll let my mom have the bed and I'll sleep on the floor.

After we drop off Mom's bags, we walk to The Crawl, which is this campus-wide event of gallery openings, concerts, and street performances. "Let's go to the Wallach first," I say. "There's supposed to be an art show about invisible civilizations and the human psyche."

"Interesting combination," Mom says. "Will there be wine and hors d'oeuvres?"

"Probably." I chuckle. "This is the Ivy League, after all."

"Right," Mom says, linking her arm through mine. "I forget how fancy you are."

She's joking but she's not joking. Mom has never tried for upper-crust sophistication; why should she when she has that international-bohemian vibe going for her instead? But Mom's come close, at times, to accusing me of trying to be something I'm not, what with my figure skating and lofty career goals.

"How are the boys?" I ask, referring to my brothers, who just started kindergarten.

"They're great. Danny is already reading at a first-grade level, and David just joined the Little Tykes soccer team."

Mom loves talking about Danny and David, which is fine, but it also serves as a reminder that she's way more interested in parenting them than she ever was with me when I was their age. Of course, with me she was a single mom and life was hard. And I doubt that I was ever very easy, at least as daughters go.

We make it to the Wallach, unlink arms, and enter the gallery. I resist silently comparing Mom to the other mothers here: her in a flowy denim skirt, a corduroy jacket, and hair pulled back in a scrunchie; them in tweeds, cashmere, and diamond stud earrings. *Appearance doesn't matter,* I tell myself, even though I don't altogether believe it. Lately, I'm thinking that appearances can mean everything.

Mom gets herself a glass of wine and we both sample some filo-dough cheese things that are divine. We also look at the paintings, like a huge mural of a cartoon-like cat eating a realistically drawn mouse, complete with blood spurting from its neck. "What do you think this has to do with civilization or the psyche?" she asks me.

"Survival of the fittest? Universality of the food chain?" I shrug. "You've got me."

My mom burps. "Excuse me," she says. "I always get indigestion after a long car trip."

"Do you need to use the bathroom?" I point toward a hallway. "I think it's down there."

Mom hands me her glass of wine and heads off to the ladies' room. I remain rooted to my spot, self-consciously wondering if some campus official might card me. So just to be defiant, I take a fortifying sip of the wine to calm my nerves.

Then a commotion comes from behind, complete with the sound of cameras clicking and people moving out of the way. Oliver Hunt is here along with Marina, and he makes a big show of draping his arm over his daughter's shoulder while loudly appreciating the art. "Love the colors," he says. "These paintings are really something."

A man in a suit approaches him, his hand outstretched. Hunt smiles and gives him a shoulder-slap in recognition. Marina, who looks like she'd rather be scrubbing down an outhouse, spots me across the room, escapes her father's grasp, and comes over.

"How's it going, Elyse?"

"Great," I say, realizing I sound totally insincere.

Marina raises an eyebrow. "Are you covering this for *The Spec?*"

"Sort of," I tell her. "I'm taking notes inside my mind so I can write something up later. But I'm also here with my mom. She's in the bathroom."

Marina's icy expression melts a little. "That's so great. Your mom dropped everything to spend Parents' Weekend with you?"

Maybe I shouldn't laugh at her sentimental tone, but I can't help it. "Why do you sound so surprised?" I ask. "It's not unheard of, for a mom and dad to clear their schedules and spend Parents' Weekend with their kid. Your dad's doing it."

Marina's voice goes flat. "Only because his PR gal said there would be image-improving photo-ops if he did." She shakes her head. "I know I shouldn't talk since I used to be into all that stuff, but seriously—I've grown out of the constant need for mass-adoration, yet he never will."

"Oh." I dare to place my hand on her shoulder, hoping she'll accept my friendly advance and not think it condescending or overly sympathetic. Thank God Marina relaxes under my touch.

"Sorry," she says. "I was feeling sorry for myself just now, and people hate it when I do that. By all appearances, I have everything."

"But do appearances even matter?" I ask, voicing my thought from just moments ago. "I mean, I understand how you feel. I *should* be happy that my mom came all the way here to visit me."

"But you're not happy?" Marina gently asks. "Why not? What's wrong?"

Her kindness unexpectedly brings tears of frustration to my eyes. "I don't know," I choke out. "I really wanted to cover this for *The Spec,* especially the part about your dad's participation, but I can't do a good job if I'm escorting her around. And I won't be at my best if I have to sleep on my dorm room floor."

Marina knits her brow. "Huh?"

I shake my head. "It's not a big deal," I state, sure that I'm failing miserably at stoicism. "But by the time my mom decided to come, it was too late to get her a guest room, and hotels in the area are outrageous. So, she'll sleep in my bed and I'll sleep on the floor."

"But that sounds awful!" Marina exclaims. "Especially with whats-her-name, that intense roommate of yours. You don't want that!"

Before I can respond, my mom re-enters the room and finds me in the same spot where I was. "Sorry I took so long." She places her hand over her belly. "My stomach is doing a number on me." Then she smiles like she's just noticed Marina standing there. "Who's your friend, Elyse?"

I know she already recognizes Marina, because we used to watch her reality show together, and Mom would scoff at all the excesses of Marina's lifestyle. Nonetheless, I introduce them to each other.

"It is so nice to meet Elyse's mom," Marina says. "Your daughter is such a great friend."

My mother's mouth twists into a confused-looking smile. I'd told her all about Aubrey on our phone conversations, but I barely mentioned Marina because I figured Mom would judge me for it.

"That's so sweet of you." Mom lets her words linger in the air, probably because she wants to pay Marina a compliment but can't figure out what's appropriate to say to a reality-tv-star/notorious litigator's daughter.

But Marina's been handed compliments her whole life and she clearly doesn't need any extra right now. "Do you two have dinner plans? I know my dad would love to treat you to a meal at Hunt Plaza, and of course, he'd want you to stay overnight as well."

I gasp. "Marina, are you sure?"

She nods. "Trust me Elyse, you'll be doing me a favor."

"That's so generous," says my mom, but I can hear the skepticism in her voice. She never has enough bad things to say about Oliver Hunt when he's bragging about his legal victories on CNN. Still, I know that pure curiosity will compel Mom to accept his generosity.

"Great, then it's settled." Marina gestures toward her dad, who is still working the room. "Come on," she says to my mother, "let me introduce you."

I'm a step behind them, trying not to stumble from the crazy 180-degree turn this evening just took.

Later, after a lavish steak dinner, my mom passes out underneath 1000-thread-count sheets atop a king-sized bed inside a deluxe Hunt Plaza Suite. "Come by my room later," Marina had said as dinner was wrapping up. "I have that coat for you."

At first, I wasn't going to go. I mean, haven't I already accepted enough handouts from Marina? But then my mind began to race, fearful that she'll think me rude or like I'm blowing her off. So, I take the elevator to the umpteenth floor and knock on the numbered door she'd told me to find. Marina answers almost instantly, wrapped in a silk kimono and holding a glass of white wine.

"Come in." She gestures me inside, and I follow her into a lavish suite decorated in alternating shades of cream, mauve, and gray. There are enough silk throw pillows in every corner of the room that she could bury someone alive with them if she wanted to.

"I can never thank you enough," I say, as soon as we're inside. "I know what you sacrificed, and I'm sure your dad must be furious. Hanging out with my mom and me hardly gave him the photo ops he was looking for."

"Don't worry about it," Marina puts down her wine and goes toward what must be a closet. "Hanging with you and your mom was way more fun than anything my dad's publicist wanted us to do."

"Well, I'm glad you think so, but I don't want to make Oliver Hunt angry, at me or at you."

Marina uses one hand to wave off that thought, like she can physically bat it away into oblivion. She uses her other hand to reach into her closet and pulls out a blousy gray jacket with a sash. "Here," she says, handing me the jacket. "It's like your sweater, only way nicer."

I take the jacket but keep my gaze focused on her. "Thank you, Marina. I really appreciate it. I hope you know that."

Marina rolls her eyes and I wonder if somehow I just said the wrong thing. "Don't make such a big deal out of everything, Elyse. I didn't sacrifice anything for you." She adjusts her silk kimono, letting an extra bit of flesh around her cleavage show. "You were exactly right for my dad's photo ops: a beautiful girl and her down-to-earth mother. It was perfect."

A lump forms in my throat. "You're just being nice."

"No, really. It was perfect." She pauses, and I notice how flushed her cheeks are, how she's parting her lips. "You're perfect, Elyse."

And then it's like she leans forward to kiss me, but that can't be right. I step back, confused, wondering if I'm inadvertently high off something or maybe I've seen one too many lesbian films.

Marina laughs, running a hand through her hair. "Wow. Don't mind me. I'm on my third glass of wine, and I guess I'm a little loopy."

"Right. Of course. Well, thanks again," I stutter, rushing away from this awkward moment and rushing away from her. Whatever that was, hopefully we can both live it down.

"Elyse!" She calls after me and I turn. "I'm sure you'll write about this evening for *The Spec.* That's fine. But you can't say anything that will make me, or my father look bad, okay?"

It's the most uncertain, the most vulnerable, I've ever heard her sound, and I have even less of an idea how to respond to her now than I did just a moment ago. I say the first thing that comes to mind. "Marina, how could I possibly say anything negative, when there's nothing negative to say?"

"Great." Marina's voice and demeanor hardens slightly around the edges. "So, you promise?"

As a journalist, I know I need to be careful, agreeing to this sort of demand. But my response slips out before I can control it. "Uh, sure."

"Wonderful. Thank you." She switches back into her officious, confident mode. "Well, goodnight."

"Good night," I say, feeling unsettled. I know I'm far from perfect, but I do pride myself on being sincere, on being honest. After all, words have power and promises have consequences. So, what sort of impossible promise did I just make?

Chapter 9

My first figure skating event of the year is a few days later, but there's no way my mom can stick around for it. That's fine; it's not even a competition, just a showcase to get people excited about our team. I'm torn about even participating, what with the election so close. Time spent skating is time I could be working for Eleanor. But if I want to keep my place on the team I must perform because my coach, Carly, thinks that with all my political work, I've lost my devotion to the ice. So, on Saturday morning we stand at the edge of the rink. I'm in sweats, still sleepy as I prepare to warmup, and she's in her Columbia coach tracksuit, already fully awake and sipping from a steaming cup of coffee. "With all the practices you've missed, I ought to just kick you off the team," she says.

"But I've been practicing on my own. I swear. I come here late at night or early in the morning, whenever I can after all my other stuff is done. You'll see. I'm as prepared as anyone else on the team."

This isn't a lie, and maybe Carly believes me, but her eyes narrow as she gives me a hard stare. "Just be grateful you don't do pairs. Being a soloist is saving you right now."

That may be, but I don't do pairs for a reason; I'm a soloist all the way. I'd much rather do a series of jumps and spins where I'm responsible for catching myself than rely on some figure-skating-arranged-marriage-buddy to catch me, hold me upside-down, and twirl me at breakneck speed, his tenuous grip the only thing keeping me from falling and cracking my head open.

"I promise I'll be at all the practices once the campaign is over," I tell Carly.

She rolls her eyes. "You'd better be."

That's my cue to get out on the ice, so I take off my skate guards and do just that. At first, I just skate lazy loops around the rink, letting my body sway as velocity propels me forward, trusting that soon all the energy I'm sort of exerting will warm me up. But Carly is watching, and I can feel her gaze, silently demanding that I step up my game and show her the benefit of all my self-scheduled practice sessions. I move faster, trying to get good edge control and speed so I can execute a decent spiral.

Then, from the corner of my eye, I spot a guy sitting in the bleachers, and I know without knowing that his eyes are on me. I start stroking across the ice, using the edges of my skates to expand my pace and gain the velocity needed to break into a flying spin. Carly will probably yell at me later. "What were you thinking," she'll chide, "doing a flying spin before you're fully warmed up? If you'd hurt yourself it would have served you right."

But I don't fall, and I don't get hurt. I catch good air with my jump and transition seamlessly into a sitting/spinning position, managing at least a half dozen rotations before I slow to a stop. Once I'm still, I stand, confident that by meeting eyes with the guy sitting in the bleachers, I'm meeting eyes with Finn.

I'm not wrong. There he is, huddled in his wool pea coat and stocking cap, his eyes looking a lighter blue than normal this morning, like they're reflecting the sheen of the ice.

I skate over to the railing. "This is a surprise," I say. "Are you a figure skating fan?"

He gives me a crooked smile, and oh God, there's that dimple. "Not really. I've watched the winter Olympics with my mom before, but this will be my first live event."

"You know it doesn't start for another four hours, right?"

He lets his mouth drop open in pretend shock. "No way. I guess that's why I got my pick of seats."

"And you also got in free. They haven't even started selling tickets yet."

"Right." He stands. "So, I'll leave and come back." He turns like he's about to walk out.

"You can't go," I say. "Not until you tell me why you're really here."

Finn hunches his shoulders into a shrug. "I woke early, went for a walk, and without meaning to, ended up at your dorm. And I thought, 'Why not ask Elyse out for waffles?' I knocked at your door. Your roommate, who seemed sort of annoyed that I'd gotten her out of bed, said you were here. But I don't suppose you can go for waffles?"

I shake my head no. "My coach would kill me."

"Okay." He arches an eyebrow. "Dinner, later?"

"Umm…" I rub my freezing fingers together, trying to increase their circulation. "I know the other night you said you'd be my friend, but I wasn't sure if that meant we'd actually spend time together, you know, in a way that wasn't accidental or random."

It could be due to the freezing temp of the ice rink, but Finn's cheeks pinken a little. "I don't believe in random accidents."

"How nice for you."

"So, will you have dinner with me later?"

Ever since the night of the fundraiser, I've analyzed and reanalyzed my encounter with Finn dozens of times. I can't *not* admit to myself that I like him, but still… he and I come from different worlds, and I don't want to be his slumming-it college romance. And, if I keep talking to him, any muscle warmth I gained during my few minutes on the ice will congeal into a damp tepidness. That's got to be a sign. Besides, I'm not normally down on myself but I know that dating him would tie me up in emotional knots because while he's lovely, there's no way either of us believes that we're right for each other. "No thanks," I say.

Then I skate away.

Finn leaves and hours later, when the showcase begins, I don't look for him in the crowd because I figure he got the message and anyway, he has his pick of girls to date. I do my routine to "Defying Gravity" from *Wicked,* which Carly has already told me I'll have to change since this year every soloist in the league will choose that song to skate to. But for today, I do my best to fly over the ice, matching my movements to the emotion of the lyrics, determined to prove that truly nothing will ever get me down.

I receive a standing ovation, but this is an easy crowd. Besides, I could do a few backwards loop-di-loops to this song, and people will still go crazy. I smile, wave, and skate towards the rink's exit, and that's when I see him. Finn *did* return, and he launches a bouquet of roses into the air. They land about two feet away from me, so I skate over to retrieve them. Once they're cradled in one of my arms, my other arm rises, and I find myself blowing him a kiss.

I guess I just got caught up in the moment.

After I've showered and changed into my street clothes, I find Finn still lingering in the arena, though most of the other spectators have left by now. When our eyes meet, he smiles like his near-stalking me is the most normal thing ever. And I smile like I'm thrilled he's returned, like I'd instantly regretted sending him away.

"How about pasta?" He says. "After skating like that, I bet you could use some carbs."

I can smell my still damp hair, finally free after being slicked up into a too-tight bun all day, and my apple-scented conditioner is making me hungry. Weirdly, it makes me hungry for marinara sauce and parmesan. "Nobody has ever told you no before, have they?"

"Lots of people have tried," Finn retorts, "but no one's ever been successful."

I release a mock-defeated sigh. "Well, who am I to make history? Let's go."

"Great." But instead of stepping toward the door, he gently reaches for a lock of my hair. "Your hair…" He looks almost dazed. "I've never seen it down before. It's so pretty." Then, he drops his hand like he's been burned. "Sorry. I don't usually go around touching people's hair. I hope that wasn't too weird."

What's weird is how turned on I am by it, but I don't tell him that. "No worries," I say, and I tighten the sash of my new parachute jacket, the castoff that Marina gave me. It's shiny and gray but it's also blousy and hangs like a sweater. Marina was right thinking that I'd like it.

"Is that a new coat?" Finn asks. "What happened to your wool sweater?"

"You really notice everything, don't you?" I laugh. "Marina insisted that I retire my sweater. And I guess this jacket is a designer brand. Alexander McQueen? Have you heard of him?"

"Of course," replies Finn. He puts his hand on the small of my back as we walk through the ice arena's doors. I have my gym bag slung over my shoulder, and I hold the roses he gave me in my other hand. Finn takes my bag, places it over his outside shoulder, and takes my hand in his, just like he did as we left the fundraiser the other night. "So, Marina gave you that coat?"

"Yeah. Not only that, she went out of her way to be sweet to my mom and me over Parents' Weekend. It was all so nice of her."

"I'm not surprised. Marina *is* nice. *Really* nice. Most people don't get that about her because she's so good looking and her dad is Oliver Hunt."

"Right." I stop walking for a second and tug on Finn's arm. "Finn," I say, using a serious voice. "I really do want to have dinner with you, but can we make a pledge that for tonight, we won't talk about either Aubrey or Marina?"

He looks at me quizzically. "I guess. But why?"

"Because I want to see if we have anything else in common."

"Okay, but I'm not that interested in what we have in common."

I tilt my head. "Umm… why not?"

He's still holding my hand, and I must admit, his grip feels like the relief that comes after making a difficult decision. It's strong and warm, tugging me in the right direction, making me fantasize about getting wrapped up in his arms, his lips pressed against mine.

"Because I have things in common with lots of people, and all they're interested in is doing what's expected and trying to make themselves look good." He squeezes my fingers. "But you're not like that."

I nod. Did he just compliment me? Should I thank him? He fills in my silent moment of hesitation. "Let's just eat dinner, Elyse," he says softly. "And we'll figure out everything else as we go. Okay?"

"Okay."

We go out for a pasta dinner. We're both ravenous, and as we sit in a booth at the low-lit Italian restaurant, we brazenly shovel in spicy, garlicy spaghetti and meatballs as if it's our one hundredth date, instead of our first. After it's over, he takes me back to my dorm room, and then I spend way too much time wondering how long it will be before I can see him again.

***

Two nights later I'm finishing a shift at Eleanor's campaign headquarters, trying to decide if I should hit the rink for a midnight practice session or go back to my dorm, get a few hours of sleep, and make Carly happy by showing up at 7:00 AM to take part in her drills. As I pack up my tote bag, I'm lost in thought, and I don't notice that someone has approached my desk.

"Do you want a ride back to campus?" she says. "We could stop and get coffee on the way."

It's Aubrey. "Oh hi," I say. "I didn't even see you come in."

"You were on the phone, and it looked like a pretty intense conversation. I didn't want to interrupt. Then I was back in my mom's office for a couple hours."

I nod. "Did you two get a lot done?"

Aubrey pulls up a chair and sinks into it. Then she shrugs in a droopy sort of way. Everything about her looks droopy right now: her hair, her mouth, her shapeless sweater, and definitely her eyes. "We got the talking points down for all our appearances next week." She exhales slowly. "I'm so tired, Elyse. I don't know how I'm going to get through the next few days with my schoolwork and all the campaign stuff. It's just too much."

"Have you told your mom that?"

"I don't need to. She knows." Aubrey moves her head from side to side, stretching her neck. "She's urging me to skip all the campaigning. But she needs me, and the country needs her. What else can I do?"

I tap a pencil against the desk where I sit, wishing I had some magic remedy, but the best I can offer is a distraction. "Hey, what are you doing for Halloween? Want to go to a party with Finn and me?"

At this, Aubrey stills her head and widens her eyes. "Are you and Finn, like, hanging out?"

I can feel my cheeks turn pink, and I cast my gaze down, staring at my worn out, clunky black boots. "I guess you could say that." I look back up, meeting her eyes. "I mean, we might be dating. What do you think about that?"

"I think Finn is a great guy, but if he's dating you, he also has excellent taste and judgement."

Suddenly energetic, she stands and tugs at my arm. "Come on, let's get coffee and you can tell me all about it."

"Sure," I say, eager to follow. Her enthusiasm is infectious, plus, there's something about Aubrey that makes it difficult to say no.

Chapter 10

On election night, we all gather in the banquet room of a Brooklyn hotel to watch the results. Eleanor is declared the winner at 11:58 PM, and Finn, who had never seemed to care about the race, sweeps me into his arms, spins me around, and kisses me hard on the mouth.

I enthusiastically return his kiss and when we finally pull away, he gazes down at me, beaming. 'It's all because of you," he says. "She won because of you."

"Don't say that too loud," I laugh. "Even if you're only kidding. There are some people in this room who might kill me for taking the credit."

"They'd have to get through me first," he jokes. "I'll protect you from all these gun-control loving Democrats."

"My hero." I say this in jest, but —my God—do I honestly mean it? Not for the first time, I fear I'm abandoning my feminist ideals and falling too hard, too fast, for Finn. We join lips again, more languidly this time. This new connection is certainly one thing that Finn and I have in common. We both like kissing each other.

But the room is too wild, too full of buoyancy, to celebrate anything other than Eleanor Adam-Drake's victory. People make toasts that are met by cheers, there's backslapping and self-congratulatory "I told you she'd win" proclamations, and the crowd becomes more drunk and giddy than any college party I've ever attended. Finn and I hold hands the whole time so as not to get separated, and late in the evening I finally spot Aubrey. She's standing in a corner near the stage with Marina by her side. Amazed that nobody is commanding their attention, I drag Finn over to them.

"Congratulations!" I capture Aubrey in a hug that I am just drunk enough to attempt. She hugs me back, so I know it's all good, that I haven't just gotten too affectionately familiar with the most highly esteemed college student in the country.

"Elyse, thank you *so much* for all your help," Aubrey says. "I will always be grateful for the dedication you put towards my mom's campaign."

I wave my hand in a dismissive, *oh please, that was nothing* sort of way. "I was happy to volunteer. It was a great opportunity."

"You are so right," Marina tells me. "Eleanor will be president someday, and now you're on a first-name basis."

"We all are," says Finn.

Yes, but for me, a nobody from West Chester, being on a first-name basis with a possible future president is epically huge. Meanwhile Finn, Marina, and Aubrey will never know what life is like without having powerful connections at their fingertips. I should count myself lucky to have cultivated a link to Eleanor, to any of them.

And I do. I count myself very, very, lucky.

"I'd better go," Aubrey says. "It's almost time for my mom's victory speech and I need to find my dad, so we can stand on stage with her."

She walks off, leaving Marina, Finn, and me standing where we were. Marina glances at Finn's and my conjoined hands. "So, you two are a couple now? That's sweet."

Finn doesn't release my hand, but I feel him lean away from me, ever so slightly. "We can thank you for introducing us," he says to Marina. "Or, at least for causing us to meet."

Marina flashes us her gleaming white smile. "Glad I could help. It's been a very productive semester for me: I got a sexual predator fired, helped get Eleanor elected, and now I can take credit for you two falling in love."

The room is noisy but it's as if there's a deafening silence nonetheless. I can't look at Finn for fear of seeing him blanch at the mention of the "L" word. Embarrassed, I unweave my fingers from Finn's and step away. "Whoa," I laugh. "It's not like we're sending out wedding invitations yet. We haven't even hired a calligrapher."

Marina returns my laugh. "Oh, Elyse, I love that you always say exactly whatever pops into your head. Your lack of filter is such a charming trait."

"Really?" I ask, unsure if she's honestly complimenting me, or if she's issuing a subtle warning.

"Sure." Marina tucks one of her smooth auburn tresses behind her ear. "It's endearing, especially to someone like me who always has to be on guard."

Finn drapes his arm over my shoulder. "Yeah, but think about it… you don't really know Elyse that well. Who knows what she's capable of?"

He's joking of course, but Marina narrows her eyes at me, as if to say, *exactly.*

Thankfully, at that moment, New York's senior senator takes the stage to introduce Eleanor. The room erupts into wild cheers, and Finn, Marina, and I pivot and stare up at the action. Eleanor arrives followed by Anton and Aubrey, who stand behind her, shining with support. Eleanor beams at the crowd, waving and throwing kisses, saying "Thank you, thank you all so much," while trying to quiet the cheers so she can commence her speech. Finally, we all pipe down so she can speak over us.

"Thank you, New York!" she cries, and there's one more burst of applause before we let her talk.

Eleanor makes her inspirational victory speech, thanks the campaign bigwigs by name, gives props to her fellow New York politicians, and of course, gushes over Anton and Aubrey.

Aubrey and Anton step forward, and together with Eleanor, they form a human chain, somehow hugging each other while also waving to the crowd. At one point, Aubrey spots Finn, Marina, and me, standing in the same spot where she left us not too long ago, and she gives a smile and special wave, just for us.

"She's the future," Marina says, and while she's got to be referring to Eleanor, it's possible Aubrey is included as well. It doesn't matter. If either of them really is the future then the future is looking good.

***

Once the campaign is over, I return to my normal routine, which is no less hectic than my abnormal one. Instead of volunteering for Eleanor, I go back to the refugee center where I work as a "resettlement" intern, meaning I help new refugees with stuff like finding work, enrolling in public benefits, and learning to ride the subway. Add in skate practices and meets, classwork, and writing for *The Spec,* and my days are so busy that it's hard to find time for hanging out with friends, or for that matter, a boyfriend. "Couldn't you skip it?" Finn asks, when I tell him I can't see him that evening because I have a shift at the refugee center. "I can't. Najmo needs me to help her with her resume. "Finn, having just taken a bite of his sandwich, wipes his mouth with a paper napkin. We're eating lunch together at a campus coffee shop during the short break between our morning and afternoon classes. "Who's Najmo?"

"She's an incredibly resilient woman who arrived here last month." I grip the edge of the table we're sitting at with both hands and lean forward, not caring if I let my intensity show. "Najmo fled both Yemen *and* an abusive husband, and she brought her three children here to New York City where she knows no one. She's never held a job, but unofficially, she did bookkeeping for her father's business. She's self-educated and incredibly bright. I need to find her something with a decent wage."

"How do the two of you communicate? You don't speak Arabic, do you?"

I hold out my hand, wiggling my fingers in that so-so gesture. "A little. My Spanish is better, so I'm more likely to get assigned refuges from Central or South America. But Najmo needed help ASAP, and like I said, she's incredibly bright. She's already taught herself some English."

Finn raises his eyebrows at me. "You speak both Arabic and Spanish?"

I shrug. "You know my mom teaches graduate studies in ESL. When I was growing up, instead of making me do chores, she'd make me learn foreign languages to earn my allowance money."

"Seriously?" He chuckles in disbelief. "What other languages do you know?"

"A bit of Chinese, Hmong, and Burmese. I mean, I'm not completely fluent in any of them, but Mom says I inherited her propensity for learning languages and that it's a skill either you're born with or not, but those who are shouldn't waste it. That's why I started volunteering at the refugee center." I sip from my iced coffee, relishing the cold rush of caffeine that I especially need today. "Besides, my mother probably would have disowned me if I didn't do something to counterbalance attending a ritzy Ivy League school. Mom believes that the best way to find meaning is to think about others over yourself, to find small ways to make life better for people who have less than you."

"She'd rather have you teach English to immigrants and stay close to home?" Finn asks in a neutral tone, seemingly curious for my answer.

"Maybe. I don't know." I look down at my sandwich that is mostly just crusts now, and then back up to Finn's eyes, which blink at me expectantly. "Just because I have a knack for picking up languages doesn't mean I'm any good at teaching English. In fact, it's kind of the opposite. Learning new languages comes so easy to me that I have trouble understanding how it could be difficult for someone else. I do better helping out in other ways."

Finn answers me with a slow, warm smile, and then he looks down at his watch. "I should go. Macroeconomics starts in ten minutes." He leans in, kissing me briefly on the mouth. "What time is your shift tonight?"

"Seven. I'll be done at ten. Should I call you later?"

"Sure," he says, and saunters off, seemingly distracted. I don't overthink the funny vibe I got from him, but I do briefly worry about it. Did I just scare him off? Sometimes people don't know how to respond to my multi-lingual activism. I mean, given my upbringing, it all seems perfectly normal to me, but I tend not to talk about it too much, for fear others will think I'm bragging.

Several hours later, I walk through the doors of the refugee center and am immediately greeted by Najmo, who hugs me while jumping up and down, apparently in glee. "What's going on?" I ask her in Arabic.

Her response is a mix of Arabic and English. "Eamal," she says. "A job!"

We sit down, and after catching her breath, Najmo manages to explain. There's a bookkeeping position at one of the Beck Real Estate offices. The center got a call, they asked for Najmo by name, and then hired her over the phone. I think, trying to fit the pieces of the puzzle together; Finn must have called his dad and asked him to find her something, saying she had bookkeeping experience. Najmo tells me that tomorrow she'll go down to the office and fill out all the necessary papers. And she asks me if I could come with her since she's nervous about finding her way on the subway on her own.

It will mean missing class, but I don't hesitate to say yes. After congratulating her, I step away, pull out my phone, and call Finn. He picks up on the first ring.

"Did Najmo tell you the news?" he asks without preamble.

"Yeah, and she's so happy. I am too. How you'd manage to find her a job?"

"Easy. I called my dad." He sighs. "Don't hate me for my methods, okay? I swear my intentions are good."

"Finn, I could never hate you. Why would you even think that?"

"I don't know. It's happened before, someone turning against me after I used my dad's money or influence to get ahead."

"But you weren't using it to get ahead. You were being altruistic."

"Not completely. I liked helping Najmo, but mostly I wanted you to come over tonight." He chuckles. "I'm joking. Sort of." Then he lowers his voice. "Hey, I'm sure you have to go. But do call me later, when you're done with your shift, okay?"

"Of course." The pull toward Finn is just too strong and my resolve is too weak. "Maybe I can cut out early and come over after all."

"Or..." he says huskily, "I could just send a car to pick you up. How's 9:30?"

My body temperature rises at the mere thought of having some alone time with him. "Perfect."

***

The months whiz by, so full of activity and purpose that I don't even realize how content I am. Junior year ends and then it's my last year at Columbia. I worry that the summer break will have messed with our connection, but in the fall I settle into a rhythm with Aubrey and Marina. The three of us spend several hours a week together either studying or going out, whichever activity seems more pressing. I become secure in my friendships with them, and even more secure in my relationship with Finn, because somehow, we balance our busy schedules and spend most free moments in each other's company. But all too soon, we're cementing our post-graduation plans. Marina will launch her own interior design company, Aubrey will travel for the Adam Foundation, and Finn secures a job on Wall Street. Meanwhile, I can't decide which way to go. I could look for something in journalism or do political work like I did for Eleanor's campaign, or I could use my language skills and experience working with refugees. But I must admit, at least to myself, that I want to do something big, that ambition is rumbling around inside me, anxious to get out and make some noise. Plus, no matter what I do, I'll be competing with a ton of other applicants for a low-paying job.

Then, one afternoon in May of senior year, Aubrey calls.

"Hey, stranger," I say into the phone. "Are you back from Thailand? How was it?"

"Amazing," she gushes, and fills me in on the details but soon switches course by asking, "So, how's the job search going?"

"Okay," I respond, trying to sound chipper, but truth is, while I've had some offers for entry level positions at area papers (most notably *The Philadelphia Inquirer*), I just can't get excited about writing metro news for a pittance. The refugee center doesn't have the budget to hire me for a paid position, and while they'd write me a stellar letter of recommendation if I wanted to apply, say at the UN Headquarters in New York, I'm not even clear on what sort of position I'd apply for, or if I can afford to stay in New York.

"Well, I hope you don't mind, but I set up an interview for you with my mom. She needs somebody on her communications staff, and she hasn't forgotten all the work you did during her campaign."

I'm stunned into silence, barely struggling out, "Thank you, Aubrey."

"It's not a sure thing," Aubrey adds. "But nail the interview, and the job is yours."

"Okay," I squeak, instantly overwhelmed with nerves. "When's the interview?"

She gives me the time and date, and I'm calculating exactly how long I have to prepare and pull myself together, when Aubrey says, "Oh, and Marina is throwing a graduation party for us all, including you."

"Huh?"

"You know Marina. Any excuse for a party, right?" She laughs. "I shouldn't say that; she's really genuine and wants to celebrate our success. We all do. *But* Marina also wants an excuse to invite Columbia people to see her newly decorated apartment. You know, so she can create buzz about her interior designs."

"Um... okay." I rub my temple, feeling disoriented. "Is Marina going to call me about this party? Should I invite people?"

"Nah. I think she has everything covered. You'll hear from her soon. But mark your calendar. It's on the 14th at 8 PM."

"Oh." I pause, not wanting to sound ungrateful. "That's the night of commencement. My mother will be in town."

"Great!" Aubrey exclaims. "Bring her to the party. I'll finally get to meet her."

"All right," I respond, because really, is there anything else to say?

So on May 14th, after the Columbia commencement ceremony, I bring my mother to Hunt Plaza. Marina holds the celebration in her impeccably decorated apartment, which feeds out onto a deck with thousands of tea lights and paper lanterns. The entire staff from *The Spec* is here, along with several professors who, during college, were so intimidating, I'd never even visited their office hours.

"Congratulations, Elyse!" Marina finds me as soon Mom and I enter the party, which is already in full swing.

"Congratulations to you too! This party is amazing. Thanks for including me, Marina."

She hugs me, and I grasp her tightly, as if to communicate through gesture what I can't put into words. When she releases me, Marina speaks to my mom, "Helen, it's so nice to see you again. You must be very proud of Elyse."

Mom is wide-eyed at all the extravagance: the powder-blue silk banners draped everywhere, each painted with silver cursive letters, *Congratulations Graduates!* And there's the champagne fountain, and the catering staff circulating with trays of bruschetta and oysters. Yet Mom retains her power of speech. "Yes. Thanks so much for having us."

"Of course! And I know Aubrey is dying to meet you." Marina looks around, trying to spot her. "Oh, she's over there," Marina says, pointing toward Aubrey in the far corner of the living room; she's speaking with the history department chair. "Let's go say hi." Mom and I start to follow Marina, but then Finn approaches and pulls me aside, without Marina or my mom noticing.

"Hey," he says softly once we're hidden in an alcove out of view. "This is for you." He hands me a G&T as if it's a gift. "I wanted to be the first to toast your success." He clinks his drink to mine, and we each take a sip. Then he leans in for a kiss, which I breathlessly return.

"Are you congratulating me for graduating or for getting the Eleanor Drake job?"

"Both. But tell me about the job."

I flush with pride, abandoning any hope of acting cool. "I think I'll mostly be writing memos, taking phone calls from constituents, communicating with the rest of her staff, making sure it's all a well-oiled machine. But Eleanor interviewed me herself, and she said there's a possibility of speech-writing in the future. Isn't that incredible?"

Finn smiles and peers at me with bedroom eyes. It's like we're alone, intimate, and I want to bask in the heat of his gaze. "Your success is well-deserved, and I'm so happy you're staying in New York."

"Really?" Months ago, I'd come to terms with the expiration date on Finn's and my romance. It was a college relationship, most likely over once we graduated. I'd enjoy the time we had left and not entertain "what if" scenarios.

"Really," he confirms, and leans in for another kiss, so soft and warm I could swoon. "But where are you going to live?"

"I have no idea. I'll have to find an apartment."

"Yeah...umm, can I ask how much she's going to pay you?"

When I tell him, his face twists into a grimace. "You'll never find a place with a rent you can afford. Not on that salary."

"Then I guess I'll need a roommate." But who will that roommate be? I didn't take the time to foster many friendships during college, and even though there's a ton of people here tonight, none except Aubrey and Marina are close friends. It's laughable to even imagine either of them rooming with me in some humble Queens apartment. I take another drink of my G&T, more of a gulp this time.

"You could move in with me," Finn says.

I laugh. "Be careful. I might take you up on that."

"No really, I'm serious."

His words hang in the air like the humidity after a sun-shower. Reluctantly, I gaze into his eyes and realize he's sincere.

"Thank you," is my stunned reply. "But I'll have to think about it."

He reaches for my hand. "Elyse," he says, "I know we have our differences and that sometimes I give you a hard time. But I also know that my life makes more sense when you're around. Please, don't agonize over this; just say yes."

But I can't, not instantly, because I wouldn't be me if I didn't agonize over a major life decision at least a bit. But I do say yes to slipping away with him later that evening when nobody will miss us, and we lock the door to one of Marina's many guest rooms. We pull at each other's clothing, gasp at each other's touch, and as we make love, he whispers my name with such tenderness that my heart stops beating for three whole seconds. It's funny how significant three seconds can feel.

So, days later I say *yes, I'll move in with you*, and now I know what I'll contribute and who I'll become. It's all forever tied to Marina, Aubrey, and Finn.

Chapter 11
New York

My phone vibrates against my desk, a text from Finn. "I'm outside."

I've lost track of time, which often happens when I write speeches for Eleanor. In the year and a half that I've been working in Eleanor's office, I've found the job to be both challenging and mundane. Today's task is less of a speech and more of an address; she's the keynote speaker at the League of Women Voters' annual luncheon next week. I must put together some inspirational words about how far we've come from the 1960s, when Eleanor's goal of holding elected office was considered a foolish pipe dream.

But while we have traveled far, our destination hasn't yet been reached...

Jeez. There must be a more compelling closing thought than that. Eleanor could find better at the greeting card aisle at Walgreens.

I close out my document, power down and shut my laptop, gather my things and make my way through the office to outside. There I find Finn, leaning against a hired car like he's Richard Gere from *Pretty Woman.* I guess that makes me Julia Roberts.

"Ready?" He says, smiling and holding out his arm, inviting me to join him.

"Yeah. This morning I told everyone I'd be leaving early today, so it's fine. They know I'll make up for it later in the week."

"I'm sure there's no doubt that you will."

He opens the car's backdoor, and we climb in. "But I can't believe you were able to leave work so early," I say. "It's not even five o'clock! You usually have at least another four hours of your workday."

He scoots in closer and kisses me as the car takes off; clearly the driver knows his destination. But I don't.

"Where are we going?" I ask.

Finn's face eases into a relaxed smile. Wide eyed, his slightly crooked jaw makes him look guileless and happy. Of all his facial expressions, this one is my favorite. "I already told you that it's a surprise!" he responds. "You'll find out soon enough."

He moves back to his own seat so he can fasten his seatbelt, but we hold hands during the drive, and Finn asks me about my day. I tell him all about what I'm writing for Eleanor and how bad it is.

"You'll figure it out," he says. "I'm always amazed by the stuff you come up with."

"And by 'stuff' you mean shameless propaganda?"

He raises my hand to his lips and kisses my knuckles. "I think you are supremely talented."

"That's sweet, but not exactly a denial that I write propaganda." Finn just laughs, and I let go of the issue. He's being especially affectionate, and I don't want to ruin the mood. Soon enough, the car pulls up at Rockefeller Center.

"Here we are!" Finn laughs, obviously proud of himself. "Welcome to date night! It's the last evening skate of the season. We're finally going skating together!"

"Okay…"

I get out of the car and follow him into the skate rental area. Finn hands them the tickets he must have purchased in advance, and he gets himself skates. Only then do I notice that he's holding a small duffle bag, which he hands to me. "I brought your skates. I figured you'd prefer them over the rentals." As we lace up, Finn says, "Are you surprised?"

"Completely. I thought you hated touristy stuff like this."

"Usually I do." He pulls on the laces of his left skate and ties them into a double-knotted bow. "But you've never been here and that just seems wrong."

"Why? What's wrong about it?" I am merely inquiring, not commenting on his date-night activity choice. I mean, obviously Finn put in a lot of thought, and that alone says something. However, there's a rink not far from where we live that I go to on weekends and the occasional evening, where I have room to really skate, unlike here, where I'll be limited to moving in a circle with the masses.

"It's wrong," Finn says as he tightens the laces of this right skate, "because New York hasn't seen you skate yet. And they deserve to know how good you are."

I laugh. "Come on, Finn."

"I'm serious." He stands, wobbling a little in his skates. "Let's go show them what you're made of, and I'll try not to fall on my ass."

I get up and we head out onto the ice. I start skating in slow loops, letting Finn get acclimated to this new activity. I'm thinking we'll hold hands and move to pop songs projected over the speakers. Finn will cling to the boards where the other non-skaters hover and I'll occasionally abandon him to spin or arabesque in the center, just because I can.

So, I'm mortified when Finn starts yelling. "Ladies and Gentlemen!" He keeps his eyes up, on the shoe-wearing spectators that peer down from the walkways surrounding the rink. "We have a world-class skater here with us tonight, and she's going to show you all how it's done." With a broad arm gesture, he points everyone's attention to me. "Elyse, take the stage."

"Have you gone insane?"

He laughs. "Maybe. But trust me for a minute. It's been so long since you've competed. You need this."

I look up and see people expectantly waiting for me to perform some sort of trick that they've seen on the Olympics. More horrifying, my eyes land on my own reflection in the ice-view window of the Rock Center Cafe. I look bigger than I feel, my cheeks are pink from embarrassment and cold, but at least I'm dressed for the occasion. "Wear a skirt," Finn had told me this morning, "but nothing too tight. And you should have on tights or something underneath."

Like I would go commando underneath a loose skirt that could be blown this way or that while standing over a street vent. But this morning I didn't question his instructions and I put on a short, knitted skirt over velvety black leggings, which is perfect for skating.

Now I'm sent back years, to my last competition, to the feeling I'd get when people were waiting for me to perform. My heart races while a firm determination settles into my arms and legs like they have a consciousness, like they know they're capable of doing whatever I need them to do.

"It's your moment, Elyse," Finn loudly states. "Show the world who you are."

I look into his eyes and am reminded that he sees me, that he already knows me for who I am and wants to let others in on the secret. It's the highest compliment he could pay. I skate to the center of the rink, channel my inner Peggy Fleming, and let my muscle memory take over. I'm carving circles and arcs into the ice, lifting my limbs and jumping, landing with a speed and grace I haven't possessed for a long time.

I don't know how much time passes, probably a minute or two tops, but common-sense returns, and I remember this rink belongs to everyone and not just me, so I end my routine. There's an eruption of applause. I wave to the spectators, and skate towards Finn. "You were right," I say. "How did you know I needed that?"

"Because I need you." His voice cracks with a self-deprecating laugh. When he speaks again, his tone is low and soft, like how he says my name in moments of passion. “Promise to never leave me, Elyse.”

For a second, I’m as frozen as the ice underneath my skates. Why would he say that? True, we don’t have much time for each other lately, but I’ve never felt that our relationship is in jeopardy.

Finn wobbles on his skates as I move close enough to drape my arms over his shoulders. “I promise,” I say, before kissing him. Then we turn into a postcard: romantic NYC couple kissing while on skates. I’m sure there are spectators snapping our image on their phones. They see Finn and me as living proof that the fairytale exists, and right now, I even believe happily ever after is possible.

Chapter 12

Only two weeks later it's cold but there's a warm breeze. Spring is in the air like an ominous party invitation; you should want to go, but there's this feeling that something bad will happen if you do. Soft air against my cheek only makes my anxiety build and the vast blue sky and shining sun are so bright I must look away. I glance down at my feet, which are standing upon a glacier. Right before my eyes, the glacier cracks and the chunks of ice float apart from each other. I'm forced into doing the splits, which makes my thighs scream, but that's nothing compared to the fear perched inside my heart.

I scramble to right myself, trying to find solid ground, but my body doesn't move as fast as my brain, and in my lame search for safety I misstep and my feet find only water. Cold, unforgiving water that turns to a black hole the instant it engulfs me. I sink, water filling my lungs so that when I try to scream, no sound comes out.

Then, mercifully, I wake up.

Reaching for my glasses on the nightstand, I put them on and look around the room, which I think of as Finn's room, because technically it belongs to him even though we both live here. The Egyptian cotton sheets stick to my sweaty body. The shadows dance across the room, increasing the rate of my racing heart.

This is not my home. But if that's true, I don't have a home. I'm homeless.

Finn's hand reaches up; it was resting by his sleeping form but now he places it on the small of my back. "You okay," he mumbles. "Another nightmare?"

"Same as usual," I answer. "About the glaciers."

"No glaciers," he slurs and sighs simultaneously. "You're safe." Then he rolls over and seemingly returns to a deep sleep.

If his comment was made to comfort me, it was an epic fail. Of course there are glaciers; I mean, there aren't any here in New York, but they do exist, at least for now. And they're melting at an alarming rate. So how am I supposed to sleep when my subconscious is sending me an urgent message that something needs to be done?

I rise from bed and wander into the living room of our Manhattan apartment. There's no way in hell I could ever afford this place on my own, but Finn's six-figure salary is more than three-times what I make working as a member of Eleanor's senate office staff.

I walk over to the living room window with its view of the Manhattan skyline. Through the glass I can hear the ambient noises of the city, which are loud, even at 3 AM. Pressing my forehead against the pane, I stare down at the sidewalk dozens of stories below. Finn and I live in the middle of a skyscraper, and I often feel suspended in motion. Maybe I'm disoriented because I prefer to be close to the ground; that's why my glacier dreams have resurfaced when I'd thought they were a thing of my adolescent past.

I move away from the window, stroll into the kitchen, and grab a diet coke from the refrigerator. Drinking anything caffeinated is the exact opposite of what I ought to do. But screw it. I'm not going back to sleep anyway. I sit down at the kitchen table where I'd left my laptop. I flip it open and immediately go to Huffington Post. *Drake is Baked,* written in huge letters, splashes across the top of the page. There's a picture of Eleanor's younger brother, Ethan

Drake, frowning and looking down. Ethan Drake has dominated the news for the last few days. He's young, charismatic, and has movie-star good looks, and the only reason he hadn't been pegged to follow in his father's footsteps and become the next Drake president is that he's twelve years younger than Eleanor. So, the nation thought she should have her shot first. Except, after what just happened, Ethan Drake's political career could be over, especially if he goes to jail.

Years ago, he and his wife bought a house in Fox Chapel, Pennsylvania, where Ethan began his political career. First, he was a state senator, and then the U.S representative for Pennsylvania's seventh district. The obvious next step was to become governor, and his campaign was going great until he spent time at his vacation home in Hawaii. He went for a drive with a woman who isn't his wife, drove headlong into an oncoming car, and both the driver and the passenger of that car were killed. Ethan Drake suffered severe injuries, enough to be hospitalized. While he made a full recovery, he now claims he doesn't remember the accident or the events leading up to it.

Meanwhile, he stands trial for manslaughter and drunk driving. Ethan's wife has filed for divorce, and the other woman admits both that she and Ethan were having an affair and that they'd been drinking that afternoon.

So, the press has gone crazy, saying that Howie Drake is using his immense influence to keep his son out of jail. Subsequently, the nation has questioned the inequities of our legal system between the haves and have nots.

I text Aubrey. *Sorry about your uncle. Hopefully none of this will affect your mom's chances.*

I'm surprised when she texts back moments later. Guess I'm not the only one suffering from insomnia. *You know how unfair politics are. Especially for women.*

Eleanor declared her presidential candidacy almost a year ago and has been battling it out in the primaries between two other candidates. She'd had a slight edge until now, but all the pundits speculate that the Drake name has been sullied. I've heard whispers that she might drop out of the race "to be a good senator, and to focus on her family." So, if this recent Drake family scandal is throwing me for a loop, I can only imagine what fresh hell Aubrey is in. I text her back asking for specifics, and she responds with, *I'd rather tell you about it in person. Will you be at Marina's party tomorrow night?*

Vaguely, I remember the email from days ago, about Marina's latest soiree. *Yes, of course,* I text her. *How could I miss one of Marina's parties*?

***

The next evening, I'm walking the sidewalk of Fifth Avenue, going at a snail's pace because I don't really care to arrive at my destination.

I still can't get used to the non-stop social calendar one seems expected to maintain while living in this city. It doesn't matter what day of the week it is, there's always something going on, whether it's meeting for drinks or a get-together in SoHo, an art opening, or a huge party in the warehouse district. Most nights I prefer to go home after a full day of work, put on my flannel pajama pants, and relax on the couch. "You're living in the wrong city for that," Finn often tells me. He is almost never done with work before 9 PM, and after that, he's usually compelled to get drinks with his co-workers. But tonight, Finn plans to meet me at Marina's party after he's done with work. I wish we were arriving together because honestly, showing up alone at Marina's deluxe apartment in her father's luxury tower makes me feel foreign. I keep expecting a security guy to arrest me for trespassing. However, my name is on the list and I'm let through. I ride up the elevator with a few other party-goers whom I don't know, self-conscious in the sleek black dress I bought and wore out of the store moments before I came here. Any time I see Marina I wonder if she's judging me for my lack of chicness, aware that my bargain basement-look pales in comparison to her Upper East Side perfection.

The elevator lands on a floor near the top, and as I exit, I scratch the back of my neck, worried I left that little plastic thingy that held the price tag to my dress. No dress of Marina's would even have a price tag, but I got this at H&M, where nobody wants to be surprised when they get to the cash register.

When I enter the party, I don't see anyone I know, not even Marina. I head to the bar and get a glass of pinot noir, which I instantly regret, because everything here - the carpet, the couches, the shelving - is all white. Her place glistens with a fresh newness, like a crisp, freshly minted $100-dollar bill, and if I was familiar with the scent of new money, I'd swear it smelled like Marina's apartment.

If you spill, you're dead, I say to myself, and I take a tentative sip of my wine. Aubrey, Marina, and I take turns hosting dinners once or a month or so, just so the three of us can catch up. Whenever we're at Marina's apartment, the place is always newly decorated, but at least one thing stays the same: half the wall space is occupied by huge, floor to ceiling picture windows. Now I stand by one, gazing out. Beside me, a man and woman who seem close to my age mingle. From overhearing snippets of their conversation, I gather that one of them is in publishing and the other is in PR. "You've got to get her a book deal," the publishing guy says to the PR woman. "Marina is a goldmine."

Their conversation ceases when the woman's mouth freezes mid-sentence, because apparently, someone shock-worthy has approached. This is a surprise, as I've been to enough of Marina's parties to know that her guests are pretty much above being star-struck. But when I look over my shoulder, I understand. Aubrey approaches with (as usual) a Secret Service guy close by, but there's also a new addition in the form of a tall, thin, prematurely balding guy who holds her hand.

"Hey there!" Aubrey cheeks are flushed as she leans in and pecks me on the cheek. "Have you been here long?"

"About ten minutes." I take another sip of my pinot, wondering if it will stain my teeth. I'm pretty sure Marina only ever drinks white wine, to match the rest of her apartment. "I haven't even seen Marina yet."

"I think she's still getting dressed," Aubrey says. Then her smile grows wide and she gestures toward the guy she's with. "Elyse, I'd like you to meet Marcus. Marcus, this is Elyse."

"So nice to meet you, Elyse." He releases Aubrey's hand to shake mine, and his Adam's apple bobs up and down as he speaks. "Aubrey talks about you a lot, says you're one of the few friends she can actually trust."

I give Aubrey a puzzled look, and she laughs. "It's true," she says. "Most people want something from me, and not just my friendship. You and Marina, and well, now Marcus—you guys are different."

I look back at Marcus. "It's nice to meet you, Marcus. But I have to say, this a surprise." I turn to Aubrey. "How come you didn't mention you were dating someone new?"

Aubrey shrugs. "You know how it is. Rumors fly, and I didn't want to jinx anything." She rolls her eyes. "Things have been so crazy lately. My grandfather is furious with Uncle Ethan, and Aunt Kim is filing for divorce, but everyone is talking damage control and pressuring her to stay. Meanwhile, my mom is about to give in."

"Why?"

"The Democratic party leader told her she should step aside, and now she's getting pressure from all sides."

We talk politics. Marcus stays engaged in our conversation, but soon I feel bad that we're not including him more, so I ask him what he does. "Investment banking at Brighton Brothers," he tells me.

"Ah," I reply. "My boyfriend is an investment banker too. I'm impressed you have time to start a new relationship, what with the crazy hours you must keep."

He widens his eyes and gives me a puzzled look. "It's not so bad."

"Really? Finn is almost never home before midnight. He's either at work or out schmoozing with the people he works with. Don't you have to do that too?"

Marcus self-consciously clears his throat. "Well, every place is different. Where did you say he works?"

I tell him the name of the firm, aware of the pitying looks both Marcus and Aubrey are giving me. I should have kept my mouth shut. Of course, it's occurred to me that Finn *could* get home earlier, that when he says he *must* work what he really means is he *wants* to work, that nothing, including me, is more captivating to him than his job. But when he and I are alone together, even though those moments are rare, they're still the highlight of my week. There are the walks we take through a dusky Central Park, hand-in-hand, finding momentary peace in the craziness of our lives, and there's ordering pizza and swigging light-beer tallboys while sitting on our living room couch, watching the final season of *Grant's Lane,* the teen soap opera we grew addicted to in college. And then there's our lovemaking, those sweet, passionate moments, the feel of our skin, our hearts beating in sync, and his mouth pressed to mine.

Aubrey changes the subject, pulling me out of my reverie. "Let's find Marina," she says. "I want to see what she's wearing tonight. She still hadn't decided when I talked to her a couple of hours ago."

We wander through Marina's opulent apartment, and every time someone new approaches Aubrey to say hello, it's like she's the best friend they haven't seen in years. Aubrey always smiles graciously, calls them by name and asks a question about some personal detail of his or her life. "She's her father's daughter," I murmur to Marcus.

He nods but says, "Yes, but I think she's a lot more like Eleanor."

Finally, we find Marina standing in the kitchen, splendidly clad in a sage-colored wrap-dress with a plunging neckline that shows off her impressive cleavage. Her hair is up in a bun, with one large wisp down and tucked behind her ear. Her lips are bright red, and large and tasteful diamonds sparkle from her ears. Instantly, my black dress from H&M feels all wrong, like it's a stiff middle school choir robe when I ought to be wearing a sexy velvet gown.

"There you are!" Marina exclaims when we approach, as if she'd been looking for us the entire time. She's been talking to someone, standing close to him and nodding her head in what seemed like an intimate conversation. My stomach drops when her companion turns, and I realize it's Finn. I don't know which is more unsettling: that he was engaged in such a cozy chat with Marina before bothering to find me at this party, or that I didn't instantly recognize him from behind. Nevertheless, when we meet eyes, my Finn becomes a paradox; he's my most familiar friend yet a stranger, someone I will never truly understand.

"Hi," he says, glancing at me before letting his eyes stray back to Marina. I suppose that when Marina is in the room, everyone's just compelled to look at her. Maybe I shouldn't expect Finn to be the exception to this rule.

But I do.

Chapter 13

On Tuesday, Eleanor wins primaries in Pennsylvania and Connecticut, but she loses Delaware, Rhode Island, and Maryland. I watch the returns with several of my co-workers at a bar close to work, where we all share drinks and a sense of doom. Even though she could stay and battle it out, we know Eleanor will drop from the race in the next couple days.

For once, I get home after Finn. He's sitting on the couch watching CNN when I walk in. "Good night for you?" he asks innocently.

I plop down next to him, suddenly bone tired. "Not really. I think Eleanor is dropping from the race tomorrow. It's just too hard, fighting against stereotypes and now the mistakes her brother made…"

Finn mutes the television but gestures to CNN's talking heads nonetheless. "Gloria Borger says the Drake political dynasty is over."

I lean my head back against the couch and groan.

"Would that be so bad?" Finn asks. "I mean, maybe it's time to pin your career goals somewhere else?"

"You know I am devoted to the Drakes."

"Yes, I do. But perhaps you should rethink your devotion," Finn replies softly. "You need to look out for yourself, Elyse."

"How can you say that?"

He scooches down so we sit face to face, and he brushes a lock of hair from my cheek. "Because I can't be the only one looking out for you. It's too big a job."

I don't know where this is coming from. I need protection? This idea that he must advocate for me is new. "I didn't know I was so helpless."

He chuckles. "You're not helpless. I'm just programmed to think about you all the time. It's in my DNA." He wraps the stray lock of my hair around his fingers. "Ever since I first saw you with your hair down, right after watching you skate. I fell for you hard and never recovered."

"Is that right?"

"Yeah." He scoots in closer and we kiss. Then the TV is flicked off, he leans into me, and I'm pressed between him and the couch. He tugs off my clothes, and I let him take me like he used to, hurried and passionate, like it's after a kegger or before some college banquet where he was expected to speak. We're limbs and breath, body parts mingled and joined, blood rushing. We're gasping each other's names.

Afterwards, we lay together on the couch, my head nestled against his chest as he strokes my hair. It feels like how it used to, when adulthood and the future were still on the back burner, and we could live in the moment and just be in love.

"I've been missing you," he says.

"Me too," I murmur into his shoulder, so softly he probably didn't hear me. We're so close yet the pang in my heart reminds me there's still distance between us. I can feel his skin and the beat of his heart, but even though we're pressed into each other, I can't quite reach him.

***

That Sunday we take a cab to his parent's Park Avenue apartment. Once a month we go there for dinner, which means sitting with

Finn's sisters, their husbands, and his mom and dad at a large, banquet-style table, eating gazpacho as a starter course and then moving on to roasted chicken with some leafy green vegetable, which is all expertly prepared by their chef. Everyone is always polite to me, like I'm eternally a guest but never a family member. I mean, even though Finn and I live together, they still struggle to remember my name.

During the taxi ride, Finn stares straight ahead, not out the window and not at me. "By the way," he says, "it might get mentioned tonight that I'm buying *The Examiner*. Just wanted to give you a head's up."

His words may as well be gibberish because I can't decipher them. "What?" I ask, stunned. "I don't get it."

He looks at me now. "I'm in the final stages of buying *The New York Examiner*. We're signing the papers next week."

"Um…"" I stammer. "Okay. Does your dad know?"

"Yeah, of course. I had to tell him. I'm getting some of the money from him."

"Oh." I gaze at Finn, noticing that tonight he's more dressed up than usual. Often, he'll wear a blazer over a crew-necked shirt, but tonight he's wearing a tie that looks desperate to be loosened. "Why didn't you say anything about this earlier?" I ask.

"I wanted to keep it to myself for a while."

"So, you didn't tell anyone but your dad?"

"Well," he hesitates. "I said something to Marina the other night at her party. But only because she knows a lot about this stuff, and I wanted her opinion."

"What do you mean? What 'stuff' does Marina know a lot about?"

Finn answers me in defeated-sounding bullet points. "Having a well-known, entrepreneur dad. Using said dad's wealth to establish yourself. Risking your reputation to create something of your own, even if technically, it will never belong to you."

I already sort of knew that he and Marina have a lot in common, but hearing Finn lay it out like that flattens me a little. It's not right that he'd confide in Marina, and not in me, his girlfriend. But I have no desire to pick a fight. "And she thinks it's a good idea?"

Finn releases a smile. "Yeah. She really, really does."

Of course Marina approves. *The New York Examiner* is written for people exactly like her: affluent and influential, with their touch on the pulse of art, politics, and culture. "But why, Finn? I thought you hated the media."

He shrugs. "People change. And if you can't beat 'em, join 'em."

"Does this mean you're going to quit investment banking?"

"Maybe. Probably. I mean, I can hire people to run the paper for me, but what's the point of buying it if I'm not going to be involved?" He turns toward me, his expression eager. "But it definitely means you can quit your job."

My head jolts back. "How do you figure?"

"Because you can work for me! Any job you want! Wasn't your original goal to be a journalist? Now you can cut the cord between you and the Drakes. I really think it's time."

The cab pulls up to the curb outside the Beck's building. Finn hands the driver a couple of twenties, telling him to keep the change. I release my seatbelt and grab my purse, my eyes avoiding Finn's face. "I don't know," I say, aware that my ingratitude is obvious but helpless to prevent that. "Let's talk about it later."

We get through dinner. Finn, apparently, is oblivious or unconcerned that inwardly I'm seething. Instead, he glows under his family's praise and basks in his father's toast: "To the next grand business venture by the Beck family!" They all say how smart he is to realize the disproportionate influence *The Examiner* has over the city's most wealthy and powerful players. With this purchase, Finn is buying the ear of everyone who matters in New York.

"Aren't you proud," one of Finn's sisters asks me. I nod and say "Yes, of course, so proud," but I could have said nothing. She wouldn't have heard me either way.

Back at our apartment, the taste of rosemary chicken and limoncello still lingering on my tongue, I finally let my annoyance rear its ugly head. "I can't believe you shut me out of such a huge decision! How long have you been working on this deal?"

He rolls his eyes at me like I'm crazy. "Calm down. It hasn't been that long."

"And you just expect me to quit my job on one of your whims!"

"Do what you want, Elyse. I don't expect anything of you." His tone is calm, but he holds his hands up as if I'm foaming at the mouth, ready to come barreling toward him. "I thought you'd be happy. The Drake ship is sinking and I'm offering you a life raft."

"I'll be the judge of that!"

"Do you *want* to be beholden to a family tied to scandal and graft?"

"You know most of that is made up!" I'm yelling, unable to see clearly through all my anger. "And I'd rather be beholden to them than to someone who's using his dad's money to buy influence!"

Finn presses his lips together and his eyes narrow. "That was low, even for you."

I feel the walls of our apartment, of *Finn's* apartment, pressing in on me. Almost nothing here belongs to me, certainly not anything big or important, like the $20,000 couch or the shiny, unused kitchen appliances that rest on the granite countertop. Every object here is part of a world of wealth and privilege to which I'll never belong. "How would you know?" I say.

"What?" He asks, confused.

"How would you know what is low, for me?" I start pacing, alternately tugging at my hair or clenching my fists, so as not to throw things. "Do you even know who I am?"

He momentarily closes his eyes as if he has a piercing headache. "God, Elyse. Don't get all existential on me. Of course I know who you are." Finn's shoulders sag and he slides onto the couch, loosening his tie. When he speaks again, his voice is soft. "It was never my plan to question our relationship. I just wanted to buy a little newspaper. Why is that so wrong?"

I stop pacing, stand opposite him, and place my hands on my hips. "You say that like it's no big deal, like you were running out to buy one newspaper at the newsstand, instead of —what?—a ten-million-dollar acquisition."

"Fifteen."

"Whatever. And if that really isn't a big deal for you, then I will never understand how your mind works. It makes me wonder why you even want me around."

He sits up, slightly more intense. "I want you around because you're the only person who always tells me the truth." His mouth hangs open for a moment, before he adds, as an afterthought, "and I love you."

I let out a tiny gasp, as if I'd been punched. Finn and I have been together for years and I can count on one hand the number of times he's told me he loves me. And that includes this time, just now. Yet I can't complain, because it's not like I've *ever* said *I love you* to him. I've said *I love you too*, but that's not the same thing. And I'm aware that our relationship is not normal, but it's the only serious relationship I've ever been in, so I have no litmus test or healthy romance to compare it to. "I love you too," I murmur.

I do love him. But he's wrong about me always telling him the truth. I lie to Finn every day, all the time, in little ways. I pretend to be comfortable in this life we've created, confident that he really does belong to me long-term, and secure when I think of what the future holds for us, as a couple. If I were honest, I'd admit that I think of us as having a time limit, an expiration date when we'll sadly realize it's time to throw out everything we've shared, and start again, each of us on our own.

I wander into the bedroom, not because I want to be in here so much as I want to be away from Finn. But suddenly I feel heavy, as if each of my limbs have just gained ten pounds and the effort to keep them upright is simply too much. I lie down on the bed, wishing for oblivion, for a deep, dreamless sleep that will prepare me for tomorrow, another tense day of sidestepping the fact that Eleanor Adam-Drake's political career might go down the drain along with her brother's. I'll go to the office, write memos, arrange meetings and draft statements, and I'll field dozens of phone calls from her campaign officials, who will either be willfully ignorant and chirpy, or terse with me, as if the inevitably of Eleanor's doom somehow rests on my shoulders.

I'm on my back, my arm covering my eyes, when I hear Finn come in. "Is that it? Is our fight already over?"

"I don't feel like fighting. I'm tired and I have a headache."

I feel his weight beside me, pressing into the mattress. "I meant what I said before."

Is he about to reassure me that he really does love me, really does value me and my truth-speaking abilities? Nope. "There's a future for you at *The Examiner*. I'd quit Eleanor Adam-Drake while you still can." As he talks my world shrinks a little, its appearance altered, like a garment that's been damaged in the dryer.

I sit up and glare at him. "What about loyalty, Finn? Doesn't that mean anything to you?"

"Loyalty means everything to me. You know that. But you're about to hit a dead-end, and I don't want to see you hurt."

"That's big of you, but you're wrong. Besides, I could never go to work for my boyfriend. I'd be a laughing-stock."

"How is working for me any worse than working for your best-friend's mom?"

I let my eyes roll to the ceiling. "I'm not sleeping with Eleanor Adam-Drake."

"Well, at least we can be thankful for that." He stands. "I'm taking a shower. Join me if you want."

Part of me does want to join him, but not enough to get up, follow him into the bathroom, and pretend like everything is fine. I stay in bed and grab a pillow to press over my face. It shuts out the light and the sound of running water. It gives me the illusion that I'm alone in this world, or at least that I'm alone in this apartment. Right now, those two things feel like one and the same.

Chapter 14

Eleanor drops from the race but states, unequivocally, that she has no regrets and will run again once "her family is in a better place." Luckily for me, Eleanor never resigned as Senator, so she still has a job, which means I still have one too. At least for now. I can feel more change is coming, not just in the tiny, insular world of the Adam-Drake Senate office, but in all of New York City. The streets seem to crackle with static electricity and as August wanes, I wait for the explosion.

That's not the only thing I'm waiting for.

"I still haven't gotten my period." I say this to Aubrey one afternoon when she stops by her mother's office to pick up a dress for a fundraising event. You would think they'd have personal assistants to handle that sort of thing, but sometimes Eleanor and Aubrey can be almost charming in their normalcy. They both get a lot of criticism for their clothes, hair, and makeup, and they take all of it to heart. This makes them trench buddies in the war of public opinion, trusting only each other.

Aubrey has her dress swathed in a garment bag and draped over her arm. The office is empty except for me and her, as it's Friday afternoon before Labor Day, and everyone has either left for happy-hour drinks or they've boarded the Jitney to the Hamptons.

"Still?" She leans against the wall, peering down at me. We last talked a couple days ago, when we'd gone to workout at the health club to which the Drakes belong, and to where Aubrey often takes me as her guest. After our workout, she'd mentioned that exercising helped ease her cramps. I'd realized that I should have cramps too, and remarked, "Huh, I wonder why I haven't gotten my period yet."

Now Aubrey scowls. "So, you're over a week late? Are you going to take a pregnancy test?"

I fiddle with my stapler. It often gets jammed and sometimes there's a bent staple, stuck and forgotten, that needs prying out. I turn the thing over, looking for a distraction. Unfortunately, my stapler is fine, refusing to provide me with the sidetracking task of unjamming it. "I might have to," I say. "But I keep hoping that I won't. I do have cramps, just no action."

"Elyse, lots of women get cramps right before they find out they're pregnant."

I shove my stapler to the edge of my desk, as if it has offended me somehow. "You're not making me feel any better."

"Sorry, I'm just saying…"

I stand. "I should get going. Finn and I are supposed to spend the long weekend at his parent's beach house in Atlantic City and we're leaving tonight."

Aubrey nods. "Sure. Have a good time. But call me, well...you know."

I'm not sure I do know, at least not specifically, yet I get her general idea. "Thanks. I'll call you if I need to."

The Atlantic City beach house owned by Finn's parents is a few dozen feet away from the boardwalk and thus from the ocean. While the house itself is normal looking, with white walls, simple furniture, and lots of small bedrooms under sloped ceilings, its location is touristy and flashy. The aroma of mini-donuts wafts through the windows during the day and at night the drunken debauchery of casino-goers can be heard as if it was a TV playing in another room. But I like going there. Somehow, all the nearby sound and fury frees me from the tension I often feel during the

Sunday night dinners at Finn's parents' apartment on the Upper East Side.

On Saturday morning, I wake early and go for a run. Finn and I hadn't spoken much on the trip down; he was focused on his phone, texting the *Examiner* staff about whichever emergency was most deserving of his attention. Once we got to his parent's house, we enjoyed a late dinner and a glass of white wine. While Finn and his dad spoke in low tones about something I couldn't decipher, Finn's mom and I talked about the pros and cons of hot yoga. (She's a fan but I prefer freezing temps for exercise.)

During my run I breathe deeply and enjoy the sights as I jog past casinos and restaurants, and the Ferris wheel at Steel Pier gets bigger and closer in my line of vision. I wonder if Finn and I should ride it this afternoon. When I reach my turnaround point, optimism at the idea of a fun, carefree day envelops me, rather than the fear I felt this morning when I woke to find that my period remains elusive. Now I slow to a walk and let my heart rate go from pounding to a mild, consistent pang. My feet slap against the deck's wooden steps up to the front door. I let myself inside where the house is silent. If Finn's parents are up, they're sitting somewhere quietly, probably in one of the house's many nooks on a plush white armchair which reflects the light bouncing off the pristine hardwood floors. This house is perfect, in that there's no clutter, no dust bunnies lurking in the corners, no careless stains left in moments of negligence, no evidence that life ever gets messy or complicated. But that doesn't mean there isn't disarray; it just remains hidden, and I wonder if I could ever live somewhere like this full time.

I still have cramps, in fact they only gain intensity as I take my shower, get dressed, and go down to the kitchen to pour myself a cup of coffee. I take my steaming mug and my iPhone out onto the deck and Google "pregnancy symptoms." Aubrey was right, menstrual-like cramps are a symptom, and so are sore boobs.

Basically, any feeling that you could interpret as PMS could also mean you're pregnant.

What if I am pregnant? Then what? I try to imagine Finn and me, raising our child in an apartment like the one we live in now, only bigger. Once our baby becomes a toddler and we bring him here for vacations, will we pray that his sippy cups don't leak, that he won't leave bright stains of grape juice against the plush white furniture, or sticky Cheerios in the cracks of the floorboards? Will I be forced to mix with high society moms and set up playdates with their kids named Atticus and London? And what sort of father would Finn be? He'd probably be fine, whenever he could tear himself away from the daily operations of *The Examiner,* so in other words, he'd have approximately twenty minutes a day to devote to parenthood. Still, between the two of us, he'd be the better parent. Finn, at least, is an adult. Meanwhile, when I look in the mirror, I'm surprised not to see the face of a teenager staring back.

Never mind, I tell myself, and with a swift swipe I close out the internet browser on my iPhone. I resolve to push the issue from my mind and enjoy the weekend. If necessary, I'll worry about taking a pregnancy test on Tuesday.

I sip from my coffee and stare at the sky which is speckled with a few puffy clouds that look like the spun cotton candy sold on the boardwalk. I'm about to go find Finn and get him to join me out here, when I hear his voice coming through the kitchen window behind me. There's no way Finn can see me, not unless he sticks his head out the window and cranes his neck. "That doesn't sound like a very good plan, Dad," he says. "It's too dangerous."

"I'm past the point of worrying about it," I hear his father answer. "If Gordon is going to give the Feds stuff on me, I'll give them stuff on him."

"Yeah, but you get the difference, don't you?" Finn's voice is careful yet tense, like he's worried his words could unintentionally draw blood. "You're setting Gordon up, and that could totally backfire."

Gordon and Finn's dad are cousins, and it's no secret that they still argue about the inheritance from their grandparents.

"It won't backfire. That asshole is dumb enough to fall for the whole thing, which is why I don't feel bad about doing it. Meanwhile, he wants to bust me, and for what? Helping the right candidate win? That shouldn't even be a crime."

Now I wish I'd gotten up right when the conversation had started, but it's too late now to make my presence known. "I'm not judging you Dad," I hear Finn say. I slowly stand up, trying not to make any noise. I'm thinking I can creep down the porch steps with my back bent, staying low down so they don't notice me. Then I'll walk, barefoot through the damp grass, around to the back and I'll enter through the sliding glass door. I'll pretend I'd been in the backyard the whole time.

"Good," his father answers. "Because you don't know how complicated it is, being the head of a family."

Finn laughs ruefully. "Of course I don't. And I don't plan to, not for a really long time."

"So, you're not going to marry Elizabeth?"

Finn's dad often refers to me as "Elizabeth" even though I've explained many times that "Elyse" is not short for anything. That's my full first name. Finn and I stopped trying to correct him years ago. But I don't care about that; I need to hear Finn's answer.

"I don't know, Dad. We're not at that point yet."

"Look, Finn, I get the attraction. She's this fiery figure skater… I bet she's pretty bendy and intense in bed, huh?"

"Dad!"

"But you can't marry her. It would never work long term. You're too different. She'll never stop being an idealist, and that will get inconvenient down the line. Find someone who understands reality a little better, especially the reality of the world we live in."

Finn doesn't answer right away. When he does, his voice is low, but I think he says, "Don't we all live in the same world?"

Finn's dad chuckles. "If you believe that, you've either been way too sheltered, or not sheltered enough."

Unfortunately, they've turned away from the window, because Finn's reply is muddled and soft to my ears. Whatever he says though, must be funny. He and his dad both laugh loud enough for me to hear as they move further away, inside the house.

Has our relationship become a huge contradiction? Finn laughs at the mere idea of marrying me, and meanwhile, the prospect of having his baby makes me wonder if I'll ever laugh again. I sink back down on the bench by the window. I no longer care if Finn and his dad know I heard their conversation. Who do they think they are, joking about me as wife-material in the same breath as they discuss their family crimes?

There's a sharp, twisting clench in my stomach that nearly takes my breath away. I get up, go inside, and make a beeline for the bathroom that adjoins the guest room where Finn and I slept last night. I close the door firmly behind me, finally confident that a pregnancy test won't be necessary. The red spot in my underwear is the most welcome sight ever, and tears of relief dribble from my eyes.

I find the tampons I packed in my cosmetic bag, and then I sit on the toilet for a while, trying to regain my equilibrium and convince myself that the world, or more specifically, my life, hasn't gone crazy. Eventually there's a knock at the door. "Hey," Finn says softly, "are you okay in there?"

I stand up, straighten my clothing, and pull myself together. When I open the bathroom door, I'm smiling, pretty sure there's no trace of my tears. "Fine," I say. "I just got my period, so I have cramps. That's all."

Finn nods sympathetically, reaching out a hand to smooth back my hair. His voice is just as intimate as the gesture. "Sorry to hear that. Will you still be able to enjoy the day?"

"Yeah, of course." I look away from him and down at the wicker wastebasket where I threw the tampon wrapper. Now is not the time for serious talks or life-altering revelations. I just don't have the energy for either. "I was thinking we could get mini-donuts and ride the Ferris wheel."

"Let's do it," he replies. He holds out his hand for me to take, which I do, and we descend the stairs to begin our day. I try to enjoy myself, even as a queasiness creeps in. What if this carefree, holiday-feel of amusement park rides, greasy junk food, and saltwater kisses is the beginning of the end for us? I mean, Finn's dad might be right. Maybe only the overly sheltered or the not-sheltered-enough could believe that Finn and I will last, together and in love, living in the same world.

***

In September New York releases a long-held breath, a blustery admission of guilt and regret, but the apology is not enough. Banks fail, the stock market crashes, and it seems more people lose their jobs than stay employed. People talk about accountability, about jail time, but nobody knows anything for sure, and the people in charge will likely remain unscathed.

The same can't be said for Finn's dad. One afternoon, Finn calls me, and even the buzzing of my iPhone seems more insistent and urgent than normal. "Hey, what's up?" I ask, knowing he wouldn't call me in the middle of the day if it wasn't for something big. I wonder if his family's fortune has been impacted, but I'm afraid to find out.

"I won't be home tonight," he answers, his syllables clipped. "My dad's just been arrested and I'm going to be tied up 24/7, meeting with lawyers and helping my mom."

I swallow roughly, trying to form a response. "Okay…" I manage. That's all I can say before Finn interjects.

"He was so stupid. I warned him not to do it. But now I must be loyal; even if my dad's guilty, I'll still stand by him. You understand that, right?"

"Umm, I guess? What exactly did your dad do?"

I swear I can hear his teeth clench on the other end of the line. "It doesn't matter, Elyse. And don't tell me that 'you guess' you understand. Is that what you told Aubrey when Ethan Drake went to jail?"

"That's a totally different situation, Finn."

"Maybe, but you're always going to be more loyal to Aubrey and the Drakes than you are to me. Well, my situation is about to get rough and it's already insane. I need to know that you're with me, 100%. Because I don't think I have time for you if you're not."

Around me, the other staff members in Eleanor Adam-Drake's senate office type away furiously on their keyboards, hold vigorous phone discussions, or do both simultaneously. Ever since the financial collapse, the pressure has intensified to full-tilt she's-about-to-blow level, as we have an endless litany of questions about proposed bank bailouts, government regulations, who's going to do what for whom, and what *to* whom, and will it be fair - but we can't do nothing, right? This is in addition to the everyday, normal activity, which was already impossible to keep up with. Finn talks about not having time for *me*? I don't have time for *this*.

"We'll have to talk about it later, Finn. I'm sorry, but right now I can't reply to an ultimatum that makes no sense."

He's silent for a moment but I can sense his tight, controlled breathing. This is Finn at his worst. "That's how you feel?" he asks.

"I have to go," I reply, which isn't really an answer to his question, but nonetheless, it tells him everything he needs to know.

Chapter 15

Finn doesn't just stay away from our apartment that night, he pretty much moves back into his parents' place. Meanwhile, I find out about his father's crimes in the same way nearly everyone else in the city does, by reading headlines in *The Times*. "Milton Beck Arrested for Illegal Campaign Contributions and Witness Tampering." The article explains how he got around campaign finance laws by making large contributions to New York Democrats through illegitimate super PACS that he'd set up and then quickly dissolve. When Milton's cousin, Gordon, began working with the Feds to bust him, Milton passed Gordon some insider-trading information that was meant to incriminate him and intimidate Gordon out of being a witness. Instead, Gordon took the information to the authorities as evidence of witness tampering, and the hot water that Milton was previously in turned to scalding.

The headlines in *The Examiner* are much more forgiving, and they're all I have as insight into Finn's current mindset. "Milton Beck Betrayed by Family Member" or, "Knife in Beck's Back Twists Tighter."

Finn is obviously waging a war of public opinion, and when he isn't doing that, he divides his time between running his father's real estate business and mounting his courtroom defense. This makes him too busy to return most of my calls, but the two times that I do hear from him, he's noncommittal about coming home and claims he has "no time" to meet for dinner, lunch, or even a cup of coffee.

Then, one day on the society page of *The Examiner*, there's a large photograph of Finn and Marina. They're caught together sipping cocktails at the hottest new club, sitting close enough to share secrets. Finn gazes into Marina's doe-eyes like she alone has the power to solve his deep, existential crisis. Marina's smile is part saint, part Jezebel.

I immediately call Aubrey. "Did you see the picture?"

"Yeah, I saw it," she answers in a dense, breathy tone. There's no doubt we're talking about the same thing. "Actually, I was there last night. It was sort of spur of the moment; Marcus wanted to go out, and I agreed even though I was super-tired, thinking we wouldn't stay long. Otherwise, I would have called you…"

Her voice trails off. I picture the evening: Aubrey and Marcus, Marina and Finn, two happy couples who epitomize NYC's powerful elite. I bet they drank artisanal cocktails made from rye whiskey, orange bitters, and lemon zest. I bet they listened to a hip, new band adept at combining punk rock with classical orchestrations. I bet that after the music was done, they pontificated together about how the world is changing even as their own, personal reach stays the same. Now the only difference is, instead of snapping their fingers to gain results, they must clap their hands.

"Elyse?" Aubrey hesitates. "Are you mad?"

"No," I reply. "Not at you. But were you going to tell me about Finn and Marina?"

"There's not much to tell. I know it's hard to believe, but that photograph was taken out of context."

"Please." My laugh lodges in my dry and sticky throat. "Finn owns the paper that ran the photograph! He chose to put it there, so his motivation is the only 'context' that exists in this scenario. And Finn obviously wants everyone, including me, to know that he and Marina are an item."

Aubrey lets out a wistful sigh. "I wish I knew what to say, Elyse."

"That's okay." I squeeze my eyes shut. "But I can't stay at Finn's apartment, not if he's seeing someone else."

"I don't think you should assume they're dating. They were just hanging out."

"Right," I answer, with absolutely no conviction. As I hang up with Aubrey, I'm already making my next phone call in my mind. It has to do with the only political contact that I've made outside of the Drake family. I know the mayor of Reading, Pennsylvania; he's sort of a neighbor of mine.

West Chester, where I grew up, is in Pennsylvania's sixth Congressional district, along with all of Chester County, and the city of Reading (which is in Berk county and is pronounced red-ing). Reading has two claims to fame. One is the long bankrupt Reading Railroad —the one represented on the Monopoly Board. The other is that in multiple years it's been rated one of the poorest cities in the U.S., a declining Rust Belt town where jobs move out but immigrants move in, and drugs, dropout rates, and graft become bigger and bigger problems for the people who live there.

But the new mayor, Peter Hawkins, is trying to fix all that. I met him six months ago because he's the son of a faculty member at West Chester University, and my mom invited their whole family to her Christmas party. She made sure to introduce us, and I wound up spending the entire party talking to this tall, black-haired, blue-eyed, youngish man with a barely contained frenetic energy and suction-cup personality.

"There's so much more the government could be doing for our people," he told me. "I want to bring the citizens of Reading hope, but also something more tangible. Right now, they believe that their only chance for a better life is to move somewhere else. That's just so wrong."

"Wow. I envy you," I told him. "You have the opportunity to get to know the people who voted for you. You could do some grassroots governing in a truly diverse city and seriously make a difference."

"You could too." Peter leveled his gaze into mine and I could feel how compelling he is. His smile gleamed all the way up to his dazzling green eyes. "Let me know if you ever decide to move back to Pennsylvania. I could use your help out there."

Now it's an easy Google search to find the phone number of his mayoral office. But will he remember me? I bet he schmoozes up impressionable young women a dozen times a day, and he probably forgot my name and my face as soon as I left his line of vision. Yet, there's no harm in giving him a call. But before I can dial, my cell phone buzzes with a call from Marina.

"We need to talk," she says. "Can you meet me for a drink?"

***

Marina removes the swivel stick from her martini and eats the olive that's attached to it. She seems deep in thought as she chews, and I find this dramatic pause unnecessary. *Just tell me what's on your mind.*

We're sitting in a booth and the lighting is low, nearly dark, save the dim lamps which cast a small pool of light over all the tables, including ours. The effect is almost dreamlike, which surely is what Oliver Hunt imagined for the lobby bar of his snazziest building. This place is out of my league, but for Marina, it's home. Finally, Marina finishes chewing her olive, washes it down with a swig of martini, and speaks. "Are you planning to leave New York?"

How did she know? I bet she figured out my potential exodus before I did. "Yes." My stomach twists as I answer.

"Why? Because of Finn? If so, I don't approve. You don't need him to be happy here."

But I do need him to pay the rent. I don't say this out loud because Marina doesn't understand economic necessity. She probably has no idea what my salary is or the kind of apartment I could afford on my own.

"It's not because of Finn, at least not completely. However, that picture of you and him in *The Examiner* was like his breakup note to me."

Marina's eyes pool with sympathy. She reaches out, placing her fingers over mine in a gesture of solace and camaraderie. I have the urge to snatch my hand away and verbally rip into her. Yet I don't, because I'm not the type to blame the "other woman" for my man's betrayal. That's just tacky and wrong.

"Elyse." Marina's voice is husky with emotion, her hand still resting over mine. "I would never intentionally do anything to hurt you. Finn and I were just talking, okay?"

"I don't know." My heart pounds as my anxiety level unexpectedly spikes. I don't know how to act when Marina is all sweet and sincere. "Maybe you were 'just talking' but that doesn't mean you don't have feelings for each other."

"We understand each other," Marina says slowly, like she needs to pace out her words. "When you come from a family like his or mine, and you live in the public eye and know everyone hates you for all your wealth and privilege… well, it can be rough. Loyalty becomes super-important. Finn said you weren't willing to offer him that, and he felt betrayed."

I slide my hand out from hers. "He never really gave me the chance. I was never disloyal; I just wanted to talk to him. I needed more details about what was going on."

She nods and stares into me. She acts like this conversation is the only thing she's thinking about or focused on, but in her mind has she already skipped ahead to the next thing? "I hope this doesn't come out wrong," she continues, "but I think Finn was expecting too much. There's no way someone from your background will automatically understand his needs in a time of crisis. He should have given you a chance to catch up, and I told him so."

I laugh even though I'm not sure what's funny. "He isn't taking your advice. Probably because he'd rather just be with you."

"I swear we were just talking, Elyse. Finn needed to vent. That's all."

"Maybe for you that's all it was, but I doubt he'd say the same." I square my shoulders and keep my voice light because this isn't about asking for pity, it's about finding my strength. "I know that look he was giving you. I've been on the receiving end of a look like that. But lately, he hasn't been around to give me any looks at all."

Marina lightly taps her long, pink nails against the table. "So, you're going to leave town?" I don't respond immediately, and she leans forward, suddenly forceful. "Why don't you fight for him?"

Internally, I start to shake. I can only hope that on the outside, I still seem calm. "I shouldn't have to."

"Elyse, let's be honest. I consider you a good friend, and I hope you consider me a good friend as well. Even if you don't want to try to save your relationship with Finn, you should think about what you're doing. You've established yourself in New York City, which is not easy to do. You have developed some amazing connections and career opportunities. Are you sure you want to throw it all away because you feel lovelorn and rejected?"

I look away from her perfectly photogenic face, to one of the lamps that seems suspended in the air, amidst a sea of dark. "Why do you care?"

She twists her face into various expressions: sympathetic smile, frown of concern, lips pursed in slight annoyance. Then, she lets her features relax into something neutral, something honest. "I don't quite know," Marina states, her voice naked with candor. "It's partly because I know Aubrey will be devastated if you stop working for her mom and move away. And it's partly because I don't like winning by default, at least not when it comes to men. But mostly, I guess I'm a little scared of what might happen if you set out on your own."

"I don't understand."

"We made you Elyse," she says. "Aubrey, Finn, and me, we've all played a part in turning you into this new person who is miles away from her humble Pennsylvania roots. Aubrey and I *chose* you and look what you've become. But now, if you set out on your own, who knows what might happen? It's like Frankenstein's monster. What if we created something—or someone—with more strength and power than we'd ever predicted?"

I level her gaze. "I can't decide if that's the most flattering thing that's ever been said to me, or the most insulting." I shake off my astonishment, trying to find some emotional equilibrium. "Either way, you've just convinced me that returning to 'humble Pennsylvania roots' is the right thing to do. As for Finn, I lost him to you a long time ago, but no worries. You can have him."

She doesn't even flinch. "Okay. Good luck in Pennsylvania."

"Thank you."

Then we sip our drinks in silence, and I realize Marina thinks I'm crazy. Someone with "my background" should be grateful for the inroads I've made into her world. But her world is crumbling around me, and I have no idea how to rebuild.

***

When I call Peter Hawkins, he remembers me instantly. "Ah yes, Elyse Gibbons. Of course I have a job for you! How soon can you move to Reading?" I tell him I'll be there just as soon as I can, but I don't go into detail about my loose ends in New York that need tying up. Most importantly, I need to explain everything to Aubrey.

At first, she seems mad when I tell her I'm leaving, or perhaps she feels betrayed. "Why didn't you come to me first?" She asks. "If I'd known you were unhappy I could have talked to my mom. She has political connections all over the country. I'm sure we could have found you something."

"I already knew I wanted to work for Peter Hawkins. He's a progressive politician at the start of his career. This is my chance to be instrumental to someone who could become really big." And, I think to myself, it might be the opportunity I need to become really big myself.

We're in Aubrey's apartment, sitting on the living room floor, eating Asian takeout that I picked up on the way over, and which her Secret Service had to inspect first. That is always the way, and Aubrey stopped apologizing and asking me not to be offended a long time ago. Now she picks at her chicken fried rice, removing a pea, which I know she doesn't like. "You've been instrumental to my mom."

"That's sweet, and I know she appreciates my hard work, but we both know it's a huge exaggeration to say I've been instrumental to her."

"Okay," she responds with a sniff. "Then you've been instrumental to me. How about that? I don't know what I'll do without my good friend, Elyse Gibbons."

"We'll always be friends, Aubrey."

Aubrey nods but she looks miserable. "Everything in my life is changing. My grandfather wants me to start work as the Associate Director of Information and Justice at the Drake Center's Manhattan Branch. And, I think Marcus is going to propose," she murmurs.

"Really?"

Aubrey nods again, still glum.

I squeeze her shoulder "But that's all good, isn't it?"

"Yeah, it's good. I can't complain about the job; it's a chance to make a difference, even if I feel like Grandpa is priming me to run for office someday."

"You can make your own decisions, Aubrey. If you don't want to be a politician, then don't be."

"It's not so easy. And as for Marcus, I love him, but that's complicated too. He got laid off last week. I know he'll be fine. He'll get another job because people like Marcus don't stay down for long. And I would be thrilled to marry him, even if he's unemployed forever. But still, I wish I could keep things just as they are for a little longer, you know? Sorry if I sound entitled and whiny, but I can't help it." She sniffs again. "And now you're leaving New York."

I set down the carton of Lo Mein and scoot closer to her. Draping my arm over her shoulder and giving her a sideways hug, I kiss her on the temple of her forehead. "We'll talk on the phone. I promise, it will be like I'm just across the city."

"Here I am, thinking only of myself. Sorry."

"It's okay."

"No, it's not. This is a crazy time for you. How can I help?"

"You can talk to your mom and make sure she isn't mad at me for leaving."

"Done," she says. "But I can speak for her already. You'll always have a job with Eleanor Adam-Drake."

Suddenly, I too am sniffing back tears. The Drakes mean way more to me than I do to them, and I can only hope Aubrey is right.

***

I end up leaving Finn a voicemail, telling him that I'm moving to Reading and if he wants his apartment back, I'll be out in a couple days. He doesn't respond.

Sunday night I'm packing boxes full of clothes and books, all things I'll need to live at my mom's house since I don't yet have an address of my own, when I hear the lock turn and then the front door opens. There stands Finn, unsmiling, radiating a nuclear sort of energy.

"Sorry," I say, as if we were in the middle of a conversation. I shove my ice skates into a box, press the flaps down, and start taping it closed. "Did you think I'd be out of here by now? I reserved the U-Haul for tomorrow morning."

His voice is hushed, like the quiet moment right before something scary happens in a horror flick. "This is how you break up with me?"

I stare at Finn, disbelieving this, disbelieving him. "You're not serious," I finally say. "*You* broke up with me, Finn, in the worst way possible. I didn't even merit a phone call or an explanation that we're through." I finish taping the box closed, my movements abrupt and erratic, and then I drop the roll of packing tape as if it was a microphone. "But I get it. I didn't pass the loyalty test, and Marina understands you way better than I ever will."

He stays annoyingly calm. "This has nothing to do with Marina."

"Right. It's all about how you could never commit to me."

"Come on, Elyse. You have nothing to back that up."

He talks like a prosecutor, but I'm ready to argue for the defense. "Oh yeah? When we were in Atlantic City, I heard you joke with your dad. You said you're not ready to start a family and you laughed at the idea of marrying me." I pause, inhale, and then let my breath out in a huff. "I think this has everything to do with Marina. She's the type of girl your family wants you to be with, and it seems you feel the same way. You were never serious about me; what we had wasn't even real."

Finn's silent stare pierces me from across the room. He takes so long to respond I almost wonder if he heard me, or maybe I only imagined I was talking just now; maybe I just spoke inside my head. But when he finally responds it's like he's been divorced from joy. "Perhaps you're right, Elyse. But what we had…" he lets his voice trail as he visibly searches for the right words, "… was better than real."

Finn steps around the boxes, navigating the maze his living room has become, to reach me, his destination. He stands so close that I'm aware of the rise and fall of his chest, so close that I can almost feel the heat of his skin even though we don't touch. "Do you remember how we met?" he whispers.

It's such a strange question for him to ask, now, right as our relationship flies into pieces. "Of course I do."

His nod is barely perceptible. "And did you realize at the time, when we were busting Professor Martin for harassment, that

Aubrey and Marina were using us? That we were just props in the scheme they'd cooked up way ahead of time?"

I shift and look at the floor. "What does that have to do with anything?"

"Just answer me. Did you realize?"

"Not until after the whole thing had blown up. Then Aubrey told me."

His blue eyes bore into me. "And yet you stayed friends with her. You became *best* friends with the girl who admitted to using you. Now you work for her mother, which means you used a lie as a springboard for your entire adult life."

"I don't see it like that, Finn." I start to turn away, but he reaches for me and pulls me into his arms. I should resist, but sorrow cripples me, as if my body demands one last embrace with him.

"I'm no better, Elyse." His lips are centimeters from mine. "I let them use me too and I enjoyed the benefits. But you're wrong if you think Marina understands me. She's not capable of understanding anyone, not even herself. But you, you've always seen me for exactly who I am."

I reach up, letting my fingers graze his arm, aware that I can't hold onto him. "Until now, right?"

He answers me with a kiss, which is both leisurely and urgent. I kiss him back, releasing all my loneliness and frustration as our tongues and mouths meet. With one swift gesture he lifts and carries me into the bedroom, and we fall into bed together, tugging off each other's clothes while our kisses become more aggressive. When we're both naked, I push him down onto the mattress and pin his shoulders by holding his arms. He could obviously overpower me, but Finn lets me dominate him.

"I'll always love you," he rasps, right before we merge together with a thrust. And despite the waves of pleasure that overtake me, our lovemaking feels like we're both clinging to the edge of a cliff, aware that if we let go, we'll fall to unknown, treacherous depths.

When it's over, we roll away from each other and then both stare at the ceiling. I reach for his hand and squeeze it; his limp fingers come to life and coil around my own. "You realize that I'm still leaving, right? That I have to go."

He continues to stare at the ceiling as he releases a wistful sigh. "What time are you picking up your U-Haul tomorrow?"

"Eight o'clock"

He breathes, in and out, in and out, like the inhales and exhales are words he wants to speak.

"I wish things were different," I tell him. "But I've got to finish packing all these boxes. I don't even know how I'll get it all done before it's time to go."

I'm almost looking for an excuse, for a reason not to break this bond with a man I love but don't recognize. Yet I know if I stay, soon I won't recognize myself.

He turns his head toward mine. I look into his eyes, already missing him. "I'll help you," he says gently.

"Thanks," I whisper. Then I unfurl my fingers from his and use my thumb to trace his cheekbone, swiping the tracks of his evaporated tears. "What am I going to do without you?"

"You'll be fine. We both will."

I nod, and then I rest my cheek against his chest. He strokes my hair and we just lie there, silent. Because there's not really anything else to say. Finn is right. We will both be fine. But that's grim consolation right now, when I want to stop time. I don't know how to face tomorrow and that moment when it's time to say goodbye, when it's time to drive away.

Chapter 16
Pennsylvania

Two weeks later, I'm standing in my mom's kitchen, helping her prepare Thanksgiving dinner.

"Can you check on the pretzels? There's nothing worse than when they're all hard and overdone."

"Sure, Mom."

I open the oven door and see the tops of the pretzels my mom bought ready to bake from a local bakery are a lovely shade of brown. "I think they're ready to come out." Grabbing a potholder, I remove the baking sheet from the oven, but it's near impossible to find anywhere to place the pretzels down. Every bit of counterspace is already occupied with either the turkey, the mushroom and sauerkraut pierogies, the red-beet eggs, and the green bean casserole. Mom likes to serve an eclectic, multi-colored meal for Thanksgiving, full of Pennsylvania traditions.

"I found an apartment in Reading," I say, scooting the box of breadcrumbs, the pitcher of gravy, and the bowl of cranberry sauce closer together to make room for the hot tray of pretzels.

Mom looks over her shoulder at me. She's been carving the turkey while listening to me with a half an ear. But my last statement got her attention. "But, why?" she asks. "You can stay here as long as you want. I told you that."

"And I told you, Mom, that I don't want such a long commute. I'd be in my car close to two hours a day." She frowns at me, as if to say, *tell me the real reason you don't want to live here.* I opt for something close to the truth. "Mom, look, I appreciate the offer, I really do. I just think that if I'm going to be working to improve Reading, I ought to be living in Reading."

"I just worry about you, living there."

"Come on. You of all people should know that just because a town is full of unemployed immigrants, that doesn't mean it's dangerous. I'll be safer there than I was in New York."

Mom scoffs. "In New York, you lived in a fancy high rise with its own security guard. I'm guessing your new apartment in Reading is nothing like that."

I picture the apartment I just leased on the second floor of a twelve-unit building. It isn't anything fancy, but it has beautiful hardwood floors, a surprisingly large cedar closet, and in the bathroom there's a clawfoot tub. It also has an ancient heating system, thin windows which I bet will rattle in the wind, and a kitchen with shoe box-sized counter space. Still, it will be my own, I can walk to work, and I can honestly afford to live there on my meager Director of Community Development salary.

"Well, no, it doesn't have a security guard. But that's okay!" My sunniness is genuine because despite my broken heart, it's not so hard to look on the bright side of things. "I feel like I'll finally be an adult. I'm starting a job that I got all on my own, I'm renting my own place that I can afford on my own, and I'll be working to improve people's lives. Mom, maybe I can actually make a difference."

Mom's face softens. "Baby, I admire your resolve. I just hope you're not disillusioned and heartbroken right away. Elyse, it's not easy to find solutions to poverty and hopelessness. If it was, we wouldn't have as many problems as we do."

I nod while looking for a spatula, and for a breadbasket in which to place the pretzels "Sure. I mean, I get what you're saying." I sigh.

"But we have to start somewhere. Didn't you always tell me that the only way to solve a big problem is to chip away at it, a little at a time?"

Mom smiles. "I had no idea you were actually listening when I told you that stuff."

I laugh. "Mom, you taught me way more than you know."

***

Peter takes me out to lunch as a special "welcome to the team" gesture. We go to a pub house and order fish and chips. The unnaturally dark space has heavy shades that block out the sun, and air that smells of beer and fried food. "Are you settling in okay?"

"Yeah, great." I pick up a thick wedge of potato, swirl it in the puddle of ketchup that sits on my plate, and take a bite. Not bad, but it's heavier fare than I'd usually eat for lunch.

"Really?" Peter's gleaming eyes narrow in skepticism. "I would think you'd have culture shock, after your lifestyle in New York."

I tilt my head back and forth, like I'm offering physical proof of contemplation. "I suppose. But my life in New York never quite felt real. And being back in Pennsylvania, close to my mom and where I grew up, and…you know, living within my means, I guess it's almost a relief."

"That's good." Peter's smile goes slack as his brow furrows, and I get the sense that there's something he's not saying.

"What?" I ask, unconcerned if I sound too demanding or too familiar. Peter just doesn't seem the type to get caught up in proper etiquette.

"Nothing, really." His smile returns suddenly, so radiant and twinkly I wonder if there was an entire page in his high school yearbook devoted to celebrating it. "It's great that you feel at home. Because, and I'm being serious here, I'm thrilled you've come to work for me. I think together we can accomplish a lot."

"Thank you."

"Of course. But..."

"Oh no." I quip. "There's a 'but.'"

He briefly places a hand on my shoulder as if to assure me everything is okay. His fingers rest gently against my cardigan sweater, warm enough that I feel their heat through the thick yarn. "No, no, it's nothing bad. I just need one thing from you before we dive into improving Reading."

"Sure. Whatever you need, consider it yours."

"Don't you want to know what it is before you agree?"

I nod. "Sure."

His tone sharpens. "Tell me that this is where you want to be."

"Okay." I laugh self-consciously. "This is where I want to be."

Peter smirks and raises an eyebrow. "You don't sound very convincing. Look, I get that it's difficult leaving New York and all the connections you worked so hard to cultivate, and friends and a relationship, and well... the life that you established. It's like you created a whole new identity for yourself, right?"

He looks at me, waiting for a reply, and I realize it's not a rhetorical question.

"I wouldn't say that," I respond. "I was eighteen when I moved to New York for college. I barely had an *old* identity. I just spent the last several years figuring out who I am."

"Well, take it from somebody who's been around the block a few times. Figuring out who you are is a life-long task because most of us are constantly changing."

"Okay. Thanks." I sip from my water glass, trying to wash down the saltiness of this meal and okay, of this conversation.

"But Elyse," Peter continues, "you didn't do anything wrong, leaving New York and coming here."

"I know." My answer is soft. "But why are you saying this to me?"

He shrugs. "Just in case you feel guilty, or in case you have doubts. You don't owe anyone anything, okay?"

I shake my head. "That can't be true."

"It is." He leans forward. "Life isn't about obligation, and it's not about doing the right thing, either."

"Then what is life about?"

"Finding something to believe in and fighting like hell for it."

***

One of my first projects as Director of Community Development in Reading is to launch an initiative meant to decrease Reading's shockingly large high school dropout rate. I interview teachers, parents, and students. I talk with state officials and members of the school board. I read about public school reform and research how other districts have turned things around. But I accomplish nothing, unless you count becoming an insomniac as an accomplishment. I lie awake at night, thinking about all the families who immigrated to the U.S. and chose Reading because the cost of living was low and they thought coming here would give their children a better life. I think about the families who have lived in Reading for generations, who stayed even as all the industry left. And now they're stuck because they have no resources to start again. I think about the teenagers who are convinced that crime or drugs, or some combination of the two, will afford them better opportunities than staying in school. How do I help any of them?

There is a silver lining. My new preoccupation gives me perspective and leaves little time to feel sorry for myself. At first, my self-pity increased exponentially every time I encountered a new internet photograph that showcased Finn, Marina, and their perfect Barbie & Ken relationship. And the reports full of little details really drove me crazy. Like the society pages of Finn's own paper, *The Examiner*, reported that Marina clearly said, "Hi, Hon," to Finn when he showed up late for an art opening. And Finn's nickname for Marina is simply "M."

But none of it bothers me now. I'm so totally over obsessing over Finn and Marina.

"You have to stop reading that stuff."

Jumping a little in my chair, I turn toward Peter, who stands close behind me. "How do you do that?" I ask breathlessly, as I close *The Examiner's* society page on my computer.

"What?" Guileless, Peter tilts his head.

"Approach me from behind without making any noise. You're like a ninja."

He laughs. "All politicians are undercover ninjas. It's how we get away with our misdeeds."

"Don't joke like that. If the wrong person overhears, you'll have a scandal on your hands."

"Elyse." He says my name like it's this back-breaking burden, and as he shakes his head, his dark curls spring ever so slightly with the motion. "Lighten up. It's time for the holiday party. Let's go."

"I'm not in a party mood."

"Neither I am, but we're both going anyway."

I meet his gaze, and there's a heaviness behind his crinkling eyes. "What's wrong?" I ask.

His chin drops and then he's speaking to the floor. "Diana filed for divorce."

"Peter, I'm sorry." I reach for him, my fingers brushing his wrist.

It's another moment of physical contact between us; there's been lots of accidental nudging, his arm pushed up against mine while we sit side-by-side in a meeting that takes forever. Each time it happens, I'm taken aback by the heat radiating from his skin, as if he always has a fever. And sure, I could move away more quickly than I usually do, and I must learn to discourage his friendly advances. After all, he's my boss, he's in the public eye, and with his fortieth birthday approaching, the age gap between us is a little too wide for comfort. Hooking up with Peter would be wrong on so many levels.

"Should we get going?" I ask, for lack of anything better to say.

"Sure," he says, and we head down to his car so we can drive together to the Polish restaurant that's hosting our holiday festivities.

"I hate the holidays," Peters says once he's behind his steering wheel and I'm strapped into the passenger side. The wool of my coat bristles against the skin of my neck, and my thin fleece gloves do little to keep my fingers warm.

"Why?" I ask.

"Because it's the worst time to be alone." He stares resolutely out at the road, his profile rigid.

"Have you always felt that way, or is it just this year because of the divorce?"

We drive through downtown past the giant Christmas tree whose lighting ceremony we both attended a few weeks ago. Now the glow from the lights reflects off Peter's face, perhaps making him look sadder than he actually is. "Always, but more so this year. Truth is, I usually feel alone."

"I understand."

He takes his gaze off the road for a moment, briefly making eye contact with me. "Do you, Elyse?" He sounds skeptical.

My first instinct is to take offense, like he's accusing me of being shallow or insincere. But my emotional response quickly shifts. "No really," I say, my voice soft. "I get it. A part of me has always felt like an outsider, even with my friends or with my mom, once she had a new family. That feeling gets worse at the holidays."

"Yeah," Peter replies, and then, it feels unnecessary to say anything else.

Once we're at the party, I hit the spiced rum punch bowl and drink cup after cup, hoping a veil of alcohol will blur the edges of my life.

"You okay?" Peter asks me at one point. I must look a mess.

"I just need to use the bathroom," I say and stumble off.

After I pee and wash my hands, I reemerge into the back hallway to find Peter standing there, hands in his pockets and a sultry gleam in his eye. No concrete thought or decision registers in my muddled mind, I just travel straight into his arms and we kiss without speaking.

But after a moment I regain my sanity and manage to break away. "No," I state, worried I'm about to slur my words. "I need to make better choices." I slip past him, already feeling the regret and the beginnings of a hangover.

Peter lets me go. I take an Uber to my apartment and preemptively decide to blame the whole incident on too much rum and misplaced sentimentality. But I can't deny that Peter and I have become friends, that we've quickly grown to rely on each other for hundreds of little affirmations throughout our workday. I've probably just ruined everything.

But on Monday, I get to the office and Peter is there, making calls and writing memos about his plan to bring new industry to Reading. It was his number-one campaign promise, and I've observed that he can be as relentless as I am when pursuing his goals.

"Hey," he says when I enter the office. "I read your notes about reducing the dropout-rate. They look great. Let's talk more later today, all right?"

"Sure," I respond, and since I can't think of anything else to say, I start the trek toward my cubicle. But his voice stops me. "Hey," he says. "What you said the other night, about making good choices? Always go with your gut, okay, Elyse?"

Our eyes meet, and something inside me relaxes, something that I hadn't even realized had been coiled.

"Thanks, Peter."

"Anytime. Now get to work. We have a lot to do."

Chapter 17

Months go by and I settle into a routine of working nonstop. Peter and I keep our distance from each other, though the potential for romance still lingers in the air around us, probably because I don't have other friends or a social life in Reading. Every morning I arrive at the office around 7:30 AM, and it's usually after 8:00 PM by the time I get home. Often, it's even later because of some evening community event I must attend: a library council meeting, a public-school task force, or the hospital's information session about launching their wellness clinic. I don't mind going because it's all about progress. Also, Peter likes to send me to these things since my Spanish is way better than his is, and my language skills come in handy with the huge Spanish-speaking community in Reading.

And that's all fine. If I were home I'd just be reading or watching TV, alone. Not that there's anything wrong with being alone, except for when the isolation compels me to ask those deep, face-the-truth questions, like, *what am I doing with my life? Will I always live like this? Is it even possible to change the world?*

I wish I could call Aubrey or Marina and have a deep, soul-searching conversation about all my angst. But Aubrey is crazy busy with her own stuff, and things are just too awkward with Marina. No, I'm on my own for a while, so I figure it's okay to fantasize about Peter from time to time. I'm only human, and a little diversion is healthy.

But this morning it's more difficult than usual for me to focus. Our office is on the second floor of the city's three-story municipal center, and our windows are exactly opposite the flagpoles that mark the building's entrance. Today it's sunny outside but there's a breeze; I know because my desk is bathed in a warm light and my gaze keeps getting diverted to the flags that gently flap in the wind.

Peter emerges from his office, his shirt sleeves rolled up, the V-neck of his sweater slightly stretched and crooked. He sighs, which I know is my cue to ask him what's wrong. So, I do.

"Nothing," he states. "But I just spent nearly two hours going through the minutes of the last Shade Tree Commission meeting. We're meeting again this evening, and I know that what's-her-name, the council liaison, is going to grill me about increasing the budget for more elms along Glendale Avenue. And yeah, shade trees are important. But I don't know where to find the money."

"Do you want me to go to the meeting in your place?"

Peter's eyes dart around the room, his fingers roam through his wavy hair, and his shoulders jut forward like he's ready to launch his escape. "Really? Because if that's a sincere offer, I'd totally take you up on it."

"No problem," I reply.

"Thank you! God, I'm starving. Let me buy you lunch?"

"Sounds great."

I stand from my desk chair, grab my sweater and purse from the coat tree, and prepare to leave. "How did this morning's meeting go?" I ask once we're out on the street. We walk toward our favorite lunch spot, which serves amazing spicy pulled pork deli sandwiches. Outside, the sun has done nothing to reduce the chilliness of the wind, but I don't mind. It's a perfect cross between winter and spring. I wrap my sweater tightly around body, but Peter is always warm. It's almost like he emits steam into the cool air, with his shirt sleeves rolled up and his lean body pitched onward, ready for motion.

He puts his hand on my shoulder, only to let it immediately drop, aware that street passersby will recognize him, and any display of too much familiarity between us could cause a stir. "It was okay. All we talked about was the need to cut the budget. I just wish it was clear how we make people work harder for less."

One of my favorite things about Peter is that he *wants* to do what's right, but he's wise enough to realize that what's right isn't always obvious. This morning's meeting was with the superintendent of Reading's public schools and the head of the school board. "How do the others feel?"

He shrugs. "I think they're looking at all the bureaucratic hurdles they'll face if we make changes, not to mention the teacher's union. Christ, the whole thing is just a massive migraine."

"What can I do to help?"

"Meet with the teacher's union and find out which of our cuts they'll object to. You know they're going to hate most of it."

"Sure. Maybe we should propose a four-day week for the high school. The fifth day could be spent doing community service, which could benefit us in all sorts of ways. And we could cut building costs and teacher salaries, without having to fire anyone. I'm sure the teachers will still be upset, but at least they'd get an additional day off."

He leans in, and with anyone else, I'd feel like my personal space was invaded. "Elyse, do you want to take the reins on this? I think after all your work on the graduation initiative, you might have a better vision for the whole thing than I do."

We've reached the café where the line is always long. The owners know Peter, realize he's the mayor, and have offered him express service. But Peter sees himself as a man of the people and feels he must stand among them. He'll wait like everyone else for his Korean barbeque on grilled naan bread. "Seriously?" I ask. "You trust me like that?"

"Of course." He smiles and sighs simultaneously. "Honestly, I'm so stressed right now with divorce proceedings, your taking this off my plate will be a relief."

"How are things going with Diana?" I ask, my voice somewhat hushed. You never know how hungry for gossip random people in a sandwich line might be.

"She wants the house and alimony."

"Oh. Did she work to put you through grad school or something?"

Peter's thumb brushes my elbow ever so quickly as he stands behind me in the sandwich line, his lips dangerously close to me ear. "No. Diana has just always felt entitled to taking whatever she wants," Peter whispers. "She doesn't have a generous heart; she's not like you."

I nod calmly, but honestly, I'd like to erect a visible physical guard, like an easy-to-pitch vinyl tent that'd protect me from hurt and humiliation and cure me of this useless, silly crush. The food sandwich line seems to move especially slowly today. I'm cold in the drafty cafe, wishing I could lean against Peter and let him wrap his arms around me to keep me warm. My cell phone buzzes in my purse. I lift it out and see that it's Aubrey. I hit answer immediately.

"Hi!" I say eagerly. "It's been forever since I've talked to you!"

"I know. Things have been so crazy! You'll still be a bridesmaid though, right?"

"Just try and stop me."

"Good. Look, I know this is short notice, but I'm having a girl's weekend for my bridesmaids at the end of the month. It's in Boca Raton. Say you'll come."

There's a fluttering inside my chest. "Where in Boca Raton, Aubrey?"

She sighs. "At Atlantis Arc. Marina is hosting, but she thought I should be the one to call you."

"Aubrey, we're standing in line for lunch, and it's just about our turn. Can I call you back?"

Her answer is deflated. "Yeah, sure."

I press end without saying goodbye.

"What was that about?" Peter asks. He obviously knows I was speaking to Aubrey. Also, we're nowhere near the front of the line.

"Aubrey wants me to come to some girl's weekend at Atlantis Arc. I guess Marina is fulfilling her maid-of-honor duties by hosting at her dad's resort. But she was too scared to invite me herself."

Peter laughs. "I love it when people are afraid of you."

"Marina isn't afraid of *me,* she's just afraid of having our first conversation since Finn dumped me for her."

"Yeah, she's definitely afraid of you." He dares to squeeze my shoulder. "And with good reason. If I were her, I'd be afraid of you too."

***

I call Aubrey back later that evening. She gives me the details of the "girl's weekend," and although it all sounds fabulous, I'm tempted to offer a reason for why I can't come. I mean, I could claim to be busy with work. That would be legit, but as usual, I can't say no to Aubrey. I even relent when she insists on paying for the ticket, claiming airfare is part of the whole deal. So, two and a half weeks later, on a late Friday evening after my usual eleven-hour workday, I board a plane to Fort Lauderdale. Early Saturday morning a limo service picks me up and takes me to Oliver Hunt's luxurious beachfront resort.

It's after 3:00 AM when I collapse onto the canopied bed. I'm exhausted, yet I still exert enough brain power to wonder why the hotel's interior designer saw fit to hang so many drapes. Was that Marina's choice? Several sets surround and cover the room's numerous windows, giving it a weight that's only compounded by the huge crystal chandelier hanging directly above the bed. My last thought before falling asleep is *don't fall on me* as I imagine my lifeless body, crushed to death by thousands of tiny glass shards.

Nonetheless, I fall into a deep, dreamless slumber. I'm woken several hours later by a knock at my door. It takes me a moment or two to remember where I am. When I do, I stumble out of bed and let my feet carry me over the spongy carpet, sure Aubrey has come to wake me.

But I'm wrong. When I open the door, it's Marina standing there. Her hair is back in a ponytail and she's wearing a light pink bikini top with a pair of white culottes. Very few people could carry that look off, but on her, it's perfect. I surmise that she's either on her way down to the beach or she's already on her way back.

"Hi," she says abruptly. "I hope I didn't wake you."

I cover my mouth as if I'm yawning, but really, I'm just scared of sharing my potent morning breath. I use my other hand to hold up a finger. "One minute," I say. "But come in."

She follows me into my suite, and I make a beeline for the bathroom where I brush my teeth and comb my hair. I went to bed in a t-shirt and underwear, and that's all I have on now, but luckily, there's a thick, white hotel robe hanging from a hook by the shower. I put it on and tighten the belt around my waist before emerging. I find Marina sitting crossed-legged in a chair that's more like a throne, which fits with the room's French renaissance décor. She's royal and ready to receive me.

"I hope you find the room comfortable," she says.

"It's perfect. Thank you, Marina."

I stand there, unsure of what I'm supposed to say next. Is she waiting for me to initiate conversation? I'm not really in chitchat mode. But finally, I add, "I got in at 3:00 AM, and I'm still sort of sleepy. Is there some activity that I'm late for?"

Marina narrows her eyes. "Not exactly, but Aubrey is really looking forward to seeing you. I thought you'd want to get going sooner rather than later..."

"No, no. of course. I suppose I've missed breakfast?"

Marina stands and takes out her cell phone. She texts while she talks. "I'm sending up some coffee and croissants. After you're dressed and ready, come down to the beach. You have a spa appointment at 11:00."

"Great. Thank you." I smooth down my hair. "Umm, what time is it now?"

"A little after 9:30."

"Right. Thanks again." Marina starts to leave, but for some reason I'm compelled to stop her. "Hey," I hear myself say, "do all the other 'girl's weekend' guests have spa appointments too? Will it be, like, a group pedicure or something?"

Marina turns back towards me, the corners of her mouth twisting into a tight smile. "Elyse, the 'girl's weekend' is just you, me, and Aubrey. But yes, she and I both have 11:00 AM spa appointments. Aubrey is getting a massage, and I'm getting a facial. It's up to you, what kind of service you want." My mouth drops open and she laughs. "What did Aubrey tell you? That this weekend was some big, extended bridal shower and bachelorette party, all packed into one?"

I step back and sit against the bed. "Pretty much. Why would she misrepresent things like that?"

"Isn't it obvious?" Marina sits back on the throne-like chair and crosses her legs. "With everything Aubrey has been through, you'd think she'd be comfortable with conflict. But nothing bothers her more."

"Okay." I pause, choosing my words carefully. "But she has so much going on. I don't see how the conflict between you and me is that bright on her radar."

"What conflict between you and me?"

Involuntarily, my jaw clenches. How do I even answer that?

Marina answers for me. "Elyse, you said I could have Finn if I wanted him, and then you left town. Did I break some unspoken sisterhood code by hooking up with him? I'm asking honestly because I don't always understand the rules that everyone else just seems to get automatically."

"Sorry," I mutter. "You did nothing wrong." I rub my eyes, wishing I could keep them shut and sleep this situation away. "It's just a bit awkward sharing the same … Oh, never mind."

"Okay." Marina examines her fingernails which are tastefully done in a sparkly near-nude pink. "Anyway, I was talking about the conflict between Aubrey and me."

"Wait, I'm confused. There's a conflict between you and Aubrey? Then, why are you her maid of honor? Why are you hosting this weekend?"

Marina words come out jumbled and breathy. "She asked me to be maid of honor a long time ago, before there was tension between us. And the last thing either of us wants is to admit we're on the outs, because then it inevitably becomes public information. So, we pretend to get along. Neither Aubrey or I wants to attract negative attention that might harm our parents."

"Oh." I could ask her to continue, but I sense she'll confess more if I just wait and let her keep talking. And, with a sigh, she does.

"You know my dad has become more politically involved lately?"

"Yes." I mean, it would have been awfully hard to have missed it. After Ethan Drake was sentenced to two years in prison for his hit and run, Oliver Hunt couldn't stop talking about the inequities of the justice system, that Ethan Drake would serve a life sentence if it wasn't for his family's connections, and that the entire Drake family is corrupt. For a while, Hunt was everywhere: *Meet the Press, This Week, 60 Minutes,* and he was a regular on Fox News. Hunt used it all as a platform to run for governor of New Jersey because "someone had to step up." He won of course, and whenever he can, he reminds the press that being governor is a sacrifice because it takes time away from his business dealings. And a day never goes by where he doesn't insinuate that for all his "supposed" mob connections and corporate acquisitions, he's still way more upfront with the American people than that "shady Drake family."

"I thought you and Aubrey always swore to keep politics out of your friendship."

"We have, but now my dad is mulling a presidential run, and of course Eleanor plans to run too, so it's just messy."

"Wait." I massage my forehead, trying to grip onto some sense of reality. "Your dad wants to be president? Why?"

Marina laughs. "Because he has a real shot."

"But why, when he keeps saying that he's losing so much money by being governor?"

"Come on, Elyse. You know that's just talk. I'm sure you realize that in the long run, there's nothing more lucrative than being president. Haven't you and Peter talked about that yet? I know how 'close' the two of you have become." She uses air-quotes when she says "close" and punctuates her sentence with a sly smile.

It's like I've been sucker-punched. "I don't know what you're talking about," I stutter out, but my mind is racing. I did tell Aubrey about the time Peter and I kissed. Could she have told Marina?

"You look pale," Marina says. "I'm sorry. I didn't mean to freak you out." She sits next to me on the bed. "You hate me right now. You think I stole Finn."

I take a deep breath, placing my palm against my stomach. The crazy twists and turns of this conversation are giving me motion sickness. "We've already talked about this, Marina." I scoot an inch away, so I can turn and look her in the eye. "I left Finn, not the other way around."

"Sure." She nods seriously, and I can't tell if she really believes that, or if she's just humoring me.

"But how do you know all this stuff, Marina? Do you have spies or something?"

She bubbles out a laugh. "Aubrey might have told me a thing or two the last time we talked, you know, before things got tense between us."

I open my mouth to laugh too, but nothing comes out. Why would Aubrey betray my secrets like that?

"Marina," I struggle to say, "you don't understand my choices and I don't understand yours. But I think, for Aubrey's sake, we should call a truce."

"I'd rather go back to being friends," Marina murmurs. "And I could use your help. I want this to be a fun, carefree weekend. I want it to be like when we were college, when it still felt like anything was possible."

There's a knock on the door. "Room service," someone calls from the other side.

Marina stands. "That must be your coffee and croissants." She opens the door, and a waiter wheels in a cart carrying the most intoxicating smells on earth. Strong, good coffee combined with fresh, buttery bread. It looks like one of the croissants is almond flavored, and suddenly I'm famished.

The waiter is gone before I think to grab my purse and offer him a tip. I say as much to Marina. "Don't worry about it," she says, "I'll make sure he's taken care of." She smiles, and if a moment ago she seemed slightly vulnerable, now she has shrugged her composure back on. "I'll let you eat breakfast. Thanks for the talk. See you down at the beach?"

"Yes, of course."

And then she's gone, and I'm left rubbing my head, trying to make sense of what just happened.

Chapter 18

"Okay, time to play a game," says Marina. With one fluid gesture, she sweeps her hair off her shoulders and lets it fall against her back into a smooth, blond curtain.

"You want to play a game at dinner?" Aubrey's incredulous, as if Marina just suggested we do a striptease on the tables. We are in the decadent dining hall of the Atlantis Arc resort with its gold and dark wood décor, muraled walls of beach scenes, and way more chandeliers than a room could ever need. The effect is stately, like the European wing of an art museum with all the heavy, realistic paintings that I walk straight past on my way to see the impressionists. But at least Oliver Hunt knows what he likes. All his properties are decorated like Midas couldn't keep his hands to himself.

"Why shouldn't we play a game?" asks Marina.

"Because this isn't Chuck E. Cheese?" Aubrey smiles as she uses her fork to aggressively stab the last cherry tomato on her salad plate. She and I ordered the same first course, described on the menu as market herbs and vegetables complimented by a yellow fin tuna carpaccio and drizzled with lemon-olive oil. Everything's so fresh, and the flavors are balanced perfectly.

But Aubrey is used to this sort of meal, used to this sort of life. She obviously hasn't been swayed by the sumptuousness of the evening and whatever grudge she holds against Marina hasn't melted like the herb butter served with steaming sourdough rolls.

I sip my chardonnay. The waiter said there's a crisp, dry honeysuckle and peach combo (with an undercurrent of buttery vanilla), and it plays on my tongue and mellows me out. Poor Marina. She's intent on making this dinner special, but Aubrey won't relax. "Playing a game could be fun," I say, "depending on what sort of game it is." I look at Marina. "What do we have to do?"

"Well, there are blindfolds involved. Think 'truth or dare' combined with 'pin the tail on the donkey.'" Aubrey and I both cock our heads and study Marina, trying to assess if she's for real. Thankfully, we get our answer when Marina laughs. I haven't seen her this playful in years. Her good mood is infectious, and I laugh too.

Marina squeezes Aubrey's shoulder. "Don't worry. The game is sort of like twenty questions, very mature and totally appropriate for the dining room."

The waiter arrives, clears away our salad plates, and sets our main courses in front of us. Aubrey got the sea bass steamed in an herbed duck broth, I got the halibut with a wild mushroom casserole, and Marina ordered the lobster, which comes with black truffle dipping butter. I'd thought about ordering the lobster because after all, nobody really cares about the price tag for the evening. But I refrained because there was no way I could eat it delicately without dripping black butter down my chin or onto my blouse, or without squeezing the claw cracker too hard, losing my grip, and making it fly across the room. I guess I should have known the wait staff would take apart the lobster for Marina, and that the butter would be thick enough not to dribble.

Still, just because Marina can eat something with grace, doesn't mean I can. And anyway, my halibut looks amazing.

"Okay." Aubrey picks up her dinner fork and contemplates her meal. With her eyes on her plate, she asks, "Am I supposed to think of something about my wedding for you two to guess?"

"Nope. You'll do the guessing!" Marina reaches for her evening bag, which hangs from a glittery chain over the side of her chair. She opens the satin flap, pulls out a piece of paper and waves it; Aubrey and I can only guess what it says. "I asked Marcus a bunch of questions the other night, and you're going to guess how he answered."

Aubrey barely responds, so I try to sound enthusiastic enough for both of us. "Awesome!" I say. "Do I get to guess too?"

"Sure," replies Marina.

"And what sort of prize do I get if I win?"

Marina smiles and again reaches into her pocketbook. She retrieves a ball of pink fabric, and when she whips it out, I see it's not as tiny as it appeared at first glance. It's small, a fitted V-neck t-shirt, but it will most likely fit Aubrey. The front is printed with black, block letters: *I'm Marrying Marcus.*

"Well," I say to Aubrey, "I guess you'd better win. I don't believe in false advertising, which means I'd have to steal your fiancé."

Aubrey shrugs. "It wouldn't be the first time someone at this table stole a guy from someone else."

Marina makes this odd sound, part laugh, part clearing her throat, and I shift in my chair, wishing that moment hadn't just happened. But Marina and I meet eyes and silently agree to just gloss over the awkwardness.

I take my first bite of halibut which is insanely delicious, but I'm more consumed with the tension between Marina and Aubrey than I am with how good everything tastes. As I swallow, I say, "Okay Marina, what's the first question?"

"What's the best trip you and Marcus ever took together?" Marina raises an eyebrow and looks at Aubrey. "Remember, you're saying what you think Marcus said."

"I think we should make a rule that I have to answer first," I say, "otherwise, I could cheat and just say whatever Aubrey says."

"Fine. What's your answer, Elyse?" Marina holds the answer sheet so only she can see it as she waits for my response.

"Umm…when they went to Iceland?"

"Aubrey?" Marina asks.

Aubrey knits her eyebrows together, contemplating. "Maybe it's Iceland, but I think I'll go with camping in the Catskills."

"Really?" I turn to her. "I don't remember you ever telling me about that trip."

Aubrey smiles. "We went last fall and it was spur of the moment. We had a weekend wide-open, with no obligations or events. So we packed the trunk with Marcus's ancient camping gear, got into the car, and set off on the road without a plan. Whenever we hit a freeway entrance, we flipped a coin to figure out if we'd go north or south, east or west. Eventually, we wound up in the Catskills."

"You're lucky you didn't wind up in Trenton," jokes Marina. "I hear the camping there is terrible."

Aubrey doesn't respond to that, and she addresses only me. "It was so great. Of course, my Secret Service detail was along, but Jud drove behind us, and once we got to the campground, he blended right in. Marcus and I were all grunged up, and when we went for an amazing hike up Panther Mountain, nobody recognized me or even gave me a second glance. And that night, sitting around the campfire, it was so quiet, I felt anonymous, like I could be anyone. It was maybe the first time Marcus and I were truly alone together for an entire weekend."

"Sounds wonderful." I sip my wine and take a bite of my wild mushroom casserole, which is so tasty, I might never enjoy mushroom pizza again. It will always pale in comparison to this. I turn to Marina. "What was Marcus's answer?"

She takes a deep breath and her smile falters. "Iceland," she says, apology filling her voice. "But Aubrey, I'm sure he wasn't thinking in the right context. The way I phrased the question, he probably thought I meant major trips, not weekend getaways."

Aubrey shrugs, but her face is all hard edges. “It’s fine. What’s the next question?”

Marina glances at the paper, even though it seems like she has the questions memorized. “How many kids does he want to have?”

“Two,” I state, as if I’m sure. Honestly, I have no idea, but two seems like the safe answer.

Aubrey shakes her head. “Five,” she says.

My mouth drops open. I look at Marina. “Is that right? He really said that he wants five kids?”

“I’m afraid so,” Marina says. She speaks to Aubrey. “What are you going to do about that? There’s no way you’re having five kids, not if you want to get anything else done.”

Aubrey takes a dainty bite of her sea bass, chews thoughtfully, and lets her gaze float toward the ceiling as if she is only now considering the issue. Finally, she swallows and proceeds to speak. “I told him I only want one kid, which isn’t really true, but that makes it easier to compromise on three. I can live with three.”

“How many kids do you actually want?”

“If it was up to me? Two.”

Marina’s mouth twists a little, into a semi-frown. “It is up to you.”

“I meant if it was up to only me.”

“Well, you should have final say,” replies Marina. “You’re the one who has to get pregnant. You’re the one who will be forced to sacrifice.”

“I don’t think of motherhood as a sacrifice,” snips Aubrey. “And I’ll be fine focusing on family over politics. It’s what I want.”

“Really?” The look Marina levels at Aubrey is a skepticism-filled assault. “What about making your mom the first female president? What about becoming president yourself one day?”

Aubrey laughs ruefully. “Please. Can you imagine me as President? Elyse here would do a better job than me, and I sincerely mean that.”

I'm struck dumb, unable to respond, torn between feeling flattered and afraid to let my ambition show.

"But anyway," Aubrey continues, "I do want to support my mom, but she won't let her political career influence my personal choices. She's not like your dad in that way."

"Come on, Aubrey. This is me you're talking to." Marina's deep breath echoes with restraint. "I've seen your family's craziness dictate your personal choices time and again. It's the story of your life. If you want to be mad at me, fine, but don't lie, don't rewrite history. It's just insulting."

"Okay," I interject, my voice just a touch too loud. "Let's keep going with the game. What's the next question?"

Marina ignores me. "And my dad doesn't pressure me about anything."

"That's because he doesn't know who you are. If he did, he would, and you know *exactly* what I mean." Aubrey's words are a chide/hiss combo. I don't think I've ever seen her look so flinty, with her eyes narrowed, her jaw set, and her cheeks slightly pink.

In turn, Marina goes pale. For a second, she stops breathing, doesn't blink, doesn't move. It makes me remember Marina's face from years ago, right after she'd tried to kiss me. I had forgotten all about it until now, when I see the same latent self-doubt lurking beneath her composed demeanor.

Of course she recovers quickly; she's Marina Hunt for God's sake. Nothing shakes her. Nothing, except for what Aubrey just said. "Careful, Aubrey," she whispers. Does she think I won't be able to hear, that I won't bear witness to this painful conversation? "Don't say something you'll regret or that you can't take back."

They silently square off, staring at each other, each refusing to speak or look away. I take a bite of my halibut which now tastes like chalk, and a sip of my wine, which does nothing to abate the tension gnawing at me. "Look," I finally say. "I get it. I mean, I think I do. You're both at a crossroads, and you both have crazy pressure from your parents, whether they mean to put it on you or not. And meanwhile, you're trying to figure out what you want, but that's hard, when your every move is public property. I can identify."

They both concede by looking away from each other and toward me. Their questioning expressions implore me to continue, to explain how I could possibly identify with their situations.

I clear my throat. "I mean, obviously my mom isn't famous, but she has strong opinions about my life and doesn't always agree with my choices. Meanwhile, I'm a big fish in a small pond. I'm a workaholic, and my only friend in Reading is Peter, the mayor who's going through a divorce. And it's like we're constantly fighting against our mutual attraction because if we give in things could get real messy and we'd be in the public eye. The whole city would assume things about me, and they'd minimize me too. I'd for sure be less effective at community development, even though my initiative to decrease the dropout rate has actually started working." I shrug that last statement off; I hadn't meant to indulge in a humble brag. "If Peter and I were to turn romantic, I'd be seen only as his mistress, and the judgement that comes with that, well…" I trail off, aware I've been rambling, aware that I'm not connecting with either of them. All I've done is made this whole thing about me, which in retrospect, was probably the wrong route to take.

"Given the chance, could you love Peter?" Aubrey asks.

"I don't know," I reply.

"Well," Aubrey says on an exhale, "you'll have to figure that one out on your own. But Elyse, don't sacrifice your goals and ideals unless you're sure. Because I know you, and I know how much you'll regret it if you do."

"Okay," I say. Gently, I ask, "What about the sacrifices you're making to be with Marcus?"

"I'm not driven like you are." Aubrey's replies, without scorn. "And I love Marcus." She switches her gaze to Marina. "I know how you feel about Finn, so we won't talk about that." Marina looks down, picks up her fork, and takes a meager bite of lobster.

"Anyway," Aubrey continues, "I don't think it's wrong to sacrifice career for family, as long as you're not sacrificing your personal identity as well."

"I agree," says Marina, looking Aubrey square in the eye. "And I hope you know that everything I do, I do with good intentions."

Aubrey blinks, holds Marina's gaze for a moment, and then looks away, embarrassed. "I know. But how far do you think your dad will take things?"

Marina shrugs. "Who knows? He'll take things as far as they can go. That's his nature. It's my nature too."

"Is he seriously going to run in the next election?"

"Maybe." Marina shrugs.

"He'd be running against my mom," says Aubrey.

"Yeah, but if anyone is tough enough to stand up to my dad, it's your mom." Marina's smile is so practiced, so glittery, that I concede to awe. She lets her cheek muscles relax ever so slightly and then picks up her list again. "Okay, let's get back to the game. What is Marcus's dirtiest sexual fantasy?"

Aubrey's mouth drops open in shock. "Tell me you're joking! You DID NOT ask him that!"

"I know this one!" I answer. "It's like soft-core porn, where he's the pizza delivery guy, and Aubrey rubs cheese and pepperoni all over her naked body!"

Aubrey balls up her napkin and throws it at me. We all laugh, and the tension finally dissipates. For now, anyway, we can just be three girlfriends enjoying the evening, an amazing meal, and the fantasy of a future without inevitable conflict between us.

Chapter 19

My phone buzzes. I look at the clock; it's nearly 2 AM. I swipe to accept the call.

"Hey," I murmur.

"Did I wake you?" Peter asks.

"Why do you always ask me that?" I laugh softly, to let him know I'm not honestly exasperated. "You know I keep my phone on silent at night, and once I'm asleep, if I ever fall asleep that is, it takes way more than buzzing to wake me."

"Okay." Peter joins me in chuckling. "What's keeping you up, tonight?"

"I watched CNN right before I went to bed, and there was a segment on oil spills and the permanent damage they do even after it's all been cleaned up."

"I thought you knew better than to watch CNN right before bed."

"Yeah, but usually it's just talking heads debating over today's most controversial issue. How was I supposed to know?" I sigh. "Why are you awake?"

"Oh, you know. The usual…"

I stretch in bed. "You're worried you might suddenly die in your sleep?"

"Nah. The other one."

"You're playing and replaying all the stuff you did and said today, and you're concerned that decades from now, some of it might be considered racist or sexist?"

"Right." He takes a deep breath. "And then I tell myself it doesn't matter, that nothing matters, and for all I know, the entire world is just a figment of my imagination, that maybe I'm not even real. After that, I really can't sleep."

"I prefer to believe we're all teeny tiny bugs living on a dust mite, like in *Horton Hears a Who.*"

"How would that make anything better?" Peters asks, sounding genuinely curious.

"It wouldn't, except to give us perspective."

"I suppose," Peter responds. "Hey, speaking of perspective, did I ever tell you about the time in college when I got to meet a Holocaust survivor?"

"No. Tell me now."

"Well, he was a guest speaker at a social justice seminar…"

I snuggle up under my covers. Nobody but Peter could tell a story about the Holocaust and make me feel cozy, but there's always something soothing about the soft tone of his voice, reaching me in the middle of the night while the rest of the world sleeps. Peter and I have been working together for well over a year now, and other than that one isolated kiss, nothing more has happened, at least not physically. But we have slipped into this habit of calling each other late at night; if one of us can't sleep, then the other must suffer too. Except, talking to him never feels like suffering.

The next day, Peter invites me to his house for dinner. "I have something important I need to talk to you about," he'd said earlier today. "Come over later? I'll make you pasta."

I agree to come, though it's probably unwise. Now that his divorce has been finalized and he's officially single, perhaps Peter is ready to take the plunge and suggest we turn our relationship romantic. If that's what he needs to "talk" to me about, I don't even know how I'll respond.

When I get to Peter's house, I knock tentatively, like I can't fully commit to being here. He opens the door so quickly it's almost as if he was waiting on the other side, hand on doorknob, ready to let me in immediately upon my arrival. "Hey," he says, smiling. He's wearing the same shirt he wore to work, an Oxford but with an extra button unbuttoned now that he's home. He changed into jeans, and his hair is ruffled, like maybe he took a nap and now has bedhead to show for it. "Thanks for coming over. Come in."

As soon as I enter, I hear soft, romantic music. There's also a tantalizing smell; I'm guessing something with marinara sauce. "I hope you don't mind a lot of garlic," Peter says. "I'm not much of a cook, so whatever I make I usually load down with garlic and spice to cover any potential mistakes."

"I think that's an excellent strategy. Here." I hand him the bottle of wine I brought, a Pinot Nior. "I don't know a lot about wine, but the label said it's won awards."

His smile broadens. "Thank you. Can I pour you a glass?"

"Please."

He expertly opens the bottle and pours us each a generous amount. We sip our wine and make nervous chitchat while Peter does the final dinner prep. I stand there, awkwardly, asking if I can help, with him saying, "No, no, you're my guest."

Finally, we're sitting across from each other, each of us facing a large plate of sausage-stuffed ziti. "This looks and smells delicious. Thanks so much for having me over."

"Thanks for coming." He raises his glass. "Let's toast, okay? To trying new things."

"To trying new things."

We clink glasses and drink. Then Peter sets down his wine and clears his throat. "Elyse, I think I should get to the point, and put us both out of our misery. I want to talk to you about our careers, and new possibilities, and well… I trust your judgement. I need your opinion on something big."

I gulp, unsure if I'm prepared for what's coming. "What is it?"

"How would you feel if I decided to run for Congress?"

My stomach drops. I don't know exactly what I was expecting, but it wasn't that.

Peter holds out his hand as if he needs to stop me from coming towards him. "Wait, before you answer, let me explain. I think a Democrat would have a real chance of winning against Harris this year, what with the national mood the way it is." Harris, an old-school Republican businessman, has represented Pennsylvania's sixth district for nearly two decades. Reading is part of his constituency, but so is all of Chester County, including West Chester, where I grew up. Reading is definitely the most diverse and economically challenged spot in the district; everywhere else is either rural or suburban and the type of place where conservatism thrives.

However, the national mood lately has been leaning liberal. Our current president is a seventy-five-year-old Republican who said during his campaign that he would only serve one term in order to get the country "back on track." But he's done nothing but bring the economy down even further than it already was after the financial crisis and people are beyond annoyed. It doesn't help that the vice president is an outspoken airhead with rock star appeal but no depth or knowledge, and every week she says something more offensive than the last offensive thing she'd said a week before. Meanwhile, pundits can't help wondering what might have been, had Eleanor Drake never taken herself out of the running for the nomination. All this has set up the midterms for a "blue wave," and Democrats across the country are hedging their bets and deciding to run.

"Elyse," Peter says to me, "I think I could have a real shot, and just think of the possibilities. I'd be working on the Hill, and you could run for mayor of Reading."

I nearly do a spit-take of my wine. "Me? Are you serious? I'm not a politician."

"But you could be. You're well-respected throughout the city, and nobody knows more about running Reading than you do, including me. I know you could win! Think about it – this could be amazing."

"But..."

Peter leans forward, his eyes gleaming, his face flushed. "And there would be other benefits too. If you and I were both elected officials but no longer working together, well..." he reaches for my hand and takes it, caressing my fingers with his thumb. "Imagine the possibilities, Elyse. We could have it all."

I lean back in my seat, the movement causing my hand to slip from Peter's grasp. "Do you really think it's possible to have it all?"

He nods. "I do. I think the future holds brilliant opportunities for us both, but only if we first get closure on our past."

"Huh?"

He gives me half a laugh. "You're going to Aubrey's wedding this weekend. You'll be reminded of everything you gave up, including Finn."

I hide my shock that Peter remembers this detail about my life, and that he's apparently given it some thought. "And?"

"I have a theory." Peter sips his wine before continuing. "You've been holding back, not wanting to turn our relationship into anything more than professional, because you're still in love with Finn."

I start to protest, but Peter shakes his head and gently speaks over me. "Wait, Elyse. I'm not judging you, but there's more. I also believe you're still in love with the Drake family. In a platonic way, of course. But you can't fully commit to this life here in Reading or to the idea of you and me being a couple because part of you wants to be back in New York, living with Finn and working for the Drakes."

I open my mouth to respond but no words come out, at least not immediately. It's like I'm struggling for air, rather than merely trying to form a coherent response. Finally, I mutter, "You're wrong."

"Okay." Peter's voice is so soft I can barely hear him above the languid tones of the music he has playing. "Just… please wait until after this weekend to tell me how you feel. Seeing Finn might be painful and uncomfortable. Seeing Aubrey and the Drake family might remind you of how much you miss them. But I think the timing is perfect. This way, if you decide you want me and Reading and this life, then I'll know you're jumping in with both feet." Peter leans back in his chair, making it creak. His shoulders seem wider when he sits like that, his whole demeanor slightly imposing. The candlelight flickers and soft shadows play across his face. "Elyse, I want you to choose me. I think we could have something great together. But I want it to be right."

"Okay," I answer, my voice nearly muted. "I want it to be right too." I take a bite of ziti and a sip of wine, both of which taste like warmth, comfort and ease. The realization that nothing will happen between Peter and me tonight creates the same sort of untightening that spreads through me after drinking the pinot. We'll finish eating dinner, and we'll talk about his potential run for Congress. And when we're done, he'll kiss me on the cheek before I walk back out through his front door, get into my secondhand Honda, and drive home to the drafty one-bedroom apartment I call home.

Chapter 20

Aubrey and Marcus are getting married on a palatial-sized estate that houses a chateau with lovely stonework, a courtyard full of mini-waterfalls and manicured rose bushes, and a panoramic view of the Hudson Valley. It's a weekend event, and everyone in the wedding party is invited to stay over after the rehearsal dinner, which is in a banquet hall lit by real candles hanging from rustic chandeliers.

Tomorrow morning I'll have an appointment at the onsite salon where, along with the other bridesmaids, my nails and makeup will be done and my hair will be swept into a stylish chignon way more complex than you'd think a chignon ever could be. But for now, I'm resigned to the idea that I'll barely speak with Aubrey for the next couple of days. She has her own "bride's attendant" for the next 48 hours, which renders me and the other bridesmaids fairly useless, except to offer emotional support when the moment arrives.

For now, that moment is still pending. And I'm wishing I had a date, a "plus one" to hold my elbow as we wade through the multitudes of Drake family friends, political bigwigs, and Liechtenstein's royalty. Having Peter here might have confused matters, but at least his presence would make it less obvious that I haven't dated anyone since Finn and I broke up.

When I walk into the dining room for cocktail hour, there's a string quartet playing Vivaldi. People mill around, effortlessly communicating that they belong. I scan the room for someone I know and see Aubrey and Marcus standing by the windows, holding hands and looking radiant as they're bathed in the warm candlelight that surrounds them. And standing with them, also holding hands, are Finn and Marina. Finn seems taller than I remember, but his hair is shorter. He's still broad in the chest, his nose still charmingly crooked, and his smile still sly and intimate. Beside him, Marina looks like an auburn-haired Grace Kelly standing next to her prince. She's flawless, wearing a chic black cocktail dress and one simple, elegant strand of pearls.

I'm wearing a midnight blue velvet dress I got off the sales rack at Bloomingdales. When I bought it, I'd thought it was understated and sophisticated, but now the longish skirt and modest neckline make me feel matronly. And I'm hit with a realization: it's like I'm inside a coffee table book about perfect weddings, perfect couples, perfect lives. Only I'm the crease in the photo, the coffee stain on an otherwise flawless presentation of what's right.

What should I be striving for? I mean, if Peter and I were to one day get married, I'm sure we'd fall short of this…of all of this. But I can't think too hard about it now because my stomach is empty. I need food, and more importantly, I need a cocktail.

I scan the room again and see that there are different stations of appetizers and drinks. I ignore my nausea and instead decide that a little stress-eating might be key. I fill up a small plate with sausages wrapped in filo dough, fried peppers and goat cheese on crostini, and tuna poke. I also find a pink cocktail that is hopefully stronger than it looks. I need to get sort of inebriated to make it through this dateless, just-saw-my-ex-for-the-first-time-since-we-broke-up evening.

I stand in a lonely spot of the vast reception space, trying to figure out how to eat from my plate of tapas when both my hands are full. I could put my cocktail down on the floor for a moment, but that seems risky. Maybe I could find a spot to sit or a table to stand by, but that would entail mingling and talking to people. Crap. I did not think this through. If only Peter were here, he could hold the plate for me. Then again, if Peter were here, I might not feel the need to get simultaneously tanked and stuffed. I sip my cocktail which tastes of champagne, vodka, and cherry juice. Not bad.

"Hello, Elyse. It's good to see you."

Holy crap. Eleanor Adam-Drake has crossed the room to speak to me. Dressed in a light gray satin sheath, she is alone, which in and of itself is incredible since people are always attempting to gain her ear, if even for a moment. "Eleanor Adam-Drake!" I try not to sound too incredulous, to not actually gasp her name, but I don't think I'm all that successful. "Thank you, err… I mean, it's good to see you too. How are you? How's the invisible primary going?"

I'm referring to the unofficial time before the actual primary, where candidates position themselves and prepare to run. "It's alright," she answers, fingers absently smoothing her newly short hair. "But I always feel like I could be doing more. Aubrey mentioned you're still living in Pennsylvania?"

"Yes, that's right."

"Any chance you'd relocate to Des Moines in a few months? I could use someone competent like you, someone who understands the working class. That first caucus is so important, and I'd really appreciate your help."

My mouth drops open. God, I wish I had at least one hand free. "Hold on, just one sec." I dart over to the nearest cocktail table, and even though it's surrounded by people, I wedge my way in between two pudgy white guys in suits. "Excuse me," I say to them both. Then I abandon my plate of food on the table that's right there.

Before she has a chance to disappear, I practically jump back to Eleanor. "Sorry," I say. "I just couldn't have this conversation while holding a plate of sausage rolls and tuna. I have a feeling this will be a big moment for me, and I don't want to remember it for the appetizers."

She laughs. "So, is that a yes? You'll work my campaign and run things for me in Iowa, through the caucus? After that, we'd move you around until the general election. You could pick from several field offices… maybe one in Pennsylvania, if you want. What do you think?"

"I think that sounds amazing! Thank you!"

We shake hands, exchange a couple pleasantries, and then she excuses herself to find Anton, who's probably talking to some head of state or maybe flirting with a CEO's trophy wife. It's not until I watch Eleanor's back recede into the crowd that I think about Peter, about how he said he might be able to love me, about how he thinks I could be Reading's next mayor.

Oops.

I down my drink in two gulps, and then, as a server walks by with a whole tray full of more pink cocktails, I grab two. "Thanks," I murmur. "One of these is for my date."

Ha. I don't need to explain that I'm my own date and that the man who thinks he could love me let me come to this weekend-wedding-event alone. It's not the server's business; it's not anyone's business but mine. I take the drink in my left hand and swallow it down, find a flat surface where I can discard the cocktail glass, and then I sip from the drink in my right hand. I plan to be delicate with this third drink, to savor and appreciate the ingredients, whatever they are. I should ask for the recipe. After all, the cocktails here must be the latest, hippest thing.

"Hello, Elyse."

The room wobbles a bit, but I know him before I see his face. I'd recognize that voice anywhere, even though we haven't talked in so long. In my sleep, he still occasionally speaks my name. "Finn," I say, letting myself take him in, "you look good, but I'm not surprised. I hear that everything's going your way."

His smile is slow and half-hearted. "How are you?"

"I'm A-Okay," I tell him, making the "okay" hand sign while trying to mask a burp. "But hey, shouldn't you be mingling with all the big names in the room? Why are you talking to me instead of standing with Marina and fielding questions about when you'll tie the knot?"

Finn shrugs. "That can wait. Marina is fine without me for a while." He says this without indignation and doesn't seem to take offense at my sardonic tone. "Besides, I saw you standing all by yourself and felt bad."

"Oh, that's totally not necessary." I take a breath, aware I'm almost loud enough to attract attention. "I was talking to Eleanor Drake like less than two minutes ago, and she offered me a job running her Des Moines office. Seriously. *Des Moines.* You can't get better than that."

"Congratulations."

"Thanks." A hiccup escapes. Dammit. "I might not take it though," I wave my hand dismissively. "Don't tell, okay? Because I just acted like I'm totally in."

He narrows his eyes at me. "Why wouldn't you take it?"

I was hoping he'd ask me that. "Because Peter implied that we might get married someday. He's got aspirations to run for Congress, and who knows where that could lead. Plus, he thinks I should run for mayor of Reading. You know, commit to my humble Pennsylvania roots. So, I sort of need to choose between that life..." I make a sweeping gesture with one hand, "or this. I told him I'd think about it." I punctuate my statement by slurping my cocktail, though I'd meant to take a dignified sip. If I wasn't so tipsy, I'd cringe with embarrassment.

Finn laughs. "Come on, Elyse. There's nothing to think about. You know exactly what you'll do."

I look him squarely in the eye. "You think you know me so well? Maybe I've changed since we were together. Maybe the possibility of a mature, affectionate relationship has altered how I see the world. I'm making a real difference in Reading, and all I ever wanted was a chance to make a difference."

"Perhaps." He steps in close, so our heads are mere centimeters apart. And when he speaks, it's in this soft, familiar tone that reminds me of all the private moments we used to share. "But where is he, Elyse? Why isn't Peter here? And why are you letting him call all the shots?"

I stare into Finn's eyes, which tonight, underneath all the candlelight, glow like sapphires. I try to respond to his questions but can't find an answer. He continues. "If he wants you to be happy and if he knows you at all, he'll recognize your ambition. He'll know that you'd go insane always letting him be the one to decide things."

"It's not like that. Peter knows who I am. He gets me."

"Really?" Finn's breath is hot on my neck, insisting upon an intimacy that might make me faint. "Does he know that you're phobic about elevators? Does he know you regret never mastering a triple toe loop? Does he know that your favorite food is tuna casserole sprinkled with potato chips, or that your favorite place to be touched is that spot on your upper right thigh?"

"You can't say these things to me anymore, Finn." I turn my head so I'm looking at the back of some lady's choker necklace rather than into Finn's ocean-blue eyes.

"Why not? You only told me about Peter to make me jealous."

I don't answer.

"So, you got what you wanted. I'm jealous."

Hot rage, in the form of a stabbing headache, pierces through my brow. In one swift, aggressive gesture, I step back and let my eyes meet his again, and my words come out in a hiss. "How can you say that when you gave up on our relationship? Sure, leaving was technically my idea, but you refused to fight for me! And now you're just messing with my head. What the fuck is wrong with you?"

His nostrils flare and pink hints at his cheeks, both sure signs that Finn is irked. "You still know me better than anyone, Elyse, so you also know the answer to that question is long and complicated. I'm in a relationship with a woman who doesn't love me and who can't give me what I want. She'll only ever give me what I need, and

I'm supposed to be okay with that. And most of the time I am, but then I see you, and I remember what real happiness is like."

I let my mouth hang open, feeling shocked back into sobriety. "Finn, honestly, I had no idea you felt that way."

"Yes, you did."

Suddenly, a huge, fake smile grows on Finn's face, as he waves across the room. "Karl, hello!" He's speaking to someone who must be approaching from behind. Without a word, Finn walks away toward this Karl guy, leaving me in a cloud of dusty confusion. What the hell was that about? Does he honestly think I should just understand everything he's going through, without a word or explanation of what he's thinking? Does he honestly still love me?

I need water.

I wander around looking for a bathroom because where there's a bathroom, there must be a water fountain. I push through clusters of people, all wearing elegant outfits, probably by Brooks Brothers or Donna Karon, and mostly in shades of mauve, burgundy, or beige. The scent of jasmine and rose mixes with the aroma of sausage rolls, and when I try to swallow down my nausea, my throat complains at the imposition. Finally, I find a water fountain and lunge towards it. I take gulp after gulp as if my life depends on it. After what must be a half-gallon's worth of water, I'm satiated.

I head straight towards the nearby bathroom, sure that my makeup needs repairing as my chin is all wet. I enter through the door and nearly bump into Marina, who is hugging Aubrey. When they see me, they pull away from each other.

"Hey, you two!" I plaster on a broad grin. I'm about to say *I'm so happy to see you both, you look beautiful, isn't love grand,* but then I notice Marina is crying. "Oh, I'm sorry," I mutter. "I didn't mean to interrupt. I can find another bathroom."

"God, Elyse, stay!" Aubrey reaches for me. "We were just thinking you ought to be here too, so the three of us could have a moment alone. It's all so overwhelming, you know? I can't get my head on straight."

"Yet I'm the one who's crying!" Marina laughs through her tears, using her index finger to swipe underneath her eyes. If it was me, my mascara would streak down my face, but Marina looks even more beautiful in her weepiness. Somehow, she's all shimmery from the extra moisture.

"Is everything alright?" I ask.

Marina nods, smiling. "I'm just emotional. Our Aubrey is getting married, and I'm simply thrilled for her." She turns to Aubrey. "If anyone deserves happiness, it's you." She hugs her again, and Aubrey meets my eyes over Marina's shoulder, giving me a confused look while returning Marina's embrace.

"We all deserve happiness, Marina," Aubrey says.

They break apart once again, and Marina laughs self-consciously. "Look at me. I'm such a mess, making it all about me, when Aubrey's the one who's supposed to have a breakdown."

"That's okay," Aubrey says. "I've broken down several times already, and I'll probably break down a couple times more before saying 'I do.'" She laughs nervously. "I can't wait to be Marcus' wife, but I also know how you feel, Marina. Sometimes life moves way too fast, and you just want to stop time, so things won't change for just a little while longer. You know?"

"Yeah," I say. "I know exactly what you mean. Time changes things, and that can be scary. But look how much we've grown and all the days we have to look forward to! We have so many possibilities and opportunities to become a better version of ourselves—we have to just jump in with both feet."

"You would say that," Marina tells me.

"Why? What do you mean?"

"You never seem afraid of change," Marina responds. "and you've always been ready to change the world."

Chapter 21

After that, everything gets easier. Dinner is served, and I have an assigned spot at an assigned table, and I understand my place in the grand scheme of Aubrey Adam-Drake's nuptials. Still, I don't want to allow for the potential of dancing with Finn during the wedding reception. The next day, I commit fully to all the bridesmaid's activities, and before I know it, I'm standing tearfully by Aubrey's side as she pledges to love Marcus forever. But as soon as the ceremony is over, I plan my escape. I figure it's safe to leave after Aubrey throws her bouquet. When she does (Marina catches it, by the way), I head back to my room, change into jeans and a sweatshirt, carry my bags down to my car, and drive back to Reading. Nobody will miss me amidst all the festivities, and now that I've decided what I want, I can't wait to share my decision with Peter.

It's a little after 2:00 AM when I pull up to the curb outside of Peter's house. I didn't mind the return trip to Pennsylvania because I was happy, heading back to a life I know and understand. Perhaps seeing Marina cry in the bathroom is what did it for me. I mean, here's a woman who has everything: beauty, brains, wealth, and the devotion of man who used to love only me. Yet I could see in her eyes the unmoored feeling of being lost, of being unable to find her bearings in the place she's most expected to fit in.

However, I know where I should be, and there's no time like the present to commit.

Sure, it might be better to wait until morning to tell Peter all this. But I know he's an insomniac and he's probably still awake. Me stopping by is like an extension of our late-night phone calls, and I'm just taking it to the next level. I figure I'll knock lightly on the door, and if he answers, it will be like the final scene of every chick flick that I secretly love. If he doesn't answer, I'll go home and wait a few hours before talking to him.

I get to his house hoping there are no watchful eyes keeping track of the comings and goings at Peter's home so early in the morning. I knock lightly, just like I'd planned, but the soft impact of my fist against wood makes the door come ajar. So, I creep inside, my feet dragging with hesitation. I half-expect Peter to jump out, wielding a baseball bat, assuming I'm an intruder. But no, there's music and the living room lights are on. "Peter?" I call, though he probably can't hear me. Jazz saxophone blares from the speakers. Above the noise, I hear laughter. Female laughter.

Oh no.

I consider turning around, running back outside and away from a scene that's sure to turn ugly and awkward, but dismayed curiosity propels me forward.

"Peter? When I reach the living room, it takes my brain a moment to register what my eyes have already taken in. Peter sits in an armchair, his pants bunched around his ankles and his shirt unbuttoned down to his belly button, while a nearly naked woman in knee-high boots straddles him.

He starts, realizing that yes, I am standing here, seeing him entwined with someone who isn't me. Then he jolts up. The woman falls from his lap, into an undignified heap on the floor. She glares at him while Peter hastily pulls up his pants and buttons his shirt. "Elyse! I thought you weren't coming back until tomorrow evening."

I can't find any words, but that's okay, because nothing can communicate this weird, offended embarrassment I feel. I take a deep breath, willing myself to stay calm.

"I'm going," the woman says. She has already managed to pull on her clothes, and while her dress and coat are perfectly in place, her well made-up face is vacant. She tosses a lock of wavy blonde hair off her shoulder, tightens the strap of her trench coat, and clicks her boot heels against Peter's hardwood floors. She travels to his backdoor and lets herself out.

Peter doesn't give her a second glance, but he does go to his stereo to hit the power button. The room is now quiet, and there's a scary sort of calm before the storm as he and I face each other. "Well," he says, "I obviously wasn't expecting you. Why did you just let yourself into my house at two in the morning?"

"Your door was practically hanging open."

"Okay, but why are you here?"

"I..." I gulp, hoping I can keep it together. "Is she a prostitute?"

"Yeah." His cheeks turn pink. At least I'm not the only one who's embarrassed.

"And do you have sex with prostitutes often?"

"No!" He runs his hand through his hair, and I hate him for looking so good right now with his shirt only partially buttoned, his face vibrant with color, his eyes gleaming and alive. He's radiating sex appeal and that is so is annoying. Why isn't he coiled into a ball, conceding to let me kick all his soft spots? "I swear, this is not a normal thing for me."

"Was it a first-time thing?"

He hesitates for a moment before he shrugs. "Not exactly."

"Okay." I can hear the tears in my voice, and that frustrates me, making me want to cry more. "I don't want the details. But why did you lead me on?"

"I meant everything I said the other night, Elyse."

"Seriously? You practically ask me to marry you and two days later you sleep with a prostitute! What the fuck is wrong you?!"

Then, strangely, I laugh because it's the second time in less than twelve hours that I've asked that question of a man I have feelings for. But I should probably question myself because obviously, when it comes to romance, I make epically bad choices.

Peter's face wrinkles in confusion. "What's so funny?" He asks.

His bewilderment sobers me, and it feels like all the air has been knocked from my lungs. "Nothing," I reply, shaking my head. "I don't want an explanation. Nothing you can say will make this all right."

Peter winces like I just pinched him. "Technically, I wasn't cheating on you, Elyse. We never even slept together, but if we had, I would have been faithful."

Arguing this point seems futile, and besides, he's right about us not ever having slept together. "I'll hand in my resignation on Monday," I tell him. "Eleanor Drake offered me a new job, so we have a built-in story for why I'm leaving. And don't worry, I won't tell anyone about your prostitute habit. But you know, if you ever want to be in Congress, you'd better kick it."

I'm proud that I can be so calm, but Peter neither appreciates nor acknowledges my composure. He looks at the floor, blinking back tears, and it's like some invisible force is pushing his shoulders down. "I really could have loved you, you know. More than you ever were going to love me."

"Oh, Peter," I sigh. "I just don't believe that."

I walk toward his door, but his voice stops me. "Don't go back to work for Eleanor Drake, Elyse. We need you more here, and I think you'd make an excellent mayor."

"I don't know."

"It's not like it's a package deal. You don't have to be with me, to be here, doing what's right."

"How would you possibly know anything about doing what's right?"

It's like I slapped him, but he recovers quickly with a guileless smile. "I read a book about it once."

I start to chuckle, appreciating his attempt to lighten the situation. Yet I stop short. Nothing about this is funny, and I should just let myself feel the pain.

"See you later," I say. And I walk out his door without looking back.

Chapter 22

At least for now, I return to work as Reading's community development director. It's honestly not so awkward since Peter is always off somewhere either getting signatures on his petition to run for Congress, or filing the necessary forms, or speaking with potential donors. And since it will be a few months before Eleanor needs me in Iowa, I continue doing my best at the job I have. When there's a protest rally in Reading to decry the governor's decision to build a new prison rather than to use the money for education, social services, or health care, it's me who takes the podium to speak on the city's behalf. "Believe me, I get it," I tell the crowd. "Pennsylvanians aren't asking for a lot; we just want the basics, right? We want safe neighborhoods, affordable healthcare, and decent schools. And where are the leaders who are strong enough to help us achieve that?"

I don't think I'm particularly eloquent or fiery, but the cameras catch me on a particularly good hair day, and when a counter-protester yells at me, saying I'm just an out-of-touch liberal who's soft on crime, I answer back. "You think I don't understand you, but I do. I'm from around here, and I've seen what poverty and the loss of jobs have done to our community. And I'll admit that sometimes I have been afraid of change. But change is going to happen no matter what, and we must come together and fight for *positive* change. We have to make it about us, and not about the people in charge or the wealthiest 1% who can rig the system." Afraid that I just sounded borderline radical, I lean into the microphone, bracing myself against both the wind and the crowd's hostility. "We may not agree on all the politics, but deep down we share more with each other than we do with any of the corrupt politicians who have refused to fight for us. It's time for us to step up, work together and bravely fight for a brighter future!"

"You're all talk!" Someone in the crowd shouted. "How the hell do we do any of that stuff?"

"We demand government reform!" I respond. "Lately, our government doesn't invest in its own people. Our government used to work for its people; it used to protect us. Now, our elected officials are only interested in protecting lobbyists or their own re-election campaigns. Well, I'm here to tell you we deserve better and we deserve more! We deserve life, liberty, and the pursuit of happiness, and we must demand that our government invest in all its citizens!"

And then, just in case some of the people gathered here today don't speak English, I repeat my last couple of sentences in Spanish and then in Chinese. And when a Chinese protester asks me how we demand change, I answer first in his language, but then I switch back to English. "*Invest in People, Not in Prisons!*"

Most of the crowd cheers, but the counter protesters aren't convinced, and they yell at me some more. I just wave my hands and lead my chant, *Invest in People, Not in Prisons!* For some reason, the clip of all this goes viral, is posted, reposted, and shared on Facebook and Twitter, and then even on places like Huffington Post and BuzzFeed. *Watch This Progressive Multi-Lingual Hottie Make a Statement!*

I have my ten minutes of fame, mostly because I'm a young, vaguely ethnic-looking woman, and I said the right words at the right time, and in three different languages. I figure my moment will pass without much fanfare, and that soon enough, if I keep my head down, life will return to normal. But my ten minutes of fame are extended to twenty when a Philadelphia local news station posts pictures of me at the protest, side-by-side with pictures of me as a bridesmaid at Aubrey's wedding, posing with Aubrey and Marina, our arms draped around one another. Marina and I have on the same dress, our hair is done in the same way, and we're even wearing similar diamond pendant necklaces, as they were our bridesmaids' gifts from Aubrey. I look like I could be just as wealthy as Marina, and at first, the press tries to turn that into a controversy.

People claim that I'm an entitled poser, pretending to understand what it's like living paycheck to paycheck. But just when I think I can never show my face in Reading again, Aubrey goes on the record for *The Philadelphia Enquirer.* "Elyse Gibbons has been my good friend ever since we knew each other at Columbia. But unlike Marina Hunt and me, she was a scholarship student, the daughter of a single mother. Elyse has worked for every opportunity that's come her way. Whether as an employee in my mom's New York Senate office or as the community development director in Reading, Elyse is committed to progressive ideals because she lives by them."

I call Aubrey immediately but get her voicemail so I leave a message. "Aubrey, I know you hate making public statements, which makes what you said and did for me even more amazing. Thank you so much… I hope we can meet up soon."

Then, I get a call from Polly Kinney, head of Pennsylvania's Democratic party.

"Let me take you to lunch," she says, and I agree to meet her, even though I'm confused about why a woman as busy as her is seeking me out. We meet at a café in Harrisburg which is sort of a halfway point between her office and mine. Sitting across from her, I realize there's something very appealing about Polly Kinney. She looks to be in her late forties and is fit, energetic, and vivacious. She seems ready to jump from her chair, sprint out the door, and start fighting for the good of the people. Over cobb salads and iced tea, she and I talk Pennsylvania politics, and I marvel at how she treats me like I'm her equal.

After the waiter clears away our plates, Polly scooches her chair back, so it's easier to meet my eyes. "Thanks so much for meeting with me today, Elyse. You must be curious what this is about."

"Is it because I might run for mayor of Reading? I'm too young, too green, right?" Funny. Even though I have every intention of leaving Pennsylvania in the next few months to work for Eleanor Adam-Drake, if Polly thinks I'm unworthy of running for mayor, then I urgently need to convince her otherwise. "Look," I say, "you should give me a chance to prove myself. I've built a lot of relationships as Community Development Director, and I think I'll have the support of the people."

Polly nods and looks like she's barely containing a laugh. "I'm sure you would. But I still don't think you should run for mayor."

"Why not?"

"Because you should run for Congress instead."

It takes a moment for her words to sink in. In fact, I'm not completely sure I heard her right. "But Peter is running for Congress."

She grimaces. "Yeah. I know he's your boss, and the two of you are friends, so you probably feel some loyalty there, but here's the thing: if Peter runs, he'll lose."

"How do you know?"

Polly sighs, obviously struggling to find the right words to explain. "Let's just say he has some skeletons in his closet. His ex-wife has already come forward, mostly out of concern because she's a lifelong Democrat, and she told us that she knows of some corruption charges, mishandling of money when he was running for mayor, and… other things too. If the press were to find out, and I expect they would—opposition research, leaks, that sort of thing—Peter would be extremely vulnerable."

I look down at my hands which are resting against the table, but all I can see is Peter with that prostitute, an image that is forever burned in my brain. I get Polly's point; if the dirt on Peter were to come out, and it sounds like it would, that would be a disaster.

"I understand," I say simply, and I look up. When our eyes meet, I know that Polly trusts that I *do* understand. "But why me? Aren't I too young?"

"You're over 25?"

"I'll be 27 in December."

"Perfect. No worries then."

"Yeah, but nobody would take a woman in her twenties seriously, not if I'm running against a late-middle-aged businessman with decades of experience." I'm referring to the Republican incumbent who has been the sixth district of Pennsylvania's Congressman forever.

"And I'm sure that would be a challenge for you. But Elyse..." Polly leans forward, widening her eyes, "...that clip of you at the protest captured people's imagination. They saw this young, fiery, attractive woman who's, what? Part Hispanic?"

I shake my head no. "My mother met my father in Ecuador, but he never even knew about me. I've always just thought of myself as white."

Polly's smile broadens. "But that's great! Your story is one people can connect with. Young people, women, minorities, anyone who's ever felt like they don't completely belong, they'll see you as someone who can represent them. You're everything that your middle-aged, male opponent isn't, and even though he'll still probably win, I really think you'd have a fighting chance."

Could that be true? "I guess I don't know what to say. I mean, I thought maybe I'd work on the Hill one day, like as a communications director or perhaps as a policy expert for a Congressional committee. In the short term, I was planning to help Eleanor Adam-Drake win the Iowa caucus."

"Why?"

I pause. "What do you mean? Why, what?"

Polly knits her brow, like she's genuinely puzzled. "Do you think that by helping Eleanor Adam-Drake become the first female president, you will fundamentally change how the world is run?"

"Yes."

"Okay." Polly firmly nods her head, just once, in a solemn sort of way. "But Elyse, perhaps you should aim higher than propping up somebody else's political career. Imagine that you ran for Congress and won. What would you do first?"

"Well..." I scratch aimlessly at my head and then remind myself to act composed. I let my hand fall to my lap, lift my chin, and straighten my spine. "I've learned a lot from listening to citizens of Reading, and it's so obvious what people need." I count off on my fingers. "Access to healthcare. Safe, affordable housing. Free college tuition or post-secondary opportunities. Jobs, but with a higher minimum wage, paid time off, sick leave, and maternity leave."

Polly smirks and answers with a touch of sarcasm. "So, you'd have a modest agenda. Anything else?"

I think for a moment. "We need to reform the justice system. We desperately need to do something about global warming and the melting of the polar icecaps. Oh... and we should bring back the Equal Rights Amendment and finally get it ratified to the Constitution."

"Okay. Good."

Polly's response makes me feel like I've just passed an oral quiz, but perhaps there's a second quiz coming, one that will be way more difficult than the first. I clear my throat. "Isn't this all irrelevant? I have no money, and everyone knows you need to be rich to run for Congress."

Polly shrugs. "Most candidates are wealthy, but if only the rich and entitled can run and win, how is that a democracy? You could probably get a lot of positive press running on the platform of leveling the economic playing field. And the Pennsylvania Democratic Party could certainly help you find donors. And..." she inhales uneasily, “your connection to the Drake family would be an asset. But Elyse, mostly you’ll need to work your butt off, develop a super-thick skin, give up down-time, sleep, privacy, and a social-life, and even then, you’ll most likely fail. How does that sound? What do you say?”

My stomach flips a million times in the space of three seconds, which is the amount of time it takes me to decide. “I say yes.”

Chapter 23

Turns out, it's easy convincing Peter not to run for Congress. There's no other serious contender for mayor, and Polly tells him that keeping his potential controversies under wraps should be doable, were he to stick with local office rather than going for federal.

What isn't so easy is getting his support for my candidacy. "Unbelievable," he hisses. "I understand that you're angry, Elyse, but you didn't have to use our personal issues as an excuse to backstab me."

"I didn't plan any of this, Peter. It all just sort of happened."

"*Please,*" Peter retorts hotly. "Nothing just 'sort of happens' to an opportunist like you."

"Fine." I can hear how I sound, all tense, wound-up, and defensive. "I guess that's it then." I should be past caring what he thinks, but I'd thought Peter and I had become close friends over the last couple years. He obviously isn't one now, and he never will be again. "I have to go. Goodbye, Peter."

If he can hear the finality in my words he doesn't respond but instead shuffles off into his office without answering. I don't go after him because I don't have time; I have a ninety-minute drive to a family-owned Mexican restaurant that's at the halfway point between Reading and Manhattan. I'm meeting Aubrey for dinner.

It will be the first time I've seen her since the wedding, and the drive feels both too long and not long enough. I emailed Eleanor yesterday about my plans to run for Congress, which of course means I won't be running her Des Moines campaign headquarters. Unsurprisingly, I haven't heard back yet. Now I grip the steering wheel, my intense focus on the road, but my mind races. How am I going to explain everything to Aubrey? Please, *please,* don't let her think I'm an opportunist like Peter does.

When I get there, Aubrey has already arrived. She sits by herself at a table, snacking on chips and guacamole, her Secret Servant agent standing off to the side trying to look inconspicuous. Aubrey stands to greet me. She's wearing drawstring pants and a beaming smile.

"How far along are you?" I ask.

She creases her brow and passes a hand over her belly. "Is it so obvious that I'm pregnant? I didn't think I was really showing yet."

"It's only obvious to people who know you well, and you look beautiful." I capture her in a tight hug. "I'm so happy for you. When is the baby due?"

"In around six months. The timing could be better, but it could also be a lot worse. Mostly, Marcus and I just feel incredibly grateful."

We end our hug and sit down across from each other.

"Does that mean you were trying to get pregnant?"

"We weren't trying *not* to get pregnant" Aubrey gives me a wicked smile. "But neither of us thought it would happen so soon. I guess when your mom plans to be president, there's no perfect time. Still, I'd prefer not to look fat on the campaign trail. The style magazines will eat me alive."

I falter, wishing to stay on the topic of babies, not on politics. But for Aubrey, there's no separating the personal from the political. "Maybe you won't have to do so much campaigning this time around, at least during the primaries. I mean, isn't Eleanor sort of a sure thing?"

Aubrey waves her hand dismissively. "Don't say that. I'm too superstitious."

The waitress approaches our table, asking me if she can get me anything to drink other than water.

"No thanks, I'm good."

"Don't be silly, Elyse." Aubrey speaks to waitress. "She'll have a house margarita."

"Aubrey!"

She shrugs, laughing. "What? I know you want one. Don't hold back on my account."

"Fine." I turn to the waitress. "I guess I'll have a house margarita."

The waitress smiles, saying she'll be back soon with my drink and to take our food order.

Aubrey sighs. "God, I'm starving. I literally want to order everything off the menu." She takes a chip, scoops it with guacamole, and eats. "For some reason, my number one craving right now is avocados. I can't stop thinking about them."

"There are far worse things you could be craving." I pick up a chip, use it to scoop up some guac, and put it in my mouth. "Delicious," I say through chews.

Aubrey swallows down her last bite. Her face breaks into a tired, self-conscious scowl as she stares at the guacamole and chips without eating any more. "It is too early for me to be this hungry. All the websites say you're supposed to be five months before you want to eat, like, everything in sight. I'm only at three and a half months, but I could devour every snack I see."

"I'm sure everyone has their own schedule for that sort of thing," I say. "If you're hungry, you should eat. The baby obviously wants guacamole."

She laughs, puts more food in her mouth and then talks, grins, and chews simultaneously. "I'm going to get huge, and everyone on social media will compare me to Marina. They'll all wonder how she manages to stay so trim on the campaign trail, while I'm as big as a house."

I shake my head and hold up my hand. "Whoa. There's so much to unpack in what you just said."

Aubrey raises her eyebrows. "*Unpack*? You sound like such a politician."

"Do I?" Momentarily, I let that concern me, but I shake off the thought. "That's not the issue."

"Then what is the issue?"

"*Your situation* is the issue." I take a deep breath. "First, you've got to let the public know you're pregnant, and soon. That will create all sorts of goodwill, and people will be afraid to criticize you. But about Marina, and the campaign trail… I mean, we haven't even gotten through the midterms yet. Is Hunt definitely going to run, and will Marina campaign for him?"

Aubrey rolls her eyes. "Marina and I haven't really been in contact. She's been weird lately."

"Oh yeah? Hey - you never told me why she was crying in the bathroom at your wedding."

"I'm not really sure myself. That's what I mean when I say she's been weird. Either she's icily composed or she's emotional for some unknown reason. I don't get it."

"Are she and Finn doing okay?"

Aubrey makes a face and rolls her eyes. "I have no idea. But Marina did mention they might announce their engagement at the beginning of election season, and then plan the wedding for late October. It would create all sorts of positive buzz and free publicity for her dad's campaign."

Wow. I didn't know that Finn and Marina were thinking so seriously about marriage, or that Oliver Hunt was hardcore planning to be president. Luckily, at that moment, the waitress arrives with my drink and to take our order, so I'm saved from immediately having to respond to Aubrey's horrifying nugget of information. But after taking a fortifying gulp of my margarita and telling the waitress I'll have the seafood chimichanga, I feel Aubrey's eyes on me. When I dare look at her, I see that she's assessing me with an expression of care and concern.

"It drives you crazy, doesn't it?"

"No!" I force myself to use a flippant, playful tone. "Watching Finn get married so he can increase the electability of the corrupt, fear-mongering dad of one of my best-friends sounds awesome. Count me in!"

Aubrey blows a strand of hair from her face, laughing just a little. "I know. But wouldn't it be worse if he was seriously in love?"

"Who's to say he's not? Isn't everyone in love with Marina?"

"I suppose. But love is a two-way street, and I'm starting to wonder if the apple hasn't fallen far from the tree."

"Meaning?"

"Meaning, Marina is a lot like her dad. She's way too focused on self-promotion to ever fall in love."

"That's kind of harsh. What's really been going on between you two?"

"It's complicated." Aubrey lowers her voice, turning serious. "Oliver Hunt is always saying false and mean-spirited stuff about my family, and meanwhile, Marina's fulltime job is making her life seem perfect on Twitter and Instagram. I guess the resentment builds up."

I sip from my drink, letting the lemon-tequila combo quell my anxiety. "I get it. But we're two years out from the presidential election. Maybe you should talk to her, before things get really intense."

"Yeah, you're right." She smiles apologetically. "Anyway, there's no way Hunt even gets nominated, so I don't know what I'm getting so worked up about."

"Exactly."

"And besides..." Aubrey takes a sip of water, maintaining eye contact with me as she does, "it sounds like the midterms are really heating up. And you should know, right?"

I let my chin drop, feeling blood rush to my face. "Your mom told you about my plans?"

"She forwarded me your email."

I raise my head, meeting her eyes. "It's because of you, Aubrey. If you hadn't defended me to *The Philadelphia Enquirer,* I bet the Pennsylvania Democrats would never have sought me out." She just raises her eyebrows in response, so I add, "Thanks again, by the way."

"You're welcome."

"So… are you and your mom mad at me?"

Aubrey's face breaks, and for a moment I think she's going to cry. "God, Elyse, of course not. We're thrilled and rooting for you all the way. Just let us know how we can help."

"Really?"

"Yes!" Aubrey laughs, reaching across the table, over the chips and guac, to grasp my hands. "You would make an excellent Congresswoman, and Pennsylvania's sixth district will be lucky to have you."

I squeeze her hand. "Slow down. I don't even have the nomination yet, and if I do get it, I'd still have to beat a four-term Washington insider."

"And that's exactly what makes you so electable. Elyse, the country is ready for change. They're ready for someone like you!"

"You think?"

She shrugs. "Honestly? You have a tough fight ahead. But I definitely think it's worth a shot."

Our food arrives, we dig in, and our conversation switches from politics to possible baby names and whether Aubrey and Marcus should move from the city to a place like Greenwich, CT. There, they could have a backyard and it wouldn't be so impossible to find a decent public school. I don't mention that I've heard that some of the neighborhoods in Greenwich are among the wealthiest in the entire country, so while you could drive from there to Reading in less than a day, the two communities are worlds apart in every other sense.

And even though Aubrey and I can each drive for less than two hours and meet somewhere as cool as this little Mexican restaurant, and even though my entry into politics could bring us closer than we've ever been, I fear that the different worlds we now inhabit will cause the distance between us to grow long and deep. But I won't worry about that now.

I have a campaign to plan.

Chapter 24

I spend a lot of hours standing on street corners, clipboard in hand, asking passersby for their signature. "I'm running to represent Pennsylvania's sixth district in the United States Congress," I state, always keeping my voice low because my natural tendency is to squeak a little every time I ask anyone for anything. "Will you sign my petition?"

"Why should I?" one lady asks. She's older, in jeans and an American Flag sweatshirt, walking a little dog with a patchy coat. "What makes you think you belong in Congress?" she demands.

I gulp. "I belong because I want to do it," I answer. "I'm just a normal American who will work hard to represent her neighbors, and that's what we need."

She grimaces but then, surprisingly, reaches for my clipboard and pen, and signs the petition.

And so it goes, one signature at a time. I have a band of volunteers, mostly students who I met when I organized Reading's youth community service program, but there are also some adults too, ones who believe in activism, ones who want change. Without them, I would not be able to get the 1,000 signatures needed to file my petition, but I have everything in order by the deadline.

Luckily, there aren't a lot of other Democrats who want to go up against Dwayne Harris, the Republican incumbent. After a lot of going door to door, attending city and town events, and talking to both individuals and groups—and with the support of Polly Kinney and the Pennsylvania Democratic party—I'm nominated as the official Democratic candidate for Congress in Pennsylvania's sixth district. That's the good news. In other news, Harris is quickly ahead of me in every poll. He has the name recognition thing going for him, and he's just one of those guys everyone respects. But Marina, who is thrilled when she hears I'm running, says I can combat that.

"I *so* need a project right now. You've got to let me help you with social media," she says. "If I learned one thing from my days as a reality TV star, it's how to project an image."

I figure I have nothing to lose and agree to let Marina send a professional photographer and videographer to follow me around for a few days while I go door to door talking to people about my platform. All my actions are captured, including me working at a Reading soup kitchen so I can speak with some of the community's poorest members, and me attending PTA meetings and forums about public safety where I listen to the concerns of all who attend. There's pictures and footage of me talking to people and listening to people, and my quiet, reflective moments as I focus intently at my laptop or speak on my phone. Oh, and there's also random shots of me preparing ramen for dinner, and of my blistered feet after I walked for miles while canvassing, and of me tying my long brown hair into my signature bun on the top of my head so it won't get in my way during the long hours of campaigning.

The whole idea is to make me seem like a woman of the people. "Which is what you are, Elyse, so you might as well embrace it."

I know Marina's right, and I don't argue with her, but I do ask why she's helping me. "Aren't your dad's political beliefs pretty different from mine?"

She gets sort of huffy. "I'm not my dad," she insists. "And I support candidates, not party affiliations." We're skyping, and the purpose of the session is to talk about the various Instagram posts she has planned for me. But then she surprises me and veers off topic. "I'm emailing you an image of your new campaign poster. Take a look! I want to see your reaction."

I find the email Marina sent and open the attachment. A painting of my head and shoulders takes up most of the space with my name (ELYSE is much larger than GIBBONS) painted behind me. On the bottom of the poster are side-by-side instructions, in both Spanish and English, to vote for me, a DEMOCRAT, for CONGRESS. It's all in red, blue, and a touch of yellow, which happens to be the colors of Ecuador's flag. I'm in profile, looking up with a slight, hopeful smile on my face, my hair pulled up in its signature bun. The look feels both vintage and modern at once, reminding me of the historic posters I've seen of Eva Peron.

"Isn't it amazing?" Marina asks. "You look like a revolutionary. People are going to LOVE it!"

Thank God I agree with her, and that most likely my campaign manager, whom Marina helped me find, will approve of the poster as well. It's no good crossing Marina once she's decided how something is going to be.

We post that image everywhere—all over Facebook, Twitter, and Instagram. Almost immediately, I gain more followers. It's the first image people see on my website which gets an increase in traffic. That means we get an increase in campaign donations as well, so we're able to invest in real paper posters and hang them wherever we can throughout all of both Chester and Berk County. But I get the most positive buzz from Eleanor and Aubrey appearing with me at an event in Philadelphia to support Planned Parenthood. After that, the gap between my poll numbers and Harris' starts to narrow. Then, Harris agrees to a debate. On the night it's going to happen, Aubrey comes to Pennsylvania to lend me some moral support.

"He's going to say I'm too young. He's going to make me seem insignificant and silly, like I'm a teenage girl whose ideals have never been tested. And in the next breath he'll call me a hypocrite, that I'm no 'woman of the people' with my fancy Ivy League education and liberal elite connections."

"Don't let him!" Aubrey kneels by the chair where I sit. We're in the auditorium's dressing room at West Chester University, where my mom works and where, in moments, Harris and I will take the stage. "If he tries to call you out, turn the tables and demand that he explain all his corporate donations and ties to special interests. Beat him at his own game, Elyse!"

"What if I can't? What if I don't know how?"

"Figure it out." Aubrey sounds more resolute than I've ever heard her. The glint in her eye is intense, like a laser she could shoot into me to fill me with power. "It's your moment and the Elyse Gibbons I know is not going to let an opportunistic oligarch mansplain anything to her." She leans back, peering at me. "You have a strand of hair loose from your bun." She smooths my hair, tucking the strays behind my ear. "I believe in you. Go win this debate."

I nod, afraid that if I speak I'll start to cry. Then I stand, breathe deep, straighten my jacket, and walk towards backstage where I am to await my entrance.

All too soon, Harris and I are called onto the stage and under the bright lights. We shake hands. The moderator asks us questions about all the issues, and Harris does exactly what I expect him to, which is imply I'm not up to the job. I don't have enough experience, he says.

"Let me tell you about my experience," I retort. "I have lived among the people in my district. Many are immigrants; most are people who work two or three jobs yet barely make ends meet. Some are young people trying to pay for their education, and some are moms and dads who want to give their kids a better life than what they can afford. These people aren't so concerned with my experience; they want someone who will value their own experiences, someone who will be their voice in Congress, and that's what I'm here to do."

The press uses that response as the predominate soundbite from the evening, and I'm declared the winner of the debate. But Harris is still the favorite to win, until tragedy strikes.

On a Wednesday in the last week of September, a student at a large public high school in Malvern, PA, brings a semi-automatic rifle with him to class where he kills three teachers and five students. While shots ring out, kids are forced to wait in closets or in dark corners of classrooms, and they wonder if they'll make it out alive. In the aftermath, a vocal group of students publicly mourn the death of their classmates and teachers, and they call on politicians to enact stricter gun control. But Dwayne Harris refuses to cut ties with the NRA, nor does he promise to vote to outlaw semi-automatic weapons.

I have no ties with the NRA to cut, and I pledge to make gun control one of my top priorities were I to make it to the Hill. Suddenly, in the wealthy suburbs in Chester County, there's a huge voter registration drive among high school seniors and college students. In addition, lots of suburban moms throw me their support. And while I hate that it's a mass shooting that could potentially put me over the top, on the first Tuesday in November, I am awaiting the campaign results at a bar in Reading. My campaign staff, volunteers, and my mom have all gathered with me.

My mom and I stand outside the bar because I desperately need to get away from the television screens, and I even more desperately need some air.

"I'm so nervous," I tell my mom. "What if I lose?"

"If you lose, at least you came close,'" she says. "And you can always try again."

"I know. But I made so many promises to my supporters, and they believe in me. They believe our ideas are worth fighting for. If I lose, I'll feel like I betrayed them. Nothing has ever felt more important to me, than winning does, right now." Suddenly dizzy, I pitch forward, lowering my head, trying to feel normal.

"Are you okay, baby?"

"No. I think I might throw up." I stand up straight, woozy but determined to get a grip. "Have you ever gone through this, Mom? Have you ever felt like everything is on the line, but you have no control over what's going to happen next?"

My mother opens her mouth to answer, but before she speaks, we hear whoops and cheers coming from inside. Adrenaline shoots through me, I rush into the bar, race through the crowd gathered around the TV, and see the graphic: My name in blue, with a 52% next to it, and Harris' name in red, with a 47% next to it. And there's a blue check by my name. Suddenly, a real-life news reporter is by me, microphone in hand, asking, "Elyse Gibbons, how does it feel to defy the odds and win the election?"

And that's just the beginning of the craziness.

Overnight, I become a celebrity. I am the youngest female ever elected to Congress. Liberals call me a social media sensation, a champion of the young and the poor, and a symbol of female empowerment. Conservatives try to dig up dirt on me, like some of the columns I wrote for *The Spec* at Columbia, and they label my views as "radically liberal." Also, they speculate that I was sleeping with Peter while he was still married and while I worked for him. And it's amazing how quickly word gets out that I once lived with the fiancé of Marina Hunt. *Fox and Friends* suggests that I used men to climb to the top and that I capitalized on tragedy by manipulating young people into voting for me after the high school shooting.

All this happens before I'm even sworn in.

"I don't understand why I make people so angry," I tell Aubrey during one of our frequent phone conversations.

"Conservatives are just mad that they underestimated you," she answers.

"Maybe." I'm standing in the new office space that I just rented in Reading; it will be my home base for when Congress isn't in session. This is where my constituents will contact me to share all their concerns that I need to take to Washington. "But all this attention is freaking me out. I'm not used to it." I open the window, even though it's only around forty degrees outside. The cool air is like ice on a wound. Outside, pedestrians scurry from cars to buildings, bundled in their coats against what, even for Reading, is a blustery mid-November day.

"Well, you'd better *get* used to it," Aubrey retorts. "Elyse, you've become a symbol, and the fact that you beat a white, middle-aged, male politician who's as establishment as they come drives people crazy. Either they see you as a beacon of hope and change or as a tremendous threat that needs warding off."

I sigh. "But I'm neither of those things. I'm still just me."

"Shh…" Aubrey's shushing noises aren't for me; they're for baby Clara, who, judging from the fussy sounds she's making, is irritated about something.

"'How's Clara today?" I ask.

"She's fine, just cranky. But I'm exhausted. Clara had me up nursing her three times last night."

"Hungry girl," I say.

"Anyway," Aubrey sighs. "I called you for a reason. I have news."

"You and Marcus found a home in Connecticut?"

"No. I mean, maybe, but that's not the news." She pauses dramatically. "Finn and Marina have announced that they're 'relocating' to DC."

"Oh." My mind wrestles for more words, ones that will express nonchalance. I can be cool about this; it's no big deal that Finn and I will be living in the same city. At least I know that's how I'm supposed to feel. Yet without permission, a memory plays vividly behind my eyes: Finn and me skating at Rockefeller Center—his rosy cheeks and twinkling eyes as he watched me spin and stretch through the air. "You're beautiful!" he'd yelled, right before kissing me.

"Hello? Elyse? Are you still there?"

"Yeah," I answer, feeling defeated. "Did they say why they are moving?"

"Because Finn wants *The Examiner* to be based in DC, and he's switching the focus of his paper to politics. But you know what that really means, right? Hunt is going to use *The Examiner* as his personal propaganda machine. And meanwhile, Marina's official job is to decorate the new Hunt hotel on Pennsylvania Avenue, but really, she'll be her dad's ambassador to DC."

My stomach turns over in a nauseous, twisty motion. "I see."

"It's like they're marking their territory in advance."

"You sound angry." As I say this I step back, accidentally bumping into my desk and knocking over the coffee mug I'd left too close to the edge. A light brown stain immediately seeps into the beige carpet. From my desk, I grab a paper napkin that came with last night's takeout and start blotting.

Aubrey takes a measured pause before answering. "I just really hate Hunt's methods. But I doubt he'll be successful at whatever he's trying to do. I'm more worried about you."

"Me? Why are you worried about me?

"Because you'll be tempted to spend time with Finn when you should focus on your Congressional career."

My paper napkin isn't nearly thick enough to soak up the coffee, so I go to grab paper towels, cursing under my breath. "Aubrey, I promise you, that won't happen." Armed with a handful of paper towels, I kneel on the floor and soak up the spilled coffee. "There's too much at stake for me to get all wound up over my ex."

"Sure, it's just... don't take this the wrong way, but I don't think you ever really got over him."

"Yes, I did," I snap. Immediately I feel bad and soften my voice. "Sorry. I've got to go. Talk to you later?"

"Sure. Call me after Finn calls you. I know he will."

Hours later, I exit my new office and get into my car. Night comes early this time of year, and I flick on the heat as soon as I turn the ignition, though right now the air coming through the vent matches the chilliness from outside. I don't turn the air down; instead I just wait for the temperature change.

When I get to where I should turn to go home, I drive right by. Instead of driving to my apartment, I wind through the poorer neighborhoods until I get to Victory Ice Arena and breathe a sigh of relief as I walk through the door.

"Hey, Tawni."

Tawni works at the front desk. She schedules practice time for the handful of hockey leagues that use the rink to practice. Hockey is sort of a wealthy, white person sport, and this neighborhood is neither white nor wealthy, so the rink doesn't get a lot of demand.

"Hey, Hon," Tawni answers, briefly looking up from the ancient computer where she puts together all her Excel spreadsheets. "Bad day?"

"Can you tell just by looking at me?"

"'Fraid so." She smiles warmly. "You gonna go skate it off?"

"That's my plan."

I traipse over the worn brown carpet, past the snack bar that serves only nachos and past the thick, black wooden benches to my locker. There's no locker room here, but at least I have a little rectangle of space to call my own, a place to store my skates and a fleece jacket. Luckily, I chose to wear a tunic and some leggings today, clothes that I can move in. But my coat, a heavy, padded corduroy affair, isn't the best for skating, so I take it off and put on the fleece instead. My mind flashes to that jacket Marina gave me all those years ago. Right now, it hangs in the back of my closet and in the back of my consciousness. It's still stylish but seeing as how it no longer fits the image I need to project, I have trouble putting it on.

Once I've laced up my skates, I pass through the doors and into the cold of the arena. The moment my blades dig into the ice is an elixir, and I immediately skate in wide, fast circles, as if I could exorcise my demons through speed, control, and strength. If only life outside the rink felt as simple as it does in here.

Later, I finally get home, heat up some noodles, and collapse onto my couch. Against my better judgement, I turn on the news, flipping back and forth between CNN, MSNBC, and FOX. I've become paranoid while watching TV, worried I'll find my face posted with some damning headline that I didn't see coming. My Twitter and Instagram followers like me to post often, both about my daily routine and my take on whatever the day's news is. Yet, a price tag comes with these posts; I never know when my critics will get all worked up over how I worded something.

Then my phone buzzes. Aubrey was right. Finn is calling me.

I put the TV on mute, place my bowl of noodles on the coffee table, and answer the call. "Hi," I say casually, as if it hasn't been forever since we've spoken. "When are you moving to DC?"

"I'm already here," he answers, and the closeness of his voice instantly diminishes years of painful distance and lies, and that's exactly what I am afraid of. "I'm staying downtown right now while I set up *The Examiner's* office and find a place for Marina and me to live. Want to meet tomorrow for a drink?"

I close my eyes and rest my head against the couch. "I'm in Reading right now."

"What about your orientation for Congress?"

"That doesn't start until Monday morning. I'm getting in on Sunday afternoon."

"Okay, so do you want to meet up on Sunday evening?"

I feel as if he'd just suggested I give him my kidney rather than meet him for a drink. With a sigh, I say, "Sure. Why not?"

He returns with, "Look, if you don't want to meet, just say so. No hard feelings."

"No, no." I take my voice up an octave, trying to sound perky and polite. "Of course I'll meet you. I'll text you later with a bar near my hotel."

"Great."

There's a pause where I know I should say something, but no words come. Finally, he says, "How are you?"

"I'm good. But I should go."

"Okay. See you Sunday?"

"Yup."

There's another awkward, silent moment, and then we say our clunky goodbyes and hang up. I pick up my bowl of noodles and realize I didn't make them hot enough. I turn up the sound on the TV only to find that all three channels have gone to commercial. I wanted to eat my hot noodles while watching the news, and instead I'm eating warmish noodles while watching an insurance commercial.

I could cry, but that would be like crying over a hangnail, stinging and red, but barely worth the band-aide that provides a temporary fix. And I know I only have myself to blame, but God, I'd rather blame Finn.

Chapter 25
Washington DC

Finn agrees to meet me at the bar in Hotel Hive, which is where I booked a room to stay during my orientation. It offers the most affordable rates of all the places that are remotely convenient to Congress. When I walk in a few minutes early, I don't see Finn, but I know that I will soon, and that puts me in the mood for a gin & tonic. I order at the bar, and then find a table by a fireplace to sit. Before Finn gets here, I snap a picture of my drink, which sits on the table beside the book I brought, *Why We Can't Wait,* by Martin Luther King Jr. The exposed brick wall, bookshelves, and cozy fireplace of the bar serve as a backdrop. "First night in DC!" I tweet. "Excited for orientation tomorrow but must chill in the meantime." Then, so I don't feel like a total poser, I pick up my book and read, letting MLK's words inspire and remind me of why I want to be here. I've read several pages and am nearly ready for my second drink when Finn enters the bar, seven minutes late.

"Sorry," he says as he sits opposite me. "I underestimated how long it would take to get here."

He looks the same, all the way down to the navy-blue Henley that peeks out from underneath his wool jacket. His hair is spikey now, probably to hide the fact that his hairline is receding, and the tension lines around his jaw are more deeply etched. But other than that, he's achingly familiar, like a recurring dream that wakes me up tired.

"This is for you." I point toward the G&T that I took the liberty of ordering for him. It sits on the table, slick with condensation and becoming increasingly watered down as its ice cubes melt. "You're lucky you got here when you did. I was about to drink it myself."

"Thanks." He holds up his drink, as if to toast. "To reunions."

I lift my nearly empty glass and tap it to his. "To winning."

"That's right." Finn smiles. "I guess congratulations are in order. Good job, Congresswoman Gibbons."

"I have your fiancé to thank for my victory. Marina's help was priceless."

"Yeah." He leans back in his chair, assessing me. I guess he's not going to acknowledge the "fiancé" part of my statement. "She's good at influencing public opinion."

"That's one way of putting it."

I mean that to sound playful, but it comes out snarky instead. Finn looks irritated. "Elyse, you know Marina thinks of you as one of her best friends, right?"

I release an angsty breath. "Sorry. I'm sort of on edge, you know, nervous about tomorrow." I grip my glass, which is now full of nothing but ice. "I need a fresh drink. Do you want another one?"

"No. But I'll take a real drink."

"What's wrong with the one I got you?"

"The gin obviously isn't top shelf." Finn laughs. "I know, I know. I'm a snob - but let me get this round." He stands, and I'm acutely aware of how, with one fluid movement, he could lean in and kiss me. My cheeks burn at the thought, and I pray Finn doesn't notice, that he doesn't hear my heart pounding. "I'll be right back," he says.

In the short amount of time he stands at the bar, all these questions race through my mind: *Why did I agree to meet him? Why did he want to meet me? Is Aubrey right? Am I really not over Finn?*

When he returns with our gin and tonics, he sits back across from me and resumes our conversation as if there had been no interruption. "I understand why you're nervous, Elyse, but don't be. Wait until you're actually sworn in for that."

"It doesn't matter. The spotlight is already on me." I ball both my hands into fists, hesitant to mention what's on the forefront of my mind. "Have you seen all the stuff the press has dug up about our relationship? I mean, it's probably madness for us to be meeting like this, especially without Marina here. Is she still in New York?"

"Yeah. She'll fly out later this week. But Marina thought it was a good idea for you and me to get a drink, even if the press does catch wind of it. That way, she can make a statement, like she knew we were meeting and that she trusts us both."

Just the thought causes a hitch in my breath. "So, there's no such thing as bad publicity?"

"Exactly."

We both pause, sip our drinks, and let the weight of our evening together settle. How can any of this be real? Feeling his gaze, I hesitate and then meet his eyes.

His nostrils flare ever so slightly, like there's something he wants to say, but can't. He sounds almost wistful when he states, "It's great to see you, Elyse. You look good."

"And you look the same," I reply. 'You seem the same too."

"Appearances can be deceiving." He raises his eyebrows. "But I'll take that as a compliment, like you're saying that I haven't aged."

"Or matured." I smile, thinking that this time, he'll get that I'm joking.

But Finn drops his chin and stares down into his drink as if it was a crystal ball. "Are you mad at me about something?"

Oh well. I may as well lay it on the line. "Not really. But the last time I saw you, at Aubrey's wedding, our conversation sent me spinning, and now I'm confused. I mean, why'd you want to see me?"

He shrugs. "I thought it would be nice."

"On my very first night in DC?"

Finn blows some air from his cheeks. "You could have said no."

Suddenly, I sneeze a violent, gushy sort of sneeze, and immediately grab for the damp cocktail napkin underneath my drink. It doesn't help much, but Finn reaches into his pocket and comes out with several unused Kleenex neatly folded into a thick rectangle. As he hands me the tissues, I'm reminded of all the little ways he used to try to care for me when were a couple.

"Thanks," I say, and then blow my nose, embarrassed and worried that I have snot all over my face.

"Are you catching a cold?"

"Probably," I reply, sniffing. "It's that time of year."

He chuckles softly. "Remember the time you had a sinus infection, and you used the neti pot I bought you?"

Ah, yes. Finn got me chicken soup, extra Advil, and a brand new neti pot which a coworker had said would work wonders. "Of course," I answer. "You were so well intentioned."

"And it was all going great until you heard that news story about neti pots and brain-eating amoebas, and then you freaked out."

I concede a smile. "I was scared to fall asleep, like I'd turn into a zombie or something. So you stayed up with me all night, watching movies." Chuckling, I meet his eye. "That was nice of you."

"Yeah, I had my moments." His return-chuckle sounds self-conscious. "But in retrospect, I shouldn't have insisted we watch *Night of the Living Dead.*"

"Really?" I reply with gentle sarcasm. "You think watching it might have exacerbated my anxiety?"

A crooked grin spreads across half his face. "Can I help it if you're intense?"

And then it's like a cloud passes over that brief moment of sunshine between us. Sure, I'm being overly sensitive, but I hate it when Finn reminds me of how flawed I am. I place both my elbows on the table. Leaning in, I shoot him my laser focus. "So, Finn, tell me why you've relocated to DC."

"It's been explained in articles on CNN, USA Today, Slate..."

"I know. I read those articles. But what's the real reason you're here?"

He squints at me. "I'm doing what's been asked of me."

"Ever the good son."

"I suppose."

I shrug away my fake nonchalance. "Fine."

We square off, staring into each other's eyes. "Yeah, it is fine," he says after a moment. "I should go."

My mouth drops open in shock. "You've been here, like, ten minutes."

He stands up to leave. "It was nice seeing you. Good luck tomorrow, Elyse." Then he walks away.

I'm left alone, sitting at my table, wondering what just happened.

Chapter 26

The next few months are a whirlwind. I complete Congressional orientation, and several weeks later, I'm sworn in as the youngest woman ever elected to the House of Representatives. Afterwards, the media's attention stays strong, partly because I openly question House leadership whenever I disagree with them on something. I use Twitter as my platform, and my rapidly growing number of followers gets me an interview on *60 Minutes* and a guest spot on *The Tonight Show.* What's more exciting, however, is my assignment to the Education and Workforce committee where I hope to continue working on the dropout rate but now at a national level.

I also find an apartment in DC., hire staff for both my Congressional office here and back home in Pennsylvania, and work day and night, reading bills, attempting to understand how things are run on the Hill. There's a learning curve, but I'm trying to keep ahead of it.

All this means I have zero time for a social life, which is good since I have no friends in DC., other than Marina and Finn, who I haven't heard from since that night at Hotel Hive. But one afternoon I notice a missed call from Marina.

Curious, I call her back.

"You have to come to the Hunt Hotel on Pennsylvania Avenue for a slumber party," Marina states, like two seconds after we say hello. "Aubrey will be in town, and it will be just like old times, the three of us hanging out. Besides, the hotel is almost ready to open, and I need to give the rooms a test-run first. What do you say?"

If the press were to catch wind of me staying at a Hunt Hotel, I'm sure I'd be criticized every which way. But I don't care. I'm lonely lately and I need downtime with my best girlfriends...okay, with my *only* girlfriends.

"Count me in, Marina! I'd love to come."

Several days later, I find myself wrapped in a thick, super-soft Hunt Hotel' s velvet bathrobe, sitting in bed with tons of pillows and a down comforter, sipping champagne from a crystal goblet, and eating a fruit parfait that contains more vitamin C than I've ingested in the last five weeks, total. I listen as Aubrey and Marina compare paparazzi harassment horror stories.

"Okay," Aubrey says. She's sitting cross-legged on the floor, wrapped in her own robe and nursing her own glass of champagne. "I bet you can't top this. A few days ago, I was pushing Clara's stroller through the neighborhood when a member of the paparazzi jumped out. I ignored him and rushed off, but he kept after me, hollering, 'Tell the truth, Aubrey! We know your uncle was arrested for child pornography! You must be so worried about little Clara!'"

Marina's mouth drops open. "Jesus, Aubrey, that is awful. The worst is when they make up vicious lies. At least Ethan can try to set the record straight."

Aubrey shrugs. "Maybe. Grandpa plans to reform Ethan's image and save the Drake family name. That includes Mom getting elected president, Ethan becoming governor of Pennsylvania, and Marcus and me moving to Connecticut so I can run for governor there."

"Seriously?" I gasp. "Aubrey, do you *want* to run for Governor?"

Aubrey collapses herself against some pillows and stares at the ceiling. "I don't know. Connecticut is so small, it probably wouldn't be that difficult to run. But we'd have to find a house super-fast if I'm going to be eligible in the next election."

"What's the rush?" Marina asks. "Wouldn't waiting be better, both for you and for your uncle? Give it some time?"

Aubrey sits up and looks Marina squarely in the eye. "I wish I could, but timing is everything. Grandpa thinks if three Drakes are simultaneously running for office, we'd *more* than triple the impact of our message and fundraising capabilities. Besides, governorships aren't vacated that often. Uncle Ethan and I both need to jump on that, so we won't be running against incumbents..." Aubrey's voice trails off and she casts her glance down. "Though I'll admit, just thinking about the whole thing makes me exhausted."

"I get it." Marina stretches her neck and arches her back. She's sitting with Aubrey on the floor, and it wouldn't be the craziest thing ever if she suddenly launched into yoga exercises, but she simply lets her muscles relax. Then she places her hand atop Aubrey's knee. "Our situations are different, but they're also the same. My dad got this idea that he could use a huge engagement party for Finn and me to announce his run for president, and then at the end of primary season, we'll have the wedding, and it would garner all sorts of free publicity and positive buzz. But I don't know if I'm on board with it all because, well..." her eyes roll toward the ceiling, "sometimes I worry that I'm not in love with Finn, at least not how I'm supposed to be, you know, in order to marry him." She pauses, letting her gaze switch back and forth between Aubrey and me and finally settling on my eyes, "Finn deserves someone who's going to love him completely, don't you think, Elyse?"

Blood rushes to my face and I must look away. I focus on the golden wallpaper with its brocade pattern of woven leaves that look like hearts hanging upside down.

"Is there something going on that I don't know about?" Aubrey asks, sounding confused.

"No!" My response is too quick and too loud. "I mean, Finn and I met for drinks a couple months ago, but I haven't spoken to him since. And I swear, Marina," I look at her, "I haven't thought about him since then either." I force out a self-deprecating laugh. "Lately, I don't know how to think about anything but work."

"Elyse, relax, okay?" Marina arches an eyebrow. "You look a little pale."

"I'm fine," I say. "Seriously, Marina, I'm happy for you, that is, if getting married is what you and Finn both want."

"Oh, I know it's what Finn wants. I'm just not sure about myself. I guess I need to figure it out, huh?"

"Don't let your dad pressure you to do things his way," Aubrey says.

"You don't need to worry about me," Marina answers. "I don't take things as seriously as you both do, especially you, Elyse."

It goes against my nature, but I know I need to shrug this off, even if that means making an honest statement in a flippant tone. "You only say that because I haven't dated anyone since Finn, and I get all pinched up and intense every time he's mentioned."

Marina smiles, but you know, one woman's smile is another woman's frown. "I can tell you're upset, but you can talk to us, okay? After all, if you can't be honest with Aubrey and me, who can you be honest with?"

She's right, except that I need to start by being honest with myself. The mere mention of loving Finn should not send me into such a tizzy. "Let's talk about something else."

Aubrey nods. "How's Congress going?"

"It's good." I bite my lip, hesitating just a moment before plunging in. "It's just, there are so many problems that need fixing and everything is so complicated. Sometimes it feels impossible to get anything done. But I *know* I want to try to empower women in a lasting way, one that will affect generations." I pause dramatically, looking back and forth between them, finally meeting eyes with Aubrey before speaking again. "So, I've decided to make it my mission to get the Equal Rights Amendment passed, once and for all."

"God, that would be amazing, wouldn't it, Elyse?" Aubrey gushes. "Just think, you could finish the work that feminists began back in the 70s and 80s!"

Marina scrunches up her brow. "Okay. I know the ERA is about equal pay, but don't we pretty much already have that?"

"No," I retort. "Not at all. And equal pay is just part of it. Passing the ERA would also give more legal protection to women who have been sexually assaulted."

"Huh." That catches Marina's attention. I can't tell if this is news to her or if she'd heard it before but it never really sank in, but her contemplative expression spurs me on.

"And it would set up women as equal citizens. I mean, in some ways it would largely be symbolic, but think of what it would mean to have finally that stated in our Constitution, that men and women are equal."

"It is long overdue," Marina agrees.

"So, what's your plan?" Aubrey asks.

"Well, I can introduce a bill that would remove the time limit for states to ratify the ERA, but then state legislatures would have to pass it, and you know, that's all about visibility. I need to get the issue out front and on everyone's radar."

Marina laughs. "Well, there you go! Consider the visibility part done! Aubrey and I can help you! It will be just like back at Columbia when we busted J.M. Only now, it's on an epic scale!"

I press my lips together. I don't want to lie, but I also don't want to admit that Marina just responded exactly how I hoped she would.

"It's an interesting idea…" There's a line of tension between Aubrey's eyes. She speaks to Marina. "But don't you think we should clear it with our families first, before we agree to band together and take on a cause? Especially since our parents are both about to run for president, you and me joining forces could cause some problems."

"Or…" I say tentatively, "it could boost both their images."

"Whatever," answers Marina. "Forget about our families. We'll do this for ourselves, and for sisterhood," she looks intensely into Aubrey's eyes. "And for our daughters. You could pass the ERA for Clara, Aubrey."

Aubrey drops her chin, but then raises her gaze back up, a resolute look on her face. "Count me in."

Chapter 27

"I can't believe you kept all this stuff, Mom." We're sorting through a box of mementos from her student days. There's a t-shirt with a huge Kelly-green circle and *ERA YES* in white letters. I look at the t-shirt and imagine a younger version of my mom wearing it, waving a sign and chanting at rallies. "Can I borrow this?"

"You can have it!" Mom looks like she might start crying happy tears again, just like she did when I first told her of my plan to get the ERA amended to the Constitution. "Wear it all the time, every day until your plan succeeds."

"I wish I could. But Congress has a dress code. They'd bust me if I showed up wearing a t-shirt." I look through the box and pull out a sash imprinted with *National ERA March* and a green ribbon also advertising *ERA.* "But maybe you and I can put on all this stuff and take some selfies?"

Mom smirks at me. "So you can post them on Twitter?"

"I mean, only if you're okay with it. But I think my supporters would love seeing you and me, advocating for the ERA together."

"Elyse, I'd pose naked in a gated yard full of rabid dogs if I thought it would get the ERA passed."

I laugh. "Let's hope it doesn't come to that. Just wear the sash and ribbon—over your clothes, of course—and that will be great."

The selfies are my way of launching the ERA publicity campaign that Marina, Aubrey, and I came up with. I do several posts over several days, accompanied with captions like, *It's time to realize the dreams of our mothers! #ERAYes.*

For her part, Aubrey also posts photos, but they're old ones—of Eleanor, Howie, and other members of the liberal Drake family advocating for the ERA back in the1970s, along with *Are we finally ready? #ERAYes.* But it's Marina who really gets the ball rolling. She posts an old headline from when we were at Columbia, fighting to bring pervy professor JM to justice. *They listened to me, but were you ignored about sexual harassment? Be heard! Please state your truth. #ERAYes.*

In two days, she gets over five million responses, and it just doesn't stop.

A lot of the replies include personal stories about sex discrimination and harassment, and some go even further, telling tales of assault. There's a consensus that it's time to do something. The media takes notice, and Aubrey, Marina, and I are interviewed both individually and together about how we want to pass the ERA. People love that the daughters of two potential presidential candidates from opposing parties have come together to fight for a common cause, and Marina convinces her father it would be politically expedient to support the ERA, that it would make him seem moderate in a way that's appealing to women voters. And when both Eleanor and Oliver go on record saying they are pro-ERA, suddenly it's an issue that "reaches across the aisle." That enables me to convince a white male Republican representative from South Carolina to co-sponsor the bill that would remove the time-limit for the ERA's ratification, pretty much assuring that the bill will pass.

Then, all that's left is to convince state senators to ratify the ERA, that is if their state failed to do so back in the 1970s. Aubrey uses the vast influence of the Drake political machine to reach the relevant elected officials, while Marina and I speak out whenever we can, arguing against claims that passing the ERA would force women into combat, or make them share public restrooms with men, or that it would mean the Supreme Court would never be able to overturn Roe v. Wade.

In just a few brief months, we get so much done, swaying public opinion, and making it possible for the amendment to move forward. Yet, it will be a while before Aubrey, Marina, and I can go out for cocktails to toast our success. I've quickly learned that getting anything done in government always takes way longer than it ought to. Meanwhile, I have a host of other goals to achieve for my constituents. I'm so busy during my first year in Congress that I barely notice how the presidential primary is heating up.

It's early spring, Oliver Hunt's approval ratings as governor of New Jersey are still high, and the polls say he's a likely contender to be the Republican nominee for president. Finn's newspaper, *The Examiner,* gives him all sorts of positive press and basically demolishes anyone who might be Hunt's opponent. I guess it's good that Finn and I haven't been in contact lately because if we were I'd probably say something rude, like asking him how he can live with himself.

But one day in mid-April, a story surfaces that *The Examiner* will never, ever cover, even if all the other news outlets in the world do.

Every single cable news channel is blaring the revelation that eleven years ago, when he was a fifty-four-year-old married man, Oliver Hunt paid for his twenty-five-year-old mistress, a weather girl on the Trenton local news, to have an abortion.

There's a lot of pontifications about how quickly the Religious Right will drop Hunt and throw their support behind a Republican Senator from Georgia who is a born-again Christian and who, by the way, doesn't support the ERA. "Without the Religious Right, there's no way Hunt gets nominated," all the talking heads decree. It doesn't take CNN long to release Hunt's old quote about Marina and her Columbia professor, where Hunt had said, "An older man should never prey on a young girl. It doesn't matter who he is; it doesn't matter who she is. Any guy who'd do that is scum, end of story."

"By Hunt's own standards, he is scum!" One CNN pundit, a Hispanic woman and Republican strategist, yells into the camera. Her rage is so thick, it's practically translucent. "And I agree! Hunt should drop from the race because he is a curse on the Republican party and on our nation!"

I'm glued to my TV, wearing sweatpants while watching the Hunt fiasco coverage and eating mac & cheese. Then it occurs to me; I shouldn't just be a spectator as this whole thing unfolds. Before I can let any second thoughts inhibit me, I grab my phone and call Finn.

He picks up almost instantly. "What do you want?"

"Nice to talk to you, too," I say. "It's been a while."

"Exactly. I haven't heard from you in months, and you choose now, when *The Examiner* is dealing with a crisis, to call."

"You didn't have to pick up."

"What do you want, Elyse?"

"I'm just curious how *The Examiner* is going to spin this story. Do you plan to cover it honestly?"

Finn lets out an epic sigh. "I have no fucking idea."

"Okay…"

"Are you home?"

"You mean in my DC apartment?" As in, the tiny barely furnished studio that still feels more like a hotel room than a home?

"Yeah."

"Yes."

"Text me your address. I'm coming over."

"Wait, Finn. Do you really think—"

But Finn hangs up on me. Without thinking about it super hard, I text him my address, realizing that it's probably a mistake, that I'm opening Pandora's box. But I can't help myself. Best- case scenario: I'll talk him through this existential crisis, and I'll convince him to do the right thing and end this weird arrangement where *The Examiner* is Hunt's personal propaganda machine. Worst case? We'll flirt, we'll argue, and then I'll tell him to go home. No big deal.

It's only a few minutes before there's a knock at my door. "You made good time," I say as I open the door. When I find him all slouched, I instantly realize that he's not in a fighting mood. His posture is like a rubber band that's lost its elasticity, and his mouth is relaxed into a neutral, wet-noodle-type shape.

"Hello, Elyse," he says, his voice velvety, and I'm reminded of when he would pick me up from my dorm room to take me out on a date. A twinge of attraction pings through me, and then I'm annoyed. Stupid sex drive. Just ask Hunt; it's capable of ruining everything.

"Come in," I say, and let him into my tiny apartment which is dominated by a queen-sized bed covered in a colorful, Mexican tiled quilt that one of my mom's students sewed by hand. "Use it for your DC apartment," my mom had insisted. "And let it serve as a reminder of who it is that you're fighting for."

Finn stands near the bed, arms at his sides. "I know what you want to say."

"Really? Well, that makes once of us."

"Come on." He cocks his head, casting his weary gaze upon me. "You want to tell me to leave Marina, to forget about Oliver Hunt, to save myself before they drag me down completely, and to salvage any ideals and credibility that I may once have had."

Shrugging, I respond. "Okay, sure. I suppose that would be a decent start."

He sighs, switching his focus to the wall above me, instead of on my face. "I've been hating myself for months, Elyse. I've used *The Examiner* to prop up Hunt, and the whole time, your voice has been inside my head. 'Stop writing propaganda, Finn. You're abandoning all your morals, Finn.' Even though I tell myself that I've published LOTS of pieces in support of the ERA, I can't get pretend-you to shut up." Finn plops down onto the edge of my bed, staring at the talking heads on TV. "This is the biggest thing to happen to cable news since Anton Adam got caught having an affair. I don't think CNN is even running commercials."

He's just stating the obvious. My breath comes out in a little huff as I sit next to Finn on the bed, keeping a good several inches between us. "How is Marina doing with all this?"

His chest heaves up and down. "I didn't talk to her. Marina and I don't talk much, not since she told me she's in love with someone else."

"Wait, what?" Did I just hear him right? Is it possible to drop a bomb without a detonation?

Finn doesn't move his eyes from the TV and he ignores me. I let two or three seconds pass. Then I get up, turn the television off, and stand in front of it. My strategy is cat-like. If I occupy the previous object of his attention, he'll automatically shift his attention to me.

This works, he lets his eyes meet mine, and I feel the wall between us come down.

"Finn, when did Marina tell you this?"

"A while ago. She confessed everything." He sits up straighter on the soft bed. "One night we went out for dinner, and over beef tartare Marina says, 'I'm in love with my friend Janet. We've had a thing for a while, and I keep meaning to break things off with her, but I don't have the heart to do it.' Then she started crying, said she didn't think she could marry me, and she was really, really sorry."

"Wow." I pause, careful of what I'll say next, hoping I won't sound harsh, but gentle instead. I sit back down next to him because it feels wrong to be standing over him at this moment. "I guess I'm not surprised that she's in love with a woman. I mean, there were signs."

He laughs bitterly, letting his head fall into his hand so he can rub his eyes. "You knew? How is it that everyone knew before me?"

"I didn't *know,* not for sure, but things she said before made me suspect. And there was this one time in college…" I let my voice trail off.

"One time in college?" Finn raises his head, meeting my gaze.

"She… for a moment I thought Marina might kiss me. But she was drunk, and then embarrassed, and I wasn't sure what had really happened…so I promised I'd never tell anyone, and I never did, until now."

Finn nods. "I get it." His tone is wistful, completely devoid of blame. "But I sure wish you had. Maybe this could have all been avoided."

I chew on my lip, contemplating. "But…why?"

Finn slouches into himself, and I wonder whether he's been drinking, if gin is to thank for his relaxed demeanor. "Are you asking me why Marina and I stay together when we both know she loves someone else?"

"Yeah."

He pushes the hair off his forehead, looking so defeated and vulnerable. It's almost physically painful not to kiss away the tension lines on his brow, not to wrap my arms around his broad shoulders, soothe him, and say that everything will be okay. "Because Hunt freaked out when she told him, said he'd disown her and cast her out if she ever went public. Then he called me in, made me tons of promises if I married her, and threatened to ruin me if I didn't."

"But Finn, you can say no! You'd survive the fallout, and maybe you'd even be happy."

"It's not that simple, Elyse."

"Why? Are you afraid of Hunt, or do you just want the power he offers you?"

"Both." He raises his hands in defeat and then lets them drop back to his lap. He tugs at the collar of his gray oxford shirt like it's been choking him. "Don't tell anyone, okay?"

"Of course I won't."

Finn laughs like I just told a joke. "Really? I just handed you a gold mine. You're not going to use it?"

I shrug. "I couldn't hurt Marina, not like that."

He looks at me, eyes glinting with gratitude. We share a smile, and I'm warmed all over. Then I remember it's not okay to feel warmed by him. "You should probably go, before anyone finds out you're here and gets the wrong idea."

Finn leans toward me and I can sense his longing. "Do you ever miss us, Elyse?"

The wall between us is slammed back into place. I jolt up. "Don't."

"What? I'm just asking a simple question."

"No, you're not. A simple question would be, 'Do you belong to a book club, Elyse?' or 'Have you ever been to Milwaukee, Elyse?' Those are simple questions. 'Do you ever miss us, Elyse?' is not simple. It's the opposite of simple."

"So… it's complicated?"

"Your grasp of the English language is stunning."

He stands, as if he's about to come forward and take me in his arms, yet thankfully his feet stay rooted to their spot. "If it's complicated, that means you have mixed emotions and strong feelings. It means that you don't always hate me. Because if you *always* hated me… that would be simple."

I let my tensed shoulders slump. "I don't hate you, Finn. I never have."

The air between us feels dense, as if there's a tangible friction I could reach out and touch. I understand that what I really want is to reach out and touch Finn, and what's worse, I want him to reach out and touch me. Now is when I should step away. Now is when I should take my eyes off his, but I can't.

"I don't hate you either, Elyse," he whispers.

"Yeah, but I never gave you cause to hate me."

"I wasn't finished." His voice is slightly louder now, slightly impatient as he begins again. "I don't hate you, Elyse, but I..." He sounds slightly strangled. "Do you really want me to say it?"

I try to laugh but it comes out as a chest-heave. "You probably shouldn't. I mean, I'm not completely sure what it is you were going to say, but if you have to ask…" I let my voice trail off.

He steps forward, close enough for me to feel him, even though we aren't yet touching. "That's all right. Some things are better left unsaid."

I don't turn away when he tilts his head down. Instead, oh God, I let his lips find my own, and when his mouth meets mine, I savor the moment as both a challenge and a caress. Hearts hammering away, in sync, we press our chests together. My blood turns to liquid lava and it pounds through my veins. The only sensation I'm aware of is insane, demanding desire.

We break apart just long enough to frantically remove each other's clothing, clumsily pulling at buttons or tugging down pants. But then muscle memory kicks in and we manage to get naked fast, because we've done this before, and it seems impossible that so many years have gone by without us loving each other.

Finn murmurs, "God, I've missed you, Elyse," and I say, "Me too, Finn," and then he pulls me to the bed and gets on top of me. I arch up to meet him and he presses his hands against my hips. I would cry out when he enters me, slick and hard and hot, but his mouth covers mine as every possible part of us becomes connected, and my relief is almost as potent as my pleasure. His flesh joined with mine; how did I get by so long without it?

He stops kissing me and looks me in the eye. As he pushes into me, deeper and deeper, his gaze gains depth as well. "I belong to you," he whispers.

I close my eyes because I can't take this, can't let this moment end, can't allow for the possibility that any of it might not be real.

Chapter 28

Two days later, Marina calls me, and I'm only slightly less terrified to answer her call than I am to ignore it. "I have to talk to you about something," she says gravely. "It's important."

And then it's like my stomach is bungee jumping off Mt. Everest, getting simultaneously burned and blisteringly cold as it rapidly plunges down to what feels like hell. And I realize I'm being overly dramatic, but I can't help it.

"What's up?" I chirp, attempting, yet failing, to sound both casual and calm.

"I need you to clear your schedule for the day after tomorrow, fly to New York, and attend an engagement party for Finn and me."

"Huh?" I'm so stunned that I stop walking and halt in the middle of the South Wing on my way down to the Capitol Café. I lean against a nearby pillar and keep my voice down. The last thing I need is for anyone, a member of the press or a fellow representative or any of their staff, to overhear this conversation. "Why are you and Finn throwing an engagement party in two days? I thought the date was weeks away."

She lets out an exasperated sigh. "Because of everything that's happened! Dad needs something to distract people from this ridiculous scandal, and a party for Finn and me is perfect. Reverend Jason James is going to lead a prayer before the cocktails, and he'll talk about what a devout man my dad is, how he's learned from his mistakes and found God. And high-profile friends from both political parties will attend, like they're silently endorsing him. Which is why I need you and Aubrey there."

I almost breathe a sigh of relief. Marina doesn't know about Finn and me, or at least she didn't call to berate me about it. But then I want to tear my hair out because Finn is getting engaged to Marina, and I'm supposed to celebrate it. And the politics of the whole thing hasn't even registered, but if I'm going to survive in DC, it must register. "Marina," I say carefully, "have you really thought this through?"

"Of course," she snaps. "Don't lecture me, Elyse. It's so not what I need right now."

"But the last time you spoke about Finn, you weren't even sure that you wanted to marry him. You weren't even sure that you love him."

"That's irrelevant. Elyse, you're a politician now, so I know you understand." She grunts out a mirthless laugh. "You realize how important it is, to keep up appearances. None of the other stuff gets done if you don't."

Unfortunately, I completely understand what she's saying, but I'd hate to be so quick to fall in line. I keep my voice slow and careful. "Marina… I'm sorry; I can't attend your party. Honestly, if it was to celebrate something that you're excited about, you couldn't keep me away. But I can't endorse a political opportunity for your dad, especially when I disagree with him about so much."

"Think again," Marina hisses. "You will attend."

"Marina, calm down."

"Stop!" With her command, it's clear she thinks I've forgotten my place. Who am *I* to tell *her* to calm down? "I can destroy all our work on the ERA!" Her words rush out, as grating as fingernails against the chalkboard. "All I have to do is say I've rethought things, that I side with the *Family First* people now, and by the way, that would totally benefit my dad. One tweet would undo all our hard work. Don't think I won't do it, Elyse. If you want the ERA passed, you'll be at my party on Friday night."

I gulp down the tumor that seems to have suddenly sprouted in my throat. "Come on, Marina. Be reasonable."

"Sorry. Wish I could, but the media is intent on ruining my dad's presidential chances. You'll be there, and Aubrey will too. Except, I need you to convince her."

"How am I supposed to do that?"

"Figure it out, Elyse. If you care about your blessed ERA, I'll see both you and Aubrey on Friday night."

Then she clicks off, leaving me breathless. I turn around, changing course back to my office. There's no need to go down to the cafeteria. I've totally lost my appetite.

***

I don't use logic or strategy when convincing Aubrey to attend Marina's party. Instead, I beg. *"Please,"* I implore. The festivities start in less than an hour. "We have to go. Marina's gone crazy. Don't make me attend this thing by myself."

I am sitting in Aubrey's dressing room, talking to her reflection. Two days ago, I'd pleaded with her about the engagement party over the phone. After I'd promised that we could show up late and leave early, and that by no means would either of us ever stand so close to Oliver Hunt that someone could snap a picture, she'd agreed to come. But now she's wavering again.

"Elyse," Aubrey sighs, "if I go, there's no way my mom doesn't find out, and then there will be hell to pay. Did you hear what Oliver Hunt said about her on his Air America interview? He said she wouldn't be able to satisfy a nation's needs when she can't even satisfy the needs of her husband."

"Yuck." I respond, "That's totally piggish, but it will harm Hunt way more than it will harm your mom."

"That's where you're wrong." Aubrey turns to face me so I'm talking to the real her, not a reflection from her massive mirror that covers the entire wall outside a closet that rivals the size of my DC apartment. "I listened to the clip. His supporters thought it was hilarious. They're ready to put it on a t-shirt. Stuff like that is why Hunt is still polling so well, even after the abortion scandal. People love that he'll do or say anything, political correctness be damned."

"I know, and I agree that he's horrible. But tonight's party is about supporting Marina, not him."

Aubrey doesn't answer. She simply frowns, turns toward her closet, disappears and reemerges a moment later, holding a burgundy halter-top dress. She places it against her body, examining her reflection. "I haven't worn this since Clara was born. I wonder if it will stretch too tightly across my stomach."

"I bet you'll look beautiful."

Aubrey tosses the dress to the floor. "No, I'll look fat, but that's not even the reason that all my instincts are screaming, 'Don't go to the party!'"

She steps over the dress, which lies in a silky pile at her feet, and comes to sit next to me on the chaise lounge where I'm perched. "Elyse, this is all wrong. Think for a second. We know their engagement is a sham. We know that Marina is trying to bully us because her father bullies her. And then there's Finn."

"What about Finn?" I ask, feeling my blood pressure spike. I haven't told Aubrey anything about what happened between Finn and me, but sometimes I suspect my friend is psychic. She seems to know things about my life even before I know them myself.

"I think you still love him. And if you attend some false celebration where you congratulate him and Marina on their engagement, you'll just be adding one lie to another."

"So what?" I look down, dusting lint off my black silk cocktail dress. "People lie all the time."

"But you don't. It may seem like no big deal, but it is, Elyse. You owe it to your constituents to be as honest as possible, whenever possible."

I stand, deciding to rescue Aubrey's crumpled dress from the floor. I pick the dress up and smooth it out. "But what about Marina? I feel like I owe her after she helped me get elected. And she says she'll destroy all our work on the ERA."

"Please." Aubrey laughs joylessly. "I know Marina thinks she could do that, but the ERA movement is bigger than her. It's bigger than all of us."

"Still, Marina might be more powerful than you realize." I wave the dress and point toward Aubrey's massive walk-in closet. "Should I just hang this up anywhere, or does it have a specific spot?"

"Here, let me." Aubrey walks over, holds out her arm, and I hand her the dress. But before she goes to hang it up, she faces me and speaks in a cast-iron sort of voice. "I know Marina is powerful. She's famous for being famous, and she knows how to play the game. But Elyse, if you're going to survive in politics, you can't let threats from Marina, or from anyone, intimidate you. You need to stay true to who you are."

Aubrey's right, of course. If fear is what's driving me to go to this party, I should skip the festivities. Even if I don't always make the best choices, I do generally try to operate from strength over weakness.

Yet I'm not feeling super strong once I'm back in my hotel room. I only feel exhausted. I'm sure my heart is beating in a lackluster rhythm, worn down from difficult, emotional decisions, and my brain might just melt into a tepid brown puddle of lost political lessons. Everything I've tried so hard to grasp over the last few weeks is congealing into a zombie-inducing mess that renders me lifeless. I'm on top of my hotel room bed, drifting off, not caring to get under the covers, when my phone dings with a text. *On my way.* It's from Finn. Moments later, there's a knock at my door. I jump up and walk across the room to look through the peephole.

"You shouldn't be here," I nearly yell. "Go back to your party."

I knew it was a bad idea to let Marina comp me a room in the same Hunt hotel where their engagement shindig is being held. I half expected it to be her knocking at my door, backed by hotel security ready to throw me out on my ass for not fulfilling my end of the bargain.

"Ah, come on. Open the door," he begs. "I need to see you."

"Go away, Finn." I grip the doorknob as if it could hold me up, give me strength, save me from falling off a cliff. "Your being here is a terrible idea."

"I won't stay long, but you really should let me in so the entire second floor doesn't eavesdrop and leak it to the press."

I unchain the security lock, twist the knob, and face him. His hair is slicked back, his tie is askew, and his face is puffy, like he's beaten down from having to smile and act happy for the last several hours.

"Hi," Finn whispers, packing enough longing into that one syllable that my knees momentarily go weak.

I regain my strength, step aside and, against my better judgement, let him in. "So, how furious is Marina at Aubrey and me?"

"I have no idea. She's been acting normal and happy all evening." He studies my eyes like he can find some truth written there. "Did you say anything to her about us?"

"No. I'm not suicidal. Why, did she say something to you?"

"Not really." He shrugs. "But Marina can be difficult to read." Finn plops down on the edge of the bed and lays the top part of his body back while keeping his feet on the floor. "I never know what she's thinking, and I'm paranoid that she's playing some cat-and-mouse game with me."

"So, you came up to my room, just to let her catch us and zero in for the kill?"

"No, I came up to your room because I thought I'd lose my mind if I stayed at that party for one second more." Finn pats the bed's empty space next to him. "Come lie down. Let's snuggle."

Nothing sounds better than curling up and spooning with Finn. He could form a protective cocoon around me, and we'd match our breaths to one another, and we'd both drift off and dream of something pleasant, like sunsets and kittens and the beach. But unfortunately, I'm still me, and I can't quite let go enough to do what I want. "But Finn, what if Marina comes up here? It would be so easy for us to get caught."

"Caught snuggling? Imagine the scandal!"

I sigh. "It would look bad. And even if we don't get caught, we still need to think about where this is going. I don't see how you and I have any sort of future. No, we should end this now."

Finn sits up. "Elyse, aren't you tired?"

"Um, of course. What does that have to do with anything?"

His chest rises and falls as his eyes bore into mine. "You work so hard, and you never let up. You never stop trying your best at every single thing you do, and you're so hard on yourself, even when you succeed."

I roll my eyes, partly just to break his gaze. "On the night of your engagement, you talk like you understand me better than anyone else does."

He exhales through his nose, his chin drops, his gaze now fixed on the floor. "I know, and I really am sorry. Not just about tonight, but for years ago. I'm sorry I didn't fight for us." Finn looks back up at me, his expression pleading, his gaze full of desire, and his mouth slightly open, like he wishes he was kissing me. "God, Elyse. I never should have let you go."

I feel myself relent, giving in to that stupid gravitational pull I have toward being in his arms. Lying in bed in with him is like coming home.

Chapter 29

Marina is true to her word. The morning after her engagement party, she tweets, "Rethinking the ERA. Don't want to make women victims in the Constitution. Will focus now on universal paid family leave. #workingmomsmatter."

"Wow," I say to Aubrey after reading Marina's tweet aloud. We are eating breakfast at Aubrey's house before I need to catch my flight back to D.C. I spear a sausage link, swirl it in maple syrup, and then bite, letting it explode in a salty/sweet mixture that's surprisingly undiminished by Marina's quest for retribution.

"I wonder how she plans to focus on paid family leave," asks Aubrey. "It's not like she holds any elected office."

I take a sip of coffee and shrug. "Oh, you know, she'll advocate for it, speak out, make it sound like it will be part of her dad's agenda if he gets elected, criticize you and me for not making it a priority even though we are, and in the end, she'll abandon the whole thing before anything gets done."

Aubrey raises her eyebrows. "That sounds awfully bitter."

"Does it?" I use my napkin to wipe my mouth, checking my attitude while I do. A little less than two hours ago, I ushered Marina's fiancé out of my hotel room, and that's just one of the ways I've betrayed her recently. I suppose I have no right to claim any sort of moral high ground, whether it's personal or political.

"Sorry," I say. "But after everything we've worked for on the ERA, I'm worried about the fallout of losing her support."

"I know," says Aubrey. "I am too, but give Marina some time. She gets mad easily, but she usually doesn't stay mad for long. I bet Marina will be over the whole thing in a week or two." Aubrey's cell phone dings, and she picks it up to read the text. "Oh my God," she exclaims. "I guess she's over it now. Marina and Finn are here."

It's a good thing I've just taken a bite of soggy, syrup-soaked waffle, instead of sausage or cantaloupe, because otherwise I'd be choking. Luckily, I'm able swallow my food down and say, "What? Why?"

Aubrey gives me a funny look. "I invited them, of course. I thought it would be better to mend fences right away, but I wasn't surprised when I didn't hear back. Until now." She gets up and goes to the front door. I stay in my seat at the kitchen table, wishing I could run, but there's no escape.

A chorus of hellos comes from the foyer as Finn and Marina walk in, and there is the imminent sound of footsteps as the three people I at once most want to see, and totally do not want to see, approach.

"Are Marcus and Clara home?" Marina asks as they walk toward the kitchen.

"No," answers Aubrey, "he took her to the park. She was up early, and we wanted her to get fresh air before she takes her morning nap."

The little exchange between Marina and Aubrey gives Finn the chance to notice me first, and as soon as our eyes meet, I know he's both surprised and happy to find me here. It's all in the slight, half smile that exposes his dimple and the way that, for a split second, his eyebrows pull together. There's only half a moment, however, before Marina notices me as well, and I can't say her response is all that enthusiastic. But then again, this is Marina, so who knows? She's all sleek and shiny, with her auburn hair tied back in a loose ponytail. She's casually clad in a black turtleneck and designer yoga pants, and I'm guessing the modesty of her outfit was chosen so that all the attention will go to the large, square-cut yellow diamond ring that glitters from her finger.

"Oh, good, Elyse you're here too! Now you can both see my ring at the same time!" She wiggles her finger and the light bounces off the diamond which must be roughly the same size as a small African nation. Or at least, I bet the cost of it could feed one.

"Holy crap!" says Aubrey, "It's beautiful."

"Yes, it really it is," I add, wiping my mouth with my napkin once again. I am suddenly worried that I'm covered in syrup. "And how was the party?"

Aubrey shoots me a bewildered look, as if it to reprimand me for bringing that up, but I figure we may as well get it out of the way.

"It was incredible," says Marina, completely genuine. She sits down at the table beside me, and Finn sits in the chair between her and Aubrey. "Everyone was so supportive and excited for us. The band was amazing, and I think people had a really good time. There was so much love in the room!"

"That's great," Aubrey states. "I am really happy for you both. Would you like some breakfast? There are waffles and sausage being kept warm in the oven, and there's cantaloupe and of course, coffee."

"I would love some," says Finn. "All of it."

"Just coffee for me," says Marina. "I'm still full after last night. The caterers did this amazing thing with lobster and caviar on crostini. I couldn't stop eating it!" She laughs. "And for dessert, the sundae bar wasn't exactly the height of sophistication, but everyone was so thrilled. We had all the toppings you could imagine! I must have eaten at least three sundaes myself, all layered with chocolate chip cookie dough and brownie bits and miles of whipped cream."

I dare to look to Finn, and a swift shake of his head tells me she's exaggerating. I bet she had half a bare scoop, tops. "Sounds wonderful," I say, as Aubrey places a plate of food in front of Finn and a steaming cup of coffee in front of Marina. "I'm glad the party went so well."

"Yup," Marina clips that word in a slightly curt sort of way. "So, why didn't you come?"

Okay. I could let Aubrey field this one, but I may as well brave the storm. "It just didn't feel right, Marina. I mean, since the party was also a political event for your dad, and since my supporters are against most of what he stands for, showing up would have seemed like a betrayal to them."

Marina scowls before she breaks into a laugh. "Oh, lighten up." Marina rolls her eyes. "Ever since you were elected to Congress, you're so serious. What happened to your sense of humor?"

Finn, who looks sort of pale and constipated, cracks a smile and speaks to his fiancé. "Don't take it personally, Darling. Elyse has always been serious. She's too focused on her agenda to be fun."

Ouch. "That's right," I say. "And Marina, because of that anti-ERA tweet you sent, I now need to be even more agenda-focused than ever. This is not a game to me, and now I have all sorts of fires to put out." I get up. "Thanks for breakfast, Aubrey. See you around." I walk past them all and go toward the front door, refusing to catch Finn's eye in case he's trying to give me a secret, conspiratorial wink.

Aubrey follows me to the foyer where my overnight bag sits, waiting for me to grab it so I can carry it to the train station, and ride to the airport to catch my flight to D.C. "Elyse, wait," Aubrey says. "Don't leave mad."

"I'm not mad at you. But I can't handle being here right now. Sorry."

She grabs my arm, leans in, and speaks softly. "Did something happen between you and Finn?"

I jerk back. "What? No! Can't I just be furious with Marina over the ERA? Why does my anger have to be about Finn?"

She answers me with an incredulous expression, widened eyes combined with a frown.

"Don't worry," I tell her, "I'm not that stupid." Perhaps it's because I want this to be true that the lie slips so easily from my mouth. Yet I can't help but flashing back to all those years ago, when I promised Aubrey Adam-Drake that I would always tell her the truth. My insides burn with shame.

"Okay," says Aubrey. "But before you go, I have news that I never got around to sharing last night."

"You're pregnant again?" I ask hopefully.

"No," Aubrey laughs self-consciously and rubs her stomach, as if to flatten it.

"Not that you look pregnant!" I exclaim. "I just thought, since you'd said you want a big family…"

"It's okay, Elyse. No, my news is that Marcus and I bought a house in Connecticut. So, I can run for Congress. Just think, Elyse! You and I could be co-workers soon!"

I search her face, trying to decipher if the excitement she's expressing is genuine, but I can't tell. "That would be great! But…I thought the plan was to run for governor."

"Yeah, but I have to be a resident of the state for several years before I'm eligible. Grandfather thought we could get around that little detail, but no dice. Anyway, Congress will be a first step, and the Drakes will have their feet in another new state."

I want to be excited for her and not be the sort of friend who'd go on about the intensely busy schedule a Congresswoman must keep. I won't mention how she'll be spending way more time in D.C., away from Clara and Marcus, then I bet she'd feel comfortable with. Not that being governor wouldn't be time-consuming, but at least Aubrey could live and work in the same place.

Since I can't genuinely express happiness at the idea of Aubrey running for Congress, and I don't have the heart to say anything negative, I settle for grabbing her and holding her in a fierce, protective hug. "I love you, Aubrey," I say.

"I love you too." Aubrey looks and sounds bewildered as she pulls away.

"I should go. I'll call you soon, okay?"

"Of course. Have a safe trip."

I nod, fighting back tears. There are any number of reasons for why I might be crying, but I can't acknowledge any of them, and it's not until I'm safely on the sidewalk, walking brusquely towards the train station, that I dare to let any tears fall.

Chapter 30

Later that night, Finn calls me. "Was that a new shirt you had on today?"

It was. I'm not used to people paying attention to what I wear, but recently *Huffington Post* did a feature on me, "Elyse Gibbons: Combining Traditional Fashion with Progressive Politics." They said I assert a new brand of feminism and embrace my femininity with a no-nonsense, stylish, just-below knee-length jersey dress layered with a boxy, pin-striped blazer in either white or light gray. According to them, my white blazer stands for women's suffrage, and the gray symbolizes the hardship women still face, but I don't wear black because I'm aware I benefit from white privilege. Finally, the jersey dress reflects that I'm an active woman on a budget who still believes that power and femininity can go hand in hand.

Truth is, I'm trying to stick to the Congressional dress code in a way I can both afford and tolerate. I've never liked pantsuits or blazers, but alas, cardigan sweaters aren't allowed. I need jackets, and when I found this softly draped, sweater-shaped one that I like, I bought it in both colors, white and light gray. But it needs to be worn over a dress, so I went online to J Crew, and when I found an affordable jersey dress with a high enough neckline and low enough hem so it fit the dress code and looked comfortable. I ordered one each in blue, maroon, and slate gray, thinking I could combine them with my two new blazers, and add accents with varying scarves so people wouldn't realize I wear the exact same thing every day.

And that became my signature look, which I've been both praised and criticized for. Either way, people have noticed my lack of variety, so I splurged and bought some tighter fitting jackets, slacks, and silky blouses. I was wearing one of those new blouses this morning, because I figured cameras would be around to capture both my arrival and departure from Aubrey's house. I wasn't wrong.

"Yeah," I reply now to Finn. "Could you tell by its lack of wrinkles?"

"Well, that too, I suppose. But the greenish collar really brought out your hazel eyes."

How had he managed to observe such a detail, and what's more, think to ask me about it? What with all the dramatic undercurrents happening at breakfast, I could have been naked, and it would be completely understandable if he hadn't noticed.

"Gosh, Finn. I'm surprised. I mean, since I have no sense of fun, doesn't that overpower everything else?"

"Oh, don't be insulted. You know I love everything about you."

It's meant to be a flippant comment, yet his words knock the wind right out of me. "Actually, no," I reply softly. "I figured there must be things about me that you don't love. Otherwise, you wouldn't have left."

He sighs. "Technically, you're the one who left me, Elyse."

"The operative word here is 'technically.'"

"And I've already said that letting you go was the worst mistake I ever made. So, can we please not argue?" He takes my silence as consent, lowers his voice, and speaks as if our heads are resting on two twin pillows, like our mouths and eyes mere centimeters apart. "Are you okay? I've been worried ever since I heard about that article in *The Philadelphia Inquirer.*"

Panicking, I rush to my laptop which rests on my bed. I open the Inquirer's homepage. "You mean there's something new? What now?" I scan the virtual newspaper, looking for whatever article Finn was referring to, but there's nothing. "Are you talking about how the Republicans plan to block our gun control legislation?"

Finn clears his throat. "Yeah, of course."

"But that's no surprise. Everyone knows they'd give up their first born before ever breaking with the NRA."

"Sure…" Finn sounds like he's stalling. "But anytime they go against you it can be damaging. I just wanted to make sure you weren't too upset."

"That's sweet," I say. "But I should go. I have a lot to read before my committee meeting tomorrow morning."

"Okay. But when can I see you again?"

"I don't know. Maybe we should lay low for a while."

"Okay. Tomorrow, then?" Finn says, ridiculously.

I laugh. "Text me."

The next day the *Inquirer* posts a story, "Drake Family to Thwart Democratic Rivals in Pennsylvania Politics." It explains that since his car accident, Ethan Drake has been rehabilitating his image by working with vehicular safety groups and serving as a state senator. He sponsored a bill to create a Pennsylvania highway safety improvement program and is now ready to increase his ambitions and run for governor. But the Drakes are wary of other political contenders, including "rising star, Elyse Gibbons." Rumor is, I'm considering a run for governor, and although the Drakes enjoyed a close alliance with me in the past, they would not hesitate to bring my vulnerabilities to light, including my far-left ideology and questionable personal life.

I'm sitting in my Congressional office as I read this article. I place down my travel mug of coffee since what I just sipped has turned sour in my stomach. I want to call Finn and ask him how he knew about this article in advance. Yet, I feel suddenly vulnerable. What if the Drakes are watching me? If I were to call Finn, the whole world might know, and the Drakes could expose me as an adulterous fraud?

Take a breath, Elyse, I tell myself three times, yet my heart still races at a rate I can feel in my throat. How much of the article did Aubrey know about? Surely, she wouldn't tell her family secrets about my "questionable personal life" just so they could mess with my career.

It must be a big misunderstanding. I'm not even thinking about running for governor, much less talking about it. And if the reporter for that article got one fact wrong, probably she got it all wrong. The Drakes don't really have it out for me. I've almost convinced myself of this, when my office phone rings.

It's Polly Kinney.

"Elyse," she says brusquely, "I assume you've read the *Inquirer* this morning?"

"Yeah," I respond.

"Look, I'm sorry about how this went down. I wanted to have a conversation with you first, but damn it, best laid plans and all that. Anyway, yeah, we're thinking you should run for governor. Don't worry about the Drakes. They're obviously already scared of you, and that, my dear, is significant."

"Slow down, Polly." I breathe in and out. "There's no way I'm running for governor. I'm not qualified."

"Of course you are! You've lived in the state for seven years, and you're a legal, adult citizen, right?"

"You know that's not what I mean."

"Elyse," Polly says slowly, "I realize this is overwhelming. You are, as the article says, a rising political star. But the thing is, I've seen stars burn out way too quickly. You've got to seize your moment and not peak too soon. I'm telling you, running against a flawed candidate like Ethan Drake, you'll win the primary and go on to get elected governor. And you know what? Many great governors have gone on to be great presidents. Governors are way more electable than Congress members."

I cough in a burst of anxiety and shock. "Are you insane?" I ask once I'm able to catch my breath. "Me? President? Come on!"

"Elyse, people are already talking about it. I'm surprised you haven't heard. You are the new voice, the new face of the democratic party. So, it's time to start some strategic planning. How about we meet this weekend?"

I agree to drive home to Pennsylvania on Friday evening where I still rent my apartment in Reading. Polly and I will have lunch on Saturday at the same restaurant where we first met. But for now, I must put all that out of my mind because I have more pressing concerns, like the passage of the ERA.

Maybe Marina wasn't overtly hostile at breakfast the other day, but she's not stopping her sabotage efforts. On *Good Morning America* she explains that she no longer supports the Equal Rights Amendment because, in her heart, she believes that women don't want government handouts or to be given special treatment. She says that the suffragettes worked for everything they got, so today's feminists should as well. When asked if she considers herself a feminist, Marina responds, "Yes. I am a feminist who puts family first and who believes in traditional values and economic conservatism." When the interviewer asks her to elaborate, Marina explains, "I support women with my idea for universal paid maternity leave. But I don't buy into all the radical, Socialist beliefs like my friend, Elyse Gibbons, does. I support marriage, and motherhood, and prioritizing goals so an entire family unit can benefit."

Lots of feminists on Twitter respond with things like, "What does Marina Hunt know about work? Her entire, entitled life is one big handout! #ERAYes!"

I respond as well, but not on Twitter. There are always news crews with cameras lurking in the halls of Congress, and when someone from MSNBC asks me about me being a "radical socialist," I state, "I am a patriot, I am an advocate, and I am an unapologetic liberal feminist who believes that when women are finally guaranteed equal rights, including the right to support their families, the entirety of our great nation will benefit. Not everyone agrees with me on this, and that's okay. Respecting each other's differences is the first step towards equality."

And as if my day wasn't already jam-packed with drama, an old-school Republican senator from Kentucky, in a column he wrote for the Wall Street Journal, calls me an "economic illiterate" because, according to him, the numbers in my education reform bill don't add up. All it takes is one naysayer to turn the tide of public opinion, and I need the public on my side if I want other lawmakers to be on my side as well.

So, when I'm not on the floor of Congress or in committee, my staff is helping me craft my response. They say that I must make it seem like I'm above reacting to it. I tweet some hopefully clever lines about how I first studied economics at Columbia, but my real economic education began in Reading where I did community development for a city stricken by poverty. Then, in a second tweet, I state, "Ah yes. God forbid a working-class Congresswoman from Reading crafts a bill and has the same power as a middle-aged male born with a silver spoon in his mouth!" But does that sound too defensive? I hate doubting myself, but it's so hard to know what's worth responding to, and what I ought to just let go.

Honestly though, my real dilemma is about Aubrey. Should I confront her about that article in the *Inquirer*, or do I pretend like there's no issue? I'm still struggling with that question hours later at home after a long day, heating soup and making cheese toast for dinner. Then, my meal preparation is interrupted by a knock on my door. I don't even bother looking through the peephole before opening, because I can feel that it's Finn.

Wordlessly, he pulls me to him, wrapping his arms around me as he uses his feet and backside to keep the door open while doing this combination of lifting and scooting me inside. Once the door is safely closed and locked behind us, Finn twirls me around, presses my back against the door, and presses himself against my front. I can smell the cold on his skin as his kisses make me hot all over.

"Is now a good time?" he asks. "I'm not disturbing you, am I?"

"Actually..." I say, as he tugs on my blouse, "I'm heating up soup and cheese toast..."

"Oh yeah?"

"Yeah. I'm really hungry." I untuck his shirt and let my hands graze his stomach, where there's a light splattering of hair that I know grows thicker as the trail travels south. "I can't wait...melted cheese on sourdough, chicken noodle..."

"Not right now," he insists. He manages to undo the last button on my blouse, and then gently pulls it off me so the fabric billows to the floor and my skin is bare. I grab his shirt, pulling it up over his head, so now we can be skin against skin. "In a few minutes I'll order in whatever sort of dinner you want. The sky's the limit."

I turn rigid in his arms. "Except, we need to order in, right? No going out for us."

Finn frowns and, stepping away, lets go of me. "That's as much about you as it is about me."

"I'm not laying blame, Finn. But this thing between us is just so seedy." I bend down, pick up my shirt, and put it back on, buttoning up each button. I walk the short distance to my kitchen where my cheese toast is slightly burned around the edges. I remove it from my toaster oven.

Finn, after putting his shirt back on, has followed me in here. "What do you want me to say, Elyse? All day, I thought only about you. I was counting down the minutes before I could see you."

"And yet you didn't bother to text or call and ask if you could come over."

"I didn't want to give you a chance to say no."

"Oh yeah?" A laugh sticks in the back of my throat. "I'm not sure what that says about us, but I don't think it's good." I turn my stove off and remove the pan of soup from its burner, but I don't pour the soup into a serving bowl. I have a feeling Finn and I are about to have a non-soup-compatible conversation. "Okay, Finn. What if I give you the chance to tell me how you knew, hours in advance, about the *Philadelphia Inquirer* article on the Drakes and me?"

I've turned to face him, and in the tight space of my kitchen, the intensity of this moment feels elevated. Finn sighs. "Yesterday, after you left breakfast, Marina and Aubrey were talking about it. I'd just assumed the article was published in the Sunday edition, but I guess not."

It's like I've been stabbed in the heart. Not only did Aubrey know about the article, she chose to speak to Marina about it and not to me. My eyes smart with tears, and I dodge past Finn, trying to escape his gaze and concern.

"Elyse," he says. "If it's any consolation, Aubrey was only talking about the whole thing because she was worried. She doesn't want to see you hurt."

"Hah! Or maybe she just feels guilty! I mean, it sounds like Aubrey shared secrets about my 'questionable personal life' with her family so they can politically destroy me!"

"No." Finn sits on my couch and pulls on my arm so I'm sitting next to him. "It's not like that. Aubrey wanted Marina's advice."

"About what?"

"How to help you, I guess. You're not used to public scrutiny, and they both are. Aubrey knows you're going to be raked over the coals no matter what, whether it's by her family or by someone else. Nobody who rises as quickly as you have escapes that sort of public vetting."

I dig my elbows into my knees and press my forehead into the palms of my hands. "I appreciate their concern, but it still feels like a betrayal."

Finn chuckles, and he gently uses his finger to draw lazy circles on my back. "I get it, but, and I mean this in the nicest possible way, you're not really in the position to complain about betrayal."

I sit up straight and meet his eyes. "You're right," I concede. "I feel like a terrible person right now."

The same finger that was stroking my back now caresses my cheek. “Don’t. You’re not a terrible person, Elyse. But if you’re going to last in Marina and Aubrey’s world, you need to toughen up. Go after what you want. And forgive yourself for wanting it.” Finn tilts his head and leans in to kiss me. I sort of return the kiss.

At the same time, my mind races with what feels like hundreds of contradictions. I want to win, but I want to concede. I want privacy, but I want power. I want to be good, but I want to be with Finn. And I realize, that at least for tonight, I don’t have the strength to fight any more battles, internal or otherwise.

“How about we eat dinner first?” I say.

Finn laughs. “Okay. If dinner comes first, what comes second?”

I raise my eyebrows and smirk, and then I lean in and give him a real kiss, a lingering, heated one. “Like you don’t know.” I stand and move back towards the kitchen. “Come on, my cheese toast is getting cold.”

***

Four days later I meet Polly Kinny for lunch. “Tell me more about running for governor,” I immediately say. “Because I’m very much interested.”

Chapter 31

Months go by and Aubrey and I barely speak, both claiming to be so tremendously busy that we can't make time for each other, which is pretty much true. When we do talk, I don't ask her about the *Inquirer* article, and she doesn't bring it up. She also doesn't ask me about my political plans, so I say nothing. I mean, it's not like the news won't come out soon enough. I either must start planning my re-election campaign for Congress, or not. And if I'm not planning for it, people are going to have questions about what's next for me, and I can only evade such questions for so long.

Still, when I finally do see Aubrey, it's not like things feel strained. Perhaps it's because we're at a party near the Virginia state capitol, as Virginia has just become the thirty-eighth state to vote to ratify the ERA, and thirty-eight states is all we need. It's official; the Equal Rights Amendment will be added to the Constitution.

Part me of still can't believe it. I was sure the ERA Yes movement would be dead in the water after Marina pulled her support, but I guess our cause had gained enough steam that it couldn't be stopped. Now I feel like my political career could end tomorrow, and I'd still have a decent legacy and something to feel proud of. Of course, I was only one small part of the movement, but when I die, maybe the trailblazers I read about in college, like Susan

B Anthony, Emmeline Pankhurst, and Elizabeth Cady Stanton, will give me a wave of welcome as I enter the afterlife.

There's a huge victory celebration, and female politicians and activists from all over the country come to this charming banquet hall in Richmond's historic Manchester district to celebrate. Outside the party, Aubrey and I pose for picture after picture, answering reporter's questions and basking in our success. Then someone from Fox News asks, "How do you feel, Representative Gibbons, knowing this amendment is largely a symbolic measure? Do you wish you'd focused your efforts on making *real* change, like with Marina Hunt's plan for paid family leave?"

I grit my teeth but smile. "Not at all. The two things aren't mutually exclusive. And I'm thrilled to have played a role in realizing a dream that my mother, and so many women of her generation, have had for decades. The Constitution now states that women deserve the same rights as men, and that is more than a symbol. It's a seismic shift which is long overdue in this country."

"Come on Elyse," Aubrey says, tugging on my arm, "let's go in and enjoy the party." I let her lead me away from the press circle, but on our trek inside we still find ourselves faced with person after person who wants to congratulate us and bend our ears for a moment or two. Finally, we're able to grab a moment to breathe as we make it to the bar, order drinks, and sigh in happiness and relief.

"I think you were in higher demand just now than I was," Aubrey remarks. "Which is kind of cool, if you think about it."

"Really?" I ask.

"You know I've never liked the spotlight."

"Does that mean you're not going to run for the House of Representatives?"

Aubrey shakes her head. "I'm going to run, and it will be fine. I can represent my district in a quiet sort of way. I don't need attention in order to be effective. I'm not like you."

The bartender hands me my gin and tonic, and a soda water with lime for Aubrey. I think I'll pass over the subtle dig Aubrey just made at me in favor of doing some digging of my own. "Why just soda water, Aubrey? Don't you feel like celebrating?"

"Sure, I do, but you and I aren't celebrating the same thing." A proud smile spreads across her face. "Marcus and I are expecting baby number two in five months."

Gripping my drink with one hand, I lean in to give her a one-armed hug. "Congratulations," I say. "I'm so happy for you." And I really am happy, yet this means Aubrey was already pregnant when the subject came up between us before. I guess she wasn't ready to tell me at the time. I mean, I get wanting to be careful, but I thought she and I shared all the big stuff. At least, we used to. Oh well. It's not like I've been especially forthcoming myself lately.

She returns my embrace, and for a moment I feel like everything between us is great, even if there are unspoken, honest conversations begging to be held. "I just hope I'll be able to make it to Finn and Marina's wedding," Aubrey says.

Then, it's like a brick is dropped inside me, from the top of my over-worked brain to the bottom of my angsty stomach. "Huh?" I utter.

"Yeah, you haven't heard?" Aubrey says. "They've set the date. Valentine's Day. On the surface it's romantic, but really, it's to coincide with primary season. Iowa and New Hampshire will be over, of course, but Nevada, South Carolina, and all the Super Tuesday states will come soon after, and Hunt figures he'll benefit from all the free publicity that the wedding generates."

I swallow like I'm trying to ingest a dust ball, wishing my G&T was a magic potion that would get me gracefully through this moment.

"I didn't know the wedding was still on," I rasp.

Aubrey gives me this compassionate look. What if she knows that lately, my "questionable personal life," includes regular trysts with Finn, where he holds me, tells me that I'm beautiful, that I'm special, and that he loves me. He says he just needs a little more time before he can break things off with Marina so we can be together for real. I'm a fool to believe him, but I've always been a fool for Finn.

"Yeah, the wedding is still on. It was never in doubt." Aubrey leans in, whispering, although nobody in this crowded room is going to overhear our trivial little conversation. "Elyse, I'm saying this as your friend, as someone who will always be on your side, even if it doesn't seem like it. Whatever your plans for your professional life may be, you need to take care of your personal life first. Because it would be so easy for one aspect of your life to destroy the other."

Our eyes meet, and the naked truth she just spoke is reflected in the strength of her gaze. "Thank you," I say softly, as a sense of urgency overtakes me. I need to deal with this now, right this second, and it cannot wait. I excuse myself to go to the bathroom, clutching my cell phone as I walk, searching for a quiet nook. I settle for an alcove right outside a back entrance to the party. It's late September, and the bite in the evening air makes me shiver. It's like a portent. Winter is coming.

Finn picks up almost immediately after my phone connects. "I was just thinking about you," He states, warmth oozing from his voice. "I've been watching the news, looking for a glimpse of you, but there hasn't been much coverage yet. Tell me what you're wearing."

I squeeze my eyes shut, wishing this was the sort of phone call where I could tell him that my black satin sheath dress dips so low that if he was here, he could place his hand against the bare small of my back. And we'd both go a little crazy, wishing we were alone. Instead, a cool breeze flaps the sides of my dress, and I feel vulnerable and exposed.

"Did you set a date for your wedding?" I ask.

Finn makes this little sound, not quite clearing his throat, not quite grunting, but somewhere in between. "Aubrey told you?"

"Yes. You're getting married on Valentine's Day. Why didn't *you* tell me?"

He sighs. "Because I'm not going to go through with it. The charade will go on for a few more weeks, and then I'll back out."

From inside, sounds of the celebration emanate out into this breezy autumn evening. Fair or not, I resent Finn for isolating me, for letting me get cold. "Finn, that's just cruel. You need to tell Marina now. Like, tonight."

"I've already told her, Elyse. She knows. Our engagement is as just as big a farce for her as it is for me. Marina's only going along with it because she's afraid to tell her dad the truth."

I'm hit with the injustice of it all. Marina doesn't love Finn and he doesn't love her, yet they're committed to each other because they both have too much to lose. If circumstances were different, maybe Finn and I could make our relationship work. Perhaps we'd be happy, but things are what they are, and the realization that there's no future for us feels like a sucker punch. A sob rises in my throat, but I push it down. "Everything about our relationship is wrong," I state, with as steady a voice as I can manage. "I can't do this anymore."

"Elyse, I understand your reaction, but I promise it will all be okay. Just give me a little more time."

"No." I flick away an errant tear, and with a lavish inhale, I summon all my strength. "You're engaged. You belong to someone else. And let's be realistic. No matter how much time I give you, you don't belong to me. And you never will."

"Come on, Elyse."

"Goodbye, Finn. Please don't call me."

Before he can respond, I end the phone call. Then I take a few more deep breaths, pull myself together, and go back into the party.

I paste on a smile, work the room, and act like I'm thrilled to be here, thrilled to talk to every single person I encounter, that I'm not actually dying inside. It's crazy to think that less than hour ago, I thought I could die happy with what I've accomplished, when I've never taken care of the basics, like finding someone to love who will love me back. But I guess that can't be my priority anymore, not that it ever really was. I'll exchange the fantasy of a personal life for the reality of a public one. I mean, I'm a politician now.

This is what I must do.

Chapter 32

Finn is good at following instructions. He doesn't call and there's radio silence from Marina as well, except for an invitation to their wedding, which will be on Valentine's Day at Hunt's Florida resort, Atlantis Arc. I'm supposed to RSVP, but the reply card sits on my entryway table beside junk mail that needs recycling. I can't find it in me to check the "Yes, I will attend," box, but at the same time, I can't seem to check the "No" box either.

I decide to just stay focused on work. Months go by and my education reform bill makes it through committee, even though the bill is vastly different now than when it was introduced. Still, if this legislation gets passed, public schools will surely benefit. But getting the bill through the House and then the Senate, and then not vetoed by the President, will most likely take more time than I have left in Congress. At some point soon, I must announce my plans to run for governor of Pennsylvania.

I try to be evasive whenever the press asks me what my plans are, but there are no true secrets in politics, just badly kept ones. So, I should be suspicious when one evening after a long day, I'm relaxing on my couch and my phone lights up with a call from Aubrey. After several months of feeling like she's avoiding me, I'm so excited to talk to her that I forget about all about the distance that has come between us. "Hi!" I exclaim. "How are you? How's Baby Anton?"

She lets out an exhausted-sounding gush, communicating a happy soft fatigue. “We’re both good, but I can’t remember the last time I slept more than three hours at a time. Anton demands to be fed several times a night, and he hates sleeping alone in his crib. He wants to be held all the time.”

“That’s got to be exhausting! But when can I come meet him? I’d love to bring you the baby gift I picked out, and I’d *really* love to see you! It’s been way too long.”

“Oh Elyse,” Aubrey sighs. “I barely know which way is up. Between caring for Anton and preparing for my Congressional run, I don’t have the time or energy to socialize.”

“Oh.” Rebuffed, I try to keep my voice light. “Well, maybe in a month or two?”

“Probably. I’ll let you know, okay?”

“Of course.”

“But Elyse,” Aubrey pauses, and the moment feels weighted. “We do need to talk. I’ve heard rumors that you’re running for governor.”

I shiver, suddenly cold, though I’m wearing flannel pajama pants and my oversized *Columbia* hoodie. “Yes,” I state.

Aubrey clears her throat. “Yes, you’re running for governor, or yes, you know there are rumors?”

“Both.”

“You’d be running against my uncle in the primary.”

“I know.”

“Well, the Drake family doesn’t want you to run.”

I tell myself not to get intense, to strive for diplomacy. “You say ‘the Drake family’ like you’re not part of it. Do you not want me to run?”

Her words come out quickly, like she’s been ready to say them for a long time. “I’m sorry, Elyse. I’ve always tried to support you, but your running for governor is a huge mistake.”

I rise from my couch. I need water, right now. I move to the kitchen and fill a glass up at the sink. “I understand you think that,

Aubrey, but your uncle is a flawed candidate who could easily lose." I pause to take a drink, surprised that Aubrey isn't already protesting. "Several prominent Pennsylvania Democrats want me to run. They think I could win."

The ensuing silence from Aubrey's end of the phone line is frosty. "You'd have to get through the primary first," she says finally, "and you have no idea what you'll put yourself through, going against the Drakes."

"I doubt it would be much worse than what the right-wing media flings at me every day." I lean against my kitchen counter, letting its edge cut into my back, hoping the discomfort will keep me from buckling under Aubrey's iciness.

"You don't get it." Aubrey clips each one of her syllables. "If you run for governor, the news of your affair with Finn will come out. Stick to Congress, Elyse. You're doing a lot of good, and as long as you know your place, the Drakes will support you."

I must force myself to breathe and not to hyperventilate. "You told your family about Finn and me? Why would you do that, Aubrey?"

"It's what I had to do. I don't expect you to understand right now, but maybe someday you will."

"Look, whatever you and your family think you know about Finn and me, it's all speculation. You have no proof."

"Of course I have proof."

"From where? From who?"

"Who do you think?"

I don't want to play games, and I almost say so, but then I realize Aubrey is deadly serious and the answer to her question is beyond obvious. "Marina gave you proof," I state flatly.

"Yes."

"How did she figure it out?"

Aubrey sighs. "Marina never had to figure anything out, Elyse. Finn has told her everything, right from the start."

That night, I cry for hours. With heavy, snot-inducing sobs, I indulge in self-pity, sorrow, and anger, bemoaning how my two best friends conspired with the man I love to betray me. I see no remedy for it, and by 2:00 AM I resolve to end my political career. I decide I'll travel abroad the way my mother once did. I could teach English in South America and live a simple life. My mother will tell me how.

But when the sun rises, I rethink giving up so easily. Once it's a suitable hour to call people, it's not my mom whom I reach out to. It's Finn. "We need to meet," I tell him. "I have questions, and if I can't see your face, I won't know if you're lying."

"Okay..." he says slowly. "but I'm surprised you're willing to risk being seen together."

"Please." I hate how harsh I sound, but I keep talking anyway. "Like that would make a difference now."

"Elyse..."

"But let's meet somewhere away from Capitol Hill. Find me at noon in Meridian Hill Park, by the Dante statue." I hang up, confident he'll do what I say.

The morning drags, and I feel like I'm hung over, even though my headache comes purely from sleep deprivation and dehydration thanks to all the tears I've recently shed. When it's finally time to meet Finn, the sunny morning has turned to a cold afternoon, with a freezing drizzle that casts a gray pallor over the nation's capital.

Finn is waiting for me as I approach the Dante statue in Meridian Park. The collar of Finn's jacket is turned up, and dewy drops of ice cling to his hair. "Hi, Elyse," he says. "It's good to see you."

I can't tell from his nearly robotic tone if he means that or not. It's not like he sounds sarcastic, rather, there's no emotion in his voice whatsoever. "Thanks for meeting me," I say.

"Yeah, of course. What's going on?"

I take a deep breath. "Aubrey called. She heard that I'm running for governor of Pennsylvania, and since her uncle is also going to run, she urged me to stay out of the primary. She said that if I run, her family would leak proof that you and I had an affair. She also said that the proof came from Marina, and that you're the one who gave it to her."

Finn winces. "None of that was a question. You said on the phone that you had something to ask me."

I push hot air out through my nose, feeling bullish. "Is Aubrey right? Does Marina have proof about you and me, proof that you gave her?"

"Oh, Elyse." Finn steps in close to me, keeping his voice low. "You have to understand, my relationship with Marina is like a business transaction. If we're not honest with each other, then the whole thing falls apart."

I step back, worried that in my rage I'll do something crazy, like slap him. "What does that mean?" I cry.

"It means what you think! Of course I was upfront with her!" Finn's cheeks turn pink, and his blue eyes are like steel in the gray light. "I had no choice; Marina knows all my passwords. She can access my phone anytime, she can figure out my location, she can read my texts from her own devices. It was non-negotiable. She'd break up with me instantly if I ever tried to hide anything."

"So what?!" I want to grab the lapels of his coat and shake him. "You don't love her. Let her breakup with you! You'd be so much happier."

"No." Finn sighs and cringes simultaneously, like what he's about to say will cause him physical pain. "I'm not strong like you, Elyse. I can't stand up to Marina, or to her dad. They'd ruin me, but if I stay loyal…"

"If you stay loyal, what?"

He shrugs. "I'll reap the benefits."

I look at him, really taking in who he's become. He's a poor man's version of the boy I fell in love with so many years ago. Then

I lift my gaze towards the statue beside us, am hit with a realization, and I laugh ruefully. "Oh my God."

"What?" Finn asks.

"It's just such a coincidence that we're here having this conversation." I point to the huge statue of Dante. We're standing in the stone man's shadow as he holds a copy of the Divine Comedy while staring down at us with a grim expression. "Dante once said something about how the darkest places in hell are reserved for people who stay neutral in times of moral crisis."

Finn's face twists into a confused sneer. "Excuse me?"

"He was talking about people like you."

"You're saying I'm going to hell?"

"Yes! And not because you betrayed me." I figure this is my very last chance to convince him, so I lean in and let my words tumble out, quick and passionate. "Finn, if you continue to enable Marina, if you continue to aid Oliver Hunt in his insane, ethically bankrupt quest to become president, if you refuse to stand up to either of them, then you are most certainly going to hell."

Finn's entire body goes stiff, like he's turned to a harder brand of stone than the Dante statue. "You're no better, Elyse. You talk a good game, but you're happy to accept Marina and Aubrey's help whenever they offer it."

"Right." There are so many differences, so many degrees which separate Finn's complicity from my own, but I get his point. "I guess you and I don't like each other very much anymore, do we?"

"I'm sorry." Finn's voice is as feeble as his sentiment, which is how I know that our relationship is so completely over. No more redos. No more second chances.

"Yeah, me too."

There's nothing else to say, nothing else to add to the pathetic mess into which our love affair has devolved.

"I should go." He reaches out like he's going to squeeze my arm, but his hand falls lamely to his side. "Take care, Elyse." Finn turns, taking off in his own direction, and I turn the opposite way, walking away from him.

I should be bereft or furious or some combination of the two, but I must have used up all my strong emotions last night. I'm just empty. And I'm consumed with navigating the icy path.

The pavement has become slick with freezing drizzle, and my shoes are flimsy ballet flats that I chose this morning, thinking the weather would be nice. They have no traction, and the layer of ice makes it nearly impossible to balance. If I had my skates on, I could be twirling and spinning, but as it is, I must navigate what feels like enemy grounds in my damp, snow-soaked slippers. Someone should throw salt and sand out here, but the park is deserted.

I take careful steps, and my feet try to escape as l lurch forward, back, and then to the side. But somehow, I regain my equilibrium and stand upright. *Glad I caught that.* Then, abruptly, both my feet fly out from under me, and I tumble down, unfortunately landing my entire body's weight on my left elbow.

"Fuck!!" I yell, my go-to profanity for whenever I am in sudden, excruciating pain. Thank God no camera crews are around to have caught that, but even if they had, my agony is too immense to care. My entire body is in shock, waves of pain and nausea rolling through me at steam engine force. The coffee I drank this morning comes right back up, and I puke it into the snow. Sick and shaken, I look around; the only presence is the cool breeze that sways the tree branches. No one is around.

I could yell and hope somebody hears me. I could call someone, but who? But calling for help seems even more intolerable than the Herculean effort it will take to stand, to walk, to hold it together. I mean, what's the alternative? I suppose I could sit here in the coffee-puke stained snow, dissolve into a puddle of vomit and tears, and wait for someone to come. Perhaps Finn will magically know I need him, but it is too cold out for me to wait and see if he comes riding up on his white horse. *Nobody is going to help you,* I think. *You're totally on your own.*

So, somehow, I stand and trudge back toward the sidewalk above the park, back towards the station for the DC Metro that I took coming here. But I realize instantly that even if I somehow miraculously make it to the metro station, I can't board a crowded, rickety train. Scared that I will pass out and fall a second time, I gasp as my elbow shards jostle around underneath my skin.

I pull my phone out, call for an Uber, and stand, shaking on the sidewalk for probably ten minutes, though it feels like a lifetime waiting for the Uber to come. I imagine what they'll say on CNN: *This is breaking news. Elyse Gibbons is a pathetic klutz with no friends to help in her time of need.* When a metallic blue Hyundai pulls up, the driver eagerly ushers me into his car. "I know you!" He exclaims. "You're that Congresswoman who's always in the news. Can I get a selfie?'

"Sure," I grunt, as I gingerly climb into his backseat. "Once we're at the hospital, okay?"

"Wait." He turns toward the backseat, observing me more closely now. "What happened? Are you hurt?"

***

The drive to the hospital is okay, and the Uber driver even offers to pull over to a convenience store so we can buy me a coke and a package of crackers. "It will help you feel less woozy," he tells me. Sure enough, he's right. The sugar/carb combo helps. I even feel good enough to pose for a selfie outside the urgent care entrance, that is if he doesn't drape his arm around me.

Yet I still nearly pass out when I get admitted into the emergency room and they take X-Rays. It's laying my arm out, as straight and flat as possible, that I just can't handle. The medical technician insists on using a wheelchair to take me back into the exam room. There I await my results, but I already know what the doctor is going to say. My elbow is obviously and seriously messed up. I don't need medical technology to know my diagnosis.

Minutes later, the doctor comes in. "Your elbow is broken straight through in three places," he tells me. He does something on his computer, flips a switch, and like magic projects my X-Ray against the office wall. Maybe he's had a long day and my non-life-threatening situation seems tedious, or maybe he doesn't like my politics. But I detect annoyance in his grunt as he points to the image of my arm. "Here, here, and here. You also managed to dislocate parts of your bone by shoving them up into the joint."

I ignore the accusatory tone, the implication that I did this to myself on purpose, for what, to get attention? "How do we fix it?" I ask.

"Surgery," he answers simply. "I'm referring you to an orthopedic surgeon right now." He scribbles something on a slip of paper and hands it to me.

"Can I have the surgery today?" I ask.

"Doubtful. They'll want to wait several days until the swelling goes down."

"But what do I do until then? I can't even move my fingers without getting an electric shock of pain."

"I'll prescribe you some Oxy," he says. "And I'll have a nurse put you in an immobilizer."

"What's that?"

"You'll see."

Then, with neither a goodbye nor a good luck, he walks out through the exam room door, his white coat tails flapping. I just sit, staring at the flu shot poster taped to the wall, and wait for the nurse. Thankfully, she comes in after a few minutes. She's carrying a black bundle which must be the immobilizer, and she whips it out with such distaste, I wonder if it insulted her somehow.

"I can never remember how these things work," the nurse sighs. "Stand up. This might take a while."

I stand, and she starts by putting the widest part of the immobilizer around my waist, attaching it with Velcro. "I think your arm goes like this," she says, carefully bending my arm and hugging it to my stomach. Then she needs to look at the instructions to figure out how to attach all the rest of the straps, but the result is my arm is now immobile and impossible to move in a way that will hurt. But it's still unprotected, and rather than being in this half-a-straight jacket, I wish for a plaster cast, or maybe some body armor.

"Thank you," I tell the nurse, who wishes me luck and ushers me out to the lobby. Once I'm out there, I'm met with cameras and a news crew.

"Tell us what happened, Representative Gibbons," a CNN anchor insists, pointing a microphone in my face.

My reply is ridiculously obvious, but they're the only words that come to mind. "I fell down."

Then I walk away.

Chapter 33

I make an appointment with the orthopedic surgeon for tomorrow. I fill my prescription at the pharmacy. I take another Uber home to my little apartment, where I try to nap. But I'm terrified I'll inadvertently roll over onto my broken arm, so I never actually drift off. Instead, I lie on top of my bed and ruminate.

You had this coming, I think. *Slipping on the ice? You've been trying to conquer ice for years, but it finally beat you. It beat you in the nation's capital, working a job where you don't belong, chasing after a man who doesn't belong to you.*

The browns and beiges that decorate my sleep area begin to fade as the Oxy sets in, and the sun sets outside my window. I'm fading too, finally on the brink of sleep, when a knock at my apartment door startles me back into reality. I roll onto my good side, warily scooting myself into standing position, yet even still, everything hurts.

I open the door, although I haven't even begun to speculate who might be on the other side. Surely, it can't be Finn, but I'm beyond caring. Turns out, I should have cared, because Marina is here to see me.

"Elyse! I heard about your fall. How are you feeling?"

It's a question of concern, but her voice is steely. Plus, with her arms crossed over her chest and her face pressed into a frown, I'm not exactly sensing a Florence Nightingale vibe. Instead, she's like a tall, auburn-haired viper, looming over me in her bright red stilettos.

"It's all over social media," Marina continues, as if prompted. "Your Uber driver posted the selfie you guys took outside the emergency room. He said you messed up your elbow pretty bad. And, of course, you know about the news crews coming to find you at the emergency room." She looks at my arm which is still wrapped up in the immobility sling. "Is it broken?"

"Yeah. Or technically, maybe it's shattered. Somewhere in between." I shift my weight, feeling woozy. I need to be lying down. "Thanks for stopping by Marina, but if you don't mind, I'd like to go back to bed."

"I do mind, actually." Marina's smile only makes her seem more sinister. "We need to talk. Please let me in."

Okay, so she just said please (which is nice, I guess) but the implication is clear: she's not making a request but a demand. I have no fight in me now, so I step aside and let her enter, realizing doom is inevitable. This impending battle was bound to happen, and I'm meant to lose.

"Would you like to sit down?" I ask. "And can I take your coat?" I hold out my good arm, as if to take the white wool that covers her. Only Marina could wear a coat like that, never inviting drips of coffee from insecure coffee lids or grunge from city streets that might mar the pristine, fashion magazine quality she always pulls off.

"No thanks. I won't stay long."

"Okay." I let my arm drop to my side. "I think I know why you're here."

Marina tilts her head. "Oh yeah? Why?"

"Finn told you about our conversation today. You want me to stay away."

Marina narrows her eyes. "Why would I choose *now* to tell you to stay away? From the way Finn told it, you two have never been more over."

"That's true." I sigh. "I guess I'm kind of loopy from taking Oxycontin, so my brain isn't working too well. Tell me why you are here, Marina."

"I'm here because, apparently, you're still planning to run for governor of Pennsylvania."

"Why do you care whether or not I run?"

"Because I don't want the world to know that Finn's been unfaithful." Marina stares into me with a tough intensity. "It would wreck the public's perception that he and I are this perfect, fairytale couple. We need to maintain that image if we want our wedding to boost my dad's campaign."

I rub my forehead. "Okay," I say, not in agreement, but to verify I've heard the craziness she just uttered. "Why did you give Aubrey information about Finn and me if you didn't want her to use it?"

"Because she told me that if I didn't, her family would leak news about my five-year affair with a woman." Marina's normally perfect posture collapses; her shoulders slump, her chest caves, and she tilts her head. "Not even my dad knows about Janet. I tried to tell him once, but he became angry before I even got out all the words. Now, he'd kill me if he knew the truth." Marina raises her face, resuming eye contact. "But Aubrey has texts that I sent to her about Janet, and a picture of the two of us kissing in Aubrey's living room. I don't know how I could have been so stupid, so careless."

Marina flops onto my couch, hanging her head in her hands. I've never seen her like this; I didn't even know Marina was capable of such defeated behavior. "Everything is all my fault," she says. "How did it all get so fucked up?"

I sit across from her, on a folding chair that's a substitute for real furniture. Here I am: a woman in her late twenties, with no real home, no real relationship, no real friends, my life and my elbow both in shards. Yet, I feel real sympathy for Marina Hunt. "Marina, don't beat yourself up. We both trusted Aubrey, and I still can't quite believe she'd betray us like this."

Marina looks up at me, her eyes gleaming, but I can't tell whether it's with tears or with rage. "Aubrey is a Drake. She's just as ruthless as the rest of them. You think my dad is corrupt? Next to the Drakes, he's a saint."

Maybe I should hate the Drakes right now; maybe I already sort of do. But my love for Aubrey and even Eleanor didn't just evaporate overnight. Besides, I'm too tired and in too much pain for this conversation, and right now I'm incapable of playing along with Marina's alternative facts. "Right. Your dad is a saint." I say this slowly and sarcastically. "Marina, it wouldn't matter if Eleanor Anton Drake personally came to my apartment and threatened to murder me, I'd still prefer her as president over your dad."

Marina's mouth drops open in surprise. "Don't forget who you're talking to, Elyse."

"I forget nothing. And I have nothing left to lose."

"That's where you're wrong." Marina leans toward me, nearly pitching herself forward. "You've become quite the sensation, haven't you? You're the freshman Congresswoman from Pennsylvania who can do no wrong, the new face of the Democratic party. But remember, Aubrey and I made you, and we can ruin you just as easily." Marina lowers her voice into a scary-sort of hush. "Don't run for governor, Elyse. You'll regret it if you do."

I grunt in exasperation, a noise from deep inside me that stems from the grips of pain, a fog of OxyContin, and a funnel of self-pity. "Go to hell, Marina."

"What?!" Marina demands. "How can you talk to me that way?"

"Because I am so sick of being told again and again, that my success is all due to you and Aubrey. I know you've helped me tremendously, but I've worked hard, and you act like I don't have some small amount of intelligence or drive. Do you understand how insulting and demeaning that is?!"

"Calm down!" says Marina. "God, you're freaking out."

Then the realization that I *do not* want Marina here, now or ever again, hits me with a powerful force, not unlike the waves of pain I've experienced all day. "You need to leave. You shouldn't have even come in the first place."

"I had to come. You gave me no choice."

So, she's the victim? I stand, walk toward my door, and open it. "Goodbye, Marina."

"I'm not leaving until you promise not to run for governor. You owe me that."

"Marina, I'm done owing you things. And if you don't leave right now, I'll scream and make a huge scene. You really don't want it in the news tomorrow that Marina Hunt harassed poor, broken Elyse Gibbons just hours after she suffered a severe injury."

Wordlessly, Marina rises and walks towards my door. She starts to leave, but before I close the door behind her, she says, "This isn't over." Then she's gone, and I don't think I've ever felt so scared or helpless. But that's only partially due to Marina's threats and mostly due to my broken elbow.

I mean, I am still in this stupid immobilizer the nurse strapped me into at the emergency room. And I'm afraid to take it off because I won't be able to put it back on, not by myself. I can't bathe or even change into a more comfortable top than the blouse I put on this morning for work. I haven't eaten, and heating something up sounds like way too much work. And other than my staff, I have no one to call, no one to take me to my doctor's appointment tomorrow.

I tell myself to stay strong, that I'll feel better if I eat something. I gingerly take a loaf of bread from the refrigerator, remove a couple of slices from the bag, and put them in the toaster. I'll make peanut butter toast. Comfort food. Growing up, it's what my mom made me after a rough skating practice or a bad day at school, and that always made me feel better. As the scent of toasting bread fills the small space of the kitchen, I *am* comforted; just the promise of warm, gooey nourishment is soothing. Then I realize it's not peanut butter toast that's making me feel better. It's the memory of my mom taking care of me.

I've been so stupid. Of course, I have someone to call.

***

"You should come home," my mom says. "Stay in our spare bedroom, heal, and let me take care of you." She sits next to me in the waiting room of the orthopedics clinic where, any minute, they'll call me in to prep for surgery. "Forget about Congress for a couple of weeks. The session can finish without you."

I don't respond. She's been saying the same thing to me over and over since she drove up to get me several days ago. Even though I've explained, several times, that there are important floor votes coming up, Mom insists that I'm living in a toxic environment, working on the Hill.

"Elyse? Did you hear me? You need a break. I don't care if you're running for governor. Your physical and emotional well-being is more important than your political career."

"Mom!" I practically growl. "Ixnay of the overnshipgay!" I say to her in pig Latin. "Especially when we're in public. You never know who might overhear."

"Fine, I'm just saying there's a reason you're alone and almost thirty, with no one to call but your mother when you break your elbow. You've made some bad choices, Elyse, and it's time for a change."

Wow. There's nothing like a harsh dose of truth right before surgery. Why doesn't she break my other elbow and finish the job?

"My point," she continues, "is that you need to get out of D.C. and out of politics. You need to meet some well-adjusted people. You need friends who aren't so narcissistic that they believe they should rule the free world. It's not too late to live a normal life, but now's your moment. I'm convinced this is a turning point for you."

I look at my mom, dressed in faded jeans and a fleece jacket, with her long, gray-streaked hair pulled back with a headband. She looks like an aging liberal, one who's never had to live outside of a progressive bubble. I suppose since she and my stepdad stick pretty close to the academic community and the yoga studio, which is where they belong, it's a fair description. But they've been happy, and she's living proof that choosing a new path in your thirties can lead to personal fulfillment. So maybe everything she said to me is spot-on.

"Elyse Gibbons?" A woman in scrubs calls my name.

"That's me." I rise, but before walking toward that doorway, I turn to my mother. "Thanks, Mom. Wish me luck, okay?"

"Don't worry, baby," she says. "Compared to what you've been through, outpatient surgery will be a breeze."

***

"Elyse, can you wake up now?"

Everything feels like a fragmented blur. I try to accommodate the nurse's request but waking up is so hard. Why is it so hard? Next to falling, waking should be easy. Yet my head is too heavy to lift, my eyelids too sticky to keep open. When I manage to glimpse to the side, I find an arm that doesn't belong to me. I've had a lifetime minus a week with a working left arm, but now it is a useless appendage, heavy and covered in gauze, here only to cause me pain.

"Can you get dressed?" the nurse asks me. "It's time to get you home."

"I think she's going to need a hospital bed," I hear my mom say. "You must have given her too much anesthesia."

"Mom," I croak.

"What is it, baby?"

My mother leans down by my bedside, and I struggle to focus on her face, on the only familiar constant in my entire life. I'm surprised by the words that come out, but for some reason they've been lingering in my subconscious and are finally ready to make an appearance. "You were right." My throat is so dry it's hard to speak, and I have no idea why, when I can barely even lift my head, it's now necessary to express life-altering revelations. "I'm at a turning point. I need to make a change."

Chapter 34
Pennsylvania

I only stay in the hospital for one night, but once released, I am unprepared for all the post-surgery effects. My hand swells up so much that I swear it will pop. My fingers are like sausages, and my knuckles look like pillows; my hand may as well be an inflated rubber glove. I must keep it elevated, but I must keep my elbow elevated too, and this is no easy feat. Sleeping is hard. So is sitting, so is everything. I've never been prone to depression, but I'm hit with this malaise, like I no longer know how to make simple decisions or how to feel happy about little things.

I give in and stay with my mom in West Chester. Congress will survive without me for a couple weeks. But will *I* survive away from DC? It's easy to talk about "turning points" when you're still drugged out after surgery, but now that reality has set in, I have no idea in which direction I should move. I can't help feeling defeated, even as I agree to meet with Polly Kinney to "discuss the options."

Currently, my options are limited. If I were back in Congress, I wouldn't even be able to comply with the dress code, not with my elaborate arm brace that slides on over a compression sleeve. I can't wear a normal long-sleeved shirt or a jacket; instead, I must wear one of several thrift store shirts that I recently bought. I've cut off one of the sleeves to accommodate my black contraption made of metal rods, Velcro straps, and a dial at the elbow. But the dial is always slipping down, which forces me to tighten those Velcro straps to the point where my circulation gets cut off.

In my physical therapist's office, I take both the brace and sleeve off and lay my arm against a heated pillow so Miguel can inspect it. I keep thinking there's no way Miguel is old enough to be a physical therapist, but perhaps his size makes him seem younger than he is. He couldn't be more than five-eight, 150 pounds, tops. With his large brown eyes framed by thick lashes, a crooked smile, and dimpled cheeks, he emits a disarming, boyish charm. It's all just a guise though; Miguel is a task-master.

"Your swelling has increased." He uses a tape measure to make this assessment, but I already knew he'd say that. Just looking at my arm makes it swell. Sometimes I'm sure my hand is simply a zit about to pop in an explosion of stress and pain, a rebuttal to my elbow and all the inconvenience it has caused.

"Yeah," I respond. "I'm not surprised. You can tell just by looking at it." We both gaze at my arm, at the lumps and dips caused by the constant pressure of those Velcro straps.

His fingers press against a protuberance in my forearm. "This is all hard tissue," he says. "You need to massage this out, several times a day." He starts rubbing it, and I let a sigh escape. But as nice as the arm rub is, I know what's coming. And it isn't good.

Too soon, Miguel says, "Okay. Let's see where you are."

That means it's time to measure my mobility, so I stand and bend and straighten my arm as best I can. I never thought such a simple action would require so much focus, so much effort. In many ways, this is a ton more difficult than executing a perfect triple-toe loop and landing in an arabesque. I keep pushing, using all my strength to increase my degrees and get my fingers ever closer to the impossibility of touching my shoulder as I bend, or to the wall behind me as I straighten. Part of it is my pride; I want to impress Miguel, to let him know I'm not a typical patient, that through sheer force of will I'll heal faster and better than any of his other patients.

It's not unlike my figure-skating days when I wanted to impress my coach into thinking I was champion-material.

Miguel uses his tape measure again, walks back to his computer, and punches in the new, magic numbers. "How'd I do?" I ask.

He frowns. "Compared to last week? You gained two degrees bending."

"That's it?" I was sure, with all my work, I'd have at least gained five.

"That's it," he answers. "And you lost one degree straightening it."

"What?" My defenses go up, like he's just thrown me a personal attack. "That can't be right! I've been working so hard, doing my exercises three times a day, I swear!"

"Are you?"

"Yes!"

I mean, what else have I got going on?

Miguel gives me a sudden smile, which unexpectedly warms his face and makes his eyes sparkle. "Don't worry. This happens. Two steps forward, one step back, you know? Come on, let's do some work."

No wonder he's smiling. He's eager at the prospect of "doing some work," which means I'll lie on a table while he presses on my elbow at odd, painful angles, forcing it to bend and straighten way more than I want it to. Physical therapists must live for "doing some work" and I've decided they're just like dentists: professional masochists. Certainly Miguel is anyway. I square my shoulders and follow him into the room next door, to where the therapy table is. What must be done, must be done.

After I settle myself onto the table, I stare at the ceiling, resolved not to break down. I will have the best, highest pain tolerance that Miguel has ever seen. I will be the toughest patient he's ever had. That means not breaking down while he works on my arm, when all I want to do is hug my broken limb up into my collapsed body, sit in a dark corner, and lick my wounds.

To distract myself, I make conversation. "So," I manage to say through stifled gasps, "how long have you been a physical therapist?"

"Six years," he responds as he pulls on my arm, obviously trying to elongate it.

"Seriously? What, did you start right out of college?"

Miguel lets out a near-laugh. "Pretty much. But it wasn't easy to get through college and get my work visa. I had to keep re-applying for DACA."

"You're a Dreamer?"

"Yeah."

"Wow." I sigh when he releases my arm after pressing on it.

"What do you mean, 'wow'?"

"Oh. Sorry. I don't mean to be rude, but I thought all Dreamers were kids."

When he speaks, I can't tell from his matter-of-fact tone if he's offended. "Actually, most Dreamers are in their twenties, so I'm on the older end. But I qualify. When I came here with my parents, I was eleven."

"Are your parents citizens?"

"No. They used to have work visas, but those ran out, and they haven't been able to renew them. And now that we're about to elect a new president, who knows?"

"Oh." I start to formulate a response, a tactful follow-up question that isn't too intrusive, but Miguel presses on my shoulder and grabs my wrist in a way that brings sudden agony. "Holy shit!" I cry. "Are you trying to kill me?"

"We don't want your shoulder to freeze up too," Miguel responds. "And that can easily happen when you're not using it enough. Trust me."

"Of course, I trust you."

"Well, that's a surprise, considering the agony I put you through."

I start to laugh, but nothing comes out except a weepy sort of exhale. I barely know Miguel, but all at once, I'm concerned with the idea of his uncertain future. If Hunt wins the presidency, he's sure to crack down on immigration, and that could destroy someone like Miguel and his family.

Miguel presses my forearm up, as if to force my hand into my shoulder, but there may as well be miles between those body parts. Miguel's eyes dart from the clock, which he usually watches to time the positions he puts me in, to my face, which must look tortured. Our eyes meet. "Does this hurt?" he asks softly.

I don't have to answer. Miguel is familiar with pain. He encounters it all the time.

It's late afternoon when I get home, and I do what I always do, turn on CNN. Yesterday was Valentine's Day, and pictures of Marina's and Finn's wedding are everywhere. And while that's big news, the bigger news is that in four days, Nevada will hold their caucus, and a week later comes South Carolina. A week after that is Super Tuesday, when Oliver Hunt will most likely secure the republican nomination for president. He has already won Iowa and New Hampshire, and with all the positive press he's been basking in lately, Hunt seems untouchable.

As for the Democrats, Eleanor Adam-Drake is the absolute favorite to win the nomination.

A pundit on CNN talks about it now, slipping into deep-analysis mode. "In such an unpredictable year, with no incumbent running, the playing field should be wide open. And yet, both parties seem set to choose their candidates early, even though both of those candidates are deeply flawed."

Her comment prompts a discussion amongst all of CNN's talking heads about how Oliver Hunt has mafia connections, and there's evidence of graft and possible illegal acts from when he was governor of New Jersey. And then there's that story of how he paid for his mistress's abortion.

Yet, Eleanor Adam-Drake is too liberal-elite. Plus, her husband cheated on her, her brother had that car accident scandal, and we all know about her father's misdeeds as president.

I pick up my phone, ready to call Aubrey to complain about how this false equivalency BS is so unfair. Then I remember that Aubrey and I aren't speaking, that she hasn't called me once since my accident, not to check in, not to wish me well, and certainly not to apologize for betraying my secrets to her family, whom I guess is now out to get me.

Crap. I drop my phone to my side, loosen the straps on my arm brace and rub at the hard tissue Miguel says needs more work, contemplating as my fingers knead my flesh. While I try to loosen the knots in my arm, I also take deep breaths. I won't let my anxiety skyrocket again. I'll never heal if I can't relax a little.

I should just turn the TV off, but I see the story has switched back to Marina's and Finn's wedding. CNN shows happy pictures of the beautiful couple, radiantly in love and gazing into each other's eyes. There's also a picture of Aubrey standing next to Marina. She's wearing a dark green strapless gown and holding a bouquet. So, I guess Aubrey was maid of honor. Knowing that she's still tight with Marina stings, way more than Finn going ahead with the marriage does. The pundits on CNN discuss the ramifications of Aubrey and Marina's friendship and that their parents seem sure to battle it out in the political arena.

"And what about Elyse Gibbons?" a blonde pundit asks. "I understand she is also a close friend. The three of them met in college, and then they worked together, advocating for the passage of the ERA. But now it seems they've had a falling out."

Another pundit smirks. "Poor Elyse Gibbons. She just can't keep from falling."

They all laugh, and the host says, "You're referring, of course, to Congresswoman Gibbon's recent fall where she broke an elbow.

I understand she's recuperating at home in West Chester, recovering from surgery and going through physical therapy."

"Yes," the blonde pundit says. "Elyse Gibbons has temporarily dropped from the political scene. However, I've heard rumors that she might be about to launch a primary battle against Ethan Drake for governor of Pennsylvania. That could explain why she and Aubrey Adam-Drake are on the outs."

And then suddenly, as if by magic, my cell phone goes off. I've been sitting on the floor, and my phone is resting on the carpet by my knee, so I reach for it. Aubrey is calling me. Is it a coincidence, or was she also watching CNN?

"Hey," I casually state, as if no time or distance separates us.

"How are you, Elyse? How's your elbow?"

"My elbow and I have both been better. How are you?"

"I'm fine." She takes a deep breath. "And I'm sorry I haven't been in touch. But you've got to drop your plans to run for governor. You don't understand how serious this is."

"Hold on." I inhale, trying to alleviate the pressure in my chest, the hurt caused by the coldness of her tone. "I haven't made any firm plans yet. But if I were to run, would that be so awful?"

"Yes! My grandfather and my uncle would take you out. Not literally, of course, but politically… you'd be dead. And I'm sorry, maybe it's unfair, but I'm furious that you're putting me in that position."

I rub at my temple, hesitant over what to say next. "What position have I put you in, Aubrey?"

She doesn't respond, and for a moment I think she's hung up. Then I hear her breathe, so I continue. "I haven't done anything wrong, not to you, and not to your family. So, don't hold your breath waiting for me to apologize, just because the Drakes intend to destroy me."

Again, there's silence, but some dam inside her must break, because with a gush she says, "Oh, Elyse. Are you okay?"

"Yeah," I answer. "I'm okay. My body will mend. But I have been lonely lately, and I don't know when that will go away."

There's a pause. Then, quietly, Aubrey states, "You brought some of it on yourself."

"No doubt," I respond. "But why were you Marina's bridesmaid? You criticize her to me, but to her face, you give her your support. It makes me wonder what the two of you say about me when I'm not around."

"Really? I believe Marina was pretty upfront about what we've been saying."

"You mean how she gave you proof of my affair with Finn? I suppose there's more bad stuff? You could lie and say I slept with Peter while he was still married. Hey, you could dig stuff up about my mom, like her anti-American statements when she traveled overseas. And if you hire private investigators you might even be able to locate my foreign, derelict dad. Or has your family already done all that?"

I hear sniffling, like maybe Aubrey is crying. "I'm not your enemy, Elyse. Please believe me; I'm trying to help you. I don't know everything that my uncle's people have done, but I do know he's panicked, and he and my grandfather are ruthless when taking out their political opponents."

I squeeze my eyes shut, as if that could will this conversation away. "Come on, Aubrey. Don't play innocent. You gave them information about Finn and me. I thought we were friends. I thought we were best friends! Why would you do that?"

She sighs. "Because my grandfather said that if I did he wouldn't make me run for Congress."

"That makes no sense."

"It does if you're a Drake." I hear more sniffling and perhaps a baby crying in the background. It's unclear who is in distress, but clearly somebody is. "I don't always like my family's methods, but I do believe their intentions are good. And I can't help feeling like, as a part of this family, I ought to fix the world."

"It's not your job to fix the world, Aubrey."

"But what if it is? What if, with all my privilege and opportunity, I was born with this obligation to do good? And if fixing the world isn't *my* job, then whose job is it?"

I stretch out my legs and scrunch my toes. I'm sitting on the floor, my broken arm resting against a pillow, and my iPad is next to me. It's still on CNN, which hasn't gone to commercial in the time since I turned it on. "I don't know, Aubrey. I think the world has gone a little crazy. Fixing it must be a group effort."

"It has to start somewhere."

"Okay. So, maybe now is our time to act. We can both do our part."

She lets out a tiny, dismayed-sounding groan. "No. I can't. You don't understand."

"But, Aubrey -"

"I mean it, Elyse. Promise that you won't run for governor."

From many feet away, I hear the outside door open. My mom, stepdad, and half-brothers are home, full of noise, energy, and bustle. "Hello! Elyse?" My mom yells for me. "Come on out. We brought home the best tamales in the world."

For my family, every Tuesday is Mexican takeout night. "Sounds great," I call. "I'll be right there."

The prospect of good food, eaten in the company of real-life people instead of the talking heads on CNN, is appealing. I tighten the straps of my arm brace in anticipation of getting up and joining my family for dinner. "I have to go, Aubrey. I'll call you tomorrow, okay?"

"Sure," she says, sounding uncertain.

We say our goodbyes, and although we're both entirely pleasant, it doesn't escape either of us that I failed to promise her something.

Chapter 35

"You have to call Finn. That's all there is to it." Mom and I walk a trail at Stroud Preserve as she makes this declaration. Right now, the land is just a flat, vast expanse of wetlands, but we're headed toward the wooded areas, to climb to a scenic overlook. For this hike, I keep my arm in a sling made from one of my mom's oversized scarves because my brace is heavy and the pressure too uncomfortable to let my arm hang to the side. It's amazing how one out-of-commission arm can slow your whole body down. I find it hard to keep pace with my mom, who's charging along, full of vim, vigor, and edicts about my life.

"Calling Finn is the last thing I want to do."

"Well, of course," she answers. "But you *should* call him. Tell him you need to talk about your screwed-up relationship. Let him believe there's a chance you'll take him back. But wear a wire. Get him to give details about his marriage with Marina and how Hunt bullies them into living a lie."

"You've seen too many movies, Mom. Wear a wire? Come on."

"Of course, wear a wire. That way, when the Drakes try to destroy you, you'll have proof that it wasn't your fault."

"Mom, that makes no sense. I'd still be at fault for sleeping with a married man."

"He was only engaged when you two were together."

"True, but I fail to see how this plan to expose Finn and Marina would help me in any sort of way."

"Maybe it wouldn't, but if it hurts Hunt, then it's worth it! He'd be a disaster as president, so you need to do whatever you can to keep him from getting elected."

I shake my head, stepping over a muddy puddle as we power-walk. Living together these last few weeks has certainly tightened the bond between my mom and me, and one night, over a pan of cooling brownies, I told her all about my affair with Finn, and the strange falling-out I've suffered with both Aubrey and Marina. It was probably a mistake telling my mom, because she won't stop harping over "what I must do."

"Elyse?"

A male voice startles me, and squinting against the sun, I realize it's Miguel who just spoke my name. "Oh! Hello!" Blood rushes to my face. I'm embarrassed for no reason.

He looks good; maybe that's why I'm suddenly so self-conscious. In jeans and a black V-neck t-shirt, Miguel has this laid-back allure that he's never displayed during our therapy sessions. There's a rip in the knee of his jeans. His t-shirt is nothing special, but his casual clothes fit his lean, muscular frame nicely.

I hold out my arm, still in its sling. "I know, I'm supposed to keep it moving as much as possible, but when we're walking like this, it's just so much more comfortable to wear a sling."

He nods seriously. "Of course. And it's good you're getting exercise. That will help your recovery."

"Sure."

My mom clears her throat.

"Sorry!" I say again. "Miguel, this my mom, Helen." I turn to my mom. "Miguel is my physical therapist. He's really helping me a lot."

"Nice to meet you," my mom says, her arm outstretched. Miguel shakes her hand.

"Do you have a day off, then?" I ask Miguel.

"Sort of. I'm meeting my parents soon. They live close to here, and I'm helping with my little brother's birthday party. He turns twelve today."

"Oh, how wonderful. How many siblings do you have?" my mother asks.

"I'm the oldest of six," Miguel answers.

"I'm not surprised" my mother says, smiling. I panic that she's about to make some borderline racist comment about how Hispanics always come from large families. But of course not; if anyone is culturally conscious, it's my mom. "Something about you seems like an eldest sibling," she says. "Just the way you talk and carry yourself: it's clear you have a keen sense of responsibility." She pats my back. "Elyse was my first child. First children always want to fix the world, you know? At least, Elyse always has. And I'm guessing you do too, or you wouldn't be a physical therapist."

Even though her comments are benign, I still cringe and resist telling my mom to shut up. But Miguel doesn't seem to mind the instant familiarity. "Thank you," he says. "I'll take that as a compliment."

"Oh good, I was hoping you would," Mom replies.

Miguel looks at me, and there's a flutter in my chest. "I'll see you Wednesday?" he asks.

He remembers when my next appointment is? I really need to get a life because that shouldn't make me so happy. "See you Wednesday," I reply.

We walk our separate ways. "He's cute," Mom remarks, and I silently pray he's safely out of earshot. "You should totally go for it with him."

"Mom!"

"But not until you've found closure over the whole mess with Aubrey, Marina, and Finn. Wait until you've figured out how you want to fix the world. Then you'll be free to go for whatever, or whomever you want."

When I get home, I'm still thinking about what my mom said, that I want to fix the world. My mom's words mirror what Aubrey said just a few days ago. Sure, Aubrey was talking about herself, and it wasn't so much that Aubrey *wants* to fix the world, it's that she feels like she has an obligation to. Meanwhile, I was born with neither Aubrey's opportunity nor her privilege, and I don't presume to know the answers to all our problems. And, while I have a great a platform as a member of Congress, I admit to wanting more.

If I was governor, I could make sure that people like Miguel and his family have sanctuary here in Pennsylvania. I could finish what I started in Reading and put a public education initiative in place that would help more kids graduate. I could work to create more jobs. I could collaborate with local industry and negotiate workable environmental guidelines that they'd agree to follow. I have so many ideas, and who knows if any of them are good, but I'd love to find out. I'd love to try.

Yet, there's this nagging fear that everything I am and everything I've done is due to Aubrey, Marina, and Finn; it hangs over me like a wet wool sweater, like the one Marina insisted I replace with that coat she gave me. What if I'd never met them, never received their support, never had them to prop me up, to make me more visible, to let my voice grow loud enough to be heard?

Moving forward means losing them, but I lost them a long time ago. What happens next is up to me.

***

Aware that Polly Kinney will probably kill me for making this impulsive, ill-planned move, I pick up my phone and turn the video camera to selfie-mode. "I'm Elyse Gibbons," I say. "You might know me as that outspoken Congresswoman on Twitter, who spouts off her progressive politics, and who knows how to stay in the spotlight. If you're aware of my existence, chances are you either love me or hate me. But I'm here to tell you this: I am not important. I don't think politics is about individual leadership, but it should be about finding the wisdom and the moral courage to do what's right. I never woke up and said to myself, 'I want to be a Congresswoman,' or 'I want to be the governor.' I just saw an opportunity to step up, so I took it, and I've tried to change things for the better. But those of you who approve of the work I've done, approve because of the ideas I represent, and know that those ideas come from all of you. We are nothing without each other. Like our forefathers had the wisdom to realize, E Pluribus Unum: out of many comes one."

I blink, biting my lip for just a moment. "I hope I'm making sense…I didn't write any of this down beforehand. It's just, I truly believe that no one person is meant to save everyone else, to fix everyone else. We can only fix each other. So, while I've made my share of mistakes, and I've been hypocritical in ways you're sure to hear about soon, I own who I am, who I've always been, and who I will become. First and foremost, I am an American, I am a daughter of Pennsylvania, and I am only as wise, as strong, and as effective as those of you who champion me. But I would like to champion all of you. That is why I am declaring my candidacy for governor of Pennsylvania."

I repeat the same message in Spanish and then I post the video to YouTube and wait for the storm to begin.

Chapter 36

But there is no storm, at least not really. Sure, reporters contact me for interviews. Plus, all the major news outlets and dozens of local Pennsylvania stations run my video. Polly Kinney calls and half berates/half praises me, saying my selfie-announcement, which I'd filmed while wearing a hoodie and without any makeup on, was reckless and genius all at once. "You're either incredibly brave or incredibly stupid," she says.

I don't feel brave, and as for stupid, well, there are no sudden, catastrophic consequences of my campaign announcement. In other words, I hear nothing from the Hunts and nothing from the Drakes.

I tell Polly I'll be returning to Congress and DC but will still drive home often to make my physical therapy appointments. "I'll be in touch," I say.

"You'd better be," Polly responds. "We have a lot to talk about, including scheduling some primary debates between you and Ethan Drake. Let me know when you've hired a campaign manager."

Almost immediately, my inbox is flooded with emails from people wanting to run my campaign. I'll have to pick someone who knows a lot about fundraising, especially since I no longer have the support of the Drake family, nor will I receive free help from Marina and her image-making miracles. That's fine by me, yet at the end of the day, I feel a little let down. I guess I was waiting for some earth-shattering bombshell to surface, some breaking news that the Drake's PI dug up, like I'm Fidel Castro's love child, a secret Communist spy who's been working to undermine our great nation since birth, and that my affair with Finn is merely a speck on my bleak, dark past.

So, while the conservative media runs and reruns their greatest hits of damaging stories about me, nothing new comes out. I guess the Drakes are keeping things on the downlow, at least for now.

This morning, I can deal with all that, and I sing along to the radio as I drive to my physical therapy appointment. I probably shouldn't be so happy at the prospect of seeing Miguel, but I'm hoping he saw my campaign announcement, and that he liked it. After my appointment, I plan to drive to DC, where I'll avoid all icy sidewalks, choosing only to tread on the steps of the capitol. For now, I get to the clinic, check in, and am called back to Miguel's little physical therapy room. I must be smiling because he takes one look at me and says, "You look like you're not in pain."

"I'm having a good day," I respond. "How are you?"

He stares straight ahead, and his eyes barely move. "I've been worse."

Miguel resists my efforts to chitchat. He rubs my arm, measures the swelling, and tests my mobility. Later, when I lie on a therapy table so he can work my arm, he's particularly relentless, pressing down, pulling, yet unwilling to participate in a conversation that might distract me from the pain. At one point, I gasp and tears run down my face. "Too much?" he says softly, releasing my arm.

"It's okay. I know you're only doing what's necessary."

"We're pretty much done," he replies. "Let's go back, and I'll measure your movements one more time."

We return to the room where we started. I push myself super-hard and impress us both when, after a slow, shaky effort, I'm able to touch the tip of my nose with the tip of my thumb. "Ta da!" I cry. "Wow! Who knew I had it in me?"

Miguel's face breaks into a full-on smile. "I knew the whole time," he laughs. "That's great, Elyse. Good job."

I start putting my brace back on, sliding it up my arm so that stupid dial is exactly over my elbow. "Next week I'll be doing handstands, right?"

"Maybe just somersaults," he jokes. Then his smile fades, and his worry lines return. "But I think I'll refer you to my coworker, Jean. She's excellent and will take good care of you."

"What?" I momentarily stop putting my brace back on and tightening the Velcro straps. "I don't understand. Why can't I continue with you?" Then, in a rush of panic, I ask. "You're not getting deported, are you? Is everything okay with you and your parents?"

"It's nothing like that."

I sigh in relief. "That's good." I search his expression for some sort of an answer, but there's nothing in his rigid jaw and downcast eyes. "Then, why?"

He runs his hand through his hair, keeping his focus not on me but on the wall. "I just think Jean will be a better fit for you. She's the best PT in our department."

"Do you transfer all your patients to her?"

"Of course not."

"Then why me?"

I'm not completely sure, but there might be some pink creeping up underneath Miguel's brown cheeks. He shakes his head. "I know you won't believe me, but I went easy on you today. I saw that you were crying so I eased up, but I should have pushed you further. It's not right."

"Okay." I say this because no other words come to mind. But it's nowhere close to okay.

Miguel's tone turns easygoing and he speaks slowly, like I might have trouble understanding if he goes too fast. "Physical therapy is hard. It's supposed to be. You shouldn't enjoy it. And you make me feel like I should entertain you."

Angry, I finish securing my brace. "Fine. Refer me to Jean." I grab my purse and head toward the door.

"Wait." Now Miguel speaks with his normal speed and tone, and it's clear he's blushing. "That came out wrong. This is my fault, not yours. I just meant that I like you more than I should, and it's hard for me, causing you pain. I don't feel like I'm doing a good job with you. Plus, I saw your video and the fact that you're running for governor makes it even more complicated, so…."

He seems unable to finish his sentence. I wait a second or two. "So, you don't want anything complicated?"

He shakes his head. "I could get fired for asking you out, and if the press were to find out, that would be a million times worse."

"What if I asked you out?"

Miguel moves his gaze sideways, rolling his eyes ever so slightly, and possibly fighting a smile. "I could also get fired for accepting."

"Even if I'm no longer your patient?"

"If you were no longer my patient, and we happened to run each other outside of the clinic, and we both wanted to make plans to do something fun… that would maybe be okay, but with the election and all the media attention on you, if that attention then got transferred to my family…"

I rub the spot of tension at my temple. "Okay," I tell him, "I understand. You've got to protect yourself. You need to worry about what's important."

"Yeah."

"Man," I murmur, "I've got a headache. I don't think I've had enough caffeine today. Is there a coffee place nearby?"

Miguel blinks a few times and hesitantly replies, "The coffee cart in the lobby has a really good Columbian brew."

"No, I want somewhere *off* clinic grounds. How is that Starbucks right across the street?"

"It's a Starbucks. They're all the same."

Is he dense, or is he just trying to get rid of me? I think about what my mom said, that I should "totally go for it" with Miguel. I've spent most of my life ignoring her advice and instead, let my gut instinct drive my choices. And look where that got me.

"Great," I tell him, "it's good to know the Starbucks across the street is up to standard. From the outside it looks nice and spacious, like a good place to get work done. By the way, if I was there, just hanging out, and I happened to run into a friend, and we made plans to meet up some time, I'd be discreet and protect that friend's privacy."

"I'm glad to hear it," Miguel says, offering a faint smile. He comes toward me and extends his hand to shake. I let my palm meet his, and he holds my fingers in his warm, dry grip for a moment longer than expected. Then he squeezes my hand in this friendly, intense way that makes my heart quiver. "Take care, Elyse."

"You too. Maybe we'll run into each other some time?"

He shrugs. "You never know. I do love Starbucks."

We leave it at that, and as I drive to DC, I replay the interaction over and over in my mind. He must like me if he feels it's a conflict of interest to keep me as a patient. But Miguel obviously plays by the rules, and that could get in our way. I suppose he needs to be a rule-follower, given his situation. Were he to break any sort of rule, the consequences could ruin his life. That makes Miguel the antithesis of Finn, who in his entire life has never had to worry about rules, consequences, or for that matter, morality.

As I drive, my right hand grips the top of the steering wheel, and my left rests against the bottom. I clumsily navigate, making it to DC and exiting the freeway so I can take side streets to my apartment. As I pull up to the curb outside my building, I see news trucks waiting outside. "Oh no," I mutter. I park several feet away and grab my phone, which I did not check more than once or twice during my drive. I guess I was too preoccupied.

Now I see that in the last ninety minutes I've gotten dozens of texts and messages. One is from *Vanity Fair*, telling me I should let them tell my side of the story, and they'll put me on the cover. Another is from Aubrey: *Call me!* The rest are from news organizations, trying to reach me for comment.

"Hey, there she is!" A reporter suddenly notices my presence. In a rush, they all swarm over to my car, knocking on the window, brandishing their cameras and microphones like weapons. "Is it true you had an affair with Finn Beck while he was engaged to Marina Hunt?"

"Did you accept illegal, in-kind donations from Marina Hunt during your Congressional campaign?"

"Did your mother and Oliver Hunt have a fling during parent's weekend while you attended Columbia?"

"Can you comment on how your father was part of a group of commandos responsible for kidnapping Ecuador's president in 1987 and that your mother was involved as well? And are you now working to hide you father, a political refugee, in the United States of America?"

I'm surrounded. I could try to drive away, but I'd rather not add accidental homicide to my already long list of negative attention-getters. No. There's only one way out of this, and it's to face it head-on. I take a deep breath, square my shoulders, and open the car door.

Chapter 37

I face down the media and answer their questions. Several hours later, Finn and Marina, in a joint televised interview on Fox News, declare their devotion to each other. Marina, demurely clad in cream-colored sweater set, says, "I'm surprised Elyse would act so selfishly. I realize that Finn is irresistible, and I suppose she never really got over it when Finn broke up with her all those years ago. But still, I thought she was my friend."

Finn states, "It was a huge mistake, falling back into old patterns with her. When she texted me her address, I should have deleted it. I should have said no." While grasping Marina's hand, Finn explains that he, like so many people in the nation, "became transfixed. I was under her spell. Thank God I came to my senses and realized the love of my life is also the most beautiful, most supportive woman in the world." He looks longingly at Marina. "I don't deserve her, and I'll spend the rest of my life trying to make up for my mistake."

What a sexist pile of crap.

But all the news outlets think it's a good story. CNN decides to dig into my entire life and, over the course of several days, releases a virtual scrapbook on my identity. I'm the student reporter who, along with Marina and Aubrey, took down a Columbia professor. I'm the ex-girlfriend of a young Finneas Beck. (Someone unearthed a photo of him and me holding hands at one of Marina's parties in

2007, and it's shown repeatedly.) I'm a staff worker and then campaign worker for Eleanor Adam-Drake. I'm the community organizer of one of the nation's poorest cities. I'm one of Aubrey Adam's bridesmaids. (There's another photo of Marina and me in our bridesmaid's gowns, posing with a radiant Aubrey on her wedding day.) I'm the unlikely Congresswoman from Pennsylvania's sixth district. And, apparently, I'm the love child of a young revolutionary, conceived during a time of Ecuadorian political unrest, when the president and several of his officials were kidnapped to negotiate the release of an insubordinate air force commander.

"He was really only on the fringes of the whole thing," my mom explains. "It was an incredibly exciting, dangerous time in Ecuador, and your dad and I were both caught up in the drama. But I was telling the truth when I said he never knew about you."

"Okay, but you knew about him. Why didn't you tell me all this stuff before?"

"Because I had no way of contacting him, and I didn't want to give you false hope. There was no way you were ever going to know each other. I have no idea how they found out about him. I didn't know those pictures even existed."

Someone, somehow, unearthed photos of him and my mom together at a party during the weekend that LFC, the president of Ecuador, was kidnapped. There are also photos of my dad with the commandos held responsible for the kidnapping. And while my dad was never arrested, he did find it prudent to leave Ecuador and never return. He's been living in Puerto Rico for nearly thirty years but hasn't sought U.S. citizenship.

The media totally runs with this theme that I am genetically predisposed to radicalism and revolution, but they quickly drop the idea that I've been hiding my dad in the U.S. Oh, but I am opportunistic, willing to sleep my way to the top, and because of my daddy-issues, I'm only interested in unavailable men. Several so-called friends from Reading go on record, declaring that Peter and I were romantically involved while he was still married to his first wife. Peter's ex-wife, when reached for comment, says that I broke up her marriage. Nobody cares about the truth, that she'd already filed for divorce by the time that Peter and I shared that one, isolated kiss.

Aubrey calls, not to apologize but to offer advice. "You need to do an interview and frame things your way."

My head is spinning. Does this mean she's back in my corner? Should I demand she say "sorry" before I talk to her at all? Ultimately, I'm too interested in what she might tell me to care.

"How am I supposed to do that?" I demand. "Your family is waiting like vultures to take me down. Anything I say in an interview will just give them more to feed upon."

"Well, I did warn you." Aubrey's voice is low and pained, like she's talking with a sore throat. "For what it's worth, both my mom and I are angry with the rest of the family. They're framing you as this hysterical female, defining you by the relationships you've had with men, and that's something my mom has had to deal with her entire life."

"How does she get through it?"

"You need to give it time, Elyse. There's no easy fix."

I run my fingers though my hair, which is falling from the bun I put it in this morning. "No, that's fine. I get it. It's better if I survive this without your help."

"Just don't give up," Aubrey chides. "This sort of negative coverage happens to my mom nearly every day! Come on, Elyse. Maybe you lost round one of the spin-war, but round two is still up for grabs."

I push two fingers up underneath my glasses and rub both my eyes. I didn't bother to put in my contacts this morning, and I know I look a mess. "Aubrey, I need to be on the floor of Congress in a few minutes, so I should go. Thanks for calling to check in." I try to sound sincere in my gratefulness, and I almost pull it off, probably because I am *almost* sincerely grateful.

"You'll survive this, Elyse, and you'll be stronger for it. Just wait and see."

"Okay, thanks."

"Good luck. Call me later."

I hang up with Aubrey and glance at myself in the mirror in my office, appraising my outfit of fitted gray blouse, knee-length skirt, and black Velcro-strapped arm brace. I'm starting to forget what life was like before I had to wear this thing. However, right now it's the least of my worries. I need to pull myself together before I face the other members of Congress. I'm sure they'll give me a hard time no matter what, but it can't seem like any of it is getting to me. I comb out my hair and put it in a low ponytail because capturing it in a decent bun is just too difficult a feat with only one working arm. I straighten my glasses and square my shoulders. I walk toward the entrance of my office, chin up, ready to face the world. I may be broken, but I am not beat.

Chapter 38

I do the interview with *Vanity Fair*, and they hire Annie Leibowitz to do the cover. I'm photographed in a simple white-collar shirt, like what a man would wear with a tie. But for me, the top three buttons are undone. My hair is swept back from my face, I have nude lipstick on, and I'm told to face the camera with an honest look on my face. This is my chance to shape my own image, to bare my soul to the world. *Vanity Fair* wants to include my family in the story as well—my mom, my stepdad, and my brothers.

"And what about your father?" The journalist asks. We're sitting in my Congressional office at a conference table, cups of coffee and nearly untouched breakfast pastries are off to the side.

"What about him?" I respond.

"Are you and he in contact? Is it true you arranged for his asylum?"

"No, and no. I've never even met him."

"And does that bother you?" The way she pushes those words out gives them an extra edge, like she already knows how I'll answer and that it will be a lie.

Still, I really contemplate the question. "Well, sure. I'd love to meet him. But I don't feel incomplete or anything, if that's what you're getting at."

"Even after what you now know, that your father was a subversive revolutionary? A lot of people say that the apple must not fall far from the tree."

I laugh. "Yeah well, I've learned not to care what 'a lot of people' say." I sip from my coffee, thinking if I act casual, I'll feel that way too. "I expect my father had his reasons for doing what he did; the politics in Ecuador at that time were pretty crazy. And perhaps with this new information the Drakes found about him, I'll be able to track him down one day. Maybe I should send the Drakes a thank you note. But I'm not beginning my search any time soon."

"Why not?"

I'd anticipated this question beforehand, and I'd already thought up my response. Still, I become a little choked with emotion as I speak. "Because the world is at once so big and so small; there are so many people to care about, and to love, and to fight for. Honestly, finding my dad would really be about finding myself. But my first step needs to be accepting the hard truths about who I am. Until I can do that, there's not a lot of point in looking for anything or anyone else."

***

A couple of weeks later I travel to Peru for the Lima Climate Change Conference, which is sort of work-related, but I'm financing the trip on my own dime. Polly Kinney says I'm crazy to leave at a time like this, that I should stay in the country and focus on my campaign and my constituents. But I heard about this conference months ago and bought my ticket on an impulsive "I have to grab this" sort of moment. The conference is all about reversing glacial melting in Peru because their glaciers have shrunk by nearly 40%. For most of the conference we sit in lecture halls and listen to experts, or we meet in breakout groups to network and brainstorm. But there is a day trip to visit a glacier. I'm all about going, except I stay on shore.

Months ago, I might have had the strength to live out my recurring dream and stand upon the ice that melts beneath my feet. Now, I can only approach the glacier and look out and take in all the damaged beauty.

On my trip back, I have a connection at the Miami airport. I'm buying a bottle of water and a bag of Sun Chips at a news stand when there it is, my face plastered on the cover of *Vanity Fair.* It's a tight shot, me staring nakedly into the camera, my good arm wrapped over my chest and my arm with the brace resting atop my knee. I buy the magazine hoping the young woman working the cash register won't recognize me in my glasses and with my hair pulled back in a bandana.

Once I'm on the plane, I dare to look inside the magazine. The article is titled "The New Power-Player Who Refuses to Get Played." *The moment she set foot in Washington, Elyse Gibbons made her message loud and clear. As the new face of the Democratic party, she means business. While she's open to constructive criticism, her agenda does not include being taken for a fool. The consensus? Only a fool will go against her.*

What follows is a profile piece about me: my childhood, my skating, my education, my politics, and my goals for the future. It's not altogether complimentary; they do mention my hypocrisy, that I've branded myself a champion of the people while reaping the benefits of my connections to Aubrey, Finn, and Marina. While none of those three cared to comment for the article, the writing is both balanced and in-depth. And there are pictures of my mom and me, including the selfie we took while wearing my mother's old green ERA gear. Underneath the photo is my mother's quote, "I tried to teach Elyse to be strong and independent, and she is. But she also has this desire to fix the world, and I don't think she got that from me."

I close the magazine and squeeze my eyes shut. Not since I was a freshman in college have I longed for my mother so much. As soon as my plane lands I'll call her and tell her she's wrong. I may have received help from Aubrey and Marina along the way, but everything about me that's important and true, all that comes from her. My mother taught me that it's possible to fix myself, and I'll need to get that done before I can ever hope to fix the world.

Chapter 39

While my *Vanity Fair* cover-story makes my stock go up on a national level, it's local politics that I need to worry about. Pennsylvanians aren't convinced they can trust me. *The Philadelphia Inquirer* endorses Ethan Drake as their choice for the Democratic nominee in the governor's race, saying, "Only Ethan Drake has the wisdom and experience to lead Pennsylvanians while facing numerous challenges that stem from changes in industry, social upheaval, and a crumbling economy." They dismiss me as a "shiny new object" who is good at getting attention, but when it comes to substance, I fall dangerously short.

Perhaps they're right. Perhaps I'm an imposter who's been fooling everyone, including myself. Yet I must wonder if someone on the Inquirer's editorial board is tight with the Drakes. Maybe I never had a chance at the newspaper's endorsement. The only thing I can do now is keep on keeping on.

During my third primary debate with Ethan Drake, he tries to label me as a liar, a fraud, a dangerous liberal who will ruin the state for the hard-working, blue-collar population whose mentality I will never understand. Inwardly, I seethe. Why isn't Ethan Drake being held to the same standard as me? He has committed adultery, he has a father accused of political rashness, and in the end, Ethan Drake's actions and misdeeds are all more extreme and consequential than any of mine have been. I mean, at least I don't have manslaughter marring my already imperfect record.

"With all due respect," I say, "I'm not here to talk about my personal life. Have I made mistakes? Yes, I have, but so Sir, have you. And I fail to see how any of it is relevant to voters. I'm here to talk about job creation and raising the minimum wage. I'm here to talk about increasing the graduation rate and giving our students a quality education. I'm here to talk about how Pennsylvania can do our part to end global warming. I'm here to talk about gun control. I'm here to talk about every single resident of the state and how we can keep each one of them safe and prosperous. To talk about anything else is just an insult and a waste of time."

That momentarily silences Ethan Drake, and it's a turning point. The post-debate spin goes my way, the media becomes more interested in giving me positive press, and my poll numbers go up a little. But I'm still way behind. Then, one evening in late June, Aubrey surprises me and stops by my apartment in Reading. At first, I'm so shocked I can barely speak. The last time Aubrey and I spoke was when she called months ago to "check in." Since then, I'd figured our friendship was over.

"I can't stay long," she says, without preamble. She's holding baby Anton in her arms, and he's squirming and whimpering like he's angry about something. "Here, take him for a minute." She hands me the baby, making this the first time I've ever held her son.

"Hello!" I say, using the high-pitched, sing-songy voice everyone uses when talking to babies. "What a big boy! It's so nice to finally meet you!" Then I turn to Aubrey and speak normally. "And it's nice to see you. Do you want to come in?"

"No time," Aubrey answers, fishing in her shoulder bag. Her hand emerges with an envelope. "This is for you," she states and signals that we should trade; I give her back her baby, and she gives me the envelope. "But I was never here, okay? And you didn't get this from me."

"Umm, okay. What's in the envelope?"

"Go inside and read it," Aubrey says. "It's my way of saying sorry." Then she reaches in and gives me a brief kiss on the cheek. "For a while, I was thinking you'd be better off all on your own. But then I realized, I owe it to you, to fix what I broke."

"Okay..." I respond, confused. "Does this mean we can go back to being friends?"

She nods, sniffs a little, and then leaves as quickly as she arrived.

I enter my apartment, intensely curious. What is so important that Aubrey felt it was necessary to hand-deliver it? I carefully use my letter opener to rip the top of the envelope. Inside, I find a printout of a series of emails between Ethan Drake and a prominent Pennsylvania steel mill owner. This guy has hundreds of millions of dollars and employs thousands of workers. In the emails, he outlines a plan to slowly shut down his factories and move them to China, where manufacturing costs are cheaper. He promises to make mega campaign donations to Ethan Drake in exchange for his help, as governor, in navigating the corporate loopholes of moving his business overseas.

And Ethan Drake responds, "Count me in. I am totally on board."

Aubrey has stuck a post-it on the first page of the printout: *Leak this to the press or use it however you want. Like I've said before, I am always on your side. Love, -Aubrey.*

I send the emails to the Philadelphia Inquirer. There's an uproar, and Ethan Drake loses the endorsement of the unions while the press talks about the legality of his negotiations. He tries to explain the whole situation away, but no platitudes can erase this huge misstep. So, on a hot Tuesday at the end of the summer, I win the primary and become the official Democratic candidate for governor.

Aubrey calls to congratulate me. "Everyone's saying it's an upset, but I had a feeling you'd get the nomination."

"How angry is your grandfather? Does he know I won because of you?"

She makes a dismissive little sound. "I have no idea what you're talking about, Elyse"

Okay, so that's our code; we'll never mention her role in this, and it will be like it never happened.

Aubrey continues. "Besides, you were gaining on Ethan before the email scandal broke. Who's to say you wouldn't have won anyway? Grandpa will get over it. He's way too worried about my mom's campaign to focus on anything else. The polls keep showing the race between her and Hunt is much too close for comfort."

She doesn't have to go into detail about the general election or how scary those poll numbers are. I read about it in the news every day. The election is still months away, but this year is already historic for the norms that have been broken. For instance, last week Oliver Hunt encouraged proponents of the Second Amendment to "take care of things" around Eleanor Adam-Drake. The implication? They should use their guns to get rid of her, once and for all. Some people in the media were upset for maybe two minutes, saying Hunt just advocated for Eleanor's assassination, and where would it end? But no matter what he does, whether he's holding a rally, working his supporters up into a violent frenzy, lying about his own record, or using hateful, racist, or misogynistic rhetoric on a daily basis, his supporters still love him. And Marina and Finn continue to smile, wave, and shrug their shoulders if ever they're asked if they approve of Oliver Hunt's methods. Meanwhile, there's a pressing concern that commentators can't stop obsessing over: Is Eleanor likable enough?

"Well," I say, "I'll work my hardest to make sure Pennsylvania goes blue." I pause, hesitant. It's been so long since Aubrey and I have had a real conversation. I must tread lightly. "But what about you? I see that you're not on the ballot in Connecticut."

"That's right," Aubrey answers. "I told my grandfather I'd continue working for the foundation, but I refused to run for office, at least until Clara and Anton are school-age. He argued at first, but after I gave him the texts between you and Finn, he took that as a compromise and let it go." She's silent for a second, save for her breathing. "I'm sorry, Elyse. And I'm sorry it took me so long to apologize. I truly hope none of what happened has caused you permanent damage. But at the very least, you survived the scandal. Compared to that, I bet the general election will be a breeze."

I laugh. "Sure. Convincing white, working class Pennsylvanian men to vote for me will be easy-peasy."

"Maybe you should just focus on everyone who isn't a white guy?"

"That's the plan." I glance around the living room of my apartment in Reading, and my eyes land on the clock. "Aubrey, I'm sorry, but I'm running late. I need to get down to campaign headquarters. Can we talk later? I'd still like to spend time with baby Anton before he's no longer a baby."

"Yes. I'll call you. I promise."

As we hang up, I realize how happy I am.

***

When I get to my campaign headquarters, they are amazingly quiet. It's the day after the primaries, and any of my volunteers who normally would be working on Wednesday afternoons are most likely still sleeping off the hangover from last night's celebration. Even my campaign manager is taking the day off, but I feel I had no choice but to come in and get some work done. Next week, I'm returning to Congress, and then I'll really need to multi-task. I'm looking through my calendar, trying to figure out which campaign events will need extensive preparation and which ones I can just wing, when I realize someone has entered my office.

"Excuse me," a male voice says. I look up. It's Miguel.

I jump from my desk and reflexively smooth my hair which all day has been resisting the elastic band I'd used to tie it back. "Miguel," I say, flustered. "Hello. What… what are you doing here?"

He smiles. "I hope you don't mind me stopping in. I kept thinking I might run into you, at the clinic, or at that Starbucks, which, you know, I've gone into dozens of times. But you're never there."

"Sorry," I reply. "Things got crazy. I don't know if you watch the news, but I was sort of in the spotlight for a while."

"Yeah, I saw."

It's like my chest could collapse. "I figured you would have seen it, and that maybe you wouldn't want to see me after hearing all the stuff they said."

"You mean about your involvement with Finneas Beck?"

For some reason, hearing Miguel say Finn's name is a shock to my system. All I can do is nod dumbly.

Miguel squints at me, like I'm too far away to read easily. "I'd be lying if I didn't admit I was a little intimidated. I think your social circle is way beyond mine."

"Oh." I laugh, but it comes out sounding forced. "I don't have a social circle. I don't have any kind of circle, I mean, unless you count work. I'm pretty much a workaholic, and that's all there is to me."

"I doubt that." He clears his throat. "I wasn't your physical therapist for long, so it's not like I know you well, but you can tell a lot about a person just by watching how they handle pain. Anyway, I never believed the worst of what anyone said about you."

Our eyes meet, and the warmth from his gaze compounds his kind words. I can't remember the last time anyone said something so nice to me. "Thank you."

"And congratulations. My family and I, we can't vote, but we appreciate your stance on immigration." Miguel shifts his weight and momentarily looks down at his shoes. They're gray canvas with brown cord ties, and they look classy, comfortable, and new. During our appointments, Miguel only ever wore this one worn pair of sneakers, so I experience a surge of hope, thinking maybe Miguel is trying to impress me with his shoes. I mean, do guys do that?

"Anyway," he continues, "I wanted you to know how much it means to me and my family, that you could be our next governor. It kills me that I won't be able to vote for you, but I was wondering if you could use more volunteers?" His face breaks into a smile that's broad and warm.

"Of course! I'd be honored to have you as a volunteer; I just wish I could..." My voice trails off, as I'm unable to finish my thought. I wish I could fix everything? Or do I simply wish to make this moment last for a while? That way, I could bask in the heat of Miguel's eyes: friendly, earnest, and focused on me.

"Hey, how's your elbow?" His question is abrupt, pulling me from my reverie.

I hold out my arm and show off my new bending capability. "I can touch my face without much effort at all. Pretty exciting, huh?"

"Yeah, and I see you're not wearing the brace."

"Just the compression sleeve."

"That's great." He smiles again, and I decide to take the plunge.

"Are you hungry? I skipped lunch today, and I'm starving. There's a Subway just a couple doors down. I could buy you a sandwich."

"No."

I'm instantly deflated, and my face burns with humiliation. How could I read this so wrong? But then Miguel keeps talking. "I mean, if I'm going to eat dinner at four in the afternoon, it needs to be worth it. No offence, but we can do better than Subway."

"Dinner? Right now?"

"Yeah. Why not?" He wrinkles his face and gestures toward the work on my desk. "Unless you're too busy."

"Nah. I've had a long week, and it's only Wednesday. I deserve to cut out early."

I pack up my things, lock the office, and we head out. "I'll drive," Miguel says, jiggling his car keys in his hand. "Do you like tapas? There's a great place about a mile from here."

"Yeah. That sounds perfect."

He motions to his car and presses the unlock button on his key. As his car blurts out an abrupt little bleep, Miguel says, "Climb in."

"Okay," I respond shyly and lift the metal door handle that has grown warm in the afternoon sun. The inside of Miguel's car is very tidy, with seat covers over what I'm guessing is worn-down upholstery and a cardboard palm-tree-shaped air freshener hanging from the rearview mirror. Miguel sits beside me, settling into the driver's seat, and turns on the ignition. "Feel free to change the radio station," he states. "I try to avoid commercials."

"Sure." I press the pre-programmed buttons and NPR comes on first, but right now I want something light and fun, not the measured tones of Michel Martin on *All Things Considered*. The next station has someone talking in Spanish, and it sounds like an ad. I press one more button, and a song I recognize comes on.

"Let's go," says Miguel, and he deftly pulls out of the parking lot and onto the road.

I ride shotgun in Miguel's two-door sedan. Sitting so close to him with the windows rolled down and pop music playing, it's like I'm nostalgic for something I've never had. I mean, sure, in high school I went out with this guy named Karl, and there were a handful of times when he drove me to play putt-putt, or out to eat at a Thai noodle place we both loved. But it was no grand romance between Karl and me, and once I got to college, we were little more than Facebook friends.

Then I started dating Finn, who has never owned a car, and who has a driver to take him places like he's royalty. I don't think Finn even knows how to drive. As for Peter, our non-relationship was always on the downlow, so I rarely rode in a car with him. Besides, as mayor, Peter hardly ever drove. It never occurred to me until now: the flipside to dating someone entitled and influential is you sacrifice your freedom, and everything becomes complicated. But right now, Miguel and I face the open road, and even if our future together is confined to this one moment, it's perfect in its simplicity.

If I were bold, I'd cover Miguel's hand, which rests on the gear shift, with my own hand. Instead, I lean my head back, letting the smile I feel inside fill me from the bottom up.

Soon, we arrive at a tapas restaurant with a shaded patio that sports fountains, palm trees, and piano music. We sit in cushioned lawn chairs and use tiny forks to spear the best spicy prawns I've ever eaten. We also drink wine, but I sip from my glass slowly, because the last thing I want is to feel dazed or removed from right now.

"Tell me about your family," I say. "How are they doing?"

Miguel finishes chewing his shrimp before answering. As he reclines in his lawn chair, the sunlight peaks through the patio roof, casting his face in both light and shadow. "They're good. My sister, Lenore, just got a full ride to study physics at Penn State."

"Wow. She must be a brainiac."

"Yeah." Miguel smiles proudly. "She takes after my mom for sure."

"Your mom must be so proud."

He lifts his hand and waves it in a so-so gesture. "She is, but it's bittersweet. Mom knows how much she'll miss Lenore once she's out of the house, and at the same time she's scared that Lenore's scholarships won't come through because of our citizenship status. Every day she's calling someone with a different job title, trying to forge some new connection so it will all work out okay. You're lucky I haven't told her that I know you, or she would have called you by now for sure."

Before I can stop myself, I state, "That would be fine. Your mom sounds great. I'd love to meet her."

Immediately I regret saying that. Geez. Who tries to worm her way into a family introduction so soon? This doesn't even count as a first real date. But Miguel nods. "Be careful what you wish for. Because then I'll invite you to Sunday dinner, and you'll have to come and sit for hours."

I shrug. "That would be okay."

Miguel arches an eyebrow and smiles with half his mouth. "All right. But you should come when she's made empanadas."

"Deal," I reply.

We both laugh, and not because anything funny has been said. But Miguel turns serious and says, "So, you've become pretty famous."

"Yes."

"That must feel strange."

"I suppose," I respond. "Sometimes I'll be watching the news, and I'll hear stuff about myself, and that's just surreal. And then there's so much going on with the presidential campaign, and a new scandal every day, and it hits me, I *know* them. This public drama is also, for me, personal, and it's almost easy to forget that because we're all so consumed and divided. But then I wonder where I fit in, and when it's all over, if I'll ever find my place."

It's like Miguel is chewing on a thought; that rugged jaw of his is slightly clenched as he mulls over what he'll say next. After a moment, in a soft voice, he states, "I don't mean to diminish what you're up against, but from the outside, it looks like you've already found your place."

I consider this, briefly closing my eyes and letting myself relax in the warmth of the late afternoon sun. Then I let my gaze meet Miguel's wide brown eyes and feel the answer. "Yeah, you're probably right. I think I'm pretty much over everything that happened in the last few months."

"Does that mean you're over Finneas Beck?"

My cheeks grow warm, and I try to hide that I'm blushing by reaching for my glass of ice water. "I don't miss him, and I don't love him anymore." I sip, hoping the action will cool my face down. "And I've come to terms over my friendships with Aubrey and Marina, how I let knowing them define me. It's all good, except for one thing. I never want to go near the ice again."

Miguel had just popped a shrimp in his mouth, yet he must feel the need to respond immediately. He speaks and chews, trying to keep his mouth closed and his words come out slightly muffled.

"Was your fall that traumatic?"

"Yes, it really was." I slide my finger down my water glass, which has grown slick with condensation from the melting ice cubes. "You see, I've always had this preoccupation with ice. When I was in school, I even competed as a figure skater. But I stopped when I was too busy with politics. So, when I fell on the ice, it reminded me of how much I've changed. I'm too scared to ever go back."

"You say that now, but you'll change your mind."

"How do you know?"

Miguel laughs self-consciously, his eyes crinkling around the corners in a charming way. "Okay, I guess I don't know for sure. But if I had to lay odds, I'd say you're the type who doesn't stay down for long. Sooner or later, you'll face your fear, and hopefully, I'll still know you when you do."

We share another smile while we enjoy the day.

Chapter 40

It's no surprise that Pennsylvania is a swing-state this year, and it's also no surprise when, at the end of October, Eleanor Adam-Drake and Oliver Hunt both have campaign events planned for the same weekend. Eleanor's event is meant to showcase the entire Democratic ticket, which means she and I will appear together on stage at the Wells Fargo Center in downtown Philadelphia. At first, I'm worried it might be awkward. Then Aubrey calls to say that she'll be there too.

Waiting backstage for the rally to begin, I think back to the victory party for when Eleanor won her New York Senate seat all those years ago. "She's the future," Marina had said, and I'd agreed. Now, both Aubrey and Eleanor approach me.

"Elyse, hello! It's so good to see you." Eleanor grasps my hand in a shake, but she also pulls me in at the same time, giving me half a hug. She looks stunning in a beige skirt topped with a brown cashmere sweater and a scalloped blue collar that peeks out. A string of pearls completes the classy ensemble. I still admire how Eleanor can combine upper-crust sophistication with a "let's get down to business" fashion sense.

"Thank you, Eleanor, it's good to see you too. I can't wait to vote for you on Tuesday."

She smiles. "Thank you, my dear. And I will be rooting for you as well. I mean that."

"That's nice of you to say."

"Elyse," Eleanor leans in, speaking to me conspiratorially. "I'm so sorry for how my brother behaved. I hope you'll forgive me for not stepping in. I thought about it, because after all, I know how it feels having Ethan Drake damage your political career. But I knew you'd not only survive, but that you'd prosper. After all, the only reason Ethan was so vicious was because he realized you have extraordinary promise. I suspect that one day you'll surpass us all."

"I… I don't know what to say."

"That's all right. But please, hear me out about one more thing. In a few days, the nation will go to the voting booth. If, after all the votes have been counted, we find that I've failed, I'll need you to do something for me." She takes a deep steadying breath. "Promise that you will not rest, that you will not give up until you've become the first female president."

My mouth drops open in shock. I was *so* not expecting her to say that. I must clear my throat before I'm able to respond. "Thank you," I gasp. "But it won't come to that. You're going to win. You've *got to* win."

She pats my shoulder. "We'll see. So, do you promise?"

I look to Aubrey, and she nods. "Please, Elyse. Promise us both."

"But what about you, Aubrey? Doesn't your grandfather want you to be president one day?"

Aubrey shakes her head. "That's not my destiny, Elyse. It never has been. But it's always been yours."

Damn it. Why am I always fighting back tears in moments that call for strength and composure? I meet eyes with my good friend, no, with my *best* friend, Aubrey Adam-Drake. I see her sincerity as clearly as if it was typed across her face. And then I know, for her, there's one last promise I must make.

"Yes, of course. I promise."

"Wonderful. Thank you, Elyse. I feel much better now." Eleanor gives me another little reassuring shoulder pat, meeting my eyes once more before she spots Pennsylvania's incumbent Senate

Democrat, who is also waiting in the wings. Eleanor moves on to speak with him, leaving Aubrey and me alone and face to face. She grins self-consciously before leaning in to hug me. "Good luck, Elyse. I know you'll make an incredible governor."

"Thank you." When she pulls away, I see tears in her eyes. "Hey, what's wrong?"

Aubrey sniffs. "Nothing, really. Mom's nervous, you know, so I am too. And then there's the stuff Marina's said today at their rally in Pittsburgh."

"What are you talking about?"

"You haven't heard?"

"No. What she'd say?"

Aubrey pulls out her phone, apparently calling up a video clip, which she then hands to me. Marina—as tall, auburn-haired, and glowing as ever—faces a huge crowd of supporters at a rally for her dad. She speaks robustly into the microphone. "Some of you may have heard that my old college friends, Aubrey Adam-Drake and Elyse Gibbons, will appear together at their own rally later today not far from here." She holds the microphone closer, lowering her voice and taking on a serious expression. "Lately, people are giving me a hard time. They say, 'Marina, how could you ever have been friends with them when they're both so corrupt, so selfish?' And I would defend them and explain that we formed a bond in college when the three of us brought down a respected man accused of being a sexual predator. At the time, I thought I was doing what's right, but the more I hear from Elyse Gibbons and her radical feminist agenda, the more scared I become. So today, I've found the strength to confess that years ago, Elyse Gibbons orchestrated the whole 'sex scandal' on Columbia University's campus. She and Aubrey Adam-Drake coerced me into entrapping a decent man. Then they forced me to tell lies about him. Well, Pennsylvania, if you want a governor who will betray the good men of this state, who will cast them as villains and destroy their reputations so she can appease the radical feminists with their extreme agendas, look no further. You can elect such a woman in just a couple of days!"

Stunned, I hand Aubrey back her phone. "Why would she lie like that?"

Aubrey shakes her head. "I think she's nervous, since we could expose her relationship with Janet if we wanted to. But mostly, Marina likes to win. She wants her dad to win, and she wants to follow in his footsteps. She believes she'll be president one day, but she also knows that you might beat her to the punch. I guess she figures she may as well take you out now."

I'm trying to process it all, to figure out how I can deny her story without calling too much attention to it, when Aubrey nudges me. "Hey, you're getting called out on stage."

I hear Polly Kinney speaking to the audience, introducing one by one all the Democratic candidates. She is using words like "brilliant" and "compassionate" and "the future," and I can't quite believe it, but the incredible stuff she's saying is about *me.* "This firebrand Congresswoman has taken the world by storm! Please join me in welcoming Pennsylvania's favorite daughter, Elyse Gibbons!"

I square my shoulders, inhale like I'm about to run out of oxygen, and smile big. Then I stride out onto stage, facing and waving to the people of my great state. As I take in their enthusiastic applause and their yells of support, I know Miguel is right. I've already found my place.

***

Later, Aubrey and I leave the event together. We exit through the back where she has a car waiting. "Do you want to get dinner?" she asks. "I'm sure you're busy, but I would love a chance to catch up."

"That sounds great."

I'm expecting to see Aubrey's limo waiting for us, so I'm startled by television cameras. But, why are they waiting for us here? Then I realize, Marina is waiting for us too. Apparently, she's orchestrated a confrontation between the three of us, and she's brought a crew along to film it.

"Marina, what the hell?" Aubrey's angry tone belongs to someone who is no longer pursuing a career in politics.

"Hello, ladies," Marina says. She seems smaller now, standing in front of us, then she did in the video clip on Aubrey's phone. "So, did you hear about my confession today, at my dad's rally?"

"You mean the lies you told?" Aubrey answers. "What is wrong with you? Who have you become?"

I have half a mind to turn around and run back inside. But I know that would look weak and guilty, so I stay where I am, wondering what I should say to absolve myself and implicate Marina. There are so many nuggets of truth to choose from, but at this second, I have nothing bad to say. Marina looks like she's fighting back tears, and although she's probably engineered this interaction to portray herself as the victim and Aubrey and me as the villains, I can't help but feel sorry for her. She's the one who is living a lie.

Marina sniffs, and then I see she's crying. Are the tears for real? "You broke my heart, Elyse. I thought we were friends, but I never should have trusted you." She turns to Aubrey. "And you. The stuff you've said during the campaign about my family is unforgivable. Don't ever talk to me again." Marina uses the back of her hand to wipe under her eyes and her now pink nose. Her mascara is slightly smudged, but it just gives her a smoky eye, and if there's such a thing as a perfect-cry-look, Marina's got it.

She lifts her chin, and with her gleaming hair slicked back into a chignon, she resembles a wronged heroine from a 1930s

Hollywood drama. "We shared so much," she says. "I thought what we had was real."

"That's the problem," Aubrey says. "You have no idea what's real, Marina. You never have. It's why you're so dangerous."

Marina looks like she could shoot venom out from her eyes. "You think I'm dangerous?" she whisper-hisses, then lowers her voice even more, so Aubrey and I must step in to hear. "That's rich. You two are the dangerous ones. Sure, I used to value our friendship, but it's time to grow up. I'm not going to let either of you ruin my image, or my future. And I am *not* going away."

Marina adopts her previously wounded expression, sniffs one more time for good measure, and walks off.

"What the hell was that?" Aubrey asks.

I sigh. "I don't know, but this close to election day, it's probably better to let it go. People are going to believe what they want to believe, anyway."

"We'll see." Aubrey's mouth sets into a defiant little line. "Don't be surprised when I give a public response. I understand why you might take the high road, but that doesn't mean I have to."

I look at my friend, and for the first time, it occurs to me that she and Marina are opposites. Aubrey is flawed, prone to saying the wrong thing, to losing her temper. But she wants to make the world a better place and insists on seeing the best in people. Meanwhile, Marina is nearly perfect. She never slips up, but unlike Aubrey, seems capable of devious, destructive acts.

Aubrey takes my hand and gives it a squeeze. "Are you all right?" she asks.

"Yeah. You?"

She nods. "Sure. Come on, let's get out of here. I'm starving"

We get into the limo, and as we ride through the streets of Philadelphia, we're both silent and pensive. I think about Marina. Maybe her father will win on Tuesday, and perhaps she'll go on to follow in his footsteps. I can't imagine how that would be good for our country, but as we drive past the Liberty Bell Pavilion, I can almost glimpse the famously flawed relic of our American Revolution. Like the bell, surely our country's foundation is stronger than a single crack. Surely, in the end, it's our imperfections that bring us wisdom.

And maybe, it's through our imperfections that we learn how to grow.

Epilogue

I suppose, given everything that's happened, it's only natural that it was Aubrey and Marina who put me over the top in my race for governor.

I was relieved when Aubrey's statement about Marina's "confession" had nothing to do with Marina's personal life. Rather, she focused on the matter at hand. "Marina Hunt is lying," Aubrey's statement read. "She and I orchestrated the scheme to take down our professor at Columbia. Elyse Gibbons was an unwitting assistant in implicating a guilty man, while Marina Hunt and I colluded together from the beginning. And I kept documentation, including texts and emails between Marina and me, which will prove my version of events as legitimate."

The story got a lot of play, and many of the young voters and suburban moms who'd voted for me for Congress were angered by it. Not only that, they were energized and made it to the voting booth in unexpectedly large numbers. This explains my upset victory.

Unfortunately, Hunt also scored an upset victory. But I'm not going into that; the pain is still too fresh. Besides, I have my own demons to conquer.

I wasn't lying when I told Miguel I'd moved on from Finn. I can honestly say I no longer miss him, but I have grown to miss the ice. Miguel says it's only natural for me to miss something so fundamental to my identity. He's right; even when I was working intense political jobs with impossible schedules, I'd still find time to skate because that was when I was the best version of myself. Perhaps that's why, on the anniversary of my fall, I decide it's time to skate again.

"Do you want me to go with you?" Miguel asks.

I kiss him lightly on the lips. "You're sweet, but this is something I need to do on my own."

"All right." Before I turn away, he pulls me in for a hug. Miguel gives the best hugs in the world: so warm and strong, that the world has become a better place by the time he lets go. Plus, his skin smells great, like lemons and mint.

"Good luck, and please come home in one piece." By *home* he means the house I recently bought in Harrisburg near the state's capitol building. Thank God I'm not required to live in the Governor's mansion. That would just feel weird, and having to explain Miguel's constant presence there would be awkward since it's not like we're engaged. At least not yet.

"See you soon," I tell Miguel. I don't promise him that I will be home in one piece, because I'm done making promises I don't know I can keep. Instead, I tell him I love him and head out to my car.

I'd had to contact the rink to where I'm headed in advance, to schedule some private skate time. Hopefully I'm not upsetting some team's hockey practice, and I promise myself I won't stay long. I arrive, discreetly head down to the rink, and lace up my skates. Since I have the place to myself, there is room to skate in large, lazy circles, and time and space to push down my fears and ignore flashbacks of falling. *You're doing great,* I tell myself, even though it's not really true. Before, when I'd skate, I would soar, completely oblivious to any possible danger, heartbreak, or bone breaks. I just didn't understand my potential for pain.

I wish that back then I'd taken more time to cherish carving my blades into the ice, spinning and leaping, being at home with speed and power. Now I'm tentative, scared of tumbling onto that cold, unforgiving surface.

But I don't have to live in fear.

I attempt a jump, and although it's small, I feel victorious when I don't land with my butt on the ice. I skate back and forth, gaining a sense of strength and security, confident I've found my power. I remember how much I love the ice. And if that love somehow leads to another fall, well, *what the hell.* Isn't taking control all about picking yourself up and, if necessary, starting again? Doesn't strength come from staying true to yourself and keeping the promises you've made?

I don't forget the promises I've made. I intend to keep them all.

THE END

Acknowledgements

(in no particular order)

Thanks to Shauna Slade for all the suggestions, support, advice, and the witty lines that you wrote for me (shh!); to Lynn Osterkamp for the proofreading & the feedback, the honest advice, and for teaching me the feminist ideals I put in my novel; to Allan Press for first suggesting the idea for *First Daughters;* to Priya Doraswamy for first believing in my novel, and for all the guidance that helped me shape it into its final version; to Mary Ellen Bramwell for the proofing and objective opinions; and to Black Rose Writing for publishing *First Daughters*! Thank you to Rich, Eli, and Pauline, who love, accept, and support me even when I'm consumed with writing. The three of you are my heart! Finally, there are some outstanding female leaders and writers I'd like to mention. These women, through their eloquence, bravery, and leadership, helped inspire me to write *Favorite Daughters:* Ruth Bader Ginsburg, Hillary Clinton, Alexandria Ocasio-Cortez and the other female House Representatives sworn in on January 3rd, 2019, Stacey Abrams, Chelsea Clinton, Margaret Atwood, Susan B Anthony, Elizabeth Cady Stanton, Emmeline Pankhurst, and Katy Tur.

About the Author

Laurel Osterkamp is a self-proclaimed political junkie from Minneapolis, where she teaches English and Creative Writing at a local high school, and runs her blog, laurellit.com. Her books, *Following My Toes, Starring in the Movie of My Life, November Surprise, The Holdout, The Next Breath*, and *Just Like the Bronte Sisters*, have received awards and rave reviews from readers, bloggers, and established sites such as Midwest Book Review, RT Book Reviews, USA Today Books, and Kirkus. Her full-length novel, *The Standout*, is a 2015 Kindle Scout Winner and was published by Kindle Press. She is currently seeking a master's degree in Creative Writing through Lindenwood University.

Note from the Author

Word-of-mouth is crucial for any author to succeed. If you enjoyed *Favorite Daughters*, please leave a review online—anywhere you are able. Even if it's just a sentence or two. It would make all the difference and would be very much appreciated.

Thanks!
Laurel Osterkamp

Made in United States
North Haven, CT
20 November 2022

26991280R00188